"Mother of Serpents" by Robert Bloch—Though he'd risen to the highest political office in Haiti, he'd forgotten that there was a power far more pervasive than politics which still ruled the land. . . .

"The Lost Boys" by Orson Scott Card—It's not easy to make friends when you're the new kid in town but in this town it might have been better to remain a stranger. . . .

"The Man with Pin-Point Eyes" by Erle Stanley Gardner—His power had given him a gateway to the past and the key to locating a long-forgotten treasure—but would the price of obtaining these hidden riches prove too high?

These are just some of the chilling encounters that await you in—

BACK FROM THE DEAD

BACK FROM THE DEAD

EDITED BY
MARTIN H. GREENBERG
& CHARLES G. WAUGH

D A W   B O O K S ,   I N C .
DONALD   A.   WOLLHEIM,   FOUNDER
375 Hudson Street, New York, NY 10014

ELIZABETH R. WOLLHEIM
SHEILA E. GILBERT
PUBLISHERS

First Printing, March 1991

1 2 3 4 5 6 7 8 9

DAW TRADEMARK REGISTERED
U.S. PAT. OFF. AND FOREIGN COUNTRIES
—MARCA REGISTRADA.
HECHO EN U.S.A.

PRINTED IN THE U.S.A.

ACKNOWLEDGMENTS

Introduction—Copyright © 1991 by Frank D. McSherry, Jr.

"The Rose-Crystal Bell" by Robert Arthur—Copyright 1954 by Ziff-Davis Publications, Inc. Reprinted by permission of the Scott Meredith Literary Agency, Inc., 845 Third Avenue, New York, NY 10022.

"Mother of Serpents" by Robert Bloch—Copyright 1936; renewed © 1964 by Robert Bloch. Reprinted by permission of the Scott Meredith Literary Agency, Inc., 845 Third Avenue, New York, NY 10022.

"The Lost Boys" by Orson Scott Card—Copyright © 1989 by Mercury Press, Inc. Reprinted by permission of the author.

"The Man with Pin-Point Eyes" by Erle Stanley Gardner—Copyright 1931 by Erle Stanley Gardner. Reprinted by permission of Curtis Brown, Ltd.

"Grave Error" by Cathie Griffith—Copyright © 1990 by Cathie Griffith. Used by arrangement with the author.

"The Outsider" by H. P. Lovecraft—Copyright 1926 by Weird Tales. Reprinted by permission of the Scott Meredith Literary Agency, Inc., 845 Third Avenue, New York, NY 10022.

"Mop-up" by Arthur Porges—Copyright 1953 by Mercury Press, Inc. Reprinted by permission of the Scott Meredith Literary Agency, Inc., 845 Third Avenue, New York, NY 10022.

"Charlie" by Talmage Powell—Copyright © 1980 by Talmage Powell. Reprinted by permission of the author.

"If the Red Slayer" by Robert Sheckley—Copyright © 1959 by Robert Sheckley. Reprinted by permission of the author.

"The Charnel God" by Clark Ashton Smith—Copyright 1934 by Weird Tales. Reprinted by permission of the Scott Meredith Literary Agency, Inc., 845 Third Avenue, New York, NY 10022.

CONTENTS

FROM DEATH'S OTHER SIDE—

by Frank D. McSherry Jr.

> ". . . that undiscovered country
> from whose bourne no traveller returns . . ."
> —Prince Hamlet

"Rise, Lazarus!"

The heavy stone was rolled away from the tomb by the waiting crowd.

"Come forth, Lazarus!"

The voice of the Teacher, Jesus of Nazareth, rose, loud and compelling, above the hot sandy plains of Palestine.

"Lazarus, come forth!"

"And he that was dead came forth, bound hand and foot with graveclothes . . ."

In a time of miracles, in a place of miracles, a man had come back from the grave, the first to know of his own personal knowledge what lay beyond the dark gates of death and able to tell us.

But—eerily—Lazarus said nothing. He simply walked away, out of the Bible; out of history. Eerie, because he was Jesus' great friend (Jesus wept when he heard of Lazarus' illness, death, and burial); his testimony of what had happened to him during his days of death could have done much to aid the spread of Christianity. (Imagine what today's televangelists could have done with that!) But if Lazarus ever spoke of what lay beyond those gates of darkness, there seems to be no record of it—

Silence, and a vast wall of blackness. What lies on the other side?

In this volume we include shuddery possibilities, presented in tales of terror by authors skilled in mystery and the macabre. Leonid Andreyev's story starts as Lazarus, just resurrected, returns home to face his awed family and friends, local authorities, and later, as his dark fame spreads, an emperor—each with the same question on his lips. . . . M. R. James, one of the great masters of the ghost story, tells of a traveler in Sweden's arctic forests, who hears how Count Magnus returned from the Crusades, bringing back with him someone—or something—the villagers do not want to talk about, even now; and learns that Count Magnus can return from domains stranger than any he visited in the Middle East. Robert Arthur takes us to Chinatown in San Francisco, where young Dr. Williams finds an anniversary wedding present for his wife—a lovely old rose-crystal bell, its clapper missing. Just as well, too, says the curio dealer; according to legend, its ringing golden peal will bring the nearest corpse back to life. Amused, Dr. Williams buys it; Mrs. Williams has a rose-crystal clapper at home that might well be the original—and learns that even the wildest legends may be based on fact. In a horror story by Robert Bloch, famed author of *Psycho*, what lies beyond death is only hinted at, but with shuddery effect, when voodoo drums beat a resurrection spell in the black heat of jungle nights in Haiti.

Medical science has made recent impressive advancements; it can now restore to health near-terminal patients whose illnesses it could hardly understand a few years before. Perhaps in the near future it may become able to restore the dead to life. If so, what would the governments of our world do with this awesome ability? Robert Sheckley suggests an all-too-likely possibility—

And many more.

Our authors include such masters of the macabre as H. P. Lovecraft, World Fantasy Award winner Manly Wade Wellman and Clark Ashton Smith, Edgar Allan Poe, Edith Wharton and Jack London; Hugo and Nebula prize winner Orson Scott Card; an original by newcomer Kathie Griffith; and (surprisingly) one by Erle Stanley Gardner—and others.

These tales express man's fascination with what may lie beyond the gates of death. A land of mist and snow, the ancient Greeks said, roamed by blood-drinking ghosts. A world of sunny meadows and castles, the Vikings believed; of constant combat where those killed at night are magically revived for the next day's battle. For the Faithful of Allah, the milk, the honey, the houris of Paradise await—

These tales are entertainment, meant only to put ice water in your blood on fireside nights. But—who knows—perhaps—possibly—one of them may touch on the secret. What lies on the other side of that dark border? Lazarus, the traveler there and back, remained silent—silent as the grave.

(So, too, did the second traveler there. Jesus of Nazareth, who was crucified and died on the cross, came out of his grave the third day. But in none of his brief speeches to disciples and public did he say anything about what he had been and what he had done there during those three days. Surely *someone* asked. . . . Apparently, like Lazarus, his lips too were sealed. Why?

"In that sleep of death," Prince Hamlet mused, "what dreams may come?"

Dreams—or nightmares?

Here's a whole book of them. . . .

LAZARUS

by Leonid Andreyev

I

When Lazarus left the grave where, for three days and
three nights, he had been under the enigmatical sway of
Death, and returned alive to his dwelling, for a long time
no one noticed in him those sinister peculiarities which,
as time went on, made his very name a horror. Glad-
dened unspeakably by the sight of him who had been
returned to life, those near to him caressed him unceas-
ingly, and satiated their burning desire to serve him, by
their solicitude for his food and drink and garments. And
they dressed him gorgeously, in bright colors of hope and
laughter, and when, like to a bridegroom in his bridal
vestures, he sat again among them at the table, and again
ate and drank, they wept, overwhelmed with tenderness.
And they summoned the neighbors to look at him who
had risen miraculously from the dead. These came and
shared the serene joy of the hosts. Strangers from far-
off towns and hamlets came and adored the miracle in
tempestuous words. Like to a beehive was the house of
Mary and Martha.

Whatever was found new in Lazarus' face and gestures
was thought to be some trace of a grave illness and of
shocks recently experienced. Evidently, the destruction
wrought by death on the corpse had been merely arrested
by some miraculous power, for its effects were still apparent, and what death had succeeded in doing with Lazarus' face and body was like an artist's unfinished sketch
seen under thin glass. On Lazarus' temples, under his

eyes, and in the hollows of his cheeks lay a deep and cadaverous lividness; cadaverously blue also were his long fingers, and around his fingernails, grown long in the grave, the livid hue had become purple and dark. On his lips the skin, swollen in the grave, had burst in places, and thin, reddish cracks were formed, shining as though covered with transparent mica. And he had grown stout. His body, puffed up in the grave, retained its monstrous size and showed those frightful swellings in which one sensed the presence of the rank moisture of decomposition. But the heavy corpse-like odor which permeated Lazarus' graveclothes, and, it seemed, his very body, soon entirely disappeared, the livid spots on his face and hands grew paler, and the reddish cracks closed up, although they never disappeared altogether. That is how Lazarus looked when he appeared before people, in his second life, but his face looked natural to those who had seen him in the coffin.

In addition to the changes in his appearance, Lazarus' temper seemed to have undergone a transformation, but this circumstance startled no one and attracted no attention. Before his death Lazarus had always been cheerful and carefree, fond of laughter and a merry joke. It was because of this brightness and cheerfulness, with not a touch of malice and darkness, that the Master had grown so fond of him. But now Lazarus had grown grave and taciturn, he never jested himself, nor responded with laughter to other people's jokes; and the words which he uttered, very infrequently, were the plainest, most ordinary and necessary words, as devoid of depth and significance as those sounds with which animals express pain and pleasure, thirst and hunger. They were the words that one can say all one's life, and yet they give no indication of what pains and gladdens the depths of the soul.

Thus, with the face of a corpse which for three days had been under the heavy sway of death, dark and taciturn, already appallingly transformed, but still unrecognized by anyone in his new self, he was sitting at the festal table, among friends and relatives, and his gorgeous nuptial garments glittered with yellow gold and

bloody scarlet. Broad waves of jubilation, now soft, now
tempestuously sonorous, surged around him; warm glances
of love were reaching out for his face, still cold with the
coldness of the grave; and a friend's warm palm caressed
his livid, heavy hand. Musicians had been summoned,
and they made merry music on tympanum and pipe, on
cithara and harp. It was as though bees were humming,
grasshoppers chirring, and birds warbling over the happy
house of Mary and Martha.

II

One of the guests incautiously lifted the veil. By a
thoughtless word he broke the serene charm and uncov-
ered the truth in all its naked ugliness. Ere the thought
formed itself in his mind, his lips uttered with a smile:

"Why dost thou not tell us what happened in the
beyond?"

And all grew silent, startled by the question. It was as
if it occurred to them only now that for three days Lazarus had been dead, and they looked at him, anxiously
awaiting his answer. But Lazarus kept silence.

"Thou dost not wish to tell us?" wondered the man.
"Is it so terrible there?"

And again his thought came after his words. Had it
been otherwise, he would not have asked this question,
which at that very moment oppressed his heart with its
insufferable horror. Uneasiness seized all present, and
with a feeling of heavy weariness they awaited Lazarus'
words, but he was silent, sternly and coldly, and his eyes
were lowered. And, as if for the first time, they noticed
the frightful lividness of his face and his repulsive obe-
sity. On the table, as though forgotten by Lazarus, rested
his bluish-purple wrist, and to this all eyes turned as if it
were from it that the awaited answer was to come. The
musicians were still playing, but now the silence reached
them, too, and even as water extinguishes scattered
embers so were their merry tunes extinguished in the
silence. The pipe grew silent; the voices of the sonorous
tympanum and the murmuring harp died away; and, as

if its strings had burst, the cithara answered with a tremulous, broken note. Silence.

"Thou dost not wish to say?" repeated the guest, unable to check his chattering tongue. But the stillness remained unbroken, and the bluish-purple hand rested motionless. And then he stirred slightly and everyone felt relieved. He lifted up his eyes, and lo! straightway embracing everything in one heavy glance, fraught with weariness and horror, he looked at them—Lazarus, who had arisen from the dead.

It was the third day since Lazarus had left the grave. Ever since then many had experienced the pernicious power of his eye, but neither those who were crushed by it forever, nor those who found the strength to resist in it the primordial sources of life (which is as mysterious as death), ever could explain the horror which lay motionless in the depth of his black pupils. Lazarus looked calmly and simply with no desire to conceal anything; he looked coldly, as one who is infinitely indifferent to those alive. Many carefree people came close to him without noticing him, and only later did they learn with astonishment and fear who that calm stout man was, who walked slowly by, almost touching them with his gorgeous and dazzling garments. The sun did not cease shining when he was looking, nor did the fountain hush its murmur, and the sky overhead remained cloudless and blue. But the man under the spell of his enigmatical look heard no more the fountain and saw not the sky overhead. Sometimes he wept bitterly, sometimes he tore his hair and in frenzy called for help; but more often it came to pass that apathetically and quietly he began to die, and so he languished many years, before everybody's very eyes, wasted away, colorless, flabby, dull, like a tree silently drying in a stony soil. And of those who gazed at him, the ones who wept madly sometimes felt again the stir of life; the others never.

"So thou dost not wish to tell us what thou hast seen yonder?" repeated the man. But now his voice was impassive and dull, and deadly gray weariness showed in Lazarus' eyes. And deadly gray weariness covered like dust all the faces, and with dull amazement the guests stared at one another and did not understand wherefore they had gathered here and were sitting at the rich table. The talk ceased. They thought it was time to go home, but could not overcome the flaccid lazy weariness which glued their muscles, and they kept on sitting there, yet apart and torn away from one another, like pale fires scattered over a dark field.

But the musicians were paid to play, and again they took their instruments, and again tunes full of studied mirth and studied sorrow began to flow and to rise. They unfolded the customary melody, but the guests hearkened in dull amazement. Already they knew not wherefore it was necessary nor why it was well that people should pluck strings, inflate their cheeks, blow into slender pipes, and produce a bizarre, many-voiced noise.

"What vile music," said someone.

The musicians took offense and left. Following them, the guests left one after another, for night was already come. And when placid darkness encircled them and they began to breathe with more ease, suddenly Lazarus' image loomed up before each one in formidable radiance: the livid face of a corpse, graveclothes gorgeous and resplendent, a cold look, in the depths of which lay motionless an unknown horror. As though petrified, they were standing far apart, and darkness enveloped them, but in the darkness blazed brighter and brighter the supernatural vision of him who for three days had been under the enigmatical sway of death. For three days had he been dead: thrice had the sun risen and set, but he had been dead; children had played, streams had murmured over pebbles, the wayfarer had stirred up the hot dust in the highroad—but he had been dead. And now he was again among them; he touched them, he looked at them—looked at them! And through the black disks of the pupils, as through darkened glass, stared the unknowable Beyond.

III

No one was taking care of Lazarus, for no friends, no relatives were left to him, and the great desert which encircled the Holy City came near the very threshold of his dwelling. And the desert entered his house and stretched on his couch, like a wife, and extinguished the fires. No one was taking care of Lazarus. One after the other his sisters—Mary and Martha—forsook him. For a long while Martha was loath to abandon him, for she knew not who would feed him and pity him; she wept and prayed. But one night, when the wind was roaming in the desert and with a soughing sound the cypresses were bending over the roof, she dressed noiselessly and left the house secretly. Lazarus probably heard the door slam; it banged against the side-post under the gusts of the desert wind, but he did not rise to go out and to look at her who was abandoning him. All the night long the cypresses soughed over his head and the door thumped plaintively, letting in the cold, greedy desert.

Like a leper he was shunned by everyone, and it was proposed to tie a bell to his neck, as is done with lepers, to warn people against sudden meetings. But someone remarked, growing frightfully pale, that it would be too horrible if by night the tinkling of Lazarus' bell were suddenly heard under the windows—and so the project was abandoned.

And since he did not take care of himself, he would probably have starved to death, had not the neighbors brought him food in fear of something that they sensed but vaguely. The food was brought to him by children; they were not afraid of Lazarus, nor did they mock him with naïve cruelty, as children are wont to do with the wretched and miserable. They were indifferent to him, and Lazarus answered them with the same coldness; he had no desire to caress their fine black curls nor to look into their innocent shining eyes. Given up to Time and to the desert, his house was crumbling down, and long since had his famishing, lowing goats wandered away to the neighboring pastures. And his bridal garments became

threadbare. Ever since that happy day, when the musicians played, he had worn them unaware of the difference of the new and the worn. The bright colors grew
dull and faded; vicious dogs and the sharp thorns of the
desert had turned the soft fabric into rags.

By day, when the merciless sun slew all things alive,
and even scorpions sought shelter under stones and
writhed there in a mad desire to sting, he sat motionless
under the sun's rays, his livid face and his uncouth, bushy
beard lifted up, bathing in the fiery flood.

When people still talked to him, he was once asked:

"Poor Lazarus, doth it please thee to sit thus and to
stare at the sun?"

And he had answered:

"Yes, it doth."

So strong, it seemed, was the cold of his three days'
grave, so deep the darkness, that there was no heat on
earth to warm Lazarus, nor a splendor that could
brighten the darkness of his eyes. That is what came to
the mind of those who spoke to Lazarus, and with a sigh
they left him.

And when the scarlet, flattened globe would sink
lower, Lazarus would set out for the desert and walk
straight toward the sun, as though striving to reach it.
He always walked straight toward the sun, and those who
tried to follow him and to spy upon what he was doing
at night in the desert retained in their memory the black
silhouette of a tall stout man against the red background
of an enormous flattened disk. Night pursued them with
her horrors, and so they did not learn of Lazarus' doings
in the desert, but the vision of black on red was forever
branded on their brains. Just as a beast with a splinter
in its eye furiously rubs its muzzle with its paws, so they,
too, foolishly rubbed their eyes, but what Lazarus had
given was indelible, and Death alone could efface it.

But there were people who lived far away who never
saw Lazarus and knew of him only by report. With daring
curiosity, which is stronger than fear and feeds upon it,
with hidden mockery, they would come to Lazarus as he
sat in the sun and enter into conversation with him. By

this time Lazarus' appearance had changed for the better and was not so terrible. The first minute they snapped their fingers and thought of how stupid the inhabitants of the Holy City were; but when the short talk was over and they started homeward, their looks were such that the inhabitants of the Holy City recognized them at once and said:

"Look, there is one more madman on whom Lazarus has set his eye," and they shook their heads regretfully, and lifted up their arms.

There came brave, intrepid warriors, with clanging weapons; happy youths came with laughter and song; busy tradesmen, jingling their money, ran in for a moment, and haughty priests leaned their staffs against Lazarus' door, and they were all strangely changed as they came back. The same terrible shadow swooped down upon their souls and gave a new appearance to the old familiar world.

Those who still had the desire to speak, expressed their feelings thus:

> All things tangible and visible grew hollow, light, and transparent—similar to lightsome shadows in the darkness of night;
>
> for that great darkness, which encompasses the whole cosmos, was dispersed neither by the sun nor by the moon and the stars, but like an immense black shroud enveloped the earth and, like a mother, embraced it;
>
> it penetrated all the bodies, it penetrated iron and stone—and the particles of the bodies having lost their ties, grew lonely; and it penetrated into the depths of the particles, and the particles of particles became lonely;
>
> for that great void, which encompasses the cosmos, was not filled by things visible; neither by the sun, nor by the moon and the stars, but reigned boundless, penetrating everywhere, severing body, particle from particle;
>
> in the void hollow trees spread hollow roots; in the void temples, palaces, and houses loomed up, threat-

ening a phantasmal fall—loomed up and they were
hollow; and in the void men moved about restlessly,
but they were light and hollow as shadows;

for, Time was no more, and the beginning of all
things came near their end: the building was still being
built, and builders were still hammering away, and its
ruins were already seen and the void in its place; a
man was still being born, but already funeral candles
were burning at his head, and now they were extinguished, and there was the void in place of the men
and of the funeral candles;

and wrapped by void and darkness the man in
despair trembled in the face of the Horror of the
Infinite.

Thus spake the men who had still a desire to speak.
But, surely, much more could have been told by those
who wished not to speak, and died in silence.

IV

At that time there lived in Rome a renowned sculptor.
In clay, marble, and bronze he wrought bodies of gods
and men, and such was their beauty that people called
them immortal. But he himself was discontented and
asserted that there was something even more beautiful
that he could not make concrete either in marble or in
bronze.

"I have not yet gathered the glowing of the moon, nor
have I drunk my fill of sunshine," he was wont to say,
"and there is no soul in my marble, no life in my beautiful bronze."

And when on moonlit nights he slowly walked along
the road, crossing the black shadows of cypresses, his
white tunic flitting under the moon, those who met him
would laugh in a friendly way and say:

"Art thou going to gather moonlight, Aurelius? Why,
then, didst thou not fetch baskets?"

And he would answer, laughing and pointing to his eyes:

"Here are the baskets wherein I gather the sheen of the moon and the glimmer of the sun."

And so it was; the moon glimmered in his eyes and the sun sparkled therein. But he could not translate them into marble, and herein lay the serene tragedy of his life.

He was descended from an ancient patrician race, had a good wife and children, and suffered from no want.

When the obscure rumor about Lazarus reached him, he consulted his wife and friends and undertook the far journey to Judaea to see him who had miraculously risen from the dead. He was somewhat weary in those days and he hoped that the road would sharpen his blunted senses. What was said of Lazarus did not frighten him: he had pondered much over Death, did not like it, but he disliked also those who confused it with life.

"On this side lies life with its splendor of beauty, on the other—Death with its enigma," he pondered, "and man can conceive naught better while he is alive than to delight in life and in the beauty of all things living."

And he even had a vainglorious desire to convince Lazarus of the truth of his own view and restore his soul to life, as his body had been restored. This seemed so much easier because the rumors, timorous and strange, did not convey the whole truth about Lazarus and but vaguely warned against something frightful.

Lazarus had just risen from a rock in order to follow the sun which was setting in the desert, when a rich Roman attended by an armed slave approached him and addressed him in a sonorous tone of voice:

"Lazarus!"

And Lazarus beheld a superb face, lit with glory, and he beheld bright raiment, and precious stones sparkling in the sun. The red light lent to the Roman's face and head the appearance of gleaming bronze—this also Lazarus noticed. He resumed obediently his place and lowered his weary eyes.

"Yea, thou art ugly, my poor Lazarus," quietly said the Roman, playing with his golden chain. "Thou art even horrible, my poor friend, and Death was not idle that day when thou didst fall so heedlessly into its clutches. But thou art as stout as a barrel, and, as the great Caesar used to say, stout people are not ill-tempered; to tell the truth, I don't understand why men fear thee. Permit me to spend the night in thy house; the hour is late, and I have no shelter."

Never had anyone asked Lazarus' hospitality.

"I have no bed," said he.

"I am somewhat of a soldier and I can sleep sitting," the Roman answered. "We shall build a fire."

"I have no fire."

"Then we shall have our talk in the darkness, like two friends. I think thou wilt find a bottle of wine."

"I have no wine."

The Roman laughed.

"Now I see why thou art so somber and dislikest thy second life. No wine! Why, then we shall do without it: there are words that make the head go round better than any Falernian."

By a sign he dismissed the slave, and they remained all alone. And again the sculptor started speaking, but it was as if, together with the setting sun, life had left his words, and they grew pale and hollow, as if they staggered on unsteady feet, as if they stumbled and fell, drunk with the heavy lees of weariness and despair. And black chasms grew up between the words—like far-off hints of the great void and the great darkness.

"Now I am thy guest, and thou wilt not be unkind to me, Lazarus!" said he. "Hospitality is the duty even of those who for three days were dead. Three days, I was told, thou didst rest in the grave. There it must be cold—and that is whence comes thy ill habit of going without fire and wine. As for me, I like fire; it grows dark here so rapidly. . . . The lines of thy eyebrows and forehead are quite, quite interesting: they are like ruins of strange palaces, buried in ashes after an earthquake. But why dost thou wear such ugly and queer garments? I have seen bridegrooms in thy country, and they wear such clothes—so mirth-provoking, so frightful. But thou art no bridegroom, art thou?"

The sun had already disappeared, a monstrous black shadow came running from the east—it was as if gigantic bare feet had begun swishing through the sand, and the wind sent a cold wave along the spine.

"In the darkness thou seemest still bigger, Lazarus, as if thou hadst grown stouter in these few moments. Dost thou feed on darkness, Lazarus? I would fain have a little fire—at least a little fire, a little fire. I feel somewhat chilly, your nights are so barbarously cold. Were it not so dark, I should say that thou wert looking at me, Lazarus. Yes, it seems to me, thou art. Why, thou art looking at me, I feel it—but there, thou art smiling."

Night came and filled the air with heavy blackness.

"How well it will be, when the sun will rise tomorrow anew! I am a great sculptor, as thou mayst know; that is what my friends call me. I create. Yes, that is the word. But I need daylight. I give life to the cold marble, I melt sonorous bronze in fire, in the bright, hot fire. . . . Why didst thou touch me with thy hand?"

"Come," said Lazarus. "Thou art my guest."

And they went to the house. And a long night enveloped the earth.

The slave, seeing that his master did not come, went to seek him, when the sun was already high in the sky. And he beheld his master side by side with Lazarus: in profound silence were they sitting right under the dazzling and scorching rays of the sun and looking upward. The slave began to weep and cried out:

"My Master! What hath befallen thee, Master?"

The very same day Aurelius left for Rome. On the way the sculptor was pensive and taciturn, staring attentively at everything—the men, the ship, the sea, as though trying to retain something. On the high sea a storm burst over them, and all through it Aurelius stayed on deck and eagerly scanned the seas looming near and then sinking with a thud.

At home his friends were frightened at the change

which had taken place in Aurelius, but he calmed them, saying meaningly:

"I have found it."

And without changing the dusty clothes he had worn on his journey, he fell to work, and the marble obediently resounded under his sonorous hammer. Long and eagerly worked he, admitting no one, until one morning he announced that the work was ready and ordered his friends to be summoned, severe critics and connoisseurs of art. And to meet them he put on bright and gorgeous garments, that glittered with the yellow of gold and the scarlet of dyed byssus.

"Behold my work," said he thoughtfully.

His friends glanced, and a shadow of profound sorrow covered their faces. It was something monstrous, deprived of all the lines and shapes familiar to the eye, but not without a hint at some new, strange image.

On a thin, crooked twig, or rather on an ugly likeness of a twig, rested askew a blind, ugly, shapeless, outspread mass of something utterly and inconceivably distorted, a mad leap of wild and bizarre fragments, all feebly and vainly striving to part from one another. And, as if by chance, beneath one of the wildly rent salients a butterfly was chiseled with divine skill, all airy loveliness, delicacy, and beauty, with transparent wings, which seemed to tremble with an impotent desire to take flight.

"Wherefore this wonderful butterfly, Aurelius?" said somebody falteringly.

"I know not," was the sculptor's answer.

But it was necessary to tell the truth, and one of his friends who loved him best said firmly:

"This is ugly, my poor friend. It must be destroyed. Give me the hammer."

And with two strokes he broke the monstrous mass into pieces, leaving only the infinitely delicate butterfly untouched.

From that time on Aurelius created nothing. With profound indifference he looked at marble and bronze, and on his former divine works, whereon everlasting beauty rested. With the purpose of arousing his former fervent passion for work and awakening his deadened soul, his friends took him to see other artists' beautiful works, but he remained as indifferent as before, and no smile warmed his tightened lips. And only after listening to lengthy talks about beauty would he retort wearily and indolently:

"But all this is a lie."

And by day, when the sun was shining, he went into his magnificent, skillfully laid-out garden and, having found a place without shadow, he exposed his bare head to the glare and heat. Red and white butterflies fluttered around; from the crooked lips of a drunken satyr water streamed down with a splash into a marble cistern, but he sat motionless and silent—like a pallid reflection of him who, in the far-off distance, at the very gates of the stony desert, sat under the fiery sun.

V

And now it came to pass that the great, deified Augustus himself summoned Lazarus. The Imperial messengers dressed him gorgeously, in solemn nuptial clothes, as if Time had legalized them, and he was to remain until his very death the bridegroom of an unknown bride. It was as though an old, rotting coffin had been gilded and furnished with new, gay tassels. And men, all in trim and bright attire, rode after him, as if in bridal procession indeed, and those at the head trumpeted loudly, bidding people to clear the way for the Emperor's messengers. But Lazarus' way was deserted: his native land cursed the hateful name of him who had miraculously risen from the dead, and people scattered at the very news of his appalling approach. The solitary voice of the brass trumpets sounded in the motionless air, and the wilderness alone responded with its languid echo.

Then Lazarus went by sea. And his was the most magnificently arrayed and the most mournful ship that ever mirrored itself in the azure waves of the Mediterranean Sea. Many were the travelers aboard, but like a tomb was the ship, all silence and stillness, and the despairing water sobbed at the steep, proudly curved prow. All alone sat Lazarus, exposing his head to the blaze of the sun, silently listening to the murmur and splash of the wavelets, and the seamen and messengers sat far from him, a vague group of weary shadows. Had the thunder burst and the wind attacked the red sails, the ship would probably have perished, for none of those aboard had either the will or the strength to struggle for life. With a supreme effort some mariners would reach the board and eagerly scan the blue, transparent deep, hoping to see a naiad's pink shoulder flash in the hollow of an azure wave, or a drunken gay centaur dash along and in frenzy splash the wave with his hoof. But the sea was like a wilderness, and the deep was mute and deserted.

With utter indifference did Lazarus set his feet on the streets of the Eternal City. As though all her wealth, all the magnificence of her palaces built by giants, all the resplendence, beauty, and music of her refined life were but the echo of the wind in the wilderness, the reflection of the desert's shifting sands. Chariots were dashing along, and through the streets moved throngs of the strong, fair, proud builders of the Eternal City and haughty participants in its life; a song sounded; fountains and women laughed their pearly laughter; drunken philosophers harangued, and the sober listened to them with a smile; hoofs pounded the stone pavements. And surrounded by cheerful noise, a stout, heavy man was moving along, a chilling blotch of silence and despair, and on his way he sowed disgust, anger, and vague, gnawing weariness. "Who dares to be sad in Rome?" the citizens wondered indignantly, and frowned. In two days the entire city already knew all about him who had miraculously risen from the dead, and apprehensively shunned him.

But some daring people there were who wanted to test their strength, and Lazarus obeyed their imprudent summons. Kept busy by state affairs, the Emperor constantly delayed the reception, and seven days did he who had risen from the dead go about visiting others.

And Lazarus came to a cheerful winebibber, and the host met him with laughter on his lips:

"Drink, Lazarus, drink!" shouted he. "Would not Augustus laugh to see thee drunk!"

And half-naked drunken women laughed, and rose petals fell on Lazarus' livid hands. But then the winebibber looked into Lazarus' eyes, and his gaiety ended forever. Drunk did he remain for the rest of his life; never did he drink aught, yet he remained drunk. But, instead of the gay reveries which wine brings with it, frightful dreams began to haunt him, the sole food of his stricken spirit. Day and night he lived in the noisome vapors of his nightmares, and death itself was not more frightful than its raving, monstrous forerunners.

And Lazarus came to a youth and his beloved, who loved each other and were most beautiful in their passion. Proudly and strongly embracing his love, the youth said with soft compassion:

"Look upon us, Lazarus, and share our joy. Is there aught stronger than love?"

And Lazarus looked. And for the rest of their life they kept on loving each other, but their passion grew gloomy and joyless, like those funereal cypresses whose roots feed on the decay of the graves and whose black summits in a still evening hour seek in vain to reach the sky. Thrown by the unknown forces of life into each other's embraces, they mingled tears with kisses, voluptuous pleasures with pain, and they felt themselves doubly slaves, obedient slaves to life, and patient servants of the silent Nothingness. Ever united, ever severed, they blazed like sparks and like sparks lost themselves in the boundless dark.

And Lazarus came to a haughty sage, and the sage said to him:

"I know all the horrors thou canst reveal to me. Is there aught thou canst frighten me with?"

But before long the sage felt that the knowledge of horror was far from being horror itself, and that the vision of death was not Death. And he felt that wisdom and folly are equal before the face of Infinity, for Infinity knows them not. And it vanished, the dividing-line between knowledge and ignorance, between truth and falsehood, between upper and nether, and shapeless thought hung suspended in the void. Then the sage clutched his gray head and cried out frantically:

"I cannot think! I cannot think!"

Thus, under the indifferent glance of him who had miraculously risen from the dead, perished everything that serves to affirm life, its significance and joys. And it was suggested that it was dangerous to let him look upon the Emperor, that it was better to kill him, and, having buried him secretly, to tell the Emperor that he had disappeared none knew whither. Already swords were being whetted, and youths devoted to the public welfare prepared for the murder, when Augustus ordered Lazarus to be brought before him next morning, thus destroying the cruel plans.

If there was no way of getting rid of Lazarus, at least it was possible to soften the terrible impression his face produced. With this in view, skillful painters, tonsorial-ists, and artists were summoned, and all night long they busied themselves over the head of Lazarus. They trimmed his beard, curled it, and gave it a neat, agreeable appearance. By means of pigments they concealed the corpse-like lividness of his hands and face. Repulsive were the wrinkles of suffering that furrowed his aged face, and they were puttied, painted, and smoothed; then, over the smooth background, wrinkles of good-tempered laughter and pleasant, carefree mirth were skillfully painted with fine brushes.

Lazarus submitted indifferently to everything that was done to him. Soon he was turned into a becomingly stout, venerable old man, into a quiet and kind grandfather of numerous offspring. It seemed that the smile, with which only a while ago he had been telling funny stories, was still lingering on his lips, and that in the corner of each eye was still lurking that serene kindliness which is the companion of old age. But they dared not change his nuptial garments, and they could

not change his eyes, two dark and frightful panes
through which the incomprehensible Beyond itself was
gazing upon men.

VI

Lazarus was not moved by the magnificence of the Imperial palace. It was as though he saw no difference
between the crumbling house closely pressed by the
desert, and the stone palace, solid and fair, and indifferently he passed into it. And the hard marble of the floors
he trod grew similar to the shifting sand of the desert,
and the multitude of richly dressed and haughty men
became like void air under his glance. No one looked
into his face as Lazarus passed by, fearing to fall under
the appalling influence of his eyes; but when the sound
of his heavy footsteps had sufficiently died down, the
courtiers raised their heads and with fearful curiosity
scrutinized the figure of a stout, tall, slightly bent old
man, who was slowly penetrating into the very heart of
the Imperial palace. Were Death itself passing, it would
be faced with no greater fear: for until then the dead
alone knew Death, and those alive knew Life only—and
there was no bridge between them. But this extraordinary man, although alive, knew Death, and enigmatical,
appalling, was his accursed knowledge.

"Woe," people thought, "he will take the life of our
great, deified Augustus," and they sent curses after Lazarus, who meanwhile kept on advancing into the interior
of the palace.

Already did the Emperor know who Lazarus was, and
prepared to meet him. But the Monarch was a brave
man, and felt his own tremendous unconquerable power,
and in his fateful duel with him who had miraculously
risen from the dead he did not want to invoke human
help. And so he met Lazarus face to face.

"Lift not thine eyes upon me, Lazarus," he commanded. "I have heard that thy face is like that of the
Medusa and turns into stone whomsoever thou lookest
at. Now, I wish to see thee and have a talk with thee,

before I turn into stone," he added in a tone of regal jocoseness, not devoid of fear.

Coming close to Lazarus, he carefully examined his face and his strange festal garments. And, although Augustus had a keen eye, he was deceived by the appearance of Lazarus.

"So. Thou dost not appear terrible, my venerable old man. But the worse for us, if horror assumes such a respectable and pleasant air. Now let us have a talk."

Augustus sat, and questioning Lazarus as much with his eyes as with words, started the conversation:

"Why didst thou not greet me upon thy entering?"

"I knew not it was needful," Lazarus answered with indifference.

"Art thou a Christian?"

"Nay."

Augustus nodded his head in approval.

" 'Tis well. I like not the Christians. They shake the tree of life ere it is covered with fruit, and scatter its fragrant bloom to the winds. But who art thou?"

"I was dead," answered Lazarus with a visible effort.

"So I have heard. But who art thou now?"

Lazarus was silent, but at last repeated in a tone of weary apathy:

"I was dead."

"Listen to me, stranger," said the Emperor, distinctly and severely giving utterance to the thought that had come to him at the beginning, "my realm is the realm of Life, my people are of the living, not of the dead. Thou art one too many here. I know not who thou art nor what thou sawest there; but if thou liest, I hate thy lies, and if thou tellest the truth, I hate thy truth. In my bosom I feel the throb of life; I feel strength in my arm, and my proud thoughts, like eagles, pierce the space. And yonder is the shelter of my rule; under the protection of laws created by me people live and toil and rejoice. Dost thou hear the battle cry, the challenge men throw into the face of the future?"

Augustus, as in prayer, stretched forth his arms and exclaimed solemnly:

"Be blessed, O great and divine Life!"

Lazarus was silent, and with growing sternness the Emperor went on:

"Thou art not wanted here, miserable scrap snatched from under Death's teeth, thou inspirest weariness and disgust with life; like a caterpillar in the fields, thou devourest the rich ear of joy and spewest forth the drivel of despair and sorrow. Thy truth is like a rusty sword in the hands of a mighty murderer—and as a murderer thou shalt be executed. But before that let me look into thine eyes. Perchance 'tis only cowards who fear them, whereas in the brave they awake the thirst for strife and victory; in that case thou shalt be rewarded and not executed. Now look at me, Lazarus."

At first it appeared to the deified Augustus that a friend was looking at him—so soft, so tenderly fascinating was Lazarus' gaze. It held a promise not of horror but sweet rest, and the Infinite seemed to the Emperor a tender mistress, a compassionate sister, a mother. But stronger and stronger grew its embraces, and already the mouth, greedy for kisses, interfered with the Monarch's breathing, and already to the surface of the soft tissues of the body came the iron of the bones and tightened the merciless circle, and unknown fangs, blunt and cold, touched his heart and languidly sank therein.

"It pains me," said the deified Augustus, turning pale. "Yet look at me, Lazarus, look at me."

It was as though ponderous gates, ever closed, were slowly moving apart, and through the increasing interstice the appalling horrors of the Infinite were pouring out, slowly and steadily. Like two shadows they entered the shoreless void and the unfathomable darkness; they extinguished the sun, ravished the earth from under the feet and the roof from overhead. No more did the congealed heart ache.

"Look on, look on, Lazarus," Augustus commanded, tottering.

Time stood still, and the beginning of each thing grew frightfully near to its end. The throne of Augustus, but recently raised up, crumbled down, and the Void was already in the place of that throne and of Augustus. Noiselessly did Rome itself crumble into dust and a new city stood on its site, and it, too, was swallowed by the void. Like fantastic giants cities, states, and countries fell and vanished in the void darkness—and with utmost indifference did the insatiable black maw of the Infinite swallow them.

"Cease!" the Emperor commanded.

In his voice already sounded a note of indifference; his hands dropped in languor, and in the vain struggle with the onrushing darkness his eagle-like eyes now blazed up, now dimmed.

"Thou hast slain me, Lazarus," said he in a spiritless, feeble voice.

And these words of hopelessness saved him. He remembered his people, whose shield he was destined to be, and keen salutary pain pierced his deadened heart.

"They are doomed to death," he reflected wearily. "Bleak shades in the darkness of the Infinite," he reflected, and horror grew within him. "Fragile vessels with living, seething blood, with hearts that know sorrow, and great joy also," he reflected within his heart, and tenderness pervaded it.

Thus pondering and oscillating between the poles of Life and Death, he slowly came back to life, to find in its sufferings and in its joys a shield against the darkness of the Void and the horror of the Infinite.

"Nay, thou hast not slain me, Lazarus," said he firmly, "but 'tis I who will take thy life. Get thee gone!"

That evening the deified Augustus partook of his meats and wines with particular joy. Now and then his lifted hand remained hovering in the air, and a dull glimmer replaced the bright sheen of his eaglelike eyes. It was the cold wave of Horror that surged at his feet. Defeated, but not undone, ever awaiting its hour, that Horror stood at the Emperor's bedside like a black shadow that pervaded all his life; it swayed his nights but yielded the days to the sorrows and joys of Life.

The following day the public executioner seared with a hot iron the eyes of Lazarus. Thereafter he was sent back to his native land. The deified Augustus dared not kill him.

Lazarus returned to the desert, and the wilderness met him with the hissing breath of its wind and the heat of its blazing sun. Again he sat on a rock, his uncouth, bushy beard lifted up, and the two black holes that had been his eyes stared at the sky with an expression of dull terror. Afar off the Holy City stirred noisily and restlessly, but around him everything was deserted and mute. No one approached the place where dwelt he who had miraculously risen from the dead, and long since his neighbors had forsaken their houses. Driven by the executioner's red-hot iron into the depth of his skull, his accursed knowledge hid there in ambush. As though leaping out of that ambush it plunged its thousand invisible eyes into man—and none dared look upon Lazarus.

And in the evening, when the sun, reddening and expanding, would come nearer and nearer the western horizon, the blinded Lazarus would slowly follow it. He would stumble against the rocks and fall, obese and weak as he was, would rise heavily to his feet and walk on again; and against the red screen of the sunset his black body and outspread hands would form a monstrous likeness of a cross.

And it came to pass that once he went out and did not come back. Thus seemingly ended the second life of him who had for three days been under the enigmatical sway of Death and had risen miraculously from the dead.

THE ROSE-CRYSTAL BELL

by Robert Arthur

Twenty years had left no trace inside Sam Kee's little shop on Mott Street. There were the same dusty jars of ginseng root and tigers' whiskers, the same little bronze Buddhas, the same gimcracks mixed with fine jade. Edith Williams gave a little murmur of pleasure as the door shut behind her and her husband.

"Mark," she said, "it hasn't changed! It doesn't look as if a thing had been sold since we were here on our honeymoon."

"It certainly doesn't," Dr. Mark Williams agreed, moving down the narrow aisle behind her. "If someone hadn't told us Sam Kee was dead, I'd believe we'd stepped back twenty years in time, as they do in those scientific stories young David reads."

"We must buy something," his wife said. "For a twentieth anniversary present for me. Perhaps a bell?"

From the shadowy depths of the shop a young man emerged, American in dress and manner despite the Oriental contours of his face and eyes.

"Good evening," he said. "May I show you something?"

"We think we want a bell." Dr. Williams chuckled. "But we aren't quite sure. You're Sam Kee's son?"

"Sam Kee, junior. My honored father passed to the halls of his ancestors five years ago. I could just say that he died——" black eyes twinkled—— "but customers

34

like the more flowery mode of speech. They think it's quaint."

"I think it's just nice, and not quaint at all," Edith Williams declared. "We're sorry your father is dead. We'd hoped to see him again. Twenty years ago when we were a very broke young couple on a honeymoon he sold us a wonderful rose-crystal necklace for half price."

"I'm sure he still made a profit." The black eyes twinkled again. "But if you'd like a bell, here are small temple bells, camel bells, dinner bells . . ."

But even as he spoke, Edith Williams's hand darted to something at the back of the shelf.

"A bell carved out of crystal!" she exclaimed. "And rose-crystal at that. What could be more perfect? A rose-crystal wedding present and a rose-crystal anniversary present!"

The young man half stretched out his hand.

"I don't think you want that," he said. "It's broken."

"Broken?" Edith Williams rubbed off the dust and held the lovely bell-shape of crystal, the size of a pear, to the light. "It looks perfect to me."

"I mean it is not complete." Something of the American had vanished from the young man. "It has no clapper. It will not ring."

"Why, that's right." Mark Williams took the bell. "The clapper's missing."

"We can have another clapper made," his wife declared. "That is, if the original can't be found?"

The young Chinese shook his head.

"The bell and the clapper were deliberately separated by my father twenty years ago." He hesitated, then added: "My father was afraid of this bell."

"Afraid of it?" Mark Williams raised his eyebrows.

The other hesitated again.

"It will probably sound like a story for tourists," he said. "But my father believed it. This bell was supposedly stolen from the temple of a sect of Buddhists somewhere in the mountains of China's interior. Just as many Occidentals believe that the Christian Judgment Day will be heralded by a blast on St. Peter's trumpet, so this small sect is said to believe that when a bell like this one is rung, a bell carved from a single piece of rose-crystal, and consecrated by ceremonies lasting ten years, any dead within sound of it will rise and live again."

"Heavenly!" Edith Williams cried. "And no pun intended. Mark, think what a help this bell will be in your practice when we make it ring again!" To the Chinese she added, smiling: "I'm just teasing him. My husband is really a very fine surgeon."

The other bowed his head.

"I must tell you," he said, "you will not be able to make it ring. Only the original clapper, carved from the same block of rose crystal, will ring it. That is why my father separated them."

Again he hesitated.

"I have told you only half of what my father told me. He said that, though it defeats death, Death cannot be defeated. Robbed of his chosen victim, he takes another in his place. Thus when the bell was used in the temple of its origin—let us say when a high priest or a chief had died—a slave or servant was placed handy for Death to take when he had been forced to relinquish his grasp upon the important one."

He smiled, shook his head.

"There," he said. "A preposterous story. Now if you wish it, the bell is ten dollars. Plus, of course, sales tax."

"The story alone is worth more," Dr. Williams declared. "I think we'd better have it sent, hadn't we, Edith? It'll be safer in the mail than in our suitcase."

"Sent?" His wife seemed to come out of some deep feminine meditation. "Oh, of course. And as for its not ringing—I shall make it ring. I know I shall."

"If the story is true," Mark Williams murmured, "I hope not . . ."

The package came on a Saturday morning, when Mark Williams was catching up on the latest medical publications in his untidy, book-lined study. He heard Edith unwrapping paper in the hall outside. Then she came in with the rose-crystal bell in her hands.

"Mark, it's here!" she said. "Now to make it ring."

She plumped herself down beside his desk. He took the bell and reached for a silver pencil.

"Just for the sake of curiosity," he remarked, "and not because I believe that delightful sales talk we were given, let's see if it will ring when I tap. It should, you know."

He tapped the lip of the bell. A muted *thunk* was the only response. Then he tried with a coin, a paper knife, and the bottom of a glass. In each instance the resulting sound was nothing like a bell ringing.

"If you've finished, Mark," Edith said then, with feminine tolerance, "let me show you how it's done."

"Gladly," her husband agreed. She took the bell and turned away for a moment. Then she shook the bell vigorously. A clear, sweet ringing trembled through the room—so thin and ethereal that small involuntary shivers crawled up her husband's spine.

"Good Lord!" he exclaimed. "How did you do that?"

"I just put the clapper back in place with some thread," Edith told him.

"The clapper?" He struck his forehead with his palm. "Don't tell me—the crystal necklace we bought twenty years ago!"

"Of course." Her tone was composed. "As soon as young Sam Kee told us about his father's separating the clapper and the bell, I remembered the central crystal pendant on my necklace. It *is* shaped like a bell clapper— we mentioned it once.

"I guessed right away we had the missing clapper. But I didn't say so. I wanted to score on you, Mark——" she smiled affectionately at him—— "and because, you know, I had a queer feeling Sam Kee, junior, wouldn't let us have the bell if he guessed we had the clapper."

"I don't think he would have." Mark Williams picked up his pipe and rubbed the bowl with his thumb. "Yet he didn't really believe that story he told us any more than we do."

"No, but his father did. And if old Sam Kee had told

it to us—remember how wrinkled and wise he seemed?—I'm sure we'd have believed the story."

"You're probably right." Dr. Williams rang the bell and waited. The thin, sweet sound seemed to hang in the air a long moment, then was gone.

"Nope," he said. "Nothing happened. Although, of course, that may be because there was no deceased around to respond."

"I'm not sure I feel like joking about the story." A small frown gathered on Edith's forehead. "I had planned to use the bell as a dinner bell and to tell the story to our guests. But now—I'm not sure."

Frowning, she stared at the bell until the ringing of the telephone in the hall brought her out of her abstraction.

"Sit still, I'll answer." She hurried out. Dr. Williams, turning the rose-crystal bell over in his hand, could hear the sudden tension in her voice as she answered. He was on his feet when she re-entered.

"An emergency operation at the hospital." She sighed. "Nice young man—automobile accident. Fracture of the skull, Dr. Amos says. He wouldn't have disturbed you but you're the only brain man in town, with Dr. Hendryx away on vacation."

"I know." Mark Williams was already in the hall, reaching for his hat. "Man's work is from sun to sun, but a doctor's work is never done," he misquoted.

"I'll drive you," Edith followed him out. "You sit back and relax for another ten minutes. . . ."

Mark Williams drew off his rubber gloves with a weary sense of failure. He had lost patients before, but never without a feeling of personal defeat. Edith said he put too much of himself into every operation. Perhaps he did. And yet—— But there was no reason for the boy to have died. Despite his injury his condition at the beginning of the operation had been excellent.

But in the middle of it he had begun to fail, his respiration to falter, his pulse to become feeble. And just as Mark Williams was completing his delicate stitching, he had ceased to breathe.

Why? Mark Williams asked himself. But there was probably no answer. Life was a flukey and unpredictable thing. Take the other lad he had operated on the night before. He had been in far worse shape than this one, and had come through with flying colors. In Room 9, just across the hall, he was gathering strength for another fifty years of life.

Young Dr. Amos, who had been the anesthetist, came over and clapped him understandingly on the shoulder as he reached for his suit coat.

"Too bad, Mark," he said. "Nobody could have done a finer job. Life just didn't want that lad, I'm afraid."

"Thanks, John." Mark tried to sound cheerful. "That's how it is, sometimes. I'd rather like an autopsy, just to satisfy myself."

"Of course. I'll order it. You look a bit tired. Go on home. Here, let me help you with your coat."

Mark Williams slid into the jacket and, when he tried to button it, became aware of the bulky object in one pocket.

"Now what's this?" he asked, and fished out the rose-crystal bell, which he had undoubtedly thrust into his pocket when the telephone call had come. "Edith's bell! She won't thank me for carrying it around this way. . . ."

"Mark, catch it!" young Amos cried as the crystal object slipped through Dr. Williams's weary fingers. It was Amos himself who caught it, a flying catch in midair that rescued the bell before it could smash on the floor. The bell tinkled abruptly, a thin, high sound, then rested silently in Amos's palm.

"That was a close one!" the younger man said. "Pretty thing. What is it?"

"A Chinese dinner bell," Mark Williams answered. "I'd better——" He didn't finish. Behind them Nurse Wythe was calling excitedly.

"Doctor! Doctor Williams! The patient's respiration is beginning! His pulse is beating. Come quickly!"

"What?" He whirled and strode back to the operating table. It was true. Pulse and respiration had re-established themselves. Even as he stood there both were gaining in strength.

"Good Lord!" breathed young Amos. "Now isn't that something! Spontaneous re-establishment of life! I never read of anything quite like this, Mark. I think we're going to save him after all."

They had saved him, quite definitely, when Nurse McGregor slipped into the operating room.

"I'm sorry to bother you, Doctor Williams," she said, in great agitation. "But could you come to the patient in Nine at once? He was doing splendidly, but five minutes ago he had a sudden relapse. I left Nurse Johnson with him and came for you—but I'm afraid he's dead."

It was lucky that traffic was light as they drove homeward. More than once Mark found himself to the left of the center line and had to pull back.

"Now why did that boy die?" he demanded. "Why, Edith? . . . By the way, here's that rose-crystal bell. Better put it in your handbag . . . He was doing fine. And then, just as we were saving one boy we thought we'd lost—we lost the one we thought we'd saved."

"These things happen, darling," she said. "You know that. A doctor can only do so much. Some of the joy always remains in the hands of Nature. And she does play tricks at times."

"Yes, confound it, I know it," her husband growled. "But I resent losing that lad. There was no valid reason for it—unless there was some complication I overlooked." He shook his head, scowling. "I ordered an autopsy but—— Yes, I'm going to do that autopsy myself. I'm going to turn back and do it now. I want to know!"

He pulled abruptly to the left to swing into a side road and turn. Edith Williams never saw the car that hit them. She heard the frantic blare of a horn and a scream of brakes, and in a frozen instant realized that there had been someone behind them, about to pass. Then the impact came, throwing her forward into the windshield and unconsciousness.

*   *   *

Edith Williams opened her eyes. Even before she realized that she was lying on the ground and that the figure bending over her was a State Trooper, she remembered the crash. Her head hurt but there was no confusion in her mind. Automatically, even as she tried to sit up, she accepted the fact that there had been a crash, help had come, and she must have been unconscious for several minutes at least.

"Hey, lady, take it easy!" the Trooper protested. "You had a bad bump. You got to lie still until the ambulance gets here. It'll be along in five minutes."

"Mark," Edith said, paying no attention. "My husband! Is he all right?"

"Now, lady, please. He's being taken care of. You——"

But she was not listening. Holding on to the State Trooper's arm, she pulled herself to a sitting position. She saw the car on its side some yards away, other cars pulled up, a little knot of staring people. Saw them and dismissed them. Her gaze found her husband, lying on the ground a few feet away, a coat folded beneath his head.

Mark was dead. She had been a doctor's wife for twenty years, and before that a nurse. She knew death when she saw it.

"Mark." The word was spoken to herself, but the Trooper took it for a question.

"Yes, lady," he said. "He's dead. He was still breathing when I got here, but he died two, three minutes ago."

She got to her knees. Her only thought was to reach his side. She scrambled across the few feet of ground to him still on her knees and crouched beside him, fumbling for his pulse. There was none. There was nothing. Just a man who had been alive and now was dead.

Behind her she heard a voice raised. She turned. A large, disheveled man was standing beside the Trooper, talking loudly.

"Now listen, officer," he was saying, "I'm telling you again, it wasn't my fault. The guy pulled sharp left right in front of me. Not a thing I could do. It's a wonder we weren't all three of us killed. You can see by the marks on their car it wasn't my fault——"

Edith Williams closed her mind to the voice. She let Mark's hand lie in her lap as she fumbled in her bag, which she somehow still clutched in her fingers. She groped for a handkerchief to stem the tears which would not be held back. Something was in the way—something smooth and hard and cold. She drew it out and heard the thin, sweet tinkle of the crystal bell.

The hand in her lap moved. She gasped and bent forward as her husband's eyes opened.

"Mark!" she whispered. "Mark, darling!"

"Edith," Mark Williams said with an effort. "Sorry—— darned careless of me. Thinking of the hospital . . ."

"You're alive!" she said. "You're *alive*! Oh, darling, darling, lie still, the ambulance will be here any second."

"Ambulance?" he protested. "I'm all right now. Help me sit up."

"But Mark——"

"Just a bump on the head." He struggled to sit up. The State Trooper came over.

"Easy, buddy, easy," he said, his voice awed. "We thought you were gone. Now let's not lose you a second time."

"Hey, I'm sure glad you're all right!" the red-faced man said in a rush of words. "Whew, fellow, you had me all upset, even though it wasn't my fault. I mean, how's a guy gonna keep from hitting you when— when——"

"Catch him!" Mark Williams cried, but the trooper was too late. The other man plunged forward to the ground and lay where he had fallen without quivering.

The clock in the hall struck two with muted strokes. Cautiously Edith Williams rose on her elbow and looked down at her husband's face. His eyes opened and looked back at her.

"You're awake," she said, unnecessarily.

"I woke up a few minutes ago," he answered. "I've been lying here—thinking."

"I'll get you another sedative pill. Dr. Amos said for you to take them and sleep until tomorrow."

"I know. I'll take one presently. You know—hearing that clock just now reminded me of something."

"Yes?"

"Just before I came to this afternoon, after the crash, I had a strange impression of hearing a bell ring. It sounded so loud in my ears I opened my eyes to see where it was."

"A—bell?"

"Yes. Just auditory hallucination, of course."

"But, Mark——"

"Yes?"

"A—a bell did ring. I mean, I had the crystal bell in my bag and it tinkled a little. Do you suppose——"

"Of course not." But though he spoke swiftly he did not sound convincing. "This was a loud bell. Like a great gong."

"But—I mean, Mark darling—a moment earlier you—had no pulse."

"No pulse?"

"And you weren't breathing. Then the crystal bell tinkled and you—you . . ."

"Nonsense! I know what you're thinking and believe me—it's nonsense!"

"But Mark." She spoke carefully. "The driver of the other car. You had no sooner regained consciousness than he——"

"He had a fractured skull!" Dr. Williams interrupted sharply. "The ambulance intern diagnosed it. Skull fractures often fail to show themselves and then—bingo, you keel over. That's what happened. Now let's say no more about it."

"Of course." In the hall, the clock struck the quarter hour. "Shall I fix the sedative now?"

"Yes—no. Is David home?"

She hesitated. "No, he hasn't got back yet."

"Has he phoned? He knows he's supposed to be in by midnight at the latest."

"No, he—hasn't phoned. But there's a school dance tonight."

"That's no excuse for not phoning. He has the old car, hasn't he?"

"Yes. You gave him the keys this morning, remember?"

"All the more reason he should phone." Dr. Williams lay silent a moment. "Two o'clock is too late for a 17-year-old boy to be out."

"I'll speak to him. He won't do it again. Now please, Mark, let me get you the sedative. I'll stay up until David——"

The ringing phone, a clamor in the darkness, interrupted her. Mark Williams reached for it. The extension was beside his bed.

"Hello," he said. And then, although she could not hear the answering voice, she felt him stiffen. And she knew. As well as if she could hear the words she knew, with a mother's instinct for disaster.

"Yes," Dr. Williams said. "Yes . . . I see . . . I understand . . . I'll come at once . . . Thank you for calling."

He slid out of bed before she could stop him.

"An emergency call." He spoke quietly. "I have to go." He began to throw on his clothes.

"It's David," she said. "Isn't it?" She sat up. "Don't try to keep me from knowing. It's about David."

"Yes," he said. His voice was very tired. "David is hurt. I have to go to him. An accident."

"He's dead." She said it steadily. "David's dead, isn't he, Mark?"

He came over and sat beside her and put his arms around her.

"Edith," he said. "Edith—— Yes, he's dead. Forty minutes ago. The car went over a curve. They have him—at the County morgue. They want me to—identify him. Identify him, Edith! You see, the car caught fire!"

"I'm coming with you," she said. "I'm coming with you!"

The taxi waited in a pool of darkness between two street lights. The long, low building which was the County morgue, a blue lamp over its door, stood below the street level. A flight of concrete steps went down to it from the sidewalk. Ten minutes before, Dr. Mark Williams had gone down those steps. Now he climbed back up them, stiffly, wearily, like an old man.

Edith was waiting in the taxi, sitting forward on the edge of the seat, hands clenched. As he reached the last step she opened the door and stepped out.

"Mark," she asked shakily, "was it——"

"Yes, it's David." His voice was a monotone. "Our son. I've completed the formalities. Now the only thing we can do is go home."

"I'm going to him!" She tried to pass. He caught her wrist. Discreetly the taxi driver pretended to doze.

"No, Edith! There's no need. You mustn't see him!"

"He's my son!" she cried. "Let me go!"

"No! What have you got under your coat?"

"It's the bell, the rose-crystal bell!" she cried. "I'm going to ring it where David can hear!"

Defiantly she brought forth her hand, clutching the little bell. "It brought you back, Mark! Now it's going to bring back David!"

"Edith!" he said in horror. "You mustn't believe that's possible. You can't. Those were coincidences. Now let me have it."

"No! I'm going to ring it." Violently she tried to break out of his grip. "I want David back! I'm going to ring the bell!"

She got her hand free. The crystal bell rang in the quiet of the early morning with an eerie thinness, penetrating the silence like a silver knife.

"There!" Edith Williams panted. "I've rung it. I know you don't believe, but I do. It'll bring David back." She raised her voice. "David!" she called. "David, son! Can you hear me?"

"Edith," Dr. Williams groaned. "You're just tormenting yourself. Come home. Please come home."

"Not until David has come back . . . David, David,

can you hear me?" She rang the bell again, rang it until
Dr. Williams seized it, then she let him take it.

"Edith, Edith," he groaned. "If only you had let me
come alone . . ."

"Mark, listen!"

"What?"

"Listen!" she whispered with fierce urgency.

He was silent. And then fingers of horror drew themselves down his spine at the clear, youthful voice that
came up to them from the darkness below.

"Mother? . . . Dad? . . . Where are you?"

"David!" Edith Williams breathed. "It's David! Let
me go! I must go to him."

"No, Edith!" her husband whispered frantically, as the
voice below called again.

"Dad? . . . Mother? . . . Are you up there? Wait for
me."

"Let me go!" she sobbed. "David, we're here! We're
up here, son!"

"Edith!" Mark Williams gasped. "If you've ever loved
me, listen to me. You mustn't go down there. David—I
had to identify him by his class ring and his wallet. He
was burned—terribly burned!"

"I'm going to him!" She wrenched herself free and
sped for the steps, up which now was coming a tall form,
a shadow shrouded in the darkness.

Dr. Williams, horror knotting his stomach, leaped to
stop her. But he slipped and fell headlong on the pavement, so that she was able to race panting down the
stairs to meet the upcoming figure.

"Oh, David," she sobbed, "David!"

"Hey, Mom!" The boy held her steady. "I'm sorry.
I'm terribly sorry. But I didn't know what had happened
until I got home and you weren't there and then one of
the fellows from the fraternity called me. I realized they
must have made a mistake, and you'd come here, and I
called for a taxi and came out here. My taxi let me off
at the entrance around the block, and I've been looking
for you down there . . . Poor Pete!"

"Pete?" she asked.

"Pete Friedburg. He was driving the old car. I lent him the keys and my driver's license. I shouldn't have—but he's older and he kept begging me. . . ."

"Then—then it's Pete who was killed?" she gasped. "Pete who was—burned?"

"Yes, Pete. I feel terrible about lending him the car. But he was supposed to be a good driver. And then their calling you, you and Dad thinking it was me——"

"Then Mark was right. Of course he was right." She was laughing and sobbing now. "It's just a bell, a pretty little bell, that's all."

"Bell? I don't follow you, Mom."

"Never mind," Edith Williams gasped. "It's just a bell. It hasn't any power over life and death. It doesn't bring back and it doesn't take away. But let's get back up to your father. He may be thinking that the bell—that the bell really worked."

They climbed the rest of the steps. Dr. Mark Williams still lay where he had fallen headlong on the pavement. The cab driver was bending over him, but there was nothing to be done. The crystal bell had been beneath him when he fell, and it had broken. One long, fine splinter of crystal was embedded in his heart.

GLÁMR

by S. Baring-Gould

At the beginning of the eleventh century there stood, a little way up the Valley of Shadows in the north of Iceland, a small farm, occupied by a worthy bonder, named Thorhall, and his wife. The farmer was not exactly a chieftain, but he was well enough connected to be considered respectable; to back up his gentility he possessed numerous flocks of sheep and a goodly drove of oxen. Thorhall would have been a happy man but for one circumstance—his sheepwalks were haunted.

Not a herdsman would remain with him; he bribed, he threatened, entreated, all to no purpose; one shepherd after another left his service, and things came to such a pass that he determined on asking advice at the next annual council. Thorhall saddled his horses, adjusted his packs, provided himself with hobbles, cracked his long Icelandic whip, and cantered along the road, and in due time reached Thingvellir.

Skapti Thorodd's son was lawgiver at that time, and as everyone considered him a man of the utmost prudence and able to give the best advice, our friend from the Vale of Shadows made straight for his booth.

"An awkward predicament, certainly—to have large droves of sheep and no one to look after them," said Skapti, nibbling the nail of his thumb, and shaking his wise head—a head as stuffed with law as a ptarmigan's crop is stuffed with blaeberries. "Now I'll tell you what— as you have asked my advice, I will help you to a shepherd; a character in his way, a man of dull intellect, to be sure, but strong as a bull."

"I do not care about his wits so long as he can look after sheep," answered Thorhall.

"You may rely on his being able to do that," said Skapti. "He is a stout, plucky fellow; a Swede from Sylgsdale, if you know where that is."

Towards the break-up of the council—"Thing" they call it in Iceland—two grayish-white horses belonging to Thorhall slipped their hobbles and strayed; so the good man had to hunt after them himself, which shows how short of servants he was. He crossed Sletha-asi, thence he bent his way to Armann's-fell, and just by the Priest's Wood he met a strange-looking man driving before him a horse laden with faggots. The fellow was tall and stalwart; his face involuntarily attracted Thorhall's attention, for the eyes, of an ashen gray, were large and staring, the powerful jaw was furnished with very white protruding teeth, and around the low forehead hung bunches of coarse wolf-grey hair.

"Pray, what is your name, my man?" asked the farmer, pulling up.

"Glámr, and please you," replied the wood-cutter.

Thorhall stared; then, with a preliminary cough, he asked how Glámr liked faggot-picking.

"Not much," was the answer; "I prefer shepherd life."

"Will you come with me?" asked Thorhall; "Skapti has handed you over to me, and I want a shepherd this winter uncommonly."

"If I serve you, it is on the understanding that I come or go as it pleases me. I tell you I am a bit truculent if things do not go just to my thinking."

"I shall not object to this," answered the bonder. "So I may count on your services?"

"Wait a moment! You have not told me whether there be any drawback."

"I must acknowledge that there is one," said Thorhall; "in fact, the sheepwalks have got a bad name for bogies."

"Pshaw! I'm not the man to be scared at shadows," laughed Glámr; "so here's my hand to it; I'll be with you at the beginning of the winter night."

Well, after this they parted, and presently the farmer found his ponies. Having thanked Skapti for his advice and assistance, he got his horses together and trotted home.

Summer, and then autumn passed, but not a word about the new shepherd reached the Valley of Shadows. The winter storms began to bluster up the glen, driving the flying snow-flakes and massing the white drifts at every winding of the vale. Ice formed in the shallows of the river; and the streams, which in summer trickled down the ribbed scarps, were now transmuted into icicles.

One gusty night a violent blow at the door startled all in the farm. In another moment Glámr, tall as a troll, stood in the hall glowering out of his wild eyes, his grey hair matted with frost, his teeth rattling and snapping with cold, his face blood-red in the glare of the fire which smouldered in the center of the hall. Thorhall jumped up and greeted him warmly, but the housewife was too frightened to be very cordial.

Weeks passed, and the new shepherd was daily on the moors with his flock; his loud and deep-toned voice was often borne down on the blast as he shouted to the sheep driving them into fold. His presence in the house always produced gloom, and if he spoke it sent a thrill through the women, who openly proclaimed their aversion for him.

There was a church near the byre, but Glámr never crossed the threshold; he hated psalmody; apparently he was an indifferent Christian. On the vigil of the Nativity Glámr rose early and shouted for meat.

"Meat!" exclaimed the housewife; "no man calling himself a Christian touches flesh to-day. To-morrow is the holy Christmas Day, and this is a fast."

"All superstition!" roared Glámr. "As far as I can see, men are no better now than they were in the bonny heathen time. Bring me meat, and make no more ado about it."

"You may be quite certain," protested the good wife, "if Church rule be not kept, ill-luck will follow."

Glámr ground his teeth and clenched his hands. "Meat! I will have meat, or——" In fear and trembling the poor woman obeyed.

The day was raw and windy; masses of grey vapor rolled up from the Arctic Ocean, and hung in piles about the mountain-tops. Now and then a scud of frozen fog, composed of minute particles of ice, swept along the glen, covering bar and beam with feathery hoar-frost. As the day declined, snow began to fall in large flakes like the down of the eider-duck. One moment there was a lull in the wind, and then the deep-toned shout of Glámr, high up the moor slopes, was heard distinctly by the congregation assembling for the first vespers of Christmas Day. Darkness came on, deep as that in the rayless abysses of the caverns under the lava, and still the snow fell thicker. The lights from the church windows sent a yellow haze far out into the night, and every flake burned golden as it swept within the ray. The bell in the lych-gate clanged for evensong, and the wind puffed the sound far up the glen; perhaps it reached the herdsman's ear. Hark! Someone caught a distant sound or shriek, which it was he could not tell, for the wind muttered and mumbled about the church eaves, and then with a fierce whistle scudded over the graveyard fence. Glámr had not returned when the service was over. Thorhall suggested a search, but no man would accompany him; and no wonder! it was not a night for a dog to be out in; besides, the tracks were a foot deep in snow. The family sat up all night, waiting, listening, trembling; but no Glámr came home. Dawn broke at last, wan and blear in the south. The clouds hung down like great sheets, full of snow, almost to bursting.

A party was soon formed to search for the missing man. A sharp scramble brought them to high land, and the ridge between the two rivers which join in Vatnsdalr was thoroughly examined. Here and there were found the scattered sheep, shuddering under an icicled rock, or half buried in a snow-drift. No trace yet of the keeper. A dead ewe lay at the bottom of a crag; it had staggered over in the gloom, and had been dashed to pieces.

Presently the whole party were called together about a trampled spot in the heath, where evidently a death-struggle had taken place, for earth and stone were tossed about, and the snow was blotched with large splashes of blood. A gory track led up the mountain, and the farm-servants were following it, when a cry, almost of agony, from one of the lads, made them turn. In looking behind a rock, the boy had come upon the corpse of the shepherd; it was livid and swollen to the size of a bullock. It lay on its back with the arms extended. The snow had been scrabbled up by the puffed hands in the death-agony, and the staring glassy eyes gazed out of the ashen-grey, upturned face into the vaporous canopy overhead. From the purple lips lolled the tongue, which in the last throes had been bitten through by the white fangs, and a discoloured stream which had flowed from it was now an icicle.

With trouble the dead man was raised on a litter, and carried to a gill-edge, but beyond this he could not be borne; his weight waxed more and more, the bearers toiled beneath their burden, their foreheads became beaded with sweat; though strong men they were crushed to the ground. Consequently, the corpse was left at the ravine-head, and the men returned to the farm. Next day their efforts to lift Glámr's bloated carcass, and remove it to consecrated ground, were unavailing. On the third day a priest accompanied them, but the body was nowhere to be found. Another expedition without the priest was made, and on this occasion the corpse was discovered; so a cairn was raised over the spot.

Two nights after this one of the thralls who had gone after the cows burst into the hall with a face blank and scared; he staggered to a seat and fainted. On recovering his senses, in a broken voice he assured all who crowded about him that he had seen Glámr walking past him as he left the door of the stable. On the following evening a houseboy was found in a fit under the farmyard wall, and he remained an idiot to his dying day. Some of the women next saw a face which, though blown out and discoloured, they recognised as that of Glámr, looking in upon them through a window of the dairy. In the twilight, Thorhall himself met the dead man, who stood and glowered at him, but made no attempt to injure his master. The haunting did not end there. Nightly a heavy tread was heard around the house, and a hand feeling along the walls, sometimes thrust in at the windows, at others clutching the woodwork, and breaking it to splinters. However, when the spring came round the disturbances lessened, and as the sun obtained full power, ceased altogether.

That summer a vessel from Norway dropped anchor in the nearest bay. Thorhall visited it, and found on board a man named Thorgaut, who was in search of work.

"What do you say to being my shepherd?" asked the bonder.

"I should very much like the office," answered Thorgaut. "I am as strong as two ordinary men, and a handy fellow to boot."

"I will not engage you without forewarning you of the terrible things you may have to encounter during the winter night."

"Pray, what may they be?"

"Ghosts and hobgoblins," answered the farmer; "a fine dance they lead me, I can promise you."

"I fear them not," answered Thorgaut; "I shall be with you at cattle-slaughtering time."

At the appointed season the man came, and soon established himself as a favorite in the house; he romped with the children, chucked the maidens under the chin, helped his fellow-servants, gratified the housewife by admiring her curd, and was just as much liked as his predecessor had been detested. He was a devil-may-care fellow, too, and made no bones of his contempt for the ghost, expressing hopes of meeting him face to face, which made his master look grave, and his mistress shudderingly cross herself. As the winter came on, strange sights and sounds began to alarm the folk, but these never frightened Thorgaut; he slept too soundly at night to hear the tread of feet about the door, and was too

short-sighted to catch glimpses of a grizzly monster striding up and down, in the twilight, before its cairn.

At last Christmas Eve came round, and Thorgaut went
out as usual with his sheep.

"Have a care, man," urged the bonder; "go not near
to the gill-head, where Glámr lies."

"Tut, tut! fear not for me. I shall be back by vespers."

"God grant it," sighed the housewife; "but 'tis not a
day for risks, to be sure."

Twilight came on: a feeble light hung over the south,
one white streak above the heath land to the south. Far
off in southern lands it was still day, but here the darkness gathered in apace, and men came from Vatnsdalr
for evensong, to herald in the night when Christ was
born. Christmas Eve! How different in Saxon England!
There the great ashen faggot is rolled along the hall with
torch and taper; the mummers dance with their merry
jingling bells; the boar's head, with gilded tusks, "bedecked
with holly and rosemary," is brought in by the steward
to a flourish of trumpets.

How different, too, where the Varanger cluster round
the imperial throne in the mighty church of the Eternal
Wisdom at this very hour. Outside, the air is soft from
breathing over the Bosphorus, which flashes tremulously
beneath the stars. The orange and laurel leaves in the
palace gardens are still exhaling fragrance in the hush of
the Christmas night.

But it is different here. The wind is piercing as a two-
edged sword; blocks of ice crash and grind along the
coast, and the lake waters are congealed to stone. Aloft,
the Aurora flames crimson, flinging long streamers to the
zenith, and then suddenly dissolving into a sea of pale
green light. The natives are waiting round the church-
door, but no Thorgaut has returned.

They find him next morning, lying across Glámr's
cairn, with his spine, his leg, and arm-bones shattered.
He is conveyed to the churchyard, and a cross is set up
at his head. He sleeps peacefully. Not so Glámr; he
becomes more furious than ever. No one will remain with
Thorhall now, except an old cowherd who has always

served the family, and who had long ago dandled his present master on his knee.

"All the cattle will be lost if I leave," said the carle; "it shall never be told of me that I deserted Thorhall from fear of a spectre."

Matters grew rapidly worse. Outbuildings were broken into of a night, and their woodwork was rent and shattered; the house door was violently shaken, and great pieces of it were torn away; the gables of the house were also pulled furiously to and fro.

One morning before dawn, the old man went to the stable. An hour later, his mistress arose, and taking her milking pails, followed him. As she reached the door of the stable, a terrible sound from within—the bellowing of the cattle, mingled with the deep notes of an unearthly voice—sent her back shrieking to the house. Thorhall leaped out of bed, caught up a weapon, and hastened to the cow-house. On opening the door, he found the cattle goring each other. Slung across the stone that separated the stalls was something. Thorhall stepped up to it, felt it, looked close; it was the cowherd, perfectly dead, his feet on one side of the slab, his head on the other, and his spine snapped in twain. The bonder now moved with his family to Tunga, another farm owned by him lower down the valley; it was too venturesome living during the midwinter night at the haunted farm; and it was not till the sun had returned as a bridegroom out of his chamber, and had dispelled night with its phantoms, that he went back to the Vale of Shadows. In the meantime, his little girl's health had given way under the repeated alarms of the winter; she became paler every day; with the autumn flowers she faded, and was laid beneath the mould of the churchyard in time for the first snows to spread a virgin pall over her small grave.

At this time Grettir—a hero of great fame, and a native of the north of the island—was in Iceland, and as the hauntings of this vale were matters of gossip throughout the district, he inquired about them, and resolved on visiting the scene. So Grettir busked himself for a cold ride, mounted his horse, and in due course of time drew

rein at the door of Thorhall's farm with the request that
he might be accommodated there for the night.

"Ahem!" coughed the bonder; "perhaps you are not
aware——"

"I am perfectly aware of all. I want to catch sight of
the troll."

"But your horse is sure to be killed."

"I will risk it. Glámr I must meet, so there's an end
of it."

"I am delighted to see you," spoke the bonder; "at
the same time, should mischief befall you, don't lay the
blame at my door."

"Never fear, man."

So they shook hands; the horse was put into the strongest stable, Thorhall made Grettir as good cheer as he
was able, and then, as the visitor was sleepy, all retired
to rest.

The night passed quietly, and no sounds indicated the
presence of the restless spirit. The horse, moreover, was
found next morning in good condition, enjoying his hay.

"This is unexpected!" exclaimed the bonder, gleefully.
"Now, where's the saddle? We'll clap it on, and then
good-bye, and a merry journey to you."

"Good-bye!" echoed Grettir; "I am going to stay here
another night."

"You had best be advised," urged Thorhall; "if misfor-
ture should overtake you, I know that all your kinsmen
would visit it on my head."

"I have made up my mind to stay," said Grettir, and
he looked so dogged that Thorhall opposed him no more.

All was quiet next night; not a sound roused Grettir
from his slumber. Next morning he went with the farmer
to the stable. The strong wooden door was shivered and
driven in. They stepped across it; Grettir called to his
horse, but there was no responsive whinny.

"I am afraid——" began Thorhall. Grettir leaped in,
and found the poor brute dead, and with its neck broken.

"Now," said Thorhall quickly. "I've got a capital
horse—a skewbald—down by Tunga, I shall not be many

hours in fetching it; your saddle is here, I think, and then you will just have time to reach——"

"I stay here another night," interrupted Grettir.

"I implore you to depart," said Thorhall.

"My horse is slain!"

"But I will provide you with another."

"Friend," answered Grettir, turning so sharply round that the farmer jumped back, half frightened, "no man ever did me an injury without rueing it. Now, your demon herdsman has been the death of my horse. He must be taught a lesson."

"Would that he were!" groaned Thorhall; "but mortal must not face him. Go in peace and receive compensation from me for what has happened."

"I must revenge my horse."

"An obstinate man will have his own way! But if you run your head against a stone wall, don't be angry because you get a broken pate."

Night came on; Grettir ate a hearty supper and was right jovial; not so Thorhall, who had his misgivings. At bedtime the latter crept into his crib, which, in the manner of old Icelandic beds, opened out of the hall, as berths do out of a cabin. Grettir, however, determined on remaining up; so he flung himself on a bench with his feet against the posts of the high seat, and his back against Thorhall's crib; then he wrapped one lappet of his fur coat round his feet, the other about his head, keeping the neck-opening in front of his face, so that he could look through into the hall.

There was a fire burning on the hearth, a smouldering heap of red embers; every now and then a twig flared up and crackled, giving Grettir glimpses of the rafters, as he lay with his eyes wandering among the mysteries of the smoke-blackened roof. The wind whistled softly overhead. The clerestory windows, covered with the amnion of sheep, admitted now and then a sickly yellow glare from the full moon, which, however, shot a beam of pure silver through the smoke-hole in the roof. A dog without began to howl; the cat, which had long been sitting demurely watching the fire, stood up with raised back and bristling tail, then darted behind some chests in a corner. The hall door was in a sad plight. It had been so riven by the spectre that it was made firm by wattles only, and the moon glinted athwart the crevices. Soothingly the river, not yet frozen over, prattled over its shingly bed as it swept round the knoll on which stood the farm. Grettir heard the breathing of the sleeping women in the adjoining chamber, and the sigh of the housewife as she turned in her bed.

Click! click!—It is only the frozen turf on the roof cracking with the cold. The wind lulls completely. The night is very still without. Hark! a heavy tread, beneath which the snow yields. Every footfall goes straight to Grettir's heart. A crash on the turf overhead! By all the saints in paradise! The monster is treading on the roof. For one moment the chimney-gap is completely darkened: Glámr is looking down it; the flash of the red ash is reflected in the two lustreless eyes. Then the moon glances sweetly in once more, and the heavy tramp of Glámr is audibly moving towards the farther end of the hall. A thud—he has leaped down. Grettir feels the board at his back quivering, for Thorhall is awake and is trembling in his bed. The steps pass round to the back of the house, and then the snapping of the wood shows that the creature is destroying some of the outhouse doors. He tires of this apparently, for his footfall comes clear towards the main entrance to the hall. The moon is veiled behind a watery cloud, and by the uncertain glimmer Grettir fancies that he sees two dark hands thrust in above the door. His apprehensions are verified, for, with a loud snap, a long strip of panel breaks, and light is admitted. Snap—snap! another portion gives way, and the gap becomes larger. Then the wattles slip from their places, and a dark arm rips them out in bunches, and flings them away. There is a cross-beam to the door, holding a bolt which slides into a stone groove. Against the grey light, Grettir sees a huge black figure heaving itself over the bar. Crack! that has given way, and the rest of the door falls in shivers to the earth.

"Oh, heavens above!" exclaims the bonder.

Stealthily the dead man creeps on, feeling at the beams as he comes; then he stands in the hall, with the firelight on him. A fearful sight; the tall figure distended with the corruption of the grave, the nose fallen off, the wandering, vacant eyes, with the glaze of death on them, the sallow flesh patched with green masses of decay; the wolf-grey hair and beard have grown in the tomb, and hang matted about the shoulders and breast; the nails, too, they have grown. It is a sickening sight—a thing to shudder at, not to see.

Motionless, with no nerve quivering now, Thorhall and Grettir held their breath.

Glámr's lifeless glance strayed round the chamber; it rested on the shaggy bundle by the high seat. Cautiously he stepped towards it. Grettir felt him groping about the lower lappet and pulling at it. The cloak did not give way. Another jerk; Grettir kept his feet firmly pressed against the posts, so that the rug was not pulled off. The vampire seemed puzzled, he plucked at the upper flap and tugged. Grettir held to the bench and bed-board, so that he was not moved, but the cloak was rent in twain, and the corpse staggered back, holding half in its hands, and gazing wonderingly at it. Before it had done examining the shred, Grettir started to his feet, bowed his body, flung his arms about the carcass, and, driving his head into the chest, strove to bend it backward and snap the spine. A vain attempt! The cold hands came down on Grettir's arms with diabolical force, riving them from their hold. Grettir clasped them about the body again; then the arms closed round him, and began dragging him along. The brave man clung by his feet to benches and posts, but the strength of the vampire was the greater; posts gave way, benches were heaved from their places, and the wrestlers at each moment neared the door. Sharply writhing loose, Grettir flung his hands round a roof-beam. He was dragged from his feet; the numbing arms clenched him round the waist, and tore at him; every tendon in his breast was strained; the strain under his shoulders became excruciating, the muscles stood out in knots. Still he held on; his fingers were bloodless; the

pulses of his temples throbbed in jerks; the breath came
in a whistle through his rigid nostrils. All the while, too,
the long nails of the dead man cut into his side, and
Grettir could feel them piercing like knives between his
ribs. Then at once his hands gave way, and the monster
bore him reeling towards the porch, crashing over the
broken fragments of the door. Hard as the battle had
gone with him indoors, Grettir knew that it would go
worse outside, so he gathered up all his remaining
strength for one final desperate struggle. The door had
been shut with a swivel into a groove; this groove was in
a stone, which formed the jamb on one side, and there
was a similar block on the other, into which the hinges
had been driven. As the wrestlers neared the opening,
Grettir planted both his feet against the stone posts,
holding Glámr by the middle. He had the advantage
now. The dead man writhed in his arms, drove his talons
into Grettir's back, and tore up great ribbons of flesh,
but the stone jambs held firm.

"Now," thought Grettir, "I can break his back," and
thrusting his head under the chin, so that the grizzly
beard covered his eyes, he forced the face from him, and
the back was bent as a hazel-rod.

"If I can but hold on," thought Grettir, and he tried
to shout for Thorhall, but his voice was muffled in the
hair of the corpse.

Suddenly one or both of the door-posts gave way.
Down crashed the gable trees, ripping beams and rafters
from their beds; frozen clods of earth rattled from the
roof and thumped into the snow. Glámr fell on his back,
and Grettir staggered down on top of him. The moon
was at her full; large white clouds chased each other
across the sky, and as they swept before her disk she
looked through them with a brown halo round her. The
snow-cap of Jorundarfell, however, glowed like a planet,
then the white mountain ridge was kindled, the light ran
down the hillside, the bright disk stared out of the veil
and flashed at this moment full on the vampire's face.
Grettir's strength was failing him, his hands quivered in
the snow, and he knew that he could not support himself

from dropping flat on the dead man's face, eye to eye, lip to lip. The eyes of the corpse were fixed on him, lit with the cold glare of the moon. His head swam as his heart sent a hot stream to his brain. Then a voice from the grey lips said—

"Thou hast acted madly in seeking to match thyself with me. Now learn that henceforth ill-luck shall constantly attend thee; that thy strength shall never exceed what is now is, and that by night these eyes of mind shall stare at thee through the darkness till thy dying day, so that for very horror thou shalt not endure to be alone."

Grettir at this moment noticed that his dirk had slipped from its sheath during the fall, and that it now lay conveniently near his hand. The giddiness which had oppressed him passed away, he clutched at the sword-haft, and with a blow severed the vampire's throat. Then, kneeling on the breast, he hacked till the head came off.

Thorhall appeared now, his face blanched with terror, but when he saw how the fray had terminated he assisted Grettir gleefully to roll the corpse on the top of a pile of faggots, which had been collected for winter fuel. Fire was applied, and soon far down the valley the flames of the pyre startled people, and made them wonder what new horror was being enacted in the upper portion of the Vale of Shadows.

Next day the charred bones were conveyed to a spot remote from the habitations of men, and were there buried.

What Glámr had predicted came to pass. Never after did Grettir dare to be alone in the dark.

BEYOND THE WALL

by *Ambrose Bierce*

Many years ago, on my way from Hongkong to New York, I passed a week in San Francisco. A long time had gone by since I had been in that city, during which my ventures in the Orient had prospered beyond my hope; I was rich and could afford to revisit my own country to renew my friendship with such of the companions of my youth as still lived and remembered me with the old affection. Chief of these, I hoped, was Mohun Dampier, an old schoolmate with whom I had held a desultory correspondence which had long ceased, as is the way of correspondence between men. You may have observed that the indisposition to write a merely social letter is in the ratio of the square of the distance between you and your correspondent. It is a law.

I remembered Dampier as a handsome, strong young fellow of scholarly tastes, with an aversion to work and a marked indifference to many of the things that the world cares for, including wealth, of which, however, he had inherited enough to put him beyond the reach of want. In his family, one of the oldest and most aristocratic in the country, it was, I think, a matter of pride that no member of it had ever been in trade nor politics, nor suffered any kind of distinction. Mohun was a trifle sentimental, and had in him a singular element of superstition, which led him to the study of all manner of occult subjects, although his sane mental health safeguarded him against fantastic and perilous faiths. He made daring incursions into the realm of the unreal without renouncing his residence in the partly surveyed and charted region of what we are pleased to call certitude.

The night of my visit to him was stormy. The Californian winter was on, and the incessant rain splashed in the deserted streets, or, lifted by irregular gusts of wind, was hurled against the houses with incredible fury. With no small difficulty my cabman found the right place, away out toward the ocean beach, in a sparsely populated suburb. The dwelling, a rather ugly one, apparently, stood in the center of its grounds, which as nearly as I could make out in the gloom were destitute of either flowers or grass. Three or four trees, writhing and moaning in the torment of the tempest, appeared to be trying to escape from their dismal environment and take the chance of finding a better one out at sea. The house was a two-story brick structure with a tower, a story higher, at one corner. In a window of that was the only visible light. Something in the appearance of the place made me shudder, a performance that may have been assisted by a rill of rain-water down my back as I scuttled to cover in the doorway.

In answer to my note apprising him of my wish to call, Dampier had written, "Don't ring—open the door and come up." I did so. The staircase was dimly lighted by a single gas-jet at the top of the second flight. I managed to reach the landing without disaster and entered by an open door into the lighted square room of the tower. Dampier came forward in gown and slippers to receive me, giving me the greeting that I wished, and if I had held a thought that it might more fitly have been accorded me at the front door the first look at him dispelled any sense of his inhospitality.

He was not the same. Hardly past middle age, he had gone gray, and had acquired a pronounced stoop. His figure was thin and angular, his face deeply lined, his complexion dead-white, without a touch of color. His eyes, unnaturally large, glowed with a fire that was almost uncanny.

He seated me, proffered a cigar, and with grave and obvious sincerity assured me of the pleasure that it gave him to meet me. Some unimportant conversation followed, but all the while I was dominated by a melancholy sense of the great change in him. This he must have perceived, for he suddenly said with a bright enough smile, "You are disappointed in me—*non sum qualis eram.*"

I hardly knew what to reply, but managed to say: "Why, really, I don't know: your Latin is about the same."

He brightened again. "No," he said, "being a dead language, it grows in appropriateness. But please have the patience to wait: where I am going there is perhaps a better tongue. Will you care to have a message in it?"

The smile faded as he spoke, and as he concluded he was looking into my eyes with a gravity that distressed me. Yet I would not surrender myself to his mood, nor permit him to see how deeply his prescience of death affected me.

"I fancy that it will be long," I said, "before human speech will cease to serve our need; and then the need, with its possibilities of service, will have passed."

He made no reply, and I too was silent, for the talk had taken a dispiriting turn, yet I knew not how to give it a more agreeable character. Suddenly, in a pause of the storm, when the dead silence was almost startling by contrast with the previous uproar, I heard a gentle tapping, which appeared to come from the wall behind my chair. The sound was such as might have been made by a human hand, not as upon a door by one asking admittance, but rather, I thought, as an agreed signal, an assurance of someone's presence in an adjoining room; most of us, I fancy, have had more experience of such communications than we should care to relate. I glanced at Dampier. If possibly there was something of amusement in the look he did not observe it. He appeared to have forgotten my presence, and was staring at the wall behind me with an expression in his eyes that I am unable to name, although my memory of it is as vivid to-day as was my sense of it then. The situation was embarrassing;

I rose to take my leave. At this he seemed to recover himself.

"Please be seated," he said; "it is nothing—no one is there."

But the tapping was repeated, and with the same gentle, slow insistence as before.

"Pardon me," I said, "it is late. May I call tomorrow?"

He smiled—a little mechanically, I thought. "It is very delicate of you," said he, "but quite needless. Really, this is the only room in the tower, and no one is there. At least—" He left the sentence incomplete, rose, and threw up a window, the only opening in the wall from which the sound seemed to come. "See."

Not clearly knowing what else to do I followed him to the window and looked out. A street-lamp some little distance away gave enough light through the murk of the rain that was again falling in torrents to make it entirely plain that "no one was there." In truth there was nothing but the sheer blank wall of the tower.

Dampier closed the window and signing me to my seat resumed his own.

The incident was not in itself particularly mysterious; any one of a dozen explanations was possible (though none has occurred to me), yet it impressed me strangely, the more, perhaps, from my friend's effort to reassure me, which seemed to dignify it with a certain significance and importance. He had proved that no one was there, but in that fact lay all the interest; and he proffered no explanation. His silence was irritating and made me resentful.

"My good friend," I said, somewhat ironically, I fear, "I am not disposed to question your right to harbor as many spooks as you find agreeable to your taste and consistent with your notions of companionship; that is no business of mine. But being just a plain man of affairs, mostly of this world, I find spooks needless to my peace and comfort. I am going to my hotel, where my fellow-guests are still in the flesh."

It was not a very civil speech, but he manifested no

feeling about it. "Kindly remain," he said. "I am grateful for your presence here. What you have heard to-night I believe myself to have heard twice before. Now I *know* it was no illusion. That is much to me—more than you know. Have a fresh cigar and a good stock of patience while I tell you the story."

The rain was now falling more steadily, with a low, monotonous susurration, interrupted at long intervals by the sudden slashing of the boughs of the trees as the wind rose and failed. The night was well advanced, but both sympathy and curiosity held me a willing listener to my friend's monologue, which I did not interrupt by a single word from beginning to end.

"Ten years ago," he said, "I occupied a ground-floor apartment in one of a row of houses, all alike, away at the other end of the town, on what we call Rincon Hill. This had been the best quarter of San Francisco, but had fallen into neglect and decay, partly because the primitive character of its domestic architecture no longer suited the maturing tastes of our wealthy citizens, partly because certain public improvements had made a wreck of it. The row of dwellings in one of which I lived stood a little way back from the street, each having a miniature garden, separated from its neighbors by low iron fences and bisected with mathematical precision by a box-bordered gravel walk from gate to door.

"One morning as I was leaving my lodging I observed a young girl entering the adjoining garden on the left. It was a warm day in June, and she was lightly gowned in white. From her shoulders hung a broad straw hat profusely decorated with flowers and wonderfully beribboned in the fashion of the time. My attention was not long held by the exquisite simplicity of her costume, for no one could look at her face and think of anything earthly. Do not fear; I shall not profane it by description; it was beautiful exceedingly. All that I had ever seen or dreamed of loveliness was in that matchless living picture by the hand of the Divine Artist. So deeply did it move me that, without a thought of the impropriety of the act, I unconsciously bared my head, as a devout Catholic or well-bred Protestant uncovers before an image of the Blessed Virgin. The maiden showed no displeasure; she merely turned her glorious dark eyes upon me with a look that made me catch my breath, and without other recognition of my act passed into the house. For a moment I stood motionless, hat in hand, painfully conscious of my rudeness, yet so dominated by the emotion inspired by that vision of incomparable beauty that my penitence was less poignant than it should have been. Then I went my way, leaving my heart behind. In the natural course of things I should probably have remained away until nightfall, but by the middle of the afternoon I was back in the little garden, affecting an interest in the few foolish flowers that I had never before observed. My hope was vain; she did not appear.

"To a night of unrest succeeded a day of expectation and disappointment, but on the day after, as I wandered aimlessly about the neighborhood, I met her. Of course I did not repeat my folly of uncovering, nor venture by even so much as too long a look to manifest an interest in her; yet my heart was beating audibly. I trembled and consciously colored as she turned her big black eyes upon me with a look of obvious recognition entirely devoid of boldness or coquetry.

"I will not weary you with particulars; many times afterward I met the maiden, yet never either addressed her or sought to fix her attention. Nor did I take any action toward making her acquaintance. Perhaps my forbearance, requiring so supreme an effort of self-denial, will not be entirely clear to you. That I was heels over head in love is true, but who can overcome his habit of thought, or reconstruct his character?

"I was what some foolish persons are pleased to call, and others, more foolish, are pleased to be called—an aristocrat; and despite her beauty, her charms and graces, the girl was not of my class. I had learned her name—which it is needless to speak—and something of her family. She was an orphan, a dependent niece of the impossible elderly fat woman in whose lodging-house she lived. My income was small and I lacked the talent for

marrying; it is perhaps a gift. An alliance with that family
would condemn me to its manner of life, part me from
my books and studies, and in a social sense reduce me
to the ranks. It is easy to deprecate such considerations
as these and I have not retained myself for the defense.
Let judgment be entered against me, but in strict justice
all my ancestors for generations should be made co-
defendants and I be permitted to plead in mitigation of
punishment the imperious mandate of heredity. To a
mésalliance of that kind every globule of my ancestral
blood spoke in opposition. In brief, my tastes, habits,
instinct, with whatever of reason my love had left me—
all fought against it. Moreover, I was an irreclaimable
sentimentalist, and found a subtle charm in an impersonal and spiritual relation which acquaintance might vul-
garize and marriage would certainly dispel. No woman,
I argued, is what this lovely creature seems. Love is a
delicious dream; why should I bring about my own
awakening?

"The course dictated by all this sense and sentiment
was obvious. Honor, pride, prudence, preservation of my
ideals—all commanded me to go away, but for that I was
too weak. The utmost that I could do by a mighty effort
of will was to cease meeting the girl, and that I did. I
even avoided the chance encounters of the garden, leaving my lodging only when I knew that she had gone to
her music lessons, and returning after nightfall. Yet all
the while I was as one in a trance, indulging the most
fascinating fancies and ordering my entire intellectual life
in accordance with my dream. Ah, my friend, as one
whose actions have a traceable relation to reason, you
cannot know the fool's paradise in which I lived.

"One evening the devil put it into my head to be an
unspeakable idiot. By apparently careless and purpose-
less questioning I learned from my gossipy landlady that
the young woman's bedroom adjoined my own, a party-
wall between. Yielding to a sudden and coarse impulse
I gently rapped on the wall. There was no response, naturally, but I was in no mood to accept a rebuke. A mad-

ness was upon me and I repeated the folly, the offense, but again ineffectually, and I had the decency to desist.

"An hour later, while absorbed in some of my infernal studies, I heard, or thought I heard, my signal answered. Flinging down my books I sprang to the wall and as steadily as my beating heart would permit gave three slow taps upon it. This time the response was distinct, unmistakable: one, two, three—an exact repetition of my signal. That was all I could elicit, but it was enough—too much.

"The next evening, and for many evenings afterward, that folly went on, I always having 'the last word.' During the whole period I was deliriously happy, but with the perversity of my nature I persevered in my resolution not to see her. Then, as I should have expected, I got no further answers. 'She is disgusted,' I said to myself, 'with what she thinks my timidity in making no more definite advances'; and I resolved to seek her and make her acquaintance and—what? I did not know, nor do I now know, what might have come of it. I know only that I passed days and days trying to meet her, and all in vain; she was invisible as well as inaudible. I haunted the streets where we had met, but she did not come. From my window I watched the garden in front of her house, but she passed neither in nor out. I fell into the deepest dejection, believing that she had gone away, yet took no steps to resolve my doubt by inquiry of my landlady, to whom, indeed, I had taken an unconquerable aversion from her having once spoken of the girl with less of reverence then I thought befitting.

"There came a fateful night. Worn out with emotion, irresolution and despondency, I had retired early and fallen into such sleep as was still possible to me. In the middle of the night something—some malign power bent upon the wrecking of my peace forever—caused me to open my eyes and sit up, wide awake and listening intently for I knew not what. Then I thought I heard a faint tapping on the wall—the mere ghost of the familiar signal. In a few moments it was repeated: one, two, three—no louder than before, but addressing a sense

alert and strained to receive it. I was about to reply when
the Adversary of Peace again intervened in my affairs
with a rascally suggestion of retaliation. She had long and
cruelly ignored me; now I would ignore her. Incredible
fatuity—may God forgive it! All the rest of the night I
lay awake, fortifying my obstinacy with shameless justifi-
cations and—listening.

"Late the next morning, as I was leaving the house, I
met my landlady, entering.

" 'Good morning, Mr. Dampier,' she said. 'Have you
heard the news?'

"I replied in words that I had heard no news; in manner, that I did not care to hear any. The manner escaped
her observation.

" 'About the sick young lady next door,' she babbled
on. 'What! you did not know? Why, she has been ill for
weeks. And now—'

"I almost sprang upon her. 'And now,' I cried, 'now
what?'

" 'She is dead.'

"That is not the whole story. In the middle of the
night, as I learned later, the patient, awakening from a
long stupor after a week of delirium, had asked—it was
her last utterance—that her bed be moved to the opposite side of the room. Those in attendance had thought
the request a vagary of her delirium, but had complied.
And there the poor passing soul had exerted its failing
will to restore a broken connection—a golden thread of
sentiment between its innocence and a monstrous base-
ness owning a blind, brutal allegiance to the Law of Self.

"What reparation could I make? Are there masses that
can be said for the repose of souls that are abroad such
nights as this—spirits 'blown about by the viewless
winds'—coming in the storm and darkness with signs and
portents, hints of memory and presages of doom?

"This is the third visitation. On the first occasion I was
too skeptical to do more than verify by natural methods
the character of the incident; on the second, I responded
to the signal after it had been several times repeated, but
without result. To-night's recurrence completes the 'fatal

triad' expounded by Parapelius Necromantius. There is no more to tell."

When Dampier had finished his story I could think of nothing relevant that I cared to say, and to question him would have been a hideous impertinence. I rose and bade him good night in a way to convey to him a sense of my sympathy, which he silently acknowledged by a pressure of the hand. That night, alone with his sorrow and remorse, he passed into the Unknown.

MOTHER OF SERPENTS

by Robert Bloch

Voodooism is a queer thing. Forty years ago it was an unknown subject, save in certain esoteric circles. Today there is a surprising amount of information about it, due to research—and an even more surprising amount of misinformation.

Recent popular books on the subject are, for the most part, sheer romantic fancy; elaborated with the incomplete theorizings of ignoramuses.

Perhaps, though, this is for the best. For the truth about voodoo is such that no writer would care, or dare, to print it. Some of it is worse than their wildest fancies. I myself have seen certain things I do not dare to discuss. It would be useless to tell people anyway, for they would not believe me. And once again, this may be for the best. Knowledge can be a thousand times more terrifying than ignorance.

I know, though, for I have lived in Haiti, the dark island. I have learned much from legend, stumbled on many things through accident, and the bulk of my knowledge comes from the one really authentic source—the statements of the blacks. They're not talkative people, as a rule, those old natives of the black hill country. It took patience and long familiarity with them before they unbent and told me their secrets.

That's why so many of the travel books are so palpably false—no writer who visits Haiti for six months or a year could possibly ingratiate himself into the confidence of those who know the facts. There are so few who really do know; so few who are not afraid to tell.

But I have learned. Let me tell you of the olden days; the old times, when Haiti rose to an empire, borne on a wave of blood.

It was many years ago, soon after the slaves had revolted. Toussaint l'Ouverture, Dessalines and King Christophe freed them from their French masters, freed them after uprisings and massacres and set up a kingdom founded on cruelty more fantastic than the despotism that reigned before.

There were no happy blacks in Haiti then. They had known too much of torture and death; the carefree life of their West Indian neighbors was utterly alien to these slaves and descendants of slaves. A strange mixture of races flourished: fierce tribesmen from Ashanti, Damballah and the Guinea Coast; sullen Caribs; dusky offspring of renegade Frenchmen; bastard admixtures of Spanish, Negro and Indian blood. Sly, treacherous half-breeds and mulattos ruled the coast, but there were even worse dwellers in the hills behind.

There were jungles in Haiti, impassable jungles, mountain-ringed and swamp-scourged forests filled with poisonous insects and pestilential fevers. White men dared not enter them, for they were worse than death. Bloodsucking plants, venomous reptiles, diseased orchids filled the forests, forests that hid horrors Africa had never known.

For that is where the real voodoo flourished, back there in the hills. Men lived there, it is said, descendants of escaped slaves, and outlaw factions that had been hunted from the coast. Furtive rumors told of isolated villages that practiced cannibalism, mixed in with dark religious rites more dreadful and perverted than anything spawned in the Congo itself. Necrophilism, phallic worship, anthropomancy and distorted versions of the Black Mass were commonplace. The shadow of Obeah was everywhere. Human sacrifice was common, the offering up of roosters and goats an accepted thing. There were orgies around the voodoo altars, and blood was drunk in honor of Baron Samedi and the old black gods brought from ancient lands.

Everybody knew about it. Each night the *rada*-drums boomed out from the hills, and fires flared over the forests. Many known *papalois* and conjure-doctors resided on the edge of the coast itself, but they were never disturbed. Nearly all the "civilized" blacks still believed in charms and philtres; even the churchgoers reverted to talismans and incantations in time of need. So-called "educated" Negroes in Port-au-Prince society were admittedly emissaries from the barbarian tribes of the interior, and despite the outward show of civilization the bloody priests still ruled behind the throne.

Of course there were scandals, mysterious disappearances, and occasional protests from emancipated citizens. But it was not wise to meddle with those who bowed to the Black Mother, or incur the anger of the terrible old men who dwelt in the shadow of the Snake.

Such was the status of sorcery when Haiti became a republic. People often wonder why there is still sorcery existent there today; more secretive, perhaps, but still surviving. They ask why the ghastly zombies are not destroyed, and why the government has not stepped in to stamp out the fiendish blood-cults that still lurk in the jungle gloom.

Perchance this tale will provide an answer; this old, secret tale of the new republic. Officials, remembering the story, are still afraid to interfere too strongly, and the laws that have been passed are very loosely enforced.

Because the Serpent Cult of Obeah will never die in Haiti—in Haiti, that fantastic island whose sinuous shoreline resembles the yawning jaws of a monstrous *snake*.

One of the earliest presidents of Haiti was an educated man. Although born on the island, he was schooled in France, and studied extensively while abroad. His accession to the highest office of the land found him an enlightened, sophisticated cosmopolite of the modern type. Of course he still liked to remove his shoes in the privacy of his office, but he never displayed his naked toes in an official capacity. Don't misunderstand—the man was no Emperor Jones; he was merely a polished ebony gentleman whose natural barbarity occasionally broke through its veneer of civilization.

He was, in fact, a very shrewd man. He had to be in order to become president in those early days; only extremely shrewd men ever attained that dignity. Perhaps it would enlighten you a bit to say that in those times the term "shrewd" was a polite Haitian synonym for "crooked." It is therefore easy to realize the president's character when you know that he was regarded as one of the most successful politicians the republic ever produced.

In his short reign he was opposed by very few enemies; and those that did work against him usually disappeared. The tall, coal-black man with the physical skull-conformation of a gorilla harbored a remarkably crafty brain beneath his beetling brow.

His ability was phenomenal. He had an insight into finance which profited him greatly; profited him, that is, in both his official and unofficial capacity. Whenever he saw fit to increase the taxes he increased the army as well, and sent it out to escort the state tax-collectors. His treaties with foreign countries were masterpieces of legal lawlessness. This black Machiavelli knew that he must work fast, since presidents had a peculiar way of dying in Haiti. They seemed peculiarly susceptible to disease— "lead poisoning," as our modern gangster friends might say. So the president worked very fast indeed, and he did a masterful job.

This was truly remarkable, in view of his humble background. For his was a success saga in the good old Horatio Alger manner. His father was unknown. His mother was a conjure woman in the hills, and though quite well-known, she had been very poor. The president had been born in a log cabin; quite the classic setting for a future distinguished career. His early years had been most uneventful, until his adoption, at thirteen, by a benevolent Protestant minister. For a year he lived with this kind man, serving as houseboy in his home. Suddenly the poor minister died of an obscure ailment; this was most unfortunate, for he had been quite wealthy and his money was alleviating much of the suffering in this particular section. Any any rate, this rich minister died, and the poor conjure woman's son sailed to France for a university education.

As for the conjure woman, she bought herself a new mule and said nothing. Her skill at herbs had given her son a chance in the world, and she was satisfied.

It was eight years before the boy returned. He had changed a great deal since his departure; he preferred the society of whites and the octoroon society people of Port-au-Prince. It is recorded that he rather ignored his old mother, too. His newly acquired fastidiousness made him painfully aware of the woman's ignorant simplicity. Besides, he was ambitious, and he did not care to publicize his relationship with such a notorious witch.

For she was quite famous in her way. Where she had come from and what her original history was, nobody knew. But for many years her hut in the mountains had been the rendezvous of strange worshipers and even stranger emissaries. The dark powers of Obeah were evoked in her shadowy altar-place amidst the hills, and a furtive group of acolytes resided there with her. Her ritual fires always flared on moonless nights, and bullocks were given in bloody baptism to the Crawler of Midnight. For she was a Priestess of the Serpent.

The Snake-God, you know, is the real deity of the Obeah cults. The blacks worshiped the Serpent in Dahomey and Senegal from time immemorial. They venerate the reptiles in a curious way, and there is some obscure linkage between the snake and the crescent moon. Curious, isn't it—this serpent superstition? The Garden of Eden had its tempter, you know, and the Bible tells of Moses and his staff of snakes. The Egyptians revered Set, and the ancient Hindus had a cobra god. It seems to be general throughout the world—the kindred hatred and reverence of serpents. Always they seem to be worshiped as creatures of evil. American Indians believed in Yig, and Aztec myths follow the pattern. And of course the Hopi ceremonial dances are of the same order.

But the African Serpent legends are particularly dreadful, and the Haitian adaptations of the sacrificial rites are worse.

At the time of which I speak some of the voodoo groups were believed to actually breed snakes; they smuggled the reptiles over from the Ivory Coast to use in their secret practices. There were tall tales current about twenty-foot pythons which swallowed infants offered up to them on the Black Altar, and about *sendings* of poisonous serpents which killed enemies of the voodoo-masters. It is a known fact that several anthropoid apes had been smuggled into the country by a peculiar cult that worshiped gorillas; so the serpent legends may have been equally true.

At any rate, the president's mother was a priestess, and equally as famous, in a way, as her distinguished son. He, just after his return, had slowly climbed to power. First he had been a tax-gatherer, then treasurer, and finally president. Several of his rivals died, and those who opposed him soon found it expedient to dissemble their hatred; for he was still a savage at heart, and savages like to torment their enemies. It was rumored that he had constructed a secret torture chamber beneath the palace, and that its instruments were rusty, though not from disuse.

The breach between the young statesman and his mother began to widen just prior to his presidential incumbency. The immediate cause was his marriage to the daughter of a rich octoroon planter from the coast. Not only was the old woman humiliated because her son contaminated the family stock (she was pure Negro, and descendant of a Niger slave-king), but she was further indignant because she had not been invited to the wedding.

It was held in Port-au-Prince. The foreign consuls were there, and the cream of Haitian society was present. The lovely bride had been convent-bred, and her antecedents were held in the highest esteem. The groom wisely did not deign to desecrate the nuptial celebration by including his rather unsavory parent.

She came, though, and watched the affair through the kitchen doorway. It was just as well that she did not make her presence known, as it would have embarrassed not only her son, but several others as well—official dignitaries who sometimes consulted her in their unofficial capacity.

What she saw of her son and his bride was not pleasing. The man was an affected dandy now, and his wife was a silly flirt. The atmosphere of the pomp and ostentation did not impress her; behind their debonair masks of polite sophistication she knew that most of those present were superstitious Negroes who would have run to her for charms or oracular advice the moment they were in trouble. Nevertheless, she took no action; she merely smiled rather bitterly and hobbled home. After all, she still loved her son.

The next affront, however, she could not overlook. This was the inauguration of the new president. She was not invited to this affair either, yet she came. And this time she did not skulk in the shadows. After the oath of office was administered she marched boldly up to the new ruler of Haiti and accosted him before the very eyes of the German consul himself. She was a grotesque figure; an ungainly little harridan barely five feet tall, black, barefooted, and clad in rags.

Her son quite naturally ignored her presence. The withered crone licked her toothless gums in terrible silence. Then, quite calmly, she began to curse him—not in French, but in native patois of the hills. She called down the wrath of her bloody gods upon his ungrateful head, and threatened both him and his wife with vengeance for their smug ingratitude. The assembled guests were shocked.

So was the new president. However, he did not forget himself. Calmly he motioned to his guards, who led the now hysterical witch-woman away. He would deal with her later.

The next night when he saw fit to go into the dungeon and reason with his mother, she was gone. Disappeared, the guards told him, rolling their eyes mysteriously. He had the jailer shot, and went back to his official chambers.

He was a little worried about that curse business. You see, he knew what the woman was capable of. He did not like those threats against his wife, either. The next day he had some silver bullets moulded, like King Henry in the old days. He also bought an *ouanga* charm from a devil-doctor of his own acquaintance. Magic would fight magic.

That night a serpent came to him in dreams; a serpent with green eyes that whispered in the way of men and hissed at him with shrill and mocking laughter as he struck at it in his sleep. There was a reptilian odor in his bedroom the next morning, and a nauseous slime upon his pillow that gave forth a similiar stench. And the president knew that only his charm had saved him.

That afternoon his wife missed one of her Paris frocks, and the president questioned his servants in his private torture chamber below. He learned some facts he dared not tell his bride, and thereafter he seemed very sad. He had seen his mother work with wax images before—little mannikins resembling men and women, dressed in parts of their stolen garments. Sometimes she stuck pins into them or roasted them over a slow fire. Always the real people sickened and died. This knowledge made the president quite unhappy, and he was still more over-wrought when messengers returned and said that his mother was gone from her old hut in the hills.

Three days later his wife died, of a painful wound in her side which no doctors could explain. She was in agony until the end, and just before her passing it was rumored that her body turned blue and bloated up to twice its normal size. Her features were eaten away as if with leprosy, and her swollen limbs looked like those of an elephantiasis victim. Loathsome tropical diseases abound in Haiti, but none of them kill in three days. . . .

After this the president went mad.

Like Cotton Mather of old, he started on a witch-hunting crusade. Soldiers and police were sent out to comb the countryside. Spies rode up to hovels on the mountain peaks, and armed patrols crouched in far-off fields where the living dead-men work, their glazed and glassy eyes staring ceaselessly at the moon. *Mamalois* were put to the question over slow fires, and possessors of forbidden books were roasted over flames fed by the very tomes they harbored. Bloodhounds yammered in the hills, and priests died on altars where they were wont to sacrifice. Only one order had been specially given: the president's mother was to be captured alive and unharmed.

Meanwhile he sat in the palace with the embers of slow insanity in his eyes—embers that flared into fiendish flame when the guards brought in the withered crone, who had been captured near that awful grove of idols in the swamp.

They took her downstairs, although she fought and clawed like a wildcat, and then the guards went away and left her son with her alone. Alone, in a torture chamber, with a mother who cursed him from the rack. Alone, with frantic fires in his eyes, and a great silver knife in his hand. . . .

The president spent many hours in his secret torture chamber during the next few days. He seldom was seen around the palace, and his servants were given orders that he must not be disturbed. On the fourth day he came up the hidden stairway for the last time, and the flickering madness in his eyes was gone.

Just what occurred in the dungeon below will never be rightly known. No doubt that is for the best. The president was a savage at heart, and to the brute, prolongation of pain always brings ecstasy. . . .

It is recorded, though, that the old witch-woman cursed her son with the Serpent's Curse in her dying breath, and that is the most terrible curse of all.

Some idea of what happened may be gained by the

knowledge of the president's revenge; for he had a grim sense of humor, and a barbarian's idea of retribution. His wife had been killed by his mother, who fashioned a waxen image. He decided to do what would be exquisitely appropriate.

When he came up the stairs that last time, his servants saw that he bore with him a great candle, fashioned of corpse-fat. And since nobody ever saw his mother's body again, there were curious surmises as to where the corpse-fat was obtained. But then, the president's mind leaned toward grisly jests. . . .

The rest of the story is very simple. The president went directly to his chambers in the palace, where he placed the candle in a holder on his desk. He had neglected his work in the last few days, and there was much official business for him to transact. For a while he sat in silence, staring at the candle with a curious satisfied smile. Then he called for his papers and announced that he would attend to them immediately.

He worked all that night, with two guards stationed outside his door. Sitting at his desk, he pored over his task in the candlelight—the candlelight from the corpse-fat taper.

Evidently his mother's dying curse did not bother him at all. Once satisfied, his blood-lust abated, he discounted all possibility of revenge. Even he was not superstitious enough to believe that the sorceress could return from her grave. He was quite calm as he sat there, quite the civilized gentleman. The candle cast ominous shadows over the darkened room, but he did not notice—until it was too late. Then he looked up to see the corpse-fat candle wriggle into monstrous life.

His mother's curse. . . .

The candle—the corpse-fat candle—was *alive*! It was a sinuous, twisting thing, weaving in its holder with sinister purpose.

The flame-tipped end seemed to glow strongly into a sudden terrible semblance. The president, amazed, saw the fiery face—his mother's; a tiny wrinkled face of flame, with a corpse-fat body that darted out toward the man with hideous ease. The candle was lengthening as if the tallow were melting; lengthening, and reaching out towards him in a terrible way.

The president of Haiti screamed, but it was too late. The glowing flame on the end snuffed out, breaking the hypnotic spell that had held the man betranced. And at that moment the candle leapt, while the room faded into dreadful darkness. It was a ghastly darkness, filled with moans, and the sound of a thrashing body that grew fainter, and fainter. . . .

It was quite still by the time the guards had entered and turned up the lights once more. They knew about the corpse-fat candle and the witch-mother's curse. That is why they were the first to announce the president's death; the first to fire a bullet into his temple and claim he committed suicide.

They told the president's successor the story, and he gave orders that the crusade against voodoo be abandoned. It was better so, for the new man did not wish to die. The guards explained why they shot the president and called it suicide, and his successor did not wish to risk the Serpent Curse.

For the president of Haiti had been strangled to death by his mother's corpse-fat candle—*a corpse-fat candle that was wound around his neck like a giant snake.*

LOST BOYS

by Orson Scott Card

I've worried for a long time about whether to tell this
story as fiction or fact. Telling it with made-up names
would make it easier for some people to take. Easier for
me, too. But to hide my own lost boy behind some phony
made-up name would be like erasing him. So I'll tell it
the way it happened, and to hell with whether it's easy
for either of us.

Kristine and the kids and I moved to Greensboro on
the first of March, 1983. I was happy enough about my
job—I just wasn't sure I wanted a job at all. But the
recession had the publishers all panicky, and nobody was
coming up with advances large enough for me to take a
decent amount of time writing a novel. I suppose I could
whip out 75,000 words of junk fiction every month and
publish them under a half dozen pseudonyms or something, but it seemed to Kristine and me that we'd do
better in the long run if I got a job to ride out the recession. Besides, my Ph.D. was down the toilet. I'd been
doing good work at Notre Dame, but when I had to take
out a few weeks in the middle of a semester to finish
Hart's Hope, the English Department was about as
understanding as you'd expect from people who prefer
their authors dead or domesticated. Can't feed your family? So sorry. You're a writer? Ah, but not one that
anyone's written a scholarly essay about. So long, boy-
oh!

So sure, I was excited about my job, but moving to
Greensboro also meant that I had failed. I had no way
of knowing that my career as a fiction writer wasn't over.

Maybe I'd be editing and writing books about computers for the rest of my life. Maybe fiction was just a phase I had to go through before I got a *real* job.

Greensboro was a beautiful town, especially to a family from the western desert. So many trees that even in winter you could hardly tell there was a town at all. Kristine and I fell in love with it at once. There were local problems, of course—people bragged about Greensboro's crime rate and talked about racial tension and what-not—but we'd just come from a depressed northern industrial town with race riots in the high schools, so to us this was Eden. There was rumors that several child disappearances were linked to some serial kidnapper, but this was the era when they started putting pictures of missing children on milk cartons—those stories were in every town.

It was hard to find decent housing for a price we could afford. I had to borrow from the company against my future earnings just to make the move. We ended up in the ugliest house on Chinqua Drive. You know the house—the one with cheap wood siding in a neighborhood of brick, the one-level rambler surrounded by split-levels and two-stories. Old enough to be shabby, not old enough to be quaint. But it had a big fenced yard and enough bedrooms for all the kids and for my office, too—because we hadn't given up on my writing career, not yet, not completely.

The little kids—Geoffrey and Emily—thought the whole thing was really exciting, but Scotty, the oldest, he had a little trouble with it. He'd already had kindergarten and half of first grade at a really wonderful private school down the block from our house in South Bend. Now he was starting over in mid-year, losing all his friends. He had to ride a school bus with strangers. He resented the move from the start, and it didn't get better.

Of course, *I* wasn't the one who saw this. *I* was at work—and I very quickly learned that success at Compute! Books meant giving up a few little things like seeing your children. I had expected to edit books written by people who couldn't write. What astonished me was that

I was editing books about computers written by people who couldn't *program*. Not all of them, of course, but enough that I spent far more time rewriting programs so they made sense—so they even *ran*—than I did fixing up people's language. I'd get to work at 8:30 or 9:00, then work straight through till 9:30 or 10:30 at night. My meals were Three Musketeers bars and potato chips from the machine in the employee lounge. My exercise was typing. I met deadlines, but I was putting on a pound a week and my muscles were all atrophying and I saw my kids only in the mornings as I left for work.

Except Scotty. Because he left on the school bus at 6:45 and I rarely dragged out of bed until 7:30, during the week I never saw Scotty at all.

The whole burden of the family had fallen on Kristine. During my years as a freelancer from 1978 to 1983, we'd got used to a certain pattern of life, based on the fact that Daddy was *home*. She could duck out and run some errands, leaving the kids, because I was home. If one of the kids was having discipline problems, I was there. Now if she had her hands full and needed something from the store; if the toilet clogged; if the xerox jammed, then she had to take care of it herself, somehow. She learned the joys of shopping with a cartful of kids. Add to this the fact that she was pregnant and sick half the time, and you can understand why sometimes I couldn't tell whether she was ready for sainthood or the funny farm.

The finer points of child-rearing just weren't within our reach at that time. She knew that Scotty wasn't adapting well at school, but what could she do? What could I do?

Scotty had never been the talker Geoffrey was—he spent a lot of time just keeping to himself. Now, though, it was getting extreme. He would answer in monosyllables, or not at all. Sullen. As if he were angry, and yet if he was, he didn't know it or wouldn't admit it. He'd get home, scribble out his homework (did they give homework when *I* was in first grade?), and then just mope around.

If he had done reading, or even watched TV, then we

wouldn't have worried so much. His little brother Geoffrey was already a compulsive reader at age five, and Scotty used to be. But now Scotty'd pick up a book and set it down again without reading it. He didn't even follow his mom around the house or anything. She'd see him sitting in the family room, go in and change the sheets on the beds, put away a load of clean clothes, and then come back in and find him sitting in the same place, his eyes open, staring at *nothing*.

I tried talking to him. Just the conversation you'd expect:

"Scotty, we know you didn't want to move. We had no choice."

"Sure. That's O.K."

"You'll make new friends in due time."

"I know."

"Aren't you ever happy here?"

"I'm O.K."

Yeah, right.

But we didn't have *time* to fix things up, don't you see? Maybe if we'd imagined this was the last year of Scotty's life, we'd have done more to right things, even if it meant losing the job. But you never know that sort of thing. You always find out when it's too late to change anything.

And when the school year ended, things *did* get better for a while.

For one thing, I saw Scotty in the mornings. For another thing, he didn't have to go to school with a bunch of kids who were either rotten to him or ignored him. And he didn't mope around the house all the time. Now he moped around outside.

At first Kristine thought he was playing with our other kids, the way he used to before school divided them. But gradually she began to realize that Geoffrey and Emily always played together, and Scotty almost never played with them. She'd see the younger kids with their squirtguns or running through the sprinklers or chasing the wild rabbit who lived in the neighborhood, but Scotty was never with them. Instead, he'd be poking a twig into the tent-fly webs on the trees, or digging around at the open skirting around the bottom of the house that kept animals out of the crawl space. Once or twice a week he'd come in so dirty that Kristine had to heave him into the tub, but it didn't reassure her that Scotty was acting normally.

On July 28th, Kristine went to the hospital and gave birth to our fourth child. Charlie Ben was born having a seizure, and stayed in intensive care for the first weeks of his life as the doctors probed and poked and finally figured out that they didn't know what was wrong. It was several months later that somebody uttered the words "cerebral palsy," but our lives had already been transformed by then. Our whole focus was on the child in the greatest need—that's what you *do*, or so we thought. But how do you measure a child's need? How do you compare those needs and decide who deserves the most?

When we finally came up for air, we discovered that Scotty had made some friends. Kristine would be nursing Charlie Ben, and Scotty'd come in from outside and talk about how he'd been playing army with Nicky or how he and the guys had played pirate. At first she thought they were neighborhood kids, but then one day when he talked about building a fort in the grass (I didn't get many chances to mow), she happened to remember that she'd seen him building that fort all by himself. Then she got suspicious and started asking questions. Nicky who? I don't know, Mom. Just Nicky. Where does he live? Around. I don't know. Under the house.

In other words, imaginary friends.

How long had he known them? Nicky was the first, but now there were eight names—Nicky, Van, Roddy, Peter, Steve, Howard, Rusty, and David. Kristine and I had never heard of anybody having more than one imaginary friend.

"The kid's going to be more successful as a writer than I am," I said. "Coming up with eight fantasies in the same series."

Kristine didn't think it was funny. "He's so *lonely*,

Scott," she said. "I'm worried that he might go over the edge."

It *was* scary. But if he was going crazy, what then? We even tried taking him to a clinic, though I had no faith at all in psychologists. Their fictional explanations of human behavior seemed pretty lame, and their cure rate was a joke—a plumber or barber who performed at the same level as a psychotherapist would be out of business in a month. I took time off work to drive Scotty to the clinic every week during August, but Scotty didn't like it and the therapist told us nothing more than what we already knew—that Scotty was lonely and morose and a little bit resentful and a little bit afraid. The only difference was that she had fancier names for it. We were getting a vocabulary lesson when we needed help. The only thing that seemed to be helping was the therapy we came up with ourselves that summer. So we didn't make another appointment.

Our homegrown therapy consisted of keeping him from going outside. It happened that our landlord's father, who had lived in our house right before us, was painting the house that week, so that gave us an excuse. And I brought home a bunch of videogames, ostensibly to review them for *Compute!*, but primarily to try to get Scotty involved in something that would turn his imagination away from these imaginary friends.

It worked. Sort of. He didn't complain about not going outside (but then, he never complained about anything), and he played the videogames for hours a day. Kristine wasn't sure she loved *that*, but it was an improvement—or so we thought.

Once again, we were distracted and didn't pay much attention to Scotty for a while. We were having insect problems. One night Kristine's screaming woke me up. Now, you've got to realize that when Kristine screams, that means everything's pretty much O.K. When something really terrible is going on, she gets cool and quiet and *handles* it. But when it's a little spider or a huge moth or a stain on a blouse, then she screams. I expected her to come back into the bedroom and tell me about this monstrous insect she had to hammer to death in the bathroom.

Only this time, she didn't stop screaming. So I got up to see what was going on. She heard me coming—I was up to 230 pounds by now, so I sounded like Custer's whole cavalry—and she called out, "Put your shoes on first!"

I turned on the light in the hall. It was hopping with crickets. I went back into my room and put on my shoes.

After enough crickets have bounced off your naked legs and squirmed around in your hands you stop wanting to puke—you just scoop them up and stuff them into a garbage bag. Later you can scrub yourself for six hours before you feel clean and have nightmares about little legs tickling you. But at the time your mind goes numb and you just do the job.

The infestation was coming out of the closet in the boys' room, where Scotty had the top bunk and Geoffrey slept on the bottom. There were a couple of crickets in Geoff's bed, but he didn't wake up even as we changed his top sheet and shook out his blanket. Nobody but us even saw the crickets. We found the crack in the back of the closet, sprayed Black Flag into it, and then stuffed it with an old sheet we were using for rags.

Then we showered, making jokes about how we could have used some seagulls to eat up our invasion of crickets, like the Morman pioneers got in Salt Lake. Then we went back to sleep.

It wasn't just crickets, though. That morning in the kitchen Kristine called me again: There were dead June bugs about three inches deep in the window over the sink, all down at the bottom of the space between the regular glass and the storm window. I opened the window to vacuum them out, and the bug corpses spilled all over the kitchen counter. Each bug made a nasty little rattling sound as it went down the tube toward the vacuum filter.

The next day the window was three inches deep again, and the day after. Then it tapered off. Hot fun in the summertime.

We called the landlord to ask whether he'd help us

pay for an exterminator. His answer was to send his father over with bug spray, which he pumped into the crawl space under the house with such gusto that we had to flee the house and drive around all that Saturday until a late afternoon thunderstorm blew away the stench and drowned it enough that we could stand to come back.

Anyway, what with that and Charlie's continuing problems, Kristine didn't notice what was happening with the videogames at all. It was on a Sunday afternoon that I happened to be in the kitchen, drinking a Diet Coke, and heard Scotty laughing out loud in the family room.

That was such a rare sound in our house that I went and stood in the door to the family room, watching him play. It was a great little videogame with terrific animation: Children in a sailing ship, battling pirates who kept trying to board, and shooting down giant birds that tried to nibble away the sail. It didn't look as mechanical as the usual videogame, and one feature I really liked was the fact that the player wasn't alone—there were other computer-controlled children helping the player's figure to defeat the enemy.

"Come on, Sandy!" Scotty said. "Come on!" Whereupon one of the children on the screen stabbed the pirate leader through the heart, and the pirates fled.

I couldn't wait to see what scenario this game would move to then, but at that point Kristine called me to come and help her with Charlie. When I got back, Scotty was gone, and Geoffrey and Emily had a different game in the Atari.

Maybe it was that day, maybe later, that I asked Scotty what was the name of that game about children on a pirate ship. "It was just a game, Dad," he said.

"It's got to have a name."

"I don't know."

"How do you find the disk to put it in the machine?"

"I don't know." And he sat there staring past me and I gave up.

Summer ended. Scotty went back to school. Geoffrey started kindergarten, so they rode the bus together. More important, things settled down with the newborn,

Charlie—there wasn't a cure for cerebral palsy, but at least we knew the bounds of his condition. He wouldn't get *worse*, for instance. He also wouldn't get well. Maybe he'd talk and walk someday, and maybe he wouldn't. Our job was just to stimulate him enough that if it turned out he wasn't retarded, his mind would develop even though his body was so drastically limited. It was do-able. The fear was gone, and we could breathe again.

Then, in mid-October, my agent called to tell me that she'd pitched my Alvin Maker series to Tom Doherty at TOR Books, and Tom was offering enough of an advance that we could live. That plus the new contract for *Ender's Game*, and I realized that for us, at least, the recession was over. For a couple of weeks I stayed on at Compute! Books, primarily because I had so many projects going that I couldn't just leave them in the lurch. But then I looked at what the job was doing to my family and to my body, and I realized the price was too high. I gave two weeks' notice, figuring to wrap up the projects that only I knew about. In true paranoid fashion, they refused to accept the two weeks—they had me clean my desk out that afternoon. It left a bitter taste, to have them act so churlishly, but what the heck. I was free. I was home.

You could almost feel the relief. Geoffrey and Emily went right back to normal; I actually got acquainted with Charlie Ben; Christmas was coming (I start playing Christmas music when the leaves turn) and all was right with the world. Except Scotty. Always except Scotty.

It was then that I discovered a few things that I simply hadn't known. Scotty never played any of the videogames I'd brought home from *Compute!* I knew that because when I gave the games back, Geoff and Em complained bitterly—but Scotty didn't even know what the missing games *were*. Most important, that game about kids in a pirate ship wasn't there. Not in the games I took back, and not in the games that belonged to us. Yet Scotty was still playing it.

He was playing one night before he went to bed. I'd been working on *Ender's Game* all day, trying to finish it before Christmas. I came out of my office about the third time I heard Kristine say, "Scotty, go to bed *now!*"

For some reason, without yelling at the kids or beating them or anything, I've always been able to get them to obey when Kristine couldn't even get them to acknowledge her existence. Something about a fairly deep male voice—for instance, I could always sing insomniac Geoffrey to sleep as an infant when Kristine couldn't. So when I stood in the doorway and said, "Scotty, I think your mother asked you to go to bed," it was no surprise that he immediately reached up to turn off the computer.

"*I'll* turn it off," I said. "Go!"

He still reached for the switch.

"Go!" I said, using my deepest voice-of-God tones.

He got up and went, not looking at me.

I walked to the computer to turn it off, and saw the animated children, just like the ones I'd seen before. Only they weren't on a pirate ship, they were on an old steam locomotive that was speeding along a track. What a game, I thought. The single-sided Atari disks didn't even hold a 100K, and here they've got two complete scenarios and all this animation and—

And there wasn't a disk in the disk drive.

That meant it was a game that you upload and then remove the disk, which meant it was completely RAM resident, which meant all this quality animation fit into a mere 48K. I knew enough about game programming to regard that as something of a miracle.

I looked around for the disk. There wasn't one. So Scotty had put it away, thought I. Only I looked and looked and couldn't find any disk that I didn't already know.

I sat down to play the game—but now the children were gone. It was just a train. Just speeding along. And the elaborate background was gone. It was the plain blue screen behind the train. No tracks, either. And then no train. It just went blank, back to the ordinary blue. I touched the keyboard. The letters I typed appeared on the screen. It took a few carriage returns to realize what was happening—the Atari was in memo-pad mode. At first I thought it was a pretty terrific copy-protection scheme, to end the game by putting you into a mode where you couldn't access memory, couldn't do anything without turning off the machine, thus erasing the program code from RAM. But then I realized that a company that could produce a game so good, with such tight code, would surely have some kind of sign-off when the game ended. And why did it end? Scotty hadn't touched the computer after I told him to stop. I didn't touch it, either. Why did the children leave the screen? Why did the train disappear? There was no way the computer could "know" that Scotty was through playing, especially since the game *had* gone on for a while after he walked away.

Still, I didn't mention it to Kristine, not till after everything was over. She didn't know anything about computers then except how to boot up and get WordStar on the Altos. It never occurred to her that there was anything weird about Scotty's game.

It was two weeks before Christmas when the insects came again. And they shouldn't have—it was too cold outside for them to be alive. The only thing we could figure was that the crawl space under our house stayed warmer or something. Anyway, we had another exciting night of cricket-bagging. The old sheet was still wadded up in the crack in the closet—they were coming from under the bathroom cabinet this time. And the next day it was daddy-long-legs spiders in the bathtub instead of June bugs in the kitchen window.

"Just don't tell the landlord," I told Kristine. "I couldn't stand another day of that pesticide."

"It's probably the landlord's father *causing* it," Kristine told me. "Remember he was here painting when it happened the first time? And today he came and put up the Christmas lights."

We just lay there in bed chuckling over the absurdity of that notion. We had thought it was silly but kind of sweet to have the landlord's father insist on putting up Christmas lights for us in the first place. Scotty went out and watched him the whole time. It was the first time

he'd ever seen lights put up along the edge of the roof—
I have enough of a case of acrophobia that you couldn't
get me on a ladder high enough to do the job, so our
house always went undecorated except the tree lights you
could see through the window. Still, Kristine and I are
both suckers for Christmas kitsch. Heck, we even play
the Carpenters' Christmas album. So we thought it was
great that the landlord's father wanted to do that for us.
"It was my house for so many years," he said. "My wife
and I always had them. I don't think this house'd look
right without lights."

He was such a nice old coot anyway. Slow, but still
strong, a good steady worker. The lights were up in a
couple of hours.

Christmas shopping. Doing Christmas cards. All that
stuff. We were busy.

Then one morning, only about a week before Christmas, I guess, Kristine was reading the morning paper
and she suddenly got all icy and calm—the way she does
when something *really* bad is happening. "Scott, read
this," she said.

"Just *tell* me," I said.

"This is an article about missing children in
Greensboro."

I glanced at the headline: CHILDREN WHO WON'T
BE HOME FOR CHRISTMAS. "I don't want to hear
about it," I said. I can't read stories about child abuse
or kidnappings. They make me crazy. I can't sleep afterward. It's always been that way.

"You've got to," she said. "Here are the names of the
little boys who've been reported missing in the last three
years. Russell DeVerge, Nicholas Tyler—"

"What are you getting at?"

"Nicky. Rusty. David. Roddy. Peter. Are these names
ringing a bell with you?"

I usually don't remember names very well. "No."

"Steve, Howard, Van. The only one that doesn't fit
is the last one, Alexander Booth. He disappeared this
summer."

For some reason the way Kristine was telling me this

was making me very upset. *She* was so agitated about it, and she wouldn't get to the point. "So *what*?" I demanded.

"Scotty's imaginary friends," she said.

"Come on," I said. But she went over them with me—she had written down all the names of his imaginary friends in our journal, back when the therapist asked us to keep a record of his behavior. The names matched up, or seemed to.

"Scotty must have read an earlier article," I said. "It must have made an impression on him. He's always been an empathetic kid. Maybe he started identifying with them because he felt—I don't know, like maybe he'd been abducted from South Bend and carried off to Greensboro." It sounded really plausible for a moment there—the same moment of plausibility that psychologists live on.

Kristine wasn't impressed. "This article says that it's the first time anybody's put all the names together in one place."

"Hype. Yellow journalism."

"Scott, he got *all* the names right."

"Except one."

"I'm so relieved."

But I wasn't. Because right then I remembered how I'd heard him talking during the pirate videogame. Come on Sandy. I told Kristine. Alexander, Sandy. It was as good a fit as Russell and Rusty. He hadn't matched a mere eight out of nine. He'd matched them all.

You can't put a name to all the fears a parent feels, but I can tell you that I've never felt any terror for myself that compares to the feeling you have when you watch your two-year-old run toward the street, or see your baby go into a seizure, or realize that somehow there's a connection between kidnappings and your child. I've never been on a plane seized by terrorists or had a gun pointed to my head or fallen off a cliff, so maybe there are worse fears. But then, I've been in a spin on a snowy freeway, and I've clung to the handles of my airplane seat while the plane bounced up and down in mid-air, and still those weren't like what I felt then, reading the whole article. Kids who just disappeared. Nobody saw anybody pick up the kids. Nobody saw anybody lurking around their houses. The kids just didn't come home from school, or played outside and never came in when they were called. Gone. And Scotty knew all their names. Scotty had played with them in his imagination. How did he know who they were? Why did he fixate on these lost boys?

We watched him, that last week before Christmas. We saw how distant he was. How he shied away, never let us touch him, never stayed with a conversation. He was aware of Christmas, but he never asked for anything, didn't seem excited, didn't want to go shopping. He didn't even seem to sleep. I'd come in when I was heading for bed—at one or two in the morning, long after he'd climbed up into his bunk—and he'd be lying there, all his covers off, his eyes wide open. His insomnia was even worse than Geoffrey's. And during the day, all Scotty wanted to do was play with the computer or hang around outside in the cold. Kristine and I didn't know what to do. Had we already lost him somehow?

We tried to involve him with the family. He wouldn't go Christmas shopping with us. We'd tell him to stay inside while we were gone, and then we'd find him outside anyway. I even unplugged the computer and hid all the disks and cartridges, but it was only Geoffrey and Emily who suffered—I still came into the room and found Scotty playing his impossible game.

He didn't ask for anything until Christmas Eve.

Kristine came into my office, where I was writing the scene where Ender finds his way out of the Giant's Drink problem. Maybe I was so fascinated with computer games for children in that book because of what Scotty was going through—maybe I was just trying to pretend that computer games made sense. Anyway, I still know the very sentence that was interrupted when she spoke to me from the door. So very calm. So very frightened.

"Scotty wants us to invite some of his friends in for Christmas Eve," she said.

"Do we have to set extra places for imaginary friends?" I asked.

"They're aren't imaginary," she said. "They're in the back yard, waiting."

"You're kidding," I said. "It's *cold* out there. What kind of parents would let their kids go outside on Christmas Eve?"

She didn't say anything. I got up and we went to the back door together. I opened the door.

There were nine of them. Ranging in age, it looked like, from six to maybe ten. All boys. Some in shirt sleeves, some in coats, one in a swimsuit. I've got no memory for faces, but Kristine does. "They're the ones," she said softly, calmly, behind me. "That one's Van. I remembered him."

"Van?" I said.

He looked up at me. He took a timid step toward me.

I heard Scotty's voice behind me. "Can they come in, Dad? I told them you'd let them have Christmas Eve with us. That's what they miss the most."

I turned to him. "Scotty, these boys are all reported missing. Where have they been?"

"Under the house," he said.

I thought of the crawl space. I thought of how many times Scotty had come in covered with dirt last summer.

"How did they get there?" I asked.

"The old guy put them there," he said. "They said I shouldn't tell anybody or the old guy would get mad and they never wanted him to be mad at them again. Only I said it was O.K., I could tell *you*."

"That's right," I said.

"The landlord's father," whispered Kristine.

I nodded.

"Only how could he keep them under there all this time? When does he feed them? When—"

She already knew that the old guy didn't feed them. I don't want you to think Kristine didn't guess that immediately. But it's the sort of thing you deny as long as you can, and even longer.

"They can come in," I told Scotty. I looked at Kristine. She nodded. I knew she would. You don't turn away lost children on Christmas Eve. Not even when they're dead.

Scotty smiled. What that meant to us—Scotty smiling. It had been so long. I don't think I really saw a smile like that since we moved to Greensboro. Then he called out to the boys. "It's O.K.! You can come in!"

Kristine held the door open, and I backed out of the way. They filed in, some of them smiling, some of them too shy to smile. "Go on into the living room," I said. Scotty led the way. Ushering them in, for all the world like a proud host in a magnificent new mansion. They sat around on the floor. There weren't many presents, just the ones from the kids; we don't put out the presents from the parents till the kids are asleep. But the tree was there, lighted, with all our homemade decorations on it— even the old needlepoint decorations that Kristine made while lying in bed with desperate morning sickness when she was pregnant with Scotty, even the little puff-ball animals we glued together for that first Christmas tree in Scotty's life. Decorations older than he was. And not just the tree—the whole room was decorated with red and green tassels and little wooden villages and a stuffed Santa hippo beside a wicker sleigh and a large chimney-sweep nutcracker and anything else we hadn't been able to resist buying or making over the years.

We called in Geoffrey and Emily, and Kristine brought in Charlie Ben and held him on her lap while I told the stories of the birth of Christ—the shepherds and the wise men, and the one from the Book of Mormon about a day and a night and a day without darkness. And then I went on and told what Jesus lived for. About forgiveness for all the bad things we do."

"Everything?" asked one of the boys.

It was Scotty who answered. "No!" he said. "Not killing."

Kristine started to cry.

"That's right," I said. "In our church we believe that God doesn't forgive people who kill on purpose. And in the New Testament Jesus said that if anybody ever hurt a child, it would be better for him to tie a huge rock around his neck and jump into the sea and drown."

"Well, it *did* hurt, Daddy," said Scotty. "They never told me about that."

"It was a secret," said one of the boys. Nicky, Kristine says, because she remembers names and faces.

"You should have told me," said Scotty. "I wouldn't have let him touch me."

That was when we knew, really knew, that it was too late to save him, that Scotty, too, was already dead.

"I'm sorry, Mommy," said Scotty. "You told me not to play with them anymore, but they were my friends, and I wanted to be with them." He looked down at his lap. "I can't even cry anymore. I used it all up."

It was more than he'd said to us since we moved to Greensboro in March. Amid all the turmoil of emotions I was feeling, there was this bitterness: All this year, all our worries, all our efforts to reach him, and yet nothing brought him to speak to us except death.

But I realized now it wasn't death. It was the fact that when he knocked, we opened the door, that when he asked, we let him and his friends come into our house that night. He had trusted us, despite all the distance between us during that year, and we didn't disappoint him. It was trust that brought us one last Christmas Eve with our boy.

But we didn't try to make sense of things that night. They were children, and needed what children long for on a night like that. Kristine and I told them Christmas stories and we told about Christmas traditions we'd heard of in other countries and other times, and gradually they warmed up until every one of the boys told all about his own family's Christmases. They were good memories. They laughed, they jabbered, they joked. Even though it was the most terrible of Christmases, it was also the best Christmas of our lives, the one in which every scrap of memory is still precious to us, the perfect Christmas in which being together was the only gift that mattered. Even though Kristine and I don't talk about it directly now, we both remember it. And Geoffrey and Emily remember it, too. They call it "the Christmas when Scotty brought his friends." I don't think they ever really understood, and I'll be content if they never do.

Finally, though, Geoffrey and Emily were both asleep. I carried each of them to bed as Kristine talked to the boys, asking them to help us. To wait in our living room until the police came, so they could help us stop the old guy who stole them away from their families and their futures. They did. Long enough for the investigating officers to get there and see them, long enough for them to hear the story Scotty told.

Long enough for them to notify the parents. They came at once, frightened because the police had dared not tell them more over the phone than this: that they were needed in a matter concerning their lost boy. They came: with eager, frightened eyes they stood on our doorstep, while a policeman tried to help them understand. Investigators were bringing ruined bodies out from under the house—there was no hope. And yet if they came inside, they would see that cruel Providence was also kind, and *this* time there would be what so many other parents had longed for but never had: a chance to say good-bye. I will tell you nothing of the scenes of joy and heartbreak inside our home that night—those belong to other families, not to us.

Once their families came, once the words were spoken and the tears were shed, once the muddy bodies were laid on canvas on our lawn and properly identified from the scraps of clothing, then they brought the old man in handcuffs. He had our landlord and a sleepy lawyer with him, but when he saw the bodies on the lawn he brokenly confessed, and they recorded his confession. None of the parents actually had to look at him; none of the boys had to face him again.

But they knew. They knew that it was over, that no more families would be torn apart as their—as ours—had been. And so the boys, one by one, disappeared. They were there, and then they weren't there. With that the other parents left us, quiet with grief and awe that such a thing was possible, that out of horror had come one last night of mercy and of justice, both at once.

Scotty was the last to go. We sat alone with him in our living room, though by the lights and talking we were aware of the police still doing their work outside. Kristine and I remember clearly all that was said, but what mattered most to us was at the very end.

"I'm sorry I was so mad all the time last summer," Scotty said. "I knew it wasn't really your fault about moving and it was bad for me to be so angry but I just was."

For him to ask *our* forgiveness was more than we could bear. We were full of far deeper and more terrible regrets, we thought, as we poured out our remorse for all that we did or failed to do that might have saved his life. When we were spent and silent at last, he put it all in proportion for us. "That's O.K. I'm just glad that you're not mad at me." And then he was gone.

We moved out that morning before daylight; good friends took us in, and Geoffrey and Emily got to open the presents they had been looking forward to for so long. Kristine's and my parents all flew out from Utah and the people in our church joined us for the funeral. We gave no interviews to the press; neither did any of the other families. The police told only of the finding of the bodies and the confession. We didn't agree to it; it's as if everybody who knew the whole story also knew that it would be wrong to have it in headlines in the supermarket.

Things quieted down very quickly. Life went on. Most people don't even know we had a child before Geoffrey. It wasn't a secret. It was just too hard to tell. Yet, after all these years, I thought it *should* be told, if it could be done with dignity, and to people who might understand. Others should know how it's possible to find light shining even in the darkest place. How even as we learned of the most terrible grief of our lives, Kristine and I were able to rejoice in our last night with our firstborn son, and how together we gave a good Christmas to those lost boys, and they gave as much to us.

AFTERWORD

In August 1988 I brought this story to the Sycamore Hill Writers Workshop. That draft of the story included a disclaimer at the end, a statement that the story was fiction, that Geoffrey is my oldest child and that no landlord of mine has ever done us harm. The reaction of the other writers at the workshop ranged from annoyance to fury.

Karen Fowler put it most succinctly when she said, as best I can remember her words, "By telling this story in first person with so much detail from your own life, you've appropriated something that doesn't belong to you. You've pretended to feel the grief of a parent who has lost a child, and you don't have a right to feel that grief."

When she said that, I agreed with her. While this story had been rattling around in my imagination for years, I had only put it so firmly in first person the autumn before, at a Halloween party with the students of Watauga College at Appalachian State. Everybody was trading ghost stories that night, and so on a whim I tried out this one; on a whim I made it highly personal, partly because by telling true details from my own life I spared myself the effort of inventing a character, partly because ghost stories are most powerful when the audience half-believes they might be true. It worked better than any tale I'd ever told out loud, and so when it came time to write it down, I wrote it the same way.

Now, though, Karen Fowler's words made me see it in a different moral light, and I resolved to change it forthwith. Yet the moment I thought of revising the story, of stripping away the details of my own life and replacing them with those of a made-up character, I felt a sick dread inside. Some part of my mind was rebelling against what Karen said. No, it was saying, she's wrong, you *do* have a right to tell this story, to claim this grief.

I knew at that moment what this story was *really* about, why it had been so important to me. It wasn't a simple ghost story at all; I hadn't written it just for fun. I should have known—I never write anything just for fun. This story wasn't about a fictional eldest child named "Scotty." It was about my real-life youngest child, Charlie Ben.

Charlie, who in the five and a half years of his life has never been able to speak a word to us. Charlie, who could not smile at us until he was a year old, who could not hug us until he was four, who still spends his days and nights in stillness, staying wherever we put him, able to wriggle but not to run, able to call out but not to speak, able to understand that he cannot do what his brother and sister do, but not to ask us why. In short, a child who is not dead and yet can barely taste life despite all our love and all our yearning.

Yet in all the years of Charlie's life, until that day at Sycamore Hill, I had never shed a single tear for him, never allowed myself to grieve. I had worn a mask of calm and acceptance so convincing that I had believed it myself. But the lies we live will always be confessed in the stories that we tell, and I am no exception. A story that I had fancied was a mere lark, a dalliance in the quaint old ghost-story tradition, was the most personal, painful story of my career—and, unconsciously, I had confessed as much by making it by far the most autobiographical of all my works.

Months later, I sat in a car in the snow at a cemetery in Utah, watching a man I dearly love as he stood, then knelt, then stood again at the grave of his eighteen-year-old daughter. I couldn't help but think of what Karen had said; truly I had no right to pretend that I was entitled to the awe and sympathy we give to those who have lost a child. And yet I knew that I couldn't leave this story untold, for that would also be a kind of lie. That was when I decided on this compromise: I would publish the story as I knew it had to be written, but then I would write this essay as an afterward, so that you would know exactly what was true and what was not true in it. Judge it as you will; this is the best that I know how to do.

THE MAN WITH PIN-POINT EYES

by *Erle Stanley Gardner*

CHAPTER 1

Victim of a Vampire Mind

If you are going to understand this story, you have got to visualize his eyes as I saw them there in that Mexicali dance hall.

I have gazed into the eyes of a swaying rattlesnake. I have seen the eyes of a mountain lion reflect a phosphorescent green from the darkness beyond my camp life. I have watched the eyes of a killer, crazed with the blood lust, his hand clawing for the holstered weapon at his side.

But I have never seen eyes that affected me as did the eyes of the man who sought me out there in that place which is known as "Cantina Gold Dollar Bar."

His eyes were gray, but not the gray of the desert. It was as though his eyes had been washed with aluminium paint. They glittered with a metallic luster, and they seemed to be all the same color—if you could call it a color.

When he got closer, I saw that the pupils were little pinpoints. You had to look close to see them. And the whites of the eyes had that same metallic luster, the same appearance of having been coated with aluminium paint.

Those eyes gave me the creeps.

He looked at me for three or four seconds and said nothing. I couldn't help watching him, couldn't keep from staring into those funny eyes. It was then I saw the pin-point pupils for the first time.

They looked as though they were turning around and around rapidly, but they always kept the same size. I've seen the pupils in a parrot's eyes do the same thing, only a parrot can change the size of its pupils. This man's eyes were always the same, always black pin-points against aluminium.

He got on my nerves.

"Well," I said, "spill it!"

He didn't speak right away, not even then, but his eyes kept boring into mine. When he finally spoke, his voice was the sort I'd expected, one of those deep, resonant voices.

"I know all about you," he said.

I thought then he must be doped up. I'd seen those little pin-point pupils before when men were all hopped up. And I'd seen gun-play start awfully fast under those circumstances, so I began to humor him along.

"Sure," I said, "I could tell that as soon as I saw you. How about a drink?"

He shook his head, not a shake back and forth the way most people would shake their heads, but a swift, single shake of his head.

"No," he said. "You don't think I know about you. Let me tell you. Your name is Sidney Rane. You had two years of college in medical school. Then your health broke down and you came to the desert. You got a job as guard for the gold shipments out of Tucson, and you've been hanging around the Southwest ever since. You are reported to know more of the desert than any man living."

He stopped then, letting his words soak in.

I glared at the pin-points.

"Who the heck are you?" I asked, and my tone must have showed irritation.

"Emilio Bender," he said, and put out his hand.

For a second or two I thought I wouldn't take that hand, but I couldn't keep from looking at those strange eyes of his, and finally I put out my hand and shook.

"Now," he said, "we'll have a drink," and led the way to the bar. We drank.

That was a hot afternoon. Flies droned about the place, or circled over the damp spots on the sticky bar. A perspiring bartender dished out the drinks as they were ordered. Half a dozen Mexicans lounged about. There were a couple of drab girls who got checks for promoting drinks. There was little tourist trade. Mostly the tourists went to the fancier places.

Bender waited until I had finished with my glass and had half turned toward him. I knew that his pin-point eyes were staring fixedly at me, trying to catch mine.

It irritated me, and I kept looking away. Finally the silence became awkward. I glanced up and his eyes locked with my gaze and held it.

"Shoot your story," I said, and knew my irritation was showing in my tone.

He lowered his voice.

"I'm a hypnotist."

"Don't try it on me," I told him. "If you want someone to practice on, go hire a Mex."

He shook his head, that single swift shake of negation again.

"Listen," he said, and led me over to a dark corner of the bar. "You've had an education. You're not a fool like some of these people. I've got something that bothers me and I want you to look at it."

He waited for me to say something. I didn't say a word.

"Hypnotism," he went on, "is something they don't know anything about; and medical science is afraid to try to learn anything about it. From the time when poor

Mesmer sat his patients around a washtub, their feet in water and an iron ring for their hands, up to the time when science proclaimed that hynotism is nothing but suggestion, science hasn't learned one thing about it."

He waited again.

After another interval of silence he said abruptly; "Do you know anything about multiple personalities?"

I'd read a little something, but I shook my head.

"They're encountered once in a while in dealing with a hypnotic subject. A woman will suddenly become some other personality. There'll be times when one personality dominates, then times when the other personality is in control."

I nodded and let it go at that.

As a matter of fact I'd heard of cases like that. Hypnotism would seem to bring out some hidden personality from the dark places of the mind. Science has recorded half a dozen instances.

"I want you to come," he said.

I kept staring into those pin-point eyes.

"Where?" I asked.

"With me," he said and started for the door.

I waited a minute, and then curiosity or the effect of suggestion or something got the best of me, and I followed him.

By that time the afternoon crowd of tourists was flowing in a stream across the United States border. The A.B.W. Club was doing a rushing business. You could hear the whir of roulette wheels, the click of chips, the clink of glasses.

I rather expected we'd turn toward the border, but we didn't. We headed down the side street which runs into the native part of old Mexicali.

It was a 'dobe house he stopped at, and it wasn't much different from the other 'dobe houses around it.

There were some dirty, half-naked children playing around in the yard. They all had drooling noses and black, questioning eyes. Their mouths were sticky from eating, and more dirt had gathered at the sticky places than on the rest of their faces.

They looked at the man with pin-point eyes, and then turned and ran, just like a bunch of quail scurrying for cover when the shadow of a hawk flits across the ground.

The house was just a square, boxlike affair with small windows and some green stuff growing in the front yard. There was a pool of surface water that smelled sour, some peppers hanging on the wall, and a door that was half open.

Bender and I walked into the house.

There were three people: an old, old woman who had a nose that looked like a withered potato, a fat woman who looked hostile, and a Mexican of the *cholo* or half-breed class. He had a low forehead, black eyes, thick lips and looked surly.

The man with pin-point eyes walked in just as if he owned the place.

"Sit down," he said to me in Mexican.

I sat down. It was a funny adventure and I wanted to see how it ended.

The fat woman snapped a shrill comment in the language of her race.

"Again!" she said. "Why don't you leave us alone?"

"Shut up," said the man with her, in a surly voice. "He is a friend."

The old woman chattered a curse.

I caught the eye of the fat woman. *"Señora,"* I said to her, "if I intrude I will go. I beg of you a thousand pardons." I spoke to her in Mexican Spanish, letting her know I was a friend.

She smiled at me, after the manner of her race, one of the most friendly races on earth—when you take 'em right.

"You are welcome," she said. "It is the other. He has come from the Evil One."

"Shut up," said the surly man again.

The woman turned to me and shrugged her shoulders.

"You see how it is, *señor*. He has sold his soul to the devil!"

I said nothing. The man with pin-point eyes said nothing.

It was warm there in the 'dobe house, close with the closeness which comes from many people sharing the same room on a hot day. Yet it was hotter outside, and the sun tortured the eyes. In the 'dobe it was dark and soothing.

CHAPTER 2

The Past Breathes

I sat and waited. Every one seemed to be waiting for something. One of the children came in the door. I motioned him over and gave him half a dollar. His eyes grew wide, and he thanked me in an undertone, then scampered out.

One by one, the other children came in and got half a dollar each. They muttered thanks. They didn't ever look toward Emilio Bender, with the aluminium eyes.

The splotch of bright sunlight from the west window moved slowly across the floor. No one said anything. They all sat and waited. I sat and waited. It was a queer sensation, like being plunged into the middle of a dream. It was all unreal.

They seemed to be watching the Mexican.

He sat in a chair, stolid, indifferent, after the manner of his race. He rolled a cigarette and smoked it, flipped the stub to the floor, looked around him with eyes that were black and inscrutable in their stolid stupidity, then rolled another cigarette.

The splotch of sunlight slid halfway across the floor.

There was a rustle. The old woman was muttering something and making the sign of the Cross. The fat woman rocked back and forth. "He comes," she said, and crossed herself again.

The man with pin-point eyes was looking at the Mexican.

I watched him, too.

I could see something was happening. The Mexican began to sit a little more erect in his chair. His head came back, and the chest was thrust out. There was something military in his bearing. The surly air of stupidity slipped from him. The dark eyes flashed with spirit. The lines of his entire face became more sensitive, more intelligent. His nostrils dilated and he got to his feet.

When he spoke his words were in a Spanish tongue, but different from the slurring idiom of the Mexican. I had to listen closely to follow what he said.

"I tell you there is a fortune in gold there! Why don't we start? Are you a coward?" he asked of the man with the aluminium-paint eyes.

Emilio Bender smiled an affable, ingratiating smile.

"We have to get our army together, my friend. It takes time."

The Mexican laughed, and there was in that laugh a note which no peon ever yet achieved. It was the laugh of a man who laughs at life.

"*Dios!* Pablo Viscente de Moreno has to wait for an army to reclaim that which is his? Bah, you make me laugh! What are you, a soldier or a coward? Bah!"

He spat out the words with a supreme contempt.

"We need provisions," said the man with pin-point eyes.

"Provisions!" said the Mexican. "Did we wait for provisions when the brave general Don Diego de Vargas went into the desert to reconquer those who had massacred our countrymen? I can show you the spot, *señor*, where we camped by the foot of a great rock, and I watched while the brave general wrote upon that rock with the point of his knife.

"I can tell you the words: '*Aquí estaba el Gen. Do. de Vargas, quién conquistó a nuestra santa fé y a la real corona todo el Nuevo Mexico a su costa, año de 1692.*'"

I translated mentally, "Here was General Diego de

Vargas, who conquered for our holy faith and the royal crown all of New Mexico at his own cost, in the year 1692."

The Mexican laughed again, that laugh that was a challenge to the universe:

"It was by camp fire that he wrote that message, and I stood beside him as he wrote. That day we had killed many Indians. We carried all before us. Those were the days! And now you babble about armies and provisions. Lead up my horse! Damn it, I will start alone! Get me my blade and dagger, give me the gray horse. He is better in the desert than the black . . . Come, let us away! I tell you there is gold to be taken!"

He whirled toward me and transfixed me with an eye that was as coldly proud as the eye of an eagle. His head was back, his shoulders squared.

The man with pin-point eyes got to his feet and made passes with his hands.

"Not now," he said soothingly. "Not now, Señor Don Pablo Viscente de Moreno; but shortly. We shall go back into the desert. To-night, by the light of the moon I will come again and we shall start. Peace. Sleep until to-night at eight. Then we shall start."

A cloud came over the proud eyes of the Mexican. The chest drooped backward, the shoulders hunched forward. The head lost its proud bearing.

The old woman swayed backward and forward in her chair, chanting a prayer. The fat woman crossed herself repeatedly.

Then the Mexican was no longer a proud soldier, but a *cholo* once more. He looked at me with dark eyes that were stolid in their animal stupidity.

"It is hot," he said, and rolled a cigarette.

Emilio Bender took me by the arm.

"We will go," he said. "Later, we will return." And he led me to the door.

There was no word of farewell from the women. The man grunted the formula which the hospitality of his race demanded. The children scuttled from the front yard and hid in the greenery at the side of the house.

*   *   *

I took a deep breath of the afternoon air.

"What," asked the man with pin-point eyes, "do you think of it?"

I was careful of my words.

"The rock he speaks of is known," I said. "It is a great sandstone cliff and is known as El Morro, or as 'Inscription Rock.' It was by the old trail of the Spaniards who sought the Seven Cities of Cibola. They camped there, and because the sandstone offered a fitting place to inscribe their names and the date of their passage, they carved inscriptions. The first starts with Don Juan de Oñate in 1605. After that many expeditions left their marks.

"There is not one person in a thousand who knows of this rock. But it is a great cliff that looks like a white castle. And there is a message from General Don Diego de Vargas upon it."

The man with the curious eyes took a deep breath.

"Then," he said, "we will start. I was not sure. They told me you could give me more information of the desert than any other man. I know now we will find gold."

"Wait a minute," I protested. "Do you think this man is at all genuine, or is he a slicker trying to promote something? Or is he hypnotized?"

Emilio Bender shrugged his shoulders.

"You have seen," he replied. "The man who talked to us is Pablo Viscente de Moreno, a soldier who marched with General Diego de Vargas when the country was yet young. I know not the history; but I gather from what the man has said on other occasions that there was a massacre, and General de Vargas was then reconquering the country."

"But," I argued, "how could a man who marched in 1692 across the desert with General Diego de Vargas speak to us in a 'dobe house in Mexicali in 1930?"

The man with pin-point eyes shrugged his shoulders.

"Do you believe in reincarnation?"

I made a gesture with my hands and answered him in Mexican: *"Quién sabe?"*

He nodded. "All right," he said; "that's the answer."

We went back to the Cantina Gold Dollar Bar and had another drink.

"We leave at eight o'clock," he said, and fastened his metallic eyes upon mine.

"What's in it for me?" I asked.

"Fifty-fifty," he said.

"The Mexican?"

"He doesn't count. We'll give him what he has to have."

I laughed at that.

"Be sure you have the half-breed personality on deck when you make the division, and not Pablo Viscente de Moreno, the soldier. You might have difficulties in getting even a cut out of the soldier."

He nodded, and his pin-point eyes seemed whirling around in spiral circles, emitting little glitters like a whirling wheel reflecting the light.

We had another drink and then I went to roll my blankets. It was adventure, even if it wasn't anything else. And how could a soldier who marched with General Diego de Vargas in 1692 talk to us in a 'dobe house in Mexicali in 1930?

It just couldn't be done.

CHAPTER 3

Warrior Without a Sword

But I rolled my blankets and met the man with pin-point eyes at eight o'clock. We went back to the 'dobe. The women crossed themselves, and the children ran and hid. But the Mexican decided to go with us.

He had another of his surly fits on, and he seemed a

little groggy as though he had been asleep and hadn't fully waked up.

Emilio Bender treated him like a dog. He put him in the back of the touring car with the rolls of blankets and cooking stuff.

"Sit there!" he snapped.

"*Si, señor,*" said the Mexican.

The car started with a lurch. The old woman crossed herself. The fat woman watched us with apathetic interest. The children were hiding in the shadows cast by the full moon. I couldn't see one of them.

We crossed the border, headed east toward Yuma. It was a hot night and a still night. The rushing ribbon of road and the drone of the motor made me sleepy. The man with pin-point eyes did the driving until we got to Yuma. Then I took the car and made Phoenix.

The Mexican slept as well as he could, what with the jouncing around on the washboard road between Yuma and the Gillespie Dam. Then we hit paving again. I gave up the wheel at Phoenix, and Emilio Bender took the car over the black cañon grade to Prescott. It was getting warm by that time, but out of Prescott we did some climbing and it was cool and nice by the time we got to Flagstaff.

Back of Winslow the road changed again to sage country, and we stopped the car in the shade of the last of the stunted cedars and had a siesta. We were on our way again by the time the moon got up. We weren't letting any grass grow under our feet.

The rock known as El Morro in New Mexico is off the beaten trail. Not many tourists get to it. It's where a mesa juts out into a valley, and a couple of cañons run together. The mesa plunges into an abrupt drop to the level of the valley. It's over two hundred feet straight down from the top to the bottom, and the sandstone sides gleam in the sun.

They've protected it from vandals. For a while people wrote their names and addresses on the rock, scratching out the messages of the early Spaniards to leave their own names. Why they did it I don't know. But they did.

*   *   *

We made a camp. The Mexican looked at me as though he were about half conscious. His head lolled around and his black eyes were utterly expressionless in their stolid stupidity.

"Wait," said the man with the aluminium-paint eyes.

So we had a siesta, cooked some beans, and warmed up some *tortillas* and waited for the moon.

It came up over the desert, casting long, black shadows. In the places where there weren't any shadows the desert gleamed like silver, and the inscription rock was like some huge castle.

We sat and watched the Mexican.

Once or twice Emilio Bender made passes with his hands and crooned low words. The Mex seemed groggy. I figured the whole thing was going to be a flop.

I don't know just what time it was, but the moon was up a good two hours and the camp fire had died down to a bed of coals before I noticed anything.

The Mex was sitting all humped over, as motionless as the rock that had weathered the countless ages, and which cast a great blob of shadow in the moonlight.

I saw his shoulders twitch and his head come back. The chin stuck out and the eyes glanced around the desert. The flesh lost its heavy look of sordid animalism and took on the fine lines of the thoroughbred. I glanced at Emilio Bender, but the man with the pin-point eyes was staring unwinkingly at the Mex.

It happened all of a sudden.

The Mexican sprang to his feet, and looked all about him. The moonlight caught his eyes, and there seemed to be fire in his glance. He looked at me and jumped back, his hand flying across his body to his left hip, groping for the hilt of his sword.

"Who are you?" he shouted. "Friend or foe? Speak, before Pablo Viscente de Moreno slits your gullet with a blade of Damascus!"

And then he frowned as his groping fingers failed to encounter the hilt of his sword.

"*Dios!* I am disarmed!" he roared. "And whence came

these clothes? What witchery is this? Where are the sentinels? How about the horses? We are in hostile country! The horses are more precious to us than gold. Where are those horses?"

He whirled and fixed the man with pin-point eyes.

"You!" he bellowed. "I've seen you before—a sniveling scribe, a hunchbacked, round-shouldered, driveling devil who is learned in something or other. Who the devil are you?"

Emilio Bender said nothing, simply continued to stare with his pin-point eyes, and the moonlight glinted from them and made them seem more than ever as though they had been coated with aluminium paint.

"Speak!" roared the Mex, and made a swift imperious stride toward the hypnotist.

Bender faltered in his glance. I mean it. He shifted his eyes quickly as does one when he is afraid. It was the first time he had ever lost that positive, unwinking stare, that incisive power.

Once more the Mexican's hand groped about his left hip.

"If I can find the devil who stole my sword I will spit him like a rabbit and leave him to writhe on the sand in the hot sunlight of to-morrow ... Where's the commander? Where is General Don Diego de Vargas?"

He paused, waiting for an answer; and as he stood there, the moonlight clothing him with a silver aura, he seemed like a man of fire. Gone was the stolid Mexican who was a peon, a *cholo*. In his place was this imperious man of fire and courage, a soldier who had made a profession of soldiering when carrying arms was not merely being a cog in a military machine.

He took a swift step toward Emilio Bender, then halted.

"*Carramba!* We have few enough men as it is, even if you are a devil of a scribe. The general would like it none too well if I should run you through. But show me where my sword is, or by the Virgin I will spit you to the gills!"

Emilio Bender made a few passes, muttered soothing words, but the passes were without effect. The Mexican turned to me.

"Crazy," he said. "It is the heat of the desert, and the constant watching for raids from savages. I have seen men so before. Tell me, comrade, where is my sword, and how come I by these clothes?"

I met his eyes, feeling a strange fascination for this man of fire.

"You left your sword and your armor at a cave where you stored much gold plunder. Have you forgotten?"

He shook his head as a swimmer shakes his head upon emerging from the water.

"Damn it, you tell the truth!" he said. "I had forgotten about that cave. It seems that I have been in a long sleep. Things are not as they should be. There is much that has intervened.

"*Bien*, we will go to the cave. Let me get my blade in my fingers once more and I will be myself. But how quiet it seems! Where are our comrades? Where is the general? Where are the horses?"

"They, too, are at the cave."

He glared at me.

"If you are lying you will be spitted like a bird!"

I shrugged my shoulders.

He looked around him at the desert.

"Strange!" he muttered. "The moon was well past the full. Now it is but turned on the wane . . . This must be the rock. Surely, this is where the general carved his name and the date of his passage. But last night it was. And to-day seems a haze. I must have had the fever. Tell me, you scrivener, have I had the fever?"

The man with pin-point eyes nodded.

"Yes," he said, "you have been sick."

The Mexican said no further word but strode across the sand toward the white silence of the glittering rock. The moonlight sent a grotesque shadow, as black as a pool of ink, accompanying him. And I trotted after.

Following me came the man with the aluminium-colored eyes, and he had to trot rapidly to keep up.

The Mexican went directly to the place on the rock where the autograph of General Vargas has been protected from vandalism by the fence. He stared at the fence.

"Done to-day!" he exclaimed.

We said nothing. He raised his eyes to the inscription on the rock and nodded.

"I had thought it was more clear. Perhaps it's the moonlight. Perhaps it's my eyes that have become dim with the fever; but it's the inscription all right."

His eye caught the yellow pasteboard box in which a roll of films had been brought to the spot by some tourist.

"What the devil?" he exclaimed, and stopped to pick it up.

We waited. He turned it over and over in his fingers.

"*Cascaras!*" he exclaimed. "There is magic in this thing, or else it is the fever."

"It is the fever," said Bender.

The Mexican glared at him. "Speak when you're spoken to, scribe. Tell me, how do we join our comrades? Which way do we go?"

"Where is the cave?" asked Bender.

He pointed toward ancient Zuñi. "It lies in that direction, a march of two days."

Bender nodded.

"Come," he said. "We have a new chariot."

And he led the way toward the automobile which had brought us.

The Mexican's breath hissed in astonishment as he saw it.

"What a chariot! But how are the horses fastened? And why make it so cursed heavy? But it has good lines; only it would do ill in battle. Mark you, my man, there is not proper arm room in which to swing a sword, and that may betray us to these savages.

"A good chariot should have a grip for the left hand so that one may lean out and swing the sword in a complete circle, free of all obstructions. But look at this! There is no grip! There is no place to lean out, and that step which runs along the side will prevent a free swing of the sword.

"But we only talk! Talk is for scriveners and women, not for men of battle. Bring on the horses and we will start."

Emilio Bender, fastened the aluminium eyes upon the man.

"First," he said, "you must sit in the chariot. We will all get in, and then the horses will come."

CHAPTER 4

An Old Battlefield

When the Mexican swung into the car, I noted that the heavy awkwardness was gone from him. He was as graceful as a race horse. I got in the back. Emilio occupied the driver's seat and stepped on the starter.

The car whirred into life and lurched forward.

The Mexican leaped out into the desert in a long arched vault of such surprising swiftness that it could not have been anticipated.

"Madre de Dios!" he exclaimed, and crossed himself. "It is magic. It shot at us from under that place in the front and it moved. I swear that it moved! Look, you can even see the tracks in the sand where it moved! And there were no horses!"

Emilio Bender got out and fastened the pin-point eyes upon the Mexican, made passes, muttered soothing words.

"It is a magic chariot. We have come from those who are powerful to take you to your comrades. We must make haste. You must enter the chariot and go with us."

The Mexican shook his head.

"No. I travel either with my horse under me, in a chariot that I can understand, or on my two feet."

"Surely," taunted Bender, "Pablo Viscente de Moreno is not afraid of a chariot that can be driven by a poor scrivener!"

That gave the Mexican something to think about. I could see his face writhe and twist in the moonlight.

"He is not!" he said, and climbed back in the car.

Bender stepped on the starter, slammed in the gears. The car lurched into motion, gathered speed, started skimming over the moonlit road.

The Mexican gazed about him at the flying landscape with eyes that seemed to bulge out beyond the line of his bushy eyebrows.

"Car-r-r-ramba!" he muttered. "Wait!" he yelled at Bender. "Such a pace will tire out the chariot within the first two miles. I tell you it is a two-day march!"

For answer Bender slammed it into high and stepped on the throttle. The Mexican tried to say something, but the words would not come. He sat on the edge of the cushioned seat, gripping the windshield support with a grip that showed the white skin over his knuckles drawn taut and pale. The car hurtled through the moonlight.

After half an hour the Mexican recovered his faculties sufficiently to glance about him for landmarks.

"This road," he said, "has no business being here. But perhaps the magic chariot makes its own road as it goes? That mountain over there is where we camped the first day's march, and the distance from here to the cave is not great. The first march is short."

Then he became interested in landmarks and seemed to forget the novelty of his means of transportation.

"There," he said, "is where we lost two men only last week. There was a scouting party of the savages. But we routed them. I charged three of the Indians over against that rock. Their bodies are there yet, if you care to go and look."

The car roared onward.

"Wait!" yelled the Mexican. "You are turning away from the direction. Over there against that hill is where we are to go. Just under the mesa that sticks up into the moonlight!"

Bender slowed the car, turned it into the native desert. The wheels bit deep into the sand, and he shifted to second.

The Mexican nodded sagely.

"I knew it could not stand that pace," he remarked. "Mark you, charioteer, you are not accustomed to these desert places. I can tell that from many things. You have probably come from Spain within a fortnight. You will soon learn that things are different here, and the greatest distance is covered by him who makes the less speed at the start."

Bender said nothing. He was pushing the car through the sand, dodging clumps of sage and greasewood.

I said nothing. It wasn't the funeral—not yet.

The car ground its way toward the base of the mesa. As the ground got higher it got harder and the laboring engine gave us a little more speed. I knew the radiator would soon be boiling at that rate. Personally, I'd have given the car a rest.

Not Bender. His greed was getting the better of his self-control, and he was pushing the car to the limit.

We covered about five miles before I could smell the motor overheating. Then it fumed like rancid butter poured on a hot stove.

"Better cool her down," I suggested to Bender.

He nodded and slowed.

The Mexican pointed to the rugged skyline of the mesa. "There to the left and down at the base. There is the entrance to the cave."

"There is much gold?" asked Bender.

"As much as two horses could carry," said the Mexican casually. "We have made these savages pay for their rebellion and the massacre of the priests."

Bender got ready again and his foot jammed the throttle to the floor boards. The wheels lurched and jumped in the sand, the car gathered momentum.

We were way off the road now, out in the desert, away from the line of sane travel. We might find anything here. I watched the line of the mesa grow larger until it loomed above us.

Then the motor halted for a second. Something clicked and from the mechanism came a clatter—clatter—clatter. The wheels ceased to spin and the car slowed.

"Connecting rod bearing," I said.

"The gold," commented the Mexican, "is but a little distance."

And Emilio Bender slammed his foot back on the throttle. Rod bearing or no rod bearing, he was going to get to that gold.

The motor lost power. The rod clattered and banged. I looked for it to thrust through the bottom of the crank case at any moment. But the wheels bit into the sand and we crawled ahead.

For several minutes the car pushed forward. Then there came a terrific noise, a hissing of hot oil on the sand, and the motor froze tight as a drum.

"Busted out the crank case," I said, not that there was any need for the comment, but I just wanted to remind him that I'd warned him.

Bender cursed, then jumped from the car. "Come on! We'll walk."

The Mexican was out of the car before the words were well clear of Bender's tongue.

"*Carajo!* It was great magic while it lasted!" And he was striding toward the wall of the mesa, his feet crunching into the sand, his black shadow marching beside him, a mere black blotch of squat darkness.

We followed as best we could. Greed was giving excessive strength to Bender, the hypnotist, and I noticed he didn't pant or tire, but jog-trotted through the sand at a steady pace, keeping almost up with the fiercely striding soldier.

We arrived at the base of the mesa. The Mexican found some long forgotten trail, and we started up.

It was a hard climb. Cloudbursts, wind and sun had done things to the trail, and the Mexican cursed from time to time.

"The Indians have been here, I tell you. We shall find where there has been a great battle. Strange I do not smell the blood or that we do not see corpses piled along the way. I tell you they are cunning. They have cut away this trail as though it had been done by a hundred years of time. Only an Indian could do that.

"Forward, my comrades! Who knows what we shall find within the cave? I wish I had my blade. It would be most awkward to be attacked now." But he kept pushing up the side of the mesa until the sheer wall frowned above us.

He stopped and pointed. "Look you at the cunning of the Indian. He has put these trees and bushes at the mouth of the cave, and he has made them look as though they had been here for years. I am afraid this means that he has conquered our men. But how could a horde of savages conquer trained soldiers?" And he looked from one to the other of us.

I shook my head and said nothing. It was Bender's party and Bender could handle the explanations.

Bender fastened those pin-point eyes of his on the Mexican and said quietly, "Who are we to fear a few savages?" and pushed aside the brush.

"Charioteer, you are a man of courage!" said the Mexican. He reached out, grasped Bender by the shoulder and jerked him to one side. "But it is the part of the soldier to go first. Only I warn you, these redskins are fiends for torture. They gouge out the eyeballs and grind hot sand into the ears. They cut the skin off the soles of one's feet and press cactus thorns into the flesh. They heat little splinters of wood and stick them into the body. They are devils when they capture one."

Bender grunted. "Never mind that stuff. Let's go ahead and get the gold."

CHAPTER 5

Dust

Moreno shrugged and marched forward, going unarmed into a cave that he thought was filled with savages, who had been dead for three hundred years. It was the act of a brave man.

There was a narrow entrance. We had to stoop to get into it, but that entrance widened out within the first twenty feet. The cave went down on a sharp incline, but there were stone steps, worn smooth by many feet, and I groped my way in the darkness.

"There should be flint and steel here, a little tinder and a candle," said the Mexican, pausing and groping.

Bender took a pocket flashlight from his coat and sent the beam flashing into the darkness.

The Mexican jumped back with an oath.

"*Cascaras*, charioteer, but you have magic of sorts! What kind of thing is that?"

"A magic light," said Bender.

The Mexican regarded it for a moment with admiring eyes. Then he reached out and took it.

"It's like the other magic: fine at first, but it may tire. I prefer the dependable light of my fathers before me. Here's the flint and the steel, but, there's no tinder. Surely that dust can't be . . . *Dios!* It is!"

He looked at me, and I could see his eyes gleaming in the reflected light from the flash.

"There is too much magic around here," he said. "I left that candle and the flint, steel, and tinder here on this rock shelf but last week. Now look at it. A hundred years might have passed, yes, two hundred years!"

And he scowled at me with an expression I didn't like.

"You," he said, "are the one who says but little. Yet you are never surprised, and you seem to know more about these magic things than this charioteer with the funny eyes. Speak!"

I smiled at him. "Better wait to argue about the magic until we find what has happened to your brave comrades.

We waste time in idle talk. It seems to me you are better at talking than at rescuing comrades."

The words snapped him out of it. He whirled.

"Right. First we will rescue those who need to be rescued. But you shall pay for those words! Blade to blade and foot to foot you shall make them good or eat them. To call Pablo Viscente de Moreno a coward, one must fight!"

And he was off down the stone stairway.

By the light of the flash I could see that it had been rounded by years and millions of feet. The very stairs had been worn in a deep passageway that bare feet alone had grooved into the rock.

"It was always here, this stairway," said the soldier, as though he could read my thoughts. "But there is much that is strange. I will be glad to see my comrades, but I fear they are trapped by these savages.

"There must be treachery somewhere, and I will smell out the traitor and have his heart spitted with my blade. I remember something now of this place. It had to do with the feeling of sickness . . . There was a fight. Hundreds of savages came pouring down into the cave. I remember that which followed— Wait! It was off here to the right. The Indians crowded me into that little chamber. There were hundreds of them. I fought them and hacked them, and they shot their arrows at me, and there were spears. I was wounded. I remember a darkness that came over everything. My torch ceased to give light and I felt a drowsy feeling. At the time I thought it was death.

"But that must have been but a swooning, for I woke up at El Morro, the rock of the inscriptions. Let us see what happened here."

He darted the beam of the flashlight into the interior of a round chamber which opened off from the main slope of the cave.

I caught the glimpse of the light on something white, and then he jumped back.

"Damn!" he cried. "I remember it now!"

For a moment he stood there, then he crossed himself and strode into the chamber.

There were skeletons there, and the floor of the cave was littered with bone dust. Bits of grinning skulls turned to dust when we touched them. There was a pile of bones in one end of the chamber from which there emerged a strip of glittering steel, reflecting in the beam of the flashlight.

The soldier leaned forward, grasped the blade from the bone heap and drew it toward him.

"Carramba!" I heard him hiss in a whisper. "It is my own. But my blade is rusted with blood. Look you, charioteeer, at the incrusted blood upon it!"

He held it out and turned the light on it.

It was a wonderfully well balanced sword of finest steel. The hilt had been ornamented and incrusted with gold. There was a coat of arms upon the upper end of it.

In the shelter of the cave, in the dry climate of the desert country the blade had kept in splendid shape, almost as it had been laid down there some three hundred years ago. And who had laid it down? To whom did those bones belong?

The same question was in mind of the soldier.

"Look you," he said. "I was left here to guard this cave and this gold. There were two other men. The general was out making a raid, and meanwhile the savages swarmed down the stairs to attack us three. That is all I remember, that fight here. I went to sleep, or I swooned from loss of blood.

"And then I woke up at the inscription rock. I am still confused on the time. It was more than two weeks ago that I stood by my chief while he wrote his name upon that rock. After that came the fight. That is the last that I remember until I awoke by the rock.

"But now I am unwounded. When I swooned I had a hundred wounds. The blood poured down my arm until the hilt of the sword slipped in my fingers through the slime of my own blood. There were dancing savages grinning at me, shooting arrows at me . . . Now I wake up two days' march away and am unwounded. What sort of magic is this?"

And he glared at Bender, with the pin-point eyes.

Emilio Bender did some tall lying, and did it fast.

"I am glad," he said, simply and in a low tone of voice. "We were in the desert and we heard the cries of savage Indians. We knew that they were torturing white men. We sneaked our way toward the place from which the cries came, and we saw little fires, and there were white men who were lashed to a heavy stake, and the fire was eating its way into their flesh.

"You were lying unconscious on one side. Your turn for the torture was to come, and my friend and I rescued you. There was a great fight with the savages. And we would have been caught had it not been for the magic chariot. But we loaded you into the chariot and took you to a safe place in the mountains. There you recovered your health, but you could not remember how or when you came there or where you had been.

"We took you back to the rock so that the sight of the inscription might bring back your memory. Your wounds have healed, and the savages now have gone."

With eyes that were clouded with thought the Mexican looked at him.

"Then," he said, "you are no charioteer at all, but a brave soldier who rescued me from the savages."

Bender nodded.

"That is right," he said.

The Mexican clapped him on the shoulder.

"Ha!" he said. "A soldier!" And his eyes glittered. He turned to me. "Then you, too, are a soldier?"

I sensed trouble coming, and I wasn't going to lie about it.

"No," I said. "I am what you'd call a charioteer. Civilization has decayed my courage and spoiled my fighting trim. If you want to list Bender as a soldier that's all right. I'm a charioteer."

He stepped back, whirled the sword in a glittering arc, made a thrust or two.

I've seen fencers in my time, but I have never seen any one who could get the things out of a sword blade that man could. The muscles seemed to have been oiled and greased, made especially for sword handling.

"But the gold," Bender was prompting him.

"My comrades!" snapped the soldier. "Is it too late to rescue them? How long was it since you found me?"

The man with the metallic eyes glittered his magnetic gaze straight into the pupils of the soldier.

"It has been more than a month," he said.

"More than a month!" repeated the Mexican in wonder.

What would he have said if he had known it had been more than three hundred years more than a month? Perhaps nothing could have surprised him very deeply after his ride in the magic chariot.

So I was treated to the spectacle of a man picking his three-hundred-year-old sword from the bony hand of his own skeleton and starting out to avenge the fate of two comrades who had been dead for a third of a thousand years.

CHAPTER 6

A Monster

I got Bender off to one side.

"You've found the cave now. But you'd better do some of your hypnotic stuff and bring this fellow back to earth. There are natives all around here, and if I have any accurate knowledge as to where we are I'd say there was an Indian pueblo within a few miles of here. This is quite a cave, and we're likely to find the Indians are familiar with it.

"If this chap runs onto some Indians down here, you

can figure what's going to happen. Better snap him out of it and we can find the gold somehow or other."

Bender looked at me, and for the first time I caught a greenish glint of panic in his aluminium-colored eyes.

"I can't hypnotize him any more," he told me. "I've tried it half a dozen times. He's dangerous, but there's nothing we can do about it. The primary personality, Ramon Ayala the Mexican, I can hypnotize any time I want. But this secondary personality has too strong a will. I can't do a thing with him."

"Where," I asked, "did this secondary personality come from?"

"It must be evidence of reincarnation," he said. "I have always believed in it. This proves it. The individual is made up of hundreds of thousands of personalities. The channel from the conscious to the subconscious is well developed, and the experiences of the conscious mind are transmitted faithfully. But the channel from the subconscious to the conscious is not developed. That is why we don't see the tangible evidence of reincarnation in—"

He was interrupted at that point by a roar.

"By my sword!" swore the soldier. "The man who has left his bones here is a robber and a thief. He has even stolen the gold chain and cross from around my neck. Look, I tell you! It is mine, and look at the shape it is in. It is blackened, the links of the chain are corroded. He well deserved slaying.

"But, mark you, my comrades, there is some foul miasma here which rots bodies quickly. For these are the bones of Indians whom I slew myself with this very sword, and but a little over a month ago. You are sure of the date?"

Blender nodded easily.

"Certain," he said. "But let's go find the gold."

"Gold!" bellowed the Mexican. "Let us go find my brave comrades, or let us avenge them."

"You are but one," tentatively suggested Bender.

"Two!" snapped the Mexican. "You forget that you are also a soldier. Two soldiers and a charioteer. *Diablo!*

What more do you want? We will avenge our brave soldiers who have died the death of the Indians' torture!"

And he was off down the main slope of the cave, brandishing his sword in a glittering arc.

Bender leaned toward me. "I left my revolver in the car. Have you a weapon?"

I shook my head. I had nothing except two fists and a jackknife.

We followed the soldier, hurrying to keep up with the circle of illumination which was cast by the flashlight. There was no time for conversation, little for thought. Bender was worrying about the gold. I was worrying about what was going to happen. Perhaps it was a presentiment, perhaps it was the uncanny atmosphere of trailing around after a warrior who had been dead for three hundred years, but there were cold chills racing along my spine.

For we couldn't control this soldier. I knew it. Bender was going to find it out, if he didn't know it already. With the passing of every single minute the strange secondary personality that was the individuality of Pablo Viscente de Moreno, a soldier who had campaigned the deserts under General Don Diego de Vargas, and who had been dead three hundred years, became more firmly ensconced in the body of a *cholo* Mexican named Ramon Ayala.

And the personality of that soldier was something to be reckoned with. Civilization has done things to us. We have become weaklings, the whole race, believe it or not. It isn't so much the physical strength that has ebbed from us, as it is the spiritual courage which we should have. Here was a man who had lived by the sword and had died by the sword. He was one who had lived his life, enjoying its every moment. His vitality showed it, made us seem as sick shadows.

Here was a man who had been raised at a time when one must be able to preserve his life in order to live. He couldn't call a cop or rely on an injunction if his neighbor got crusty. He had to stand and fight, and that was the life he enjoyed.

We talk proudly of our hardy forebears who went westward across the plains of Eighteen Forty-nine. But how of those soldiers who campaigned the deserts in Sixteen Hundred-odd? Those men were traversing trackless wastes whose very nature and extent they knew nothing of. They didn't have covered wagons and sturdy oxen. They didn't have a green and fertile goal at the end of their march.

No, they simply headed their horses into the dry and burning desert, surrounded by hostile tribes, armed only with the weapons of ancient warfare, and knowing not what was before them.

Such was the man who strode in front of me, whirling his sword in a glittering arc for the very joy of life and combat.

And in the chamber behind me were the bones of this very man, dead three hundred years.

Is it any wonder that the cool air of the cave made the perspiration on my forehead seem dank and clammy?

We came to a place where the cave widened out into a great chamber. The flashlight couldn't penetrate the darkness far enough to disclose all the walls; only a stray outthrust of rock here, or a bit of lowhung ceiling there.

The soldier stopped and sent the beam of the electric flash in a long circle.

"I have got to look for landmarks here," he said. "I was only here a few times, and it has been over a month ago, and I have been sick in that month . . . Wait! There should be a branch of the main cave over here to the left." And he walked confidently forward into the darkness.

"If anything happens we'll have a hard time getting out of here," I whispered to Emilio Bender.

"There is gold here," he said, and his voice quavered with eagerness.

I said nothing further. I could take my chances with the rest. I had been taken along to see the thing through, and that was what I was going to do.

The flashlight hit the walls again, and there was an arched opening.

"This is the place," said the soldier, and started to run.

We followed.

When he stopped short we almost ran him down. The beam of the flashlight was glittering from something white again, and I knew what it would be.

"*Madre de Dios!* Another fight. More bones. *Carramba*, there is another blade, and it is the sword of Juan Bautiste de Alvarado!"

And he stooped and picked up another red-incrusted blade of finest steel.

"Here, soldier," he said, as he thrust the hilt into the limp hand of Emilio Bender. "Here is the sword of one who was brave of heart and steady of hand. Take it and bear it well and with honor."

He took another step forward and stooped to the floor of the cave. He presently turned to me with another blade, dulled with three hundred years of disuse.

"Here, señor charioteer, take this. You are unworthy of it. It is the blade of a brave man, but it is the fortunes of war, and you may have to stand shoulder to shoulder with us before you quit the place.

"Remember that a cut is faster and more terrifying, but a thrust is the means of piling a corpse at your feet to make a partial barricade. But, when you thrust, be sure to thrust true and be careful to pull your blade out before the weight of the falling man jerks the hilt from your hand . . . Come."

And he started forward again, his feet grinding the bones beneath him to a powder.

"There is some horrid miasma about this place," he muttered. "Think of the bodies that are only a month old turning to dust!"

I said nothing. Bender had started the explanations. He could finish them.

CHAPTER 7

A Medieval Raid

The room opened out into a wide circle, then narrowed again. There was the sound of running water, and my nostrils fancied they could detect the odor of wood smoke. I spoke of it in a whisper to Bender, but he shook his head.

"Gold," he said in a hoarse whisper, and hurried on.

We came to a little alcove which had been carved out of the cave by the action of prehistoric waters. The soldier walked into this alcove, then stopped and swore.

"Here it was," he said. "Now look!"

We crowded at his shoulders to look.

We saw the remains of a stout chest, bound with hasps of iron, bolted with some strangely designed bolts. The chest had been battered and splintered. It was empty, save for several inches of dust.

Bender pushed his eager fingers in the dust, fished around with them for a few moments, then uttered a cry. He withdrew his hand, and there, in his fingers, was a great ornament of gold.

The Mexican nodded casually.

"There were hundreds more," he said.

The man with pin-point eyes slipped the golden ornament into the pocket of his coat, where it bulged out the pocket and sagged the garment. Then he started groping once more in the dust. When he had finished he knew that there was no hope of additional loot. The chest was empty.

He sat down on a rock. I thought for a moment he was going to swear.

"Where would they have taken it?" he asked.

"Back to their villages. They were, for the most part, ornaments which adorned the temples they erected to their heathen gods . . . But hold. There was a private store of gold. This was the treasure chest which all were to share in; but there were some ornaments, some melted gold in bars, some of their turquoise jewelry which was mine. I hid it in another part of the cave. Perhaps they were not so fortunate in finding that. Come with me."

Bender needed no second invitation. He was on his feet and striding forward.

I thought the light from the flash was getting just a trifle more dim.

"Better turn off the flash for a minute or two and save the battery," I warned.

"Later," said Bender. "Hurry on."

And the soldier hurried on.

With us trailing after, our strange guide went back to the main chamber, ran along the dust-covered floor which sent his footfalls thudding back at us in muffled echoes, and shot the beam of the flashlight toward the west end of the chamber.

There was nothing here but wall.

The soldier muttered, sent the beam along the wall, up one side, down the other, stepping back a few paces, muttering to himself.

"It should be here," he said. "See you, there is the head of a lion in the stone, and that to the left looks like an old man . . . Ha, now I remember! It is off to the left."

And he strode confidently to the left. There seemed to be nothing but solid rock, but as we approached nearer a little vault opened out.

"This is the place," he said. "We must stoop."

We stooped, and as we got our heads near the floor of the cave there was a gentle draft of air which smote my nostrils with the unmistakable odor of wood smoke.

But the others either did not smell it, or if they did, gave it no heed. Eagerly trailing the three hundred year old secret, they entered the chamber.

It was really an entrance to another cave, or to another branch of caves shooting out from the main chamber. I could see that there was a long passageway, and then an arched roof, and I thought I could detect a glint of light coming from some faintly discerned opening in the distant darkness.

"It was in this little cleft to the right of the opening," said the Mexican, and turned the beam of the flashlight.

I saw a long cleft some little distance away, and I saw also that the beam of the flashlight was weaker now. The light was no longer a brilliant pencil of white light, but was taking on a reddish hue.

Emilio Bender ran forward, getting his shadow so that it danced along the wall in a grotesque blob of ebony silhouette.

"To one side," yelled the soldier. "I cannot see."

And, at that instant, the light went out.

"More of your damned magic that gets tired!" shouted the Mexican, and dashed the flashlight to the floor of the cave. There sounded the tinkle of broken glass and then darkness was about us, a soul-chilling darkness that seemed as tangible as a smothering blanket thrown about our heads.

"Fool!" ranted Emilio Bender.

But his ranting did no good. The flashlight might have recuperated enough strength in the battery to have given us a few flashes that would have enabled us to find the gold and make our escape from the cave.

"I can't even find the cleft where the gold is," whined the man of the pin-point eyes.

"Bah!" scoffed the Mexican. "Are we men or are we babies? Why whimper about a little darkness? I have seen darkness before. Doubtless I will see it again!"

"Come back, come back! We must get the gold!" yelled Emilio Bender.

"It is my gold, not yours. This is a private store of my own plunder. I do not share it with soldiers who are cowards. There is much more gold in the Indian temples. Go to them and get your own store of plunder. As for me, I am going to go to the other cave."

And I could hear the Mexican's feet ringing on the stone floor as he strode away.

"How many matches have you got?" asked Bender of me, and his voice was wheedling.

"I have a number, but we need them to get out of here," I said.

"Strike one, just one that I may see where we stand."

I struck just the one, and as I did so knew that I had made a mistake. For the light of that match showed me the greenish glitter of those aluminium-colored eyes staring into mine from the dark background of the cave.

"Hold that match, steady," said the man.

I wanted to shake it out. Some inner voice told me to dash it to the floor of the cave and step on it. But I hesitated too long.

The pin-points of the eyes became rapiers, thrusting long tongues of flame into my brain. The whole side of the cave seemed to be a fathomless depth of aluminium-colored darkness from which radiated twin streamers of lambent flame.

"Give me the matches."

The voice was low and vibrant, and I could feel my hand starting toward his with the matches. But I brought all my will power to my aid, and held them back.

Once more came the command.

"Give—me—the—matches!"

The pin-points of the eyes seared the volition from my brain. I did not know that I was holding out the matches. I knew only that I was no longer master of myself.

The next I knew, the match I was holding had burned my fingers, and a cold hand had closed about the box of matches I was holding out toward Bender.

The darkness was welcome, but I was still haunted by the memory of those pin-points in their aluminium-colored background.

The next I heard was the scrape of a match on the rock wall, the sputter of flame, and the dancing of grotesque shadows as Bender moved the light slowly along, nursing the flame between cupped hands.

In a little while he found the place in the cleft where something had been thrust into a hole in the rocks. He lit another match, put in his hand and pulled out a bit of what had been cloth. Now it was but a few rags of scattered remnants. But from the openings gleamed the unmistakable yellow of gold.

"Gold!" he cried.

Then, as though it had been an echo to his shout, the cave reverberated with a blood-curdling scream which came from the distant darkness.

Emilio Bender jumped back.

"What was that?" he asked me.

"A woman's scream and a man's yell mingled together," I said.

We waited, tense, listening.

Something was coming toward us. I could see the little flickers of ruddy light which were cast by a moving flame. The woman screamed again. I could hear the pound of shod feet.

Then, from a distance, there was a bedlam of sound.

Around the corner of a passageway came the flicker of a smoking torch, and there was the Mexican, holding to him the screaming form of a young woman.

He was laughing, and there was blood on his face, marks of where her nails had raked down the skin. In his right hand, held with his sword, was a smoking wood torch, a pine knot that was filled with pitch. The girl was Indian, young, attractive, and frightened. She was held in his left arm so that her feet barely touched the floor of the cave, and the soldier was laughing, the happy carefree laugh of an adventurer.

"Forward, *amigos!*" he cried. "There are other women to be had for the taking, and then there will be a splendid fight. The warriors are coming in force. This is life! And I have been as one dead for over a month!"

And he laughed again.

The woman was kicking, squirming in his embrace like an eel fresh from the water. Her lithe body was a beautiful nut-brown. Her well-turned legs writhed and twisted like twin snakes as she sought to get some purchase from which she could add to the efficacy of her struggles.

"Go," said the soldier, and threw the torch from him in a long arc of whirling fire. Then the pitch knot hit the floor of the cave and rolled along, bouncing, giving off red embers of fire.

And the soldier was gone in the darkness with a mocking laugh.

CHAPTER 8

Battle

Ahead of me I saw a barrier of grim shadow outlined against the light of that pine knot, and then heard the sound of naked feet pattering upon the floor. A torch gleamed from around the corner of one of the passageways, and I saw a young buck Indian, almost naked, running swiftly, low to the ground, a spear in his hand.

He saw me as soon as I saw him, and flung up the spear.

I am no swordsman, but desperation stirred dormant cells of dead instinct in my brain. I acted without conscious skill, but I swung that sword at just the right angle to parry the thrust.

Then we were at it, the Indian thrusting with the spear, my sword seeming to bite through the darkness and ward off the thrusts as though it was the sword that guided the arm instead of the arm that must have guided the sword.

There were half a dozen torches, now, and there were others coming on the run. Arrows whizzed about me, and the cave reverberated to the thunder of a rifle. A bullet fanned my cheek and spatted against the wall back of me.

Another Indian was on my left, and I caught the gleam of a dagger as he struck. Out of the corner of my eye, I could see Bender standing against the wall, his sword glittering in a mad frenzy as he fought off the Indians.

Then came more men and more torches. The red flames gave a weird illumination to the scene of battle. The black smoke went up in streamers until it clung to the distant roof of the chamber. And something thudded against my sword arm with numbing force. I tried to raise the blade and the muscles refused to function.

I sensed a hurtling body coming through the air, and the sword clattered to the rock floor. I swung my left. The fist connected and the man went down. Then the half darkness fairly seemed to rain hurtling brown shapes that ran forward in close formation. Naked arms shot around my knees and I was dragged down. Something hit me on the head, and my brain exploded into a flash of light.

For an instant or two I was unconscious. When I knew anything again I was being bound swiftly and securely. I could hear groans from my left where Bender was lying, two Indians banging his head on the rocks.

There were shouts from one of the side chambers, and my captors, finished with their job of binding me, ran toward those shouts.

I raised my head, and for a few seconds saw such a battle as few living men have seen.

Our soldier had dropped the woman now, and his teeth were gleaming in the light of the torches as he fought and laughed. They did not shoot him because the very press of Indians about him prevented a bullet's being placed with any accuracy.

But they crowded upon him with grim and relentless fury. There were hunting knives that glittered red in the torchlight, and there were spears that were thrust forward by lean brown arms that rippled with wire-hard muscles.

And moving with effortless ease, his glittering blade flashing in a swift circle of defense, the man held them at bay and laughed at them.

Never had I believed it possible that a slender bit of steel could move with such bewildering speed, or could offer so perfect a defense against pressing numbers.

A swift circling cut, and a man jumped back, his right arm dangling, a knife clattering to the rock. A pointed thrust that made of the sword a mere glittering tongue of naked steel, and a savage cried out in pain and toppled forward to join the piled bodies that were slumped in a half circle around the soldier's feet, forming a barrier which hampered the movements of those who sought to attack.

The sword slittered with red for a second or two, then as it whirled in its hissing circle, it cleared again and the light reflected from the smooth steel.

It was a rock that got him, a rock expertly thrown. At that there must have been an element of luck in it, for the rock was thrown by the young girl who had crawled to the outer edge of the circle of combatants.

It arched over the heads of the warriors, and dropped from the half darkness, squarely upon the top of the soldier's head.

He would have shaken off the daze in a few seconds, but he was too hard pressed to stop even for an instant. The sword wavered for a moment in its glittering speed, and then they were on him like a pack of brown wolves dragging down a wounded buck. The whole place became but a swarming mass of seething bodies, and then the motion gradually subsided.

I moved my arms, testing the bonds which held me to see if there was any chance of escape. There was none. My arms might as well have been gripped in a vise.

Then the circle of red figures fell apart and I saw our warrior raised to his feet. His head was bleeding heavily from the cut the rock had inflicted. His arms were circled with cords, and there was still the half-dazed look in his eyes I have seen in the eyes of prize fighters when some unexpected blow has caught them with deadly force in the middle of conflict.

But he was still laughing, and I could see the gleam of his teeth.

About us gathered the enraged Indians. Many had wounds and they were in a deadly humor.

"Explain to them. Otherwise they will put us to death," chattered Emilio Bender.

Explain! As well have tried to explain cold-blooded murder to twelve men in a jury box. All the smoldering enmity of these Indians against the white man had been fanned to life. They had captured us in the act of raiding them in their sacred cave. All we could hope for was that the end would be merciful. But that was a vain hope. They had been too careful to catch us alive.

If our Mexican could throw himself back three hundred years into some past incarnation under the influence of hypnotism, then these savage Indians could throw themselves back under the influence of rage until the traditions of millions of years of ancestors swayed them in what they were to do.

They jerked us together, tied the three of us with a rope which went around our necks. Many of them had nasty wounds from which blood was flowing in veritable rivulets. But they paid them no heed. Their obsidian-like eyes were glittering with a deadly rage.

The voice of the swordsman rang out. He was fully conscious once more.

"What sort of soldiers are you?" he cried at us. "Why didn't you hold them here? You two should have had no trouble holding off the tribe. But you didn't hold one. You let the whole band come down upon me. Soldiers! Bah!

"Where are the circles of dead bodies that should be in front of you? Not a body. You are both tied like a couple of rabbits being taken to the spit! Bah, you have disgraced the swords you carried!

"You, charioteer, did the best that could be expected of you. But how of you, soldier? Soldier indeed! You will answer to me for that falsehood! You are not a soldier. You are not even a charioteer!"

He would have said more, but they jerked on the rope which circled our necks, and we perforce shuffled forward in the half darkness.

Behind us, men looked to their own wounds, or gave treatment to the wounds of others. Ahead of us, some half dozen of the Indians jerked on the rope and took us forward at a half run.

"Don't stumble," I warned Emilio Bender, "or they

will drag you to death, and the weight of your body will strangle us all."

I knew something of Indian methods, and knew how hard it was to rush at a half trot through the darkness with hands tied.

Bender yammered some reply, but I could not catch it nor did I care greatly what it was. But he did not stumble.

I did not warn the Mexican. He had heard my warning to Bender, and he was not the sort to stumble, that soldier of a distant past, come to life to plunge us all into a conflict which mocked at history.

We came at length to a lighted chamber. There was a big fire in the center and the walls were black with smoke. This must have been the council chamber of the tribe for countless centuries.

They lined us up against the wall and there were iron loops driven into the solid rock of that wall. They tied us to these loops, and I could hear the laugh of the Mexican as the rope bit into his flesh.

"These are the loops we put into the wall to tie our prisoners to. Now they have turned the tables!"

I found nothing to laugh about, nor did Emilio Bender.

CHAPTER 9

The Magic of Gold

The Indians squatted in a circle to hold a conclave, and they talked in low tones.

"Will they kill us?" asked Bender.

"Ha!" chuckled the soldier. "Will they kill us! My white-livered scrivener, who talked like a soldier and fought like a coward—they will kill us by inches! Look you to the lofty walls of the cave. From those walls your screams of agony will echo back to you before another twenty-four hours have crossed the pathway of time."

The remark got on Bender's nerves.

"Yours, too!" he snapped.

"No," said the soldier, simply. "I will not scream."

I spoke to Bender in a low voice. "I have heard of a tribe which dwells in a secret pueblo. They come in to Zuñi to trade; and once or twice when I have been in Zuñi I have seen members of what I considered a new tribe. This is their secret: They make headquarters in this cave. If they are ever surprised on the outside, they pretend to be the ordinary run of Pueblo Indians. How savage they are I don't know. Perhaps when they have had time to cool off I can barter with them. Remember, we know where there is a store of golden plunder which doubtless they consider sacred ornaments. For the present, our hope is that they will save us and not put us to immediate death."

Bender grunted at that.

The soldier laughed aloud. "What a fight it would have been had the comrades of my army been with me!"

I turned to him. "Whatever possessed you to grab that girl?"

"Because I wanted to," he said promptly enough. "I could see that there were not so many men but that three soldiers could hold them at bay. But you are a charioteer and would not know the pleasure of battle."

That was, to him, sufficient reason. We stood there in a line against the wall, ropes knotted around our necks, ropes binding our arms behind us.

About the fire squatted the Indians in council. From time to time stragglers, more or less seriously wounded, came into the chamber of the cave. The women were treating those who had suffered the most, and in the distance I could hear that wailing cry of savage sorrow with which primitive people mourn for a loved one who is dead.

As the fire died down, fresh wood was piled on it. I noticed the shape of that wood. Plainly it had been cut short in order to be dragged in through an opening; it would not have been cut in such lengths to be hauled in over the long trail we had used. Nor was there any evidence of the entrance we had used being known to the Indians.

I hoped it was a secret entrance about which they did not know. That would give us a break—if we could find our way back to that hole, and if we had the chance to get loose.

The council droned into the small hours of the night. From what I could hear I gathered that the Indians were worried lest others should know that we had come to the cave. Before they decided what to do they wanted to make certain we were alone.

After several hours of powwow, they seemed to reach some decision, and slept. They left a man to watch us and see that we didn't work loose from the ropes which held us.

But we had been tied by Indians, and there wasn't much chance of working loose.

The guard regarded us with eyes in which glittered a hatred that made chills ripple the spine. It was clear that his sole desire was to wreak vengeance upon us.

"I've got to lie down. I'm weak and the cords are hurting my arms. There's no feeling in my finger tips," said Bender.

I laughed at that. They meant to keep us standing, without sleep. If we so much as relaxed our muscles and slumped forward against the bonds, the rope around our necks would strangle us to death unless they decided to loosen the knot after it had bit into our wind, and save us for a more horrible death. I explained as much to Bender.

He seemed to be thinking things over.

"What about the car?" he asked.

"I don't understand all they said," I told him. "It's a mixture of part Spanish, part Indian, and part of a dialect I've never heard before. But they've set fire to the automobile and covered the wreckage over with sand. They're worried about how we got into the cave. They think we came in past their guards. But they'll trail us when it comes daylight and find the entrance we came in by."

He let his aluminium-colored eyes narrow in thought, and I got an idea.

"Can you hypnotize the guard?" I asked.

He suddenly stiffened to alert attention. "I can try. Talk to him in a low voice. Get his attention on you. Then, when I start to talk, you keep silent."

I told him I would. The Mexican was listening to us with a frown of perplexity on his features.

Soon the guard came close.

"Would you like gold?" I asked of him.

He scorned to answer me, after the fashion of an Indian.

"Gold, lots of gold, a fortune in sacred gold," I told him, and let my voice sink to a droning monotone. "You could be wealthy. You could traffic with the white men and buy all that you desired. You would never need to hunt, never need to work. You could have everything that any one in the tribe could have, and a thousand times more. You would be powerful, you would be chief."

He approached me and spat in my face.

I waited a few moments, then droned again: "Gold, gold, gold, ever the thing of power. There is plenty of gold. You can have sacred gold, precious gold . . ."

And then, from my right, the voice of the man with pin-point eyes took up the refrain.

"Gold, gold, gold," he said, speaking in Spanish. "Gold, gold, gold. Look at me, gaze into my eyes. In them you will see that there is honesty.

"Gold, gold, gold. You are feeling drowsy. Sleep is coming to you. Gold, gold, gold. Always there is the glitter of gold. The firelight on the wall is like gold in the rocks. You see it and the light hurts your eyes. You close them to shut out the sight of the gold, gold, gold."

And I noticed that the Indian was indeed closing his eyes. He fought against the drooping lids, but the fight was a losing one.

"Gold, gold, gold," droned the man with pin-point eyes. "And before you go to sleep you must kill the white men. You hate me. You want to kill me. When I am dead you can sleep. But you must kill me first. Take your knife from your belt, hold it in your hand, ready to cut."

And the brown hand sleepily went to the belt, took out the knife, and looked stupidly at it.

"Gold, gold, gold," droned the voice in its monotone of sleepy intonations. "Gold, gold, gold. The easiest way for you to kill me is to cut my arteries. See, I am tied up with my arteries, and my arteries stretch to the others. They are not ropes, but arteries in which there courses blood.

"Cut those arteries and watch us slowly die in great agony. Then you can sleep. You cannot call out, you cannot stay awake. You have to sleep, and then you will wake up and find gold. Gold, gold, gold."

And I saw the hand that held the knife raise it and start sawing at the ropes. As the first of the ropes parted I could see the expression upon the savage features.

Never have I seen such an expression of horrible blood lust before, nor do I care to again. It was as though I could study, through the lens of a slow-motion picture camera, the face of a man who was murdering me in a burst of savage hatred.

The eyes were maniacal. The lips slavered. The facial muscles writhed with the animal pleasure of torture inflicted upon an enemy.

"I groan, I scream, I cry out in my anguish," purred the man with the aluminium-colored eyes, "and the sound is as music to your ears. Not too fast do you work the knife, but just fast enough to let the blood flow from my arteries and leave me in agony. The warm blood is splashing upon your arms now. You are bathed in it, and you are being revenged. And presently you will sleep, and when you wake up you will find gold, gold, gold."

The words droned on while the Indian cut through the bonds that held us together and anchored us to the wall.

"Now I am dead and you can sleep," said the droning voice. "You will lie back upon the floor and your eyes will close. You will relax your hold upon the knife. You have avenged your tribe. And you will sleep a deep and dreamless slumber. When you awaken it will be to find gold. Gold, gold, gold."

The Indian slumped to the rocky floor, flung one arm under his head and instantly went to sleep.

"What magic is this?" demanded the Mexican.

"Shut up!" I hissed at him in a whisper.

The council fire was some little distance from us, and the men slept about it like logs of wood. I knew the Indian delicacy of sense. They would be almost certain to hear us before we could make good our escape. But every second was precious now.

I sat down on the rock floor and inched my way toward the sleeping Indian, took the knife from his nerveless fingers, and held it rigid in my hand.

By an effort I got to my feet. The aluminium-eyed man leaned against the blade of the knife and sawed the last of his bonds across it. When they had dropped to the floor he took the knife and cut my ropes, then those of the soldier.

CHAPTER 10

Through the Blackness

Our swords had been taken from us and flung into a corner of the rock chamber. We retrieved them, and I was barely able to restrain the soldier from then and there giving his battle cry by pointing out to him in a whisper that he was accompanied only by a charioteer and a scrivener who were worse than useless in battle. He regretfully agreed, and then we wormed our way silently toward the arched opening through which we had been marched.

In one of the pockets carved in the rock wall by the action of the elements, were stacked some pitch knots to be used as torches, and I gathered up two or three of these.

"You have the matches?" I asked of Bender.

He nodded.

Back of us some one stirred.

"Run!" I whispered.

There was a shout from behind us, but it was the confused shout of one who is not in full possession of his faculties.

Some sleeping Indian, hearing the faint sound of our feet, had doubtless awakened, looked toward the wall and seen that we had gone. But he did not know in which direction.

"Feel your way through the darkness," I cautioned them. "Do not show a light and do not make noise. They don't know which way we have gone."

They followed my instructions, although the Mexican grumbled at being forced to flee from a horde of ignorant heathens.

I had no time to explain to him the development of the modern revolver, or the repeating rifle. I could only urge him to run by warning him that he was with two cowards. It was the only argument which moved him.

I doubt if we could have found our way back to the place where the gold was stored had it not been for the uncanny sense of perception of the Mexican. He seemed able to see in the darkness, and he must have known the inside of that cave as a river pilot knows his stream. For he took us on a swift but silent walk until I could hear the wailing of women, and knew that we were approaching the scene of our conflict.

We had some light here, the light of a distant camp fire in the other chamber of the cave. The women had taken the bodies out into this chamber and built a fire. About this fire they rocked back and forth, wailing their thin chant of mourning.

They were as hypnotized with their grief as the Indian guard had been with the droned words of Emilio Bender.

*　　*　　*

Getting past them was easy, but we had to use considerable care to keep some of the children from spotting us. It was the older girls who made the trouble. They sat in on the mourning party, but youth is ever unable to concentrate for long upon any emotion other than love; and we could see the slender forms of the girls flitting about the mourning fire, putting on additional wood.

We finally reached the cleft where the gold had been stored. It was still there, intact.

Emilio Bender raked out the gold pieces and struck one of the matches. He devoured them with his eyes. There were golden ornaments, little gold images, even gold arrowheads.

In the greed of that moment, the man with the strange, aluminium-colored eyes forgot himself. He scooped such things as he desired into his pockets.

"This is *my* third," he said, heedless of the fact he had taken a good three-quarters. "You two divide the rest and we'll get going."

It must have been the silence which warned him. It was the silence which precedes a storm, and Emilio Bender looked up to encounter the flaming gaze of the man who claimed to be Pablo Viscente de Moreno, a soldier who had marched the deserts three hundred-odd years ago.

"So!" yelled the soldier. "You would loot the plunder of a soldier, eh? You who claim to be a soldier, but are not even a charioteer!"

And the right hand of the soldier whipped the naked blade in a hissing arc.

"Arise and account!" shouted the soldier.

There was only the faintest light from the distant camp fires. They glinted in half reflections from the polished blade, and served to show the men as half-formed shadows moving against the chalklike wall of the cave.

"But think," said Emilio Bender in his droning voice, "of what you can buy with that gold! Think of the sleep you have lost . . ."

I still believe that if he had surrendered the gold instead of trying to use his hypnotism he could have saved himself. But he was flushed by his success with the Indian and emboldened by greed.

"Sleep, sleep, sleep," he droned. "You need to rest, to relax, to let your senses become warm and drowsy. You feel a strange quiet . . ."

It was then that the Mexican said something which has puzzled me, and will always puzzle me. Some of what had happened could be explained through the theory of dual personalities. But this remark tended to show that he knew.

"Quiet!" he shouted. "Sleep, you say! I have slept for three hundred years. Now look out for yourself!"

It happened so quickly that I could not interfere even had I wanted to. These two men had come to the final show-down, and that show-down was inevitable. The hypnotist had virtually created this strange man who was now challenging him. And the greed of the man with eyes like pin-points was bound to bring about such a conflict, sooner or later. As well sooner as later.

I heard the rasp of steel on steel, and an exclamation from the soldier.

"You would try to slip a blade into my stomach from below, would you? Then stand up and fight, man to man."

"Quick!" yelled Bender to me. "Run him through in the back and we will divide the gold."

I know of no remark that better illustrated the character of the man. It was his last.

There was the whirl of a blade, a cut, a thrust, a groan and something staggered back and slumped to the rock.

"Fool!" grunted the soldier. "You would pose as a soldier and turn out a thief!"

I groped for the pulse of the man with pin-point eyes. There was no pulse. His wrist was limp and already chilling with death.

The soldier saw my motion and laughed bitterly. "Am I so clumsy then that when I run my blade through their hearts you can feel a beat in the wrist? He is dead, I tell you. Come."

He stooped and took the gold from the pockets of the dead man, and he made a rough division with me.

"Thus do soldiers share their spoils upon the field of battle," he said.

I crammed my gold into my pockets.

From the main body of the cave was a terrific clamor of noise. The Indians were loose and on the trail, rushing down the cave toward us.

"Quick, run!" I yelled.

"Run? Why? Are we not two soldiers?"

"They have guns," I said. "We have no chance against them."

I doubt if I could have moved him, but, of a sudden, he spoke in a thicker, slower tone.

"Very well, then, let us run. I know this cave. Follow me."

He ran; and as he ran his steps became more heavy, slower. The body gradually lost the spring and became as the muscle-bound body of a *cholo* laborer.

We ran through the dark, he leading the way.

"Stoop here," he called; and I stooped, felt a low archway graze my body.

"There is another entrance, a secret entrance," he said. "I hope I can find it. I am getting drowsy. Some one is shouting in my ear to go away and leave his body alone. Why should I have some one shout at me to leave my own body?

"*Carramba!* It's all because of that man with the funny eyes. I know now that I must die because I killed him. As his corpse gets cold, so does my own soul get cold. I am paying a price, and yet it is not a price. It is something I have already paid . . . Here, *amigo*, take all the gold. I would rather you had it than the strange man who is pushing me out of my skin. How he pushes! And he is slow and stolid. He could never oust me but for the death of the man with the strange eyes. I can feel an inner chill."

He stopped in his tracks, thrust golden ornaments and turquoise necklaces into my hands.

"Fill—your—pockets . . . *Adios, amigo!*"

And he was gone. I knew instantly when the other came into possession of his body.

"*Que es?* What is it?" he demanded, Mexican fashion, and his tone was dull as the tone of a man who is slowly awakening from a long sleep.

"We are in a cave," I said. "Follow me."

He accepted the statement with the unreasoning stolidity of his kind. I led the way in the same general direction the soldier had been piloting me. It was dark, and yet it was not entirely dark. There was a half light in the air, and a freshness which reminded me of dawn.

We pushed forward, seeing the vague shape of walls and minarets on our sides. I thought there was an opening overhead and glanced upward. I saw the pale glow of a star, pin-pointing out before the dawn, and I thought of the man with pin-point eyes.

Somewhere, we had left the cave and were in a cañon which towered on either side in great cliffs. The cliffs spread apart. The floor of the cañon became rough and bowlder-strewn. We fought our way forward. The light grew stronger, and dawn smells were in the air.

We found a deer trail angling from the floor of the cañon to the side of the mountain, around it to the desert plain below the mesa. I led the way along this. There were no signs of Indians.

The Mexican looked down at the sword he was using for a walking stick. It was stained with sticky red, and even now the flies were commencing to drone about it.

"What is this?" he asked in his thick, suspicious voice, and raised it to his eyes. Then he flung it far down the cañon. It clattered upon the rocks. He crossed himself, looked at me with eyes which were showing a glint of expression, an expression of wonderment.

"It is nothing," I said. "Come."

"Where is the other man, the Señor Bender?"

"He has remained behind. Come."

We struck the shoulder of the mountain, zigzagged to the plain. The sun came up and tinted us with its reddish rays. Far off in the distance I saw a cloud of dust and knew that it was an automobile.

I followed the course of the road, figured where we might intersect it, and ran down the sloping plain, shouting at the Mexican to hurry.

He ran with a heavy-footed pace which covered the ground but slowly. We would have missed it, but the automobile driver saw us and waited while we covered the last half mile. He was a bronzed rancher who was inclined to be suspicious, but he gave us a lift.

I had taken the things from the pockets of my coat, taken off my coat, and rolled the treasure stuff into a ball within the coat. The rancher looked at it suspiciously, but I offered no explanation. He took us to Gallup, and from there we caught a train to Los Angeles.

I had purchased a suitcase for my treasure stuff.

At Los Angeles I secured a car from a friend, and drove the Mexican back to Mexicali.

I deemed it better to transfer a portion of the gold into money and pay him his half in coin. It amounted to more than twelve thousand dollars at the prices I was able to get. Many of the things were museum pieces, even without an authentic history. And I gave no history.

But I did not pay him until I had him back in his 'dobe, and was ready to leave. His women folks commented on the wounds on his face, on the scratch marks which stretched from forehead to chin.

"Where is the evil one?" asked the old woman, when there had been mutually evasive comments on the wounds of the man.

"He remained behind."

She rocked back and forth on her chair and crooned some charm, or perhaps it was a curse. The words were unintelligible.

I shrugged my shoulders.

"He was evil, very evil," she said at length.

"He was a devil-man," said the fat woman.

The Mexican spoke simply.

"He made me very sleepy," he said.

I made no comments. The children came trooping in and climbed all over me. I gave them a *peso* apiece. Then, when I was ready to go, I took an envelope from my pocket and handed it to the Mexican.

"*Señor,*" I said, "I have the honor to wish you good day, and to express regrets at the parting and appreciation for the association."

He muttered some formal courtesy. It was the fat woman who opened the envelope and saw the crisp five-hundred-dollar bills that were in it. I heard her scream as I left the door.

From the sidewalk I could hear her voice through the open window. She was explaining the amount of the money to the more stolid and ignorant husband. The old woman was keeping up a shrill chattering of words and phrases which had almost no meaning, although once or twice I caught the expression "Devil Man."

I have no explanation. I have given you the facts as they happened; but to understand them you must be able to visualize the eyes of the man as I saw them there in that Mexicali dance hall, aluminium-colored eyes that had pupils that were mere pin-points.

If you had seen those eyes, the story would have seemed but the natural sequence of events, rather than something bizarre. Strange things happen on the border desert; strange whispers seep through the ear-aching silence of the desert spaces.

But never again have I seen a man with eyes like those—only the once. And that is enough. Emilio Bender lies asleep in a cave of death beneath a mesa in New Mexico. Perhaps, if there is anything in the Buddhist law of reincarnation and repayment, some hypnotist of three hundred years hence will disturb his rest and summon him back to the land of the living.

Personally, I do not know.

GRAVE ERROR

by Cathie Griffiths

Juan and Eddie sweated against the stairway wall as two of Little Rock's finest waddled by.

"Where we gonna have lunch, Smitty?"

"How about Su Chow's, Ames? I feel like Chinese food."

"You look more like a German dumpling to me."

"Ha, ha, ha! Very funny, Ames. Don't you think so boys?"

Juan and Eddie nodded furiously.

"And what do you suppose you look like," said Smitty as the two reached the lower landing.

"Jesus Cristee," whispered Juan. "What have you gotten us into, Eddie?"

Eddie poked him onward with the rolled newspaper. Soon they reached the second floor.

At the hall light, Eddie squinted at the ad again.

"I am dying of a rare, incurable disease. For a small fee, I will take messages to your friends or loved ones who have passed on, when I, too, pass on. Delivery of your message is guaranteed. Come, in person, to 125, 23rd Street, #8."

Juan looked at the big oak door in front of him and bit his lip. "Eddie, you sure this is okay? I dunno if we should be sending no message to the Boss. I mean, what if he comes back to haunt us or somethin'?"

"C'mon, Juanito. Let's be charitable with our new-

156

found wealth. I gotta message I wanna send the Boss. Guess what it is?"

Juan couldn't help but laugh as he replied, "Hey, Boss, who's the flaming idiot now?"

They collapsed into such helpless merriment they had to hold their guts to keep their sides from splitting. In the middle of their fun, the door was opened by a frowsy looking woman, and they tried to mask their laughs with coughs.

She motioned them into the dark and threadbare living room. "You coming to leave a message with Delbert?"

Eddie cleared his throat. "Yes, ma'am. Is he well enough to see us?"

"I'll go see, Messers . . . ?"

"Juan and Eddie, ma'am," Juan answered, a little jerk in his voice.

She left them and headed down the dim hall.

"Eddie, this place give me the creeps, man. Why don't she turn on some lights? I can hardly see my fingers before my face. And it smells funny. Like rotten eggs. Like that plant where they processed chemicals back home." Juan looked decidedly nervous.

"Maybe there's a sulfur plant near here." Eddie snapped.

"I didn't smell it outside."

Eddie crowded into Juan's face. "So, what do you think it is, Juanito? Fire and brimstone, the Devil?"

Juan jumped as a tabby cat leapt up onto the chair next to him. "Man, don' say that!" he whispered fiercely.

Eddie could tell he'd really freaked Juan, which calmed him down. Being in control made him feel much more competent. But when the lady suddenly tapped his shoulder, he shrieked.

"Delbert will see you now."

The three of them walked single file down the corridor to Delbert's bedroom. When the door clicked behind the two men, their first impression was of entombment. Their second was of two flashing disembodied blue eyes.

Juan gasped and grabbed Eddie's arm, as if to pull him from the room. At the same time, Delbert flicked on the bedside lamp. The pool of light transformed him into a wafer-thin, wasted old man. Unless he and his wife had a July-December relationship, his illness probably made him look older than he was. At his summons, Eddie and Juan moved in lockstep to the two chairs by the bed.

"Money, please." said the breathless voice.

Juan laid a five and two tens on the night table.

"Your message and to whom?"

"It's to the Boss, Gus Jeanette, and we want to ask him, 'Who's the flaming idiot, now?' " Eddie replied. He tipped his chair back, feigning confidence.

"Is that all?" the old man whispered, eyes burning like blue flames.

"Ah, yessir, he's . . . uh . . . deceased now and we thought he'd like a little joke. . . ." Eddie's voice tailed off, begging Juan's help. But Juan stayed still as a jacklit deer.

Delbert shut his eyes. "I'm just the messenger. You don't have to explain anything to me."

"Well, then," Juan said, a little too heartily. "Thank you. We'll be going now." They almost broke the stairs bolting from the building.

In mutual, silent agreement, they headed for Huey's, a favorite watering hole for young toughs and semi-toughs.

They sat at a table by the window, cradling ice-cold beers, and watched the rain, which was not cooling anything off, despite the steam it sent bouncing off the pavement. Neither one spoke until Eddie got up and brought back their third round. Then, without looking up, Juan traced the graffiti of a devil cut into the dark wooden table.

"Eddie, *la puerta no se abierta . . .*"

"Juan, speak English, or don't speak at all, man!" Eddie interrupted nervously.

"The door, Eddie, when first I tried the door, it would not open!" Juan ended in soprano.

"So, his old lady locked us in, it was a con job, man." Eddie scoffed.

Juan waved off his friend. "No, amigo, the handle turned just fine. It just wouldn't open."

"Well, what kind of chickens were we anyway, trying to run away, huh?" Eddie questioned with some heat.

Juan went back to tracing and they finished their beers morosely.

Eddie looked at his watch and suddenly brightened up. "Hey, Juanito, didja forget we've got dates tonight with those two hot chiquitas? Let's get back to the crib and shower and change, now, or we're gonna be late. Cheer up man, you can wear your new leather pants even if it is over 100. With those babes you won't wear them long enough to sweat."

The two chiquitas turned out hotter than either Juan or Eddie expected. So it's not hard to imagine the next couple of days. But, as hot chiquitas are expensive, Juan and Eddie were forced—after Joyce and Buffy left with kisses and promises—to dig up more cash if they wanted to see the girls again next weekend.

Monday morning found Juan and Eddie eating enormous breakfasts as Juan combed through the newspaper to ensure they weren't in it. Suddenly, Juan grabbed Eddie's shoulder, inducing a spate of swearing by Eddie as coffee splashed across the funnies.

But Eddie's curses were broken off by Juan's dramatic urgency. "Eddie, he's died! Delbert, he's in the obitchilary! He died yesterday!" Juan paled and crossed himself, his face becoming grave, "We shoulda never left that message, Eddie."

"Forget it, Juan. The guy probably went to heaven and he'll never even see the Boss. It was a charitable act, man. We just helped to keep his wife off welfare. Now, help me clean up this mess. We got work to do today."

"I think we oughta just dig up all the dough and keep it here. If the cops ain't found us by now, they ain't going to."

"I dunno, Eddie." Juan pulled two posters from his jacket pocket and unfolded them. Those bank cameras in St. Louis got our pictures, man. I told you we shoulda worn stockings."

"Look man, if you're so worried, why don't you throw

those FBI posters away?" The question was rhetorical, as Eddie enjoyed impressing his friends with them as much as Juan did. Eddie continued, in soothing tones, "Don't worry. St. Louis is long ago and far away."

Following Eddie's lead, Juan pulled a leather satchel from the closet, and together they walked downtown until they could hail a cab.

"Rolling Oaks Cemetery, please," Eddie said to the driver, as they settled back.

Juan, extremely tense, said nothing as the city flew by in shades of gray and green. Juan's attitude prevented Eddie from spinning a quickly improvised, and totally untrue yarn to the cab driver about the family member who'd been buried at Rolling Oaks and left, as a condition of her will, instructions that he visit the cemetery every week for the next five years if he wanted to inherit his million dollars. (Eddie considered this kind of on-the-spot improvisation on-the-job training, and practiced it constantly.) Instead, he satisfied himself today by simply checking the people out, nudging Juan when he saw a particularly good-looking chick.

"Hey, that looks like a great place to take Joyce and Buffy this weekend." Eddie was pointing to the city's finest Italian restaurant, on the way through the ritzy section of town. Juan sighed morosely.

"Just let us out right at the gates, man," Eddie said as they pulled alongside the tall, white wrought iron gates. The cemetery had a sort of deserted, semi-unkempt look, with the paint chipping off the iron fence and the grass about a week past due for mowing. Some of the headstones leaned a little, like tipsy revelers. Eddie and Juan pushed through the creaking gate and headed straight to the new grave beside the old oak tree. In another one of Eddie's jokes, the fifty thousand they made off with in the St. Louis heist—engineered by, but not long survived by, the Boss—had been buried on top of his coffin.

Eddie and Juan took their fold-up camping shovels from their satchels, slung the bags to the ground, and began to dig.

The sun continued to sink lower and lower as the afternoon wore on, but the temperature did not drop, nor did any breezes blow in the hot, oppressive air. After several hours of hard digging, Eddie and Juan were stripped to the waist, with soaking hair and ill-tempers. They stopped digging and rested against the tree trunk.

"It's hotter-n-hell out here, Eddie," Juan complained.

"Look, don't start whining, Juan. You've been draggin'me down all day, so just shut up." Eddie shot back, tired and angry from the heat. "C'mon, let's dig some more." Eddie got up, shoveled a couple of shovel loads full, and before Juan could even get started, shouted "Pay dirt, Juanito!"

They pushed the heavy bank sacks of money, five of them altogether, out of the deep hole, and stacked them up.

"Hey, Eddie, you smell something funny?"

"Yeah, Juan, I think there's another sulfur plant around here somewhere."

"Think again, boys!" a familiar voice boomed.

Juan and Eddie clutched each other and turned 180 degrees in unison. Unbelievably, they saw the Boss, sitting casually on his headstone, not five feet away. He seemed not to mind that he was in flames. As he spoke, flames would rise up, even covering his face on occasion. Then they would die down to dance along his feet, playfully reaching up for his knees.

"B–B–B . . . Boss!" Eddie was quaking.

"I got your message," the Boss replied in evident, dangerous good humor. He crossed his legs, sending up showers of sparks. "You know, boys, I was gonna forget the whole thing. Figured I'd let bygones be bygones, and let my idiot buddies Juan and Eddie have the loot. Even though you, Eddie, were stupid enough to accidentally shoot me in the foot, preventing my getaway." Here the flames rose and covered the Boss' face entirely.

Juan and Eddie cowered, too frightened to try to sneak away.

"Yeah," the Boss went on meditatively. "I was going to forget it was your fault that I was nabbed and caught pneumonia in that damp, filthy Missouri jail and died. I was even going to forget about your burying the money on top of me as a crude form of joke. And, then I got your smart aleck message." Flames positively engulfed the Boss. "That was a real hot joke boys. A real scorcher! But I have a flare for humor, too. If you get my point."

As Juan and Eddie stood rooted to the spot in horror, the Boss gestured in their direction, hurling tentacles of fire from his fingertips to their pants.

Two blocks away, patrolmen Smitty and Ames sat in their black and white under a tree, chewing gum and debating the pros and cons of various foods for dinner.

"Ames, I want chicken, not chili! It's too hot for chili."

"Smitty, is that smoke over there by the cemetery?"

"Yea. It's probably someone burning trash, but maybe we better check it out."

"Well, that settles it, then," Ames answered, starting up the engine. "The cemetery is on the way to Charlies' Chicken Hut."

What they saw as they pulled up was Juan and Eddie, buck naked, apparently alone, and jumping up and down tarentellalike beside a freshly opened grave—as if trying to escape the fires of Hades, while a mound of clothes burned briskly nearby.

"What the hell is going on here?" bellowed Smitty, reaching for his handcuffs.

A freak wind whipped the wanted posters from Juan's discarded jacket, and cracked them open in Smitty's face.

He snatched the pictures away with his left hand. Eyes bulging, he gawked at the dancing men. "Christ, they're bank robbers!" He dropped the cuffs and pulled his .38 with his right hand. "POLICE, freeze!"

Juan and Eddie stood paralyzed by this new misfortune.

"You know, Ames, if I'm not mistaken, these are the dopes that plugged one of their partners during a robbery. 'Bout as dumb as they come. And, now we find them torching their clothes and partying while digging for the loot. What do you make of it?"

"Just crazy, I guess." Ames was taciturn, feeling even hungrier now that he realized he was going to sacrifice supper.

Smitty pointed at Eddie. "Pick up them money bags son, and bring 'em here. Seems like there's a lot there. So that, at least, should make it easier on you."

Eddie started forward, but stumbled as a shooting pain crippled his right foot. He threw his arms up for balance and watched incredibly as the bags arced from his hands, slowly tumbled onto the burning clothes, and exploded like a string of Molotov cocktails.

Smitty and Ames picked themselves up, backhanding soot from their faces, and angrily advanced upon Juan and Eddie, who lay flash-burned lobster-red and hairless, as familiar, sepulchral laughter echoed through their heads. "Jesus H. Christ," ranted Smitty, "what a bunch of FLAMING IDIOTS." He continued swearing splendidly, but Juan and Eddie heard no more, seared, as they were, by this sudden illumination of unrelenting revenge. From now on, all would curse them with the boss' words.

And it would never end.

THE TORTOISE

by W. F. Harvey

One word as to the documentary part of my story.

The letter was written by Tollerton, the butler, five weeks before his death. Sandys, to whom he addressed it, was, I believe, his brother; in any case the man was not known at Revelstoke Mansions, and the letter came back to Baldby Manor unopened.

I read it twice before it dawned upon me that the man was writing of himself. I then remembered the diary which, with the rest of his belongings, had never been claimed. Each partly explains the other. Nothing to my mind will ever explain the tortoise.

Here is the letter—

"BALDBY MANOR

"My dear Tom.—You asked in your last for particulars. I suppose, as the originator of the story, I am the only person able to supply them, but the task is rather hard. First as to the safety of the hero. You need not be alarmed about that; my stories have always ended happily.

"You wonder how it all came about so successfully. Let me give you the general hang of the plot. To begin with, the man was old, a miser, and consequently eccentric. The villain of the piece (the same in this case as the hero, you know) wanted money badly, and moreover knew where the money was kept.

"Do you remember Oppenheim's *Forensic Medicine*, and how we used to laugh over the way they always bungled these jobs? There was no bungling here, and

consequently no use for the luck that attended the hero.
(I still think of him as hero, you see; each man is a hero
to himself.)

"The victim occasionally saw the doctor, and the doctor knew that the old fellow was suffering from a disease
which might end suddenly. The hero knew what the
graver symptoms of the disease were, and with diabolical
cunning told the doctor's coachman how his master had
begun to complain, but refused to see any medical man.
Three days later that 'intelligent old butler—I rather
think he must have come down in the world, poor fellow'—is stopped in the village street by Æsculapius.

" 'How is your master, John?' 'Very bad, sir.' Then
follows an accurate account of signs and symptoms, carefully cribbed up from old Banks's *Handbook.* Æsculapius
is alarmed at the gravity of the case, but delighted at the
accuracy of the observations. The butler suggests that an
unofficial visit should be paid on the morrow; he com-
plains of the responsibility. Æsculapius replies that he
was about to suggest the very same thing himself. 'I fear
I can do little,' he adds as he drives away.

"The old man sleeps soundly at night. The butler goes
his usual round at twelve, and enters his master's room
to make up the fire, and then—well, after all the rest
can be imagined. De Quincey himself would have approved
of the tooling, cotton-wool wrapped in a silk handkerchief. There was no subsequent bleeding, no fracture of
the hyoid or thyroid, and this because the operator
remembered that aphorism in Oppenheim, that murder-
ers use unnecessary violence. Only gold is taken, and
only a relatively small quantity. I have invented another
aphorism: The temperate man is never caught.

"Next day the butler enters the bedroom with his master's breakfast. The tray drops to the floor with a crash,
he tugs frantically at the bell-rope, and the servants rush
into the room. The groom is sent off post haste for help.
The doctor comes, shakes his head, and says, 'I told you
so; I always feared the end would be this!'

"Even if there had been an inquest, nothing would
have been discovered. The only thing at all suspicious

was a slight hæmorrhage into the right conjunctiva, and that would be at best a very doubtful sign.

"The butler stays on; he is re-engaged by the new occupier, a half-pay captain, who has the sincerity not to bemoan his cousin's death.

"And here comes a little touch of tragedy. When the will is read, a sum of two hundred pounds is left to John the butler, as 'some slight reward for faithful service rendered.' Question for debate: 'Would a knowledge of the will have induced a different course of action?' It is difficult to decide. The man was seventy-seven and almost in his dotage, and, as you say, the option of taking up those copper shares is not a thing to be lightly laid aside.

"It's not a bad story, is it? But I am surprised at your wanting to hear more than I told you at first. One of the captain's friends—I have forgotten his name—met you last winter in Nice; he described you as 'respectability embalmed.' We hear all these things in the servants' hall. That I got from the parlourmaid, who was uncertain of the meaning of the phrase. Well, so long. I shall probably chuck this job at the end of the year.

"*P.S.*—Invest anything that is over in Arbutos Rubbers. They are somewhere about 67 at present, but from a straight tip I overheard in the smoke-room, they are bound is rise."

That is the letter. What follows are extracts from Tollerton's diary.

"Kingsett came in this morning with a large tortoise they had found in the kitchen-garden. I suppose it is one of the half-dozen Sir James let loose a few years ago. The gardeners are always turning them out, like the ploughshares did the skulls in that rotten poem we used to learn at school about the battle of Blenheim. This one I haven't seen before. He's much bigger than the others, a magnificent specimen of Chelonia what's-its-name.

"They brought it into the conservatory and gave it some milk, but the beast was not thirsty. It crawled to the back of the hot-water pipes, and there it will remain until the children come back from their aunt's. They are rather jolly little specimens, and like me are fond of animals.

***

"The warmth must have aroused the tortoise from its lethargy, for this morning I found it waddling across the floor of the hall. I took it with me into my pantry; it can sleep very well with the cockroaches in the bottom cupboard. I rather think tortoises are vegetable feeders, but I must look the matter up.

***

"There is something fascinating in a tortoise. This one reminds one of a cat in a kennel. Its neck muscles are wonderfully active, especially the ones that withdraw the head. There is something quite feline in the eyes—wise eyes, unlike a dog's in never for a moment betraying the purpose of the brain behind them.

***

"The temperature of the pantry is exactly suited to the tortoise. He keeps awake and entertains me vastly, but has apparently no wish to try the draughty passages again. A cat in a kennel is a bad simile; he is more like a god in a shrine. The shrine is old, roofed with a great ivory dome. Only occasionally do the faithful see the dweller in the shrine, and then nothing but two eyes, all-seeing and all-knowing. The tortoise should have been worshipped by the Egyptians.

***

"I still hear nothing from Tom; he ought to have replied by now. But he is one of those rare men whom one can trust implicitly. I often think of the events of the past two months, not at night, for I let nothing interfere with that excellent habit of sleeping within ten minutes from the time my head has touched the pillow, but in the daytime when my hands are busy over their work.

"I do not regret what I have done, though the two hundred would weigh on my mind if I allowed it to do so. I am thankful to say I bore my late master no ill-will. I never annoyed him; he always treated me civilly. If there had been spite or malice on my side I should never have acted as I did, for death would only have removed him beyond my reach. I have found out by bitter experience that by fostering malice one forfeits that peaceable equanimity which to my mind is the crown of life, besides dwarfing one's nature. As it is, I can look back with content to the years we have spent together, and if in some future existence we should meet again, I, for my part, shall bear no grudge.

"Tortoises do not eat cockroaches. Mine has been shut up in a box for the last half-hour with three of the largest I can find. They are still undevoured.

***

"Some day I shall write an essay upon tortoises, or has the thing been already botched by some one else? I should lead off with that excellent anecdote of Sydney Smith's. A child, if I remember, was found by that true-hearted divine stroking the back of a tortoise. 'My dear,' he said, 'you might as well stroke the dome of St. Paul's in order to propitiate the Dean and Chapter.' Tortoises are not animals to be fondled. They have too much dignity, they are far too aloof to be turned aside from their purpose by any of our passing whims.

***

"The pantry has grown too warm, and the tortoise has taken to perambulating the passages, returning always at night to the cupboard. He seems to have been tacitly adopted as an indoor fixture, and what is more, he has been named. I named him. The subject cropped up at lunchtime. The captain suggested 'Percy' because he was so 'Shelley,' a poor sort of joke with which to honour the illustrious dead, but one which of course found favour with a table full of limerick makers. There followed a host of inappropriate suggestions. I am the last person to deny the right of an animal to a name, but there is invariably one name, and one name only, that is suitable. The guests seemed to think as I did, for all agreed that there was some one of whom the beast was the very image, not the vicar, not Dr. Baddely, not even Mrs. Gilchrist of the Crown. As they talked, I happened to notice an enlargement of an old portrait of Sir James, which had just come back from being framed. It showed him seated in his bath-chair, the hood of which was drawn down. He was wrapped up in his great sealskin cape; his sealskin cap was on his head, with the flaps drawn close over his ears. His long, scraggy neck, covered with shrivelled skin, was bent forward, and his eyes shone dark and penetrating. He had not a vestige of eyebrow to shade their brilliance. The captain laughingly turned to me to end their dispute. The old man's name was on my lips. As it was, I stuttered out 'Jim,' and so Jim he is in the dining-room. He will never be anything else than Sir James in the butler's pantry.

"Tortoises do not drink milk; or, to avoid arguing from the particular to the general, Sir James does not drink milk, or indeed anything at all. If it were not so irreverent I should dearly like to try him with some of our old port.

***

"The children have come back. The house is full of their laughter. Sir James, of course, was a favourite at once. They take him with them everywhere, in spite of his appalling weight. If I would let them they would be only too glad to keep him upstairs in the dolls'-house: as it is, the tortoise is in the nursery half the day, unless he is being induced to beat his own record from the night-nursery door to the end of the passage.

"I still have no news of Tom. I have made up my mind to give notice next month; I well deserve a holiday.

"Oh, I must not forget. Sir James does, as I thought, take port. One of the gentlemen drank too deep last night; I think it must have been the Admiral. Anyhow there was quite a pool of dark liquid on the floor that

exactly suited my purpose. I brought Sir James in. He
lapped it up in a manner that seemed to me uncanny. It
is the first time I ever used that word, which, till now,
has never conveyed any meaning to my mind. I must try
him some day with hot rum and water.

***

"I was almost forgetting the fable of the hare and the
tortoise. That must certainly figure in my essay; for the
steady plod plod of Sir James as he follows one (I have
taught him to do that) would be almost pathetic if one
did not remember that perseverance can never be pathetic,
since perseverance means ultimate success. He reminds
me of those old lines, I forget whose they are, but I think
they must be Elizabethan—

> 'Some think to lose him
> By having him confined;
> And some do suppose him,
> Poor heart, to be blind;
> But if ne'er so close ye wall him,
> Do the best that ye may,
> Blind love, if so ye call him,
> He will find out his way.
>
> 'There is no striving
> To cross his intent;
> There is no contriving
> His plots to prevent;
> But if once the message greet him
> That his True Love doth stay,
> If Death should come and meet him
> Love will find out the way.'

"I have given notice. The captain was exceedingly
kind. Kindness and considerate treatment to servants
seem to belong to the family. He said that he was more
than sorry to lose me, but quite understood my wish to
settle down. He asked me if there was any favour he
could do me. I told him yes, I should like to take 'Jim'

with me. He seemed amused, but raised no objection, but I can imagine the stormy scenes in the nursery.

"Mem. important.—There is a broken rail in the balustrade on the top landing overlooking the hall. The captain has twice asked me to see it, as he is afraid one of the children might slip through. Only the bottom part of the rail is broken, and there should be no fear of any accidents. I cannot think how with a good memory like mine I have forgotten to see to this."

These are the only extracts from Tollerton's diary that have a bearing upon what followed. They are sufficient to show his extraordinary character, his strong imagination, and his stronger self-control.

I, the negligible half-pay captain of his story, little dreamed what sort of a man had served me so well as butler; but strange as his life had been, his death was stranger.

The hall at Baldby Manor is exceedingly lofty, extending the full height of the three-storied house. It is surrounded by three landings; from the uppermost a passage leads to the nursery. The day after the last entry in the diary I was crossing the hall on my way to the study, when I noticed the gap in the banisters. I could hear distinctly the children's voices as they played in the corridor. Doubly annoyed at Tollerton's carelessness (he was usually the promptest and most methodical of servants), I rang the bell. I could see at once that he was vexed at his own forgetfulness. "I made a note of it only last night," he said. Then as we looked upward a curious smile stole across his lips. "Do you see that?" he said, and pointed to the gap above. His sight was keener than mine, but I saw at last the thing that attracted his gaze— the two black eyes of the tortoise, the withered head, the long, protruded neck stretched out from the gap in the rail. "You'll excuse a liberty, sir, I hope, from an old servant, but don't you see the extraordinary resemblance between the tortoise and the old master? He's the very image of Sir James. Look at the portrait behind you." Half instinctively I turned. I must have passed the picture scores of times in the course of a day, I must have seen it in sunlight and lamplight, from every point of view; it was a clever picture, well painted, if the subject was not exactly a pleasing one, but that was all.

Yes, I knew at once what the butler meant. It was the eyes—no, the neck—that caused the resemblance, or was it both? together with the half-open mouth with its absence of teeth.

I had been used to think of the smile as having something akin to benevolence about it; time had seemed to be sweetening a nature once sour. Now I saw my mistake—the expression was wholly cynical. The eyes held me by their discerning power, the lips with their subtle mockery.

Suddenly the silence was broken by a cry of terror, followed by an awful crash.

I turned round in amazement.

The body of Tollerton lay stretched on the floor, strangely limp; in falling he had struck the corner of a heavy oak table.

His head lay in a little pool of blood, which the tortoise—I shudder as I think of it—was lapping greedily.

THE ADVENTURE OF THE GERMAN STUDENT

by *Washington Irving*

On a stormy night, in the tempestuous times of the French revolution, a young German was returning to his lodgings, at a late hour, across the old part of Paris. The lightning gleamed, and the loud claps of thunder rattled through the lofty narrow streets—but I should first tell you something about this young German.

Gottfried Wolfgang was a young man of good family. He had studied for some time at Gottingen, but being of a visionary and enthusiastic character, he had wandered into those wild and speculative doctrines which have so often bewildered German students. His secluded life, his intense application, and the singular nature of his studies, had an effect on both mind and body. His health was impaired; his imagination diseased. He had been indulging in fanciful speculations on spiritual essences, until, like Swedenborg, he had an ideal world of his own around him. He took up a notion, I do not know from what cause, that there was an evil influence hanging over him; an evil genius or spirit seeking to ensnare him and ensure his perdition. Such an idea working on his melancholy temperament, produced the most gloomy effects. He became haggard and desponding. His friends discovered the mental malady preying upon him, and determined that the best cure was a change of scene; he was sent, therefore, to finish his studies amidst the splendors and gayeties of Paris.

Wolfgang arrived at Paris at the breaking out of the revolution. The popular delirium at first caught his enthusiastic mind, and he was captivated by the political and philosophical theories of the day: but the scenes of blood which followed shocked his sensitive nature; disgusted him with society and the world, and made him more than ever a recluse. He shut himself up in a solitary apartment in the *Pays Latin*, the quarter of students. There, in a gloomy street not far from the monastic walls of the Sorbonne, he pursued his favorite speculations. Sometimes he spent hours together in the great libraries of Paris, those catacombs of departed authors, rummaging among their hoards of dusty and obsolete works in quest of food for his unhealthy appetite. He was, in a manner, a literary ghoul, feeding in the charnel-house of decayed literature.

Wolfgang, though solitary and recluse, was of an ardent temperament, but for a time it operated merely upon his imagination. He was too shy and ignorant of the world to make any advances to the fair, but he was a passionate admirer of female beauty, and in his lonely chamber would often lose himself in reveries on forms and faces which he had seen, and his fancy would deck out images of loveliness far surpassing the reality.

While his mind was in this excited and sublimated state, a dream produced an extraordinary effect upon him. It was of a female face of transcendent beauty. So strong was the impression made, that he dreamt of it again and again. It haunted his thoughts by day, his slumbers by night; in fine, he became passionately enamored of this shadow of a dream. This lasted so long that it became one of those fixed ideas which haunt the minds of melancholy men, and are at times mistaken for madness.

Such was Gottfried Wolfgang, and such his situation at the time I mentioned. He was returning home late one stormy night, through some of the old and gloomy streets of the *Marais*, the ancient part of Paris. The loud claps of thunder rattled among the high houses of the narrow streets. He came to the Place de Gréve, the square where public executions are performed. The lightning quivered about the pinnacles of the ancient Hôtel de Ville, and shed flickering gleams over the open space in front. As Wolfgang was crossing the square, he shrank back with horror at finding himself close by the guillotine. It was the height of the reign of terror, when this dreadful instrument of death stood ever ready, and its scaffold was continually running with the blood of the virtuous and the brave. It had that very day been actively employed in the work of carnage, and there it stood in grim array, amidst a silent and sleeping city, waiting for fresh victims.

Wolfgang's heart sickened within him, and he was turning shuddering from the horrible engine, when he beheld a shadowy form, cowering as it were at the foot of the steps which led up to the scaffold. A succession of vivid flashes of lightning revealed it more distinctly. It was a female figure, dressed in black. She was seated on one of the lower steps of the scaffold, leaning forward, her face hid in her lap; and her long dishevelled tresses hanging to the ground, streaming with the rain which fell in torrents. Wolfgang paused. There was something awful in this solitary monument of woe. The female had the appearance of being above the common order. He knew the times to be full of vicissitude, and that many a fair head, which had once been pillowed on down, now wandered houseless. Perhaps this was some poor mourner whom the dreadful axe had rendered desolate, and who sat here heart-broken on the strand of existence, from which all that was dear to her had been launched into eternity.

He approached, and addressed her in the accents of sympathy. She raised her head and gazed wildly at him. What was his astonishment at beholding, by the bright glare of the lightning, the very face which had haunted him in his dreams. It was pale and disconsolate, but ravishingly beautiful.

Trembling with violent and conflicting emotions, Wolfgang again accosted her. He spoke something of her being exposed at such an hour of the night, and to the fury of such a storm, and offered to conduct her to her friends. She pointed to the guillotine with a gesture of dreadful signification.

"I have no friend on earth!" said she.

"But you have a home," said Wolfgang.

"Yes—in the grave!"

The heart of the student melted at the words.

"If a stranger dare make an offer," said he, "without danger of being misunderstood, I would offer my humble dwelling as a shelter; myself as a devoted friend. I am friendless myself in Paris, and a stranger in the land; but if my life could be of service, it is at your disposal, and should be sacrificed before harm or indignity should come to you."

There was an honest earnestness in the young man's manner that had its effect. His foreign accent, too, was in his favor; it showed him not to be a hackneyed inhabitant of Paris. Indeed, there is an eloquence in true enthusiasm that is not to be doubted. The homeless stranger confided herself implicitly to the protection of the student.

He supported her faltering steps across the Pont Neuf, and by the place where the statue of Henry the Fourth had been overthrown by the populace. The storm had abated, and the thunder rumbled at a distance. All Paris was quiet; that great volcano of human passion slumbered for a while, to gather fresh strength for the next day's eruption. The student conducted his charge through the ancient streets of the *Pays Latin*, and by the dusky walls of the Sorbonne, to the great dingy hotel which he inhabited. The old portress who admitted them stared with surprise at the unusual sight of the melancholy Wolfgang with a female companion.

On entering his apartment, the student, for the first time, blushed at the scantiness and indifference of his dwelling. He had but one chamber—an old-fashioned saloon—heavily carved, and fantastically furnished with the remains of former magnificence, for it was one of those hotels in the quarter of the Luxembourg palace which had once belonged to nobility. It was lumbered with books and papers, and all the usual apparatus of a student, and his bed stood in a recess at one end.

When lights were brought, and Wolfgang had a better opportunity of contemplating the stranger, he was more than ever intoxicated by her beauty. Her face was pale, but of a dazzling fairness, set off by a profusion of raven hair that hung clustering about it. Her eyes were large and brilliant, with a singular expression approaching almost to wildness. As far as her black dress permitted her shape to be seen, it was of perfect symmetry. Her whole appearance was highly striking, though she was dressed in the simplest style. The only thing approaching to an ornament which she wore, was a broad black band round her neck, clasped by diamonds.

The perplexity now commenced with the student how to dispose of the helpless being thus thrown upon his protection. He thought of abandoning his chamber to her, and seeking shelter for himself elsewhere. Still he was so fascinated by her charms, there seemed to be such a spell upon his thoughts and senses, that he could not tear himself from her presence. Her manner, too, was singular and unaccountable. She spoke no more of the guillotine. Her grief had abated. The attentions of the student had first won her confidence, and then, apparently, her heart. She was evidently an enthusiast like himself, and enthusiasts soon understand each other.

In the infatuation of the moment, Wolfgang avowed his passion for her. He told her the story of his mysterious dream, and how she had possessed his heart before he had even seen her. She was strangely affected by his recital, and acknowledged to have felt an impulse towards him equally unaccountable. It was the time for wild theory and wild actions. Old prejudices and superstitions were done away; every thing was under the sway of the "Goddess of Reason." Among other rubbish of the old times, the forms and ceremonies of marriage began to be considered superfluous bonds for honorable minds. Social compacts were the vogue. Wolfgang was too much of a theorist not to be tainted by the liberal doctrines of the day.

"Why should we separate?" said he; "our hearts are united; in the eye of reason and honor we are as one. What need is there of sordid forms to bind high souls together?"

The stranger listened with emotion: she had evidently received illumination at the same school.

"You have no home nor family," continued he; "let me be every thing to you, or rather let us be every thing to one another. If form is necessary, form shall be observed—there is my hand. I pledge myself to you for ever."

"For ever?" said the stranger, solemnly.

"For ever!" repeated Wolfgang.

The stranger clasped the hand extended to her: "Then I am yours," murmured she, and sank upon his bosom.

The next morning the student left his bride sleeping, and sallied forth at an early hour to seek more spacious apartments suitable to the change in his situation. When he returned, he found the stranger lying with her head hanging over the bed, and one arm thrown over it. He spoke to her, but received no reply. He advanced to awaken her from her uneasy posture. On taking her hand, it was cold—there was no pulsation—her face was pallid and ghastly.—In a word—she was a corpse.

Horrified and frantic, he alarmed the house. A scene of confusion ensued. The police was summoned. As the officer of police entered the room, he started back on beholding the corpse.

"Great heaven!" cried he, "how did this woman come here?"

"Do you know any thing about her?" said Wolfgang, eagerly.

"Do I?" exclaimed the police officer; "she was guillotined yesterday."

He stepped forward; undid the black collar round the neck of the corpse, and the head rolled on the floor!

The student burst into a frenzy. "The fiend! the fiend

has gained possession of me!" shrieked he: "I am lost for ever."

They tried to soothe him, but in vain. He was possessed with the frightful belief that an evil spirit had reanimated the dead body to ensnare him. He went distracted, and died in a mad-house.

Here the old gentleman with the haunted head finished his narrative.

"And is this really a fact?" said the inquisitive gentleman.

"A fact not to be doubted," replied the other. "I had it from the best authority. The student told it me himself. I saw him in a mad-house at Paris."

COUNT MAGNUS

by M. R. James

By what means the papers out of which I have made a connected story came into my hands is the last point which the reader will learn from these pages. But it is necessary to prefix to my extracts from them a statement of the form in which I possess them.

They consist, then, partly of a series of collections for a book of travels, such a volume as was a common product of the forties and fifties. Horace Marryat's *Journal of a Residence in Jutland and the Danish Isles* is a fair specimen of the class to which I allude. These books usually treated of some unfamiliar district on the Continent. They were illustrated with woodcuts or steel plates. They gave details of hotel accommodation, and of means of communication, such as we now expect to find in any well-regulated guide-book, and they dealt largely in reported conversations with intelligent foreigners, racy innkeepers and garrulous peasants. In a word, they were chatty.

Begun with the idea of furnishing material for such a book, my papers as they progressed assumed the character of a record of one single personal experience, and this record was continued up to the very eve, almost, of its termination.

The writer was a Mr. Wraxall. For my knowledge of him I have to depend entirely on the evidence his writings afford, and from these I deduce that he was a man past middle age, possessed of some private means, and very much alone in the world. He had, it seems, no settled abode in England, but was a denizen of hotels and boarding-houses. It is probable that he entertained the idea of settling down at some future time which never came; and I think it also likely that the Pantechnicon fire in the early seventies must have destroyed a great deal that would have thrown light on his antecedents, for he refers once or twice to property of his that was warehoused at the establishment.

It is further apparent that Mr. Wraxall had published a book, and that it treated of a holiday he had once taken in Brittany. More than this I cannot say about his work, because a diligent search in bibliographical works has convinced me that it must have appeared either anonymously or under a pseudonym.

As to his character, it is not difficult to form some superficial opinion. He must have been an intelligent and cultivated man. It seems that he was near being a Fellow of his college at Oxford—Brasenose, as I judge from the Calendar. His besetting fault was pretty clearly that of over-inquisitiveness, possibly a good fault in a traveller, certainly a fault for which this traveller paid dearly enough in the end.

On what proved to be his last expedition, he was plotting another book. Scandinavia, a region not widely known to Englishmen forty years ago, had struck him as an interesting field. He must have lighted on some old books of Swedish history or memoirs, and the idea had struck him that there was room for a book descriptive of travel in Sweden, interspersed with episodes from the history of some of the great Swedish families. He procured letters of introduction, therefore, to some persons of quality in Sweden, and set out thither in the early summer of 1863.

Of his travels in the North there is no need to speak, nor of his residence of some weeks in Stockholm. I need only mention that some *savant* resident there put him on the track of an important collection of family papers belonging to the proprietors of an ancient manor-house in Vestergothland, and obtained for him permission to examine them.

The manor-house, or *herrgård*, in question is to be

called Råbäck (pronounced something like Roebeck), though that is not its name. It is one of the best buildings of its kind in all the country, and the picture of it in Dahlenberg's *Suecia antiqua et moderna*, engraved in 1694, shows it very much as the tourist may see it today. It was built soon after 1600, and is, roughly speaking, very much like an English house of that period in respect of material—red-brick with stone facings—and style. The man who built it was a scion of the great house of De la Gardie, and his descendants possess it still. De la Gardie is the name by which I will designate them when mention of them becomes necessary.

They received Mr. Wraxall with great kindness and courtesy, and pressed him to stay in the house as long as his researches lasted. But, preferring to be independent, and mistrusting his powers of conversing in Swedish, he settled himself at the village inn, which turned out quite sufficiently comfortable, at any rate during the summer months. This arrangement would entail a short walk daily to and from the manor-house of something under a mile. The house itself stood in a park, and was protected—we should say grown up—with large old timber. Near it you found the walled garden, and then entered a close wood fringing one of the small lakes with which the whole country is pitted. Then came the wall of the demesne, and you climbed a steep knoll—a knob of rock lightly covered with soil—and on the top of this stood the church, fenced in with tall dark trees. It was a curious building to English eyes. The nave and aisles were low, and filled with pews and galleries. In the western gallery stood the handsome old organ, gaily painted, and with silver pipes. The ceiling was flat, and had been adorned by a seventeenth-century artist with a strange and hideous "Last Judgment," full of lurid flames, falling cities, burning ships, crying souls, and brown and smiling demons. Handsome brass coronæ hung from the roof; the pulpit was like a doll's-house, covered with little painted wooden cherubs and saints; a stand with three hour-glasses was hinged to the preacher's desk. Such sights as these may be seen in many a church in Sweden now, but what distinguished this one was an addition to the original building. At the eastern end of the north aisle the builder of the manor-house had erected a mausoleum for himself and his family. It was a largish eight-sided building, lighted by a series of oval windows, and it had a domed roof, topped by a kind of pumpkin-shaped object rising into a spire, a form in which Swedish architects greatly delighted. The roof was of copper externally, and was painted black, while the walls, in common with those of the church, were staringly white. To this mausoleum there was no access from the church. It had a portal and steps of its own on the northern side.

Past the churchyard the path to the village goes, and not more than three or four minutes bring you to the inn door.

On the first day of his stay at Råbäck Mr. Wraxall found the church door open, and made those notes of the interior which I have epitomized. Into the mausoleum, however, he could not make his way. He could by looking through the keyhole just descry that there were fine marble effigies and sarcophagi of copper, and a wealth of armorial ornament, which made him very anxious to spend some time in investigation.

The papers he had come to examine at the manor-house proved to be of just the kind he wanted for his book. There were family correspondence, journals, and account-books of the earliest owners of the estate, very carefully kept and clearly written, full of amusing and picturesque detail. The first De la Gardie appeared in them as a strong and capable man. Shortly after the building of the mansion there had been a period of distress in the district, and the peasants had risen and attacked several châteaux and done some damage. The owner of Råbäck took a leading part in suppressing the trouble, and there was reference to executions of ringleaders and severe punishments inflicted with no sparing hand.

The portrait of this Magnus de la Gardie was one of the best in the house, and Mr. Wraxall studied it with no little interest after his day's work. He gives no detailed

description of it, but I gather that the face impressed him
rather by its power than by its beauty or goodness; in
fact, he writes that Count Magnus was an almost phe-
nomenally ugly man.

On this day Mr. Wraxall took his supper with the family, and walked back in the late but still bright evening.

"I must remember," he writes, "to ask the sexton if
he can let me into the mausoleum at the church. He
evidently has access to it himself, for I saw him to-night
standing on the steps, and, as I thought, locking or
unlocking the door."

I find that early on the following day Mr. Wraxall had
some conversation with his landlord. His setting it down
at such length as he does surprised me at first; but I soon
realized that the papers I was reading were, at least in
their beginning, the materials for the book he was medi-
tating, and that it was to have been one of those quasi-
journalistic productions which admit of the introduction
of an admixture of conversational matter.

His object, he says, was to find out whether any traditions of Count Magnus de la Gardie lingered on in the
scenes of that gentleman's activity, and whether the popular estimate of him were favourable or not. He found
that the Count was decidedly not a favourite. If his ten-
ants came late to their work on the days which they owed
to him as Lord of the Manor, they were set on the
wooden horse, or flogged and branded in the manor-
house yard. One or two cases there were of men who
had occupied lands which encroached on the lord's
domain, and whose houses had been mysteriously burnt
on a winter's night, with the whole family inside. But
what seemed to dwell on the innkeeper's mind most—
for he returned to the subject more than once—was that
the Count had been on the Black Pilgrimage, and had
brought something or someone back with him.

You will naturally inquire, as Mr. Wraxall did, what
the Black Pilgrimage may have been. But your curiosity
on the point must remain unsatisfied for the time being,
just as his did. The landlord was evidently unwilling to
give a full answer, or indeed any answer, on the point,

and, being called out for a moment, trotted off with obvious alacrity, only putting his head in at the door a few
minutes afterwards to say that he was called away to
Skara, and should not be back till evening.

So Mr. Wraxall had to go unsatisfied to his day's work
at the manor-house. The papers on which he was just
then engaged soon put his thoughts into another channel,
for he had to occupy himself with glancing over the correspondence between Sophia Albertina in Stockholm and
her married cousin Ulrica Leonora at Råbäck in the years
1705–1710. The letters were of exceptional interest from
the light they threw upon the culture of that period in
Sweden, as anyone can testify who has read the full edition of them in the publications of the Swedish Historical
Manuscripts Commission.

In the afternoon he had done with these, and after
returning the boxes in which they were kept to their
places on the shelf, he proceeded, very naturally, to take
down some of the volumes nearest to them, in order to
determine which of them had best be his principal subject
of investigation next day. The shelf he had hit upon was
occupied mostly by a collection of account-books in the
writing of the first Count Magnus. But one among them
was not an account-book, but a book of alchemical and
other tracts in another sixteenth-century hand. Not being
very familiar with alchemical literature, Mr. Wraxall
spends much space which he might have spared in setting
out the names and beginnings of the various treatises:
The book of the Phœnix, book of the Thirty Words, book
of the Toad, book of Miriam, Turba philosophorum, and
so forth; and then he announces with a good deal of
circumstance his delight at finding, on a leaf originally
left blank near the middle of the book, some writing of
Count Magnus himself headed "Liber nigræ peregrina-
tionis." It is true that only a few lines were written, but
there was quite enough to show that the landlord had
that morning been referring to a belief at least as old as
the time of Count Magnus, and probably shared by him.
This is the English of what was written:

"If any man desires to obtain a long life, if he would

obtain a faithful messenger and see the blood of his enemies, it is necessary that he should first go into the city
of Chorazin, and there salute the prince. . . ." Here
there was an erasure of one word, not very thoroughly
done, so that Mr. Wraxall felt pretty sure that he was
right in reading it as *aëris* ("of the air"). But there was
no more of the text copied, only a line in Latin: "Quære
reliqua hujus materiei inter secretiora" (See the rest of
this matter among the more private things).

It could not be denied that this threw a rather lurid
light upon the tastes and beliefs of the Count; but to Mr.
Wraxall, separated from him by nearly three centuries,
the thought that he might have added to his general
forcefulness alchemy, and to alchemy something like
magic, only made him a more picturesque figure; and
when, after a rather prolonged contemplation of his picture in the hall, Mr. Wraxall set out on his homeward
way, his mind was full of the thought of Count Magnus.
He had no eyes for his surroundings, no perception of
the evening scents of the woods or the evening light on
the lake; and when all of a sudden he pulled up short,
he was astonished to find himself already at the gate of
the churchyard, and within a few minutes of his dinner.
His eyes fell on the mausoleum.

"Ah," he said, "Count Magnus, there you are. I
should dearly like to see you."

"Like many solitary men," he writes, "I have a habit
of talking to myself aloud; and, unlike some of the Greek
and Latin particles, I do not expect an answer. Certainly,
and perhaps fortunately in this case, there was neither
voice nor any that regarded: only the woman who, I suppose, was cleaning up the church, dropped some metallic
object on the floor, whose clang startled me. Count Magnus, I think, sleeps sound enough."

That same evening the landlord of the inn, who had
heard Mr. Wraxall say that he wished to see the clerk or
deacon (as he would be called in Sweden) of the parish,
introduced him to that official in the inn parlour. A visit
to the De la Gardie tomb-house was soon arranged for
the next day, and a little general conversation ensued.

Mr. Wraxall, remembering that one function of Scandinavian deacons is to teach candidates for Confirmation, thought he would refresh his own memory on a Biblical point.

"Can you tell me," he said, "anything about Chorazin?"

The deacon seemed startled, but readily reminded him how that village had once been denounced.

"To be sure," said Mr. Wraxall; "it is, I suppose, quite a ruin now?"

"So I expect," replied the deacon. "I have heard some of our old priests say that Antichrist is to be born there; and there are tales——"

"Ah! what tales are those?" Mr. Wraxall put in.

"Tales, I was going to say, which I have forgotten," said the deacon; and soon after that he said good night.

The landlord was now alone, and at Mr. Wraxall's mercy; and that inquirer was not inclined to spare him.

"Herr Nielsen," he said, "I have found out something about the Black Pilgrimage. You may as well tell me what you know. What did the Count bring back with him?"

Swedes are habitually slow, perhaps, in answering, or perhaps the landlord was an exception. I am not sure; but Mr. Wraxall notes that the landlord spent at least one minute in looking at him before he said anything at all. Then he came close up to his guest, and with a good deal of effort he spoke:

"Mr. Wraxall, I can tell you this one little tale, and no more—not any more. You must not ask anything when I have done. In my grandfather's time—that is, ninety-two years ago—there were two men who said: 'The Count is dead; we do not care for him. We will go to-night and have a free hunt in his wood'—the long wood on the hill that you have seen behind Råbäck. Well, those that heard them say this, they said: 'No, do not go; we are sure you will meet with persons walking who should not be walking. They should be resting, not walking.' These men laughed. There were no forest-men to keep the wood, because no one wished to hunt there. The family

were not here at the house. These men could do what
they wished.

"Very well, they go to the wood that night. My grandfather was sitting here in this room. It was the summer,
and a light night. With the window open, he could see
out to the wood, and hear.

"So he sat there, and two or three men with him, and
they listened. At first they hear nothing at all; then they
hear someone—you know how far away it is—they hear
someone scream, just as if the most inside part of his
soul was twisted out of him. All of them in the room
caught hold of each other, and they sat so for three-
quarters of an hour. Then they hear someone else, only
about three hundred ells off. They hear him laugh out
loud: it was not one of those two men that laughed, and,
indeed, they have all of them said that it was not any
man at all. After that they hear a great door shut.

"Then, when it was just light with the sun, they all
went to the priest. They said to him:

" 'Father, put on your gown and your ruff, and come
to bury these men, Anders Bjornsen and Hans Thorbjorn.'

"You understand that they were sure these men were
dead. So they went to the wood—my grandfather never
forgot this. He said they were all like so many dead men
themselves. The priest, too, he was in a white fear. He
said when they came to him:

" 'I heard one cry in the night, and I heard one laugh
afterwards. If I cannot forget that, I shall not be able to
sleep again.'

"So they went to the wood, and they found these men
on the edge of the wood. Hans Thorbjorn was standing
with his back against a tree, and all the time he was
pushing with his hands—pushing something away from
him which was not there. So he was not dead. And they
led him away, and took him to the house at Nykjoping,
and he died before the winter; but he went on pushing
with his hands. Also Anders Bjornsen was there; but he
was dead. And I tell you this about Anders Bjornsen,
that he was once a beautiful man, but now his face was

not there, because the flesh of it was sucked away off
the bones. You understand that? My grandfather did not
forget that. And they laid him on the bier which they
brought, and they put a cloth over his head, and the
priest walked before; and they began to sing the psalm
for the dead as well as they could. So, as they were
singing the end of the first verse, one fell down, who was
carrying the head of the bier, and the others looked back,
and they saw that the cloth had fallen off, and the eyes
of Anders Bjornsen were looking up, because there was
nothing to close over them. And this they could not bear.
Therefore the priest laid the cloth upon him, and sent
for a spade, and they buried him in that place.''

The next day Mr. Wraxall records that the deacon
called for him soon after his breakfast, and took him to
the church and mausoleum. He noticed that the key of
the latter was hung on a nail just by the pulpit, and it
occurred to him that, as the church door seemed to be
left unlocked as a rule, it would not be difficult for him
to pay a second and more private visit to the monuments
if there proved to be more of interest among them than
could be digested at first. The building, when he entered
it, he found not unimposing. The monuments, mostly
large erections of the seventeenth and eighteenth centuries, were dignified if luxuriant, and the epitaphs and
heraldry were copious. The central space of the domed
room was occupied by three copper sarcophagi, covered
with finely-engraved ornament. Two of them had, as is
commonly the case in Denmark and Sweden, a large
metal crucifix on the lid. The third, that of Count Magnus, as it appeared, had, instead of that, a full-length
effigy engraved upon it, and round the edge were several
bands of similar ornament representing various scenes.
One was a battle, with cannon belching out smoke, and
walled towns, and troops of pikemen. Another showed
an execution. In a third, among trees, was a man running
at full speed, with flying hair and outstretched hands.
After him followed a strange form; it would be hard to
say whether the artist intended it for a man, and was
unable to give the requisite similitude, or whether it was

intentionally made as monstrous as it looked. In view of the skill with which the rest of the drawing was done, Mr. Wraxall felt inclined to adopt the latter idea. The figure was unduly short, and was for the most part muffled in a hooded garment which swept the ground. The only part of the form which projected from that shelter was not shaped like any hand or arm. Mr. Wraxall compares it to the tentacle of a devil-fish, and continues: "On seeing this, I said to myself, 'This, then, which is evidently an allegorical representation of some kind—a fiend pursuing a hunted soul—may be the origin of the story of Count Magnus and his mysterious companion. Let us see how the huntsman is pictured: doubtless it will be a demon blowing his horn.' " But, as it turned out, there was no such sensational figure, only the semblance of a cloaked man on a hillock, who stood leaning on a stick, and watching the hunt with an interest which the engraver had tried to express in his attitude.

Mr. Wraxall noted the finely-worked and massive steel padlocks—three in number—which secured the sarcophagus. One of them, he saw, was detached, and lay on the pavement. And then, unwilling to delay the deacon longer or to waste his own working-time, he made his way onward to the manor-house.

"It is curious," he notes, "how on retracing a familiar path one's thoughts engross one to the absolute exclusion of surrounding objects. To-night, for the second time, I had entirely failed to notice where I was going (I had planned a private visit to the tomb-house to copy the epitaphs), when I suddenly, as it were, awoke to consciousness, and found myself (as before) turning in at the churchyard gate, and, I believe, singing or chanting some such words as 'Are you awake, Count Magnus? Are you asleep, Count Magnus?' and then something more which I have failed to recollect. It seemed to me that I must have been behaving in this nonsensical way for some time."

He found the key of the mausoleum where he had expected to find it, and copied the greater part of what he wanted; in fact, he stayed until the light began to fail him.

"I must have been wrong," he writes, "in saying that one of the padlocks of my Count's sarcophagus was unfastened; I see to-night that two are loose. I picked both up, and laid them carefully on the window-ledge, after trying unsuccessfully to close them. The remaining one is still firm, and, though I take it to be a spring lock, I cannot guess how it is opened. Had I succeeded in undoing it, I am almost afraid I should have taken the liberty of opening the sarcophagus. It is strange, the interest I feel in the personality of this, I fear, somewhat ferocious and grim old noble."

The day following was, as it turned out, the last of Mr. Wraxall's stay at Råbäck. He received letters connected with certain investments which made it desirable that he should return to England; his work among the papers was practically done, and travelling was slow. He decided, therefore, to make his farewells, put some finishing touches to his notes, and be off.

These finishing touches and farewells, as it turned out, took more time than he had expected. The hospitable family insisted on his staying to dine with them—they dined at three—and it was verging on half-past six before he was outside the iron gates of Råbäck. He dwelt on every step of his walk by the lake, determined to saturate himself, now that he trod it for the last time, in the sentiment of the place and hour. And when he reached the summit of the churchyard knoll, he lingered for many minutes, gazing at the limitless prospect of woods near and distant, all dark beneath a sky of liquid green. When at last he turned to go, the thought struck him that surely he must bid farewell to Count Magnus as well as the rest of the De la Gardies. The church was but twenty yards away, and he knew where the key of the mausoleum hung. It was not long before he was standing over the great copper coffin, and, as usual, talking to himself aloud. "You may have been a bit of a rascal in your time, Magnus," he was saying, "but for all that I should like to see you, or, rather——"

"Just at that instant," he says, "I felt a blow on my foot. Hastily enough I drew it back, and something fell on the pavement with a clash. It was the third, the last of the three padlocks which had fastened the sarcophagus. I stooped to pick it up, and—Heaven is my witness that I am writing only the bare truth—before I had raised myself there was a sound of metal hinges creaking, and I distinctly saw the lid shifting upwards. I may have behaved like a coward, but I could not for my life stay for one moment. I was outside that dreadful building in less time than I can write—almost as quickly as I could have said—the words; and what frightens me yet more, I could not turn the key in the lock. As I sit here in my room noting these facts, I ask myself (it was not twenty minutes ago) whether that noise of creaking metal continued, and I cannot tell whether it did or not. I only know that there was something more than I have written that alarmed me, but whether it was sound or sight I am not able to remember. What is this that I have done?"

Poor Mr. Wraxall! He set out on his journey to England on the next day, as he had planned, and he reached England in safety; and yet, as I gather from his changed hand and inconsequent jottings, a broken man. One of several small notebooks that have come to me with his papers gives, not a key to, but a kind of inkling of, his experiences. Much of his journey was made by canal-boat, and I find not less than six painful attempts to enumerate and describe his fellow-passengers. The entries are of this kind:

"24. Pastor of village of Skane. Usual black coat and soft black hat.
"25. Commerical traveller from Stockholm going to Trollhättan. Black cloak, brown hat.
"26. Man in long black cloak, broad-leafed hat, very old-fashioned."

This entry is lined out, and a note added: "Perhaps identical with No. 13. Have not yet seen his face." On referring to No. 13, I find that he is a Roman priest in a cassock.

The net result of the reckoning is always the same. Twenty-eight people appear in the enumeration, one being always a man in a long black cloak and broad hat, and the other a "short figure in dark cloak and hood." On the other hand, it is always noted that only twenty-six passengers appear at meals, and that the man in the cloak is perhaps absent, and the short figure is certainly absent.

On reaching England, it appears that Mr. Wraxall landed at Harwich, and that he resolved at once to put himself out of the reach of some person or persons whom he never specifies, but whom he had evidently come to regard as his pursuers. Accordingly he took a vehicle—it was a closed fly—not trusting the railway, and drove across country to the village of Belchamp St. Paul. It was about nine o'clock on a moonlight August night when he neared the place. He was sitting forward, and looking out of the window at the fields and thickets—there was little else to be seen—racing past him. Suddenly he came to a cross-road. At the corner two figures were standing motionless; both were in dark cloaks; the taller one wore a hat, the shorter a hood. He had no time to see their faces, nor did they make any motion that he could discern. Yet the horse shied violently and broke into a gallop, and Mr. Wraxall sank back into his seat in something like desperation. He had seen them before.

Arrived at Belchamp St. Paul, he was fortunate enough to find a decent furnished lodging, and for the next twenty-four hours he lived, comparatively speaking, in peace. His last notes were written on this day. They are too disjointed and ejaculatory to be given here in full, but the substance of them is clear enough. He is expecting a visit from his pursuers—how or when he knows not—and his constant cry is "What has he done?" and "Is there no hope?" Doctors, he knows, would call him mad, policemen would laugh at him. The parson is away. What can he do but lock his door and cry to God?

*   *   *

People still remembered last year at Belchamp St. Paul
how a strange gentleman came one evening in August
years back; and how the next morning but one he was
found dead, and there was an inquest; and the jury that
viewed the body fainted, seven of 'em did, and none of
'em wouldn't speak to what they see, and the verdict was
visitation of God; and how the people as kep' the 'ouse
moved out that same week, and went away from that
part. But they do not, I think, know that any glimmer
of light has ever been thrown, or could be thrown, on
the mystery. It so happened that last year the little house
came into my hands as part of a legacy. It had stood
empty since 1863, and there seemed no prospect of letting it; so I had it pulled down, and the papers of which
I have given you an abstract were found in a forgotten
cupboard under the window in the best bedroom.

A THOUSAND DEATHS

by Jack London

I had been in the water about an hour, and cold, exhausted, with a terrible cramp in my right calf, it seemed as though my hour had come. Fruitlessly struggling against the strong ebb tide, I had beheld the maddening procession of the waterfront lights slip by; but now I gave up attempting to breast the stream and contended myself with the bitter thoughts of a wasted career, now drawing to a close.

It had been my luck to come of good, English stock, but of parents whose account with the bankers far exceeded their knowledge of child-nature and the rearing of children. While born with a silver spoon in my mouth, the blessed atmosphere of the home circle was to me unknown. My father, a very learned man and a celebrated antiquarian, gave no thought to his family, being constantly lost in the abstractions of his study; while my mother, noted far more for her good looks than her good sense, sated herself with the adulation of the society in which she was perpetually plunged. I went through the regular school and college routine of a boy of the English bourgeoisie, and as the years brought me increasing strength and passions, my parents, suddenly became aware that I was possessed of an immortal soul, and endeavored to draw the curb. But it was too late; I perpetrated the wildest and most audacious folly, and was disowned by my people; ostracized by the society I had so long outraged, and with the thousand pounds my father gave me, with the declaration that he would neither see me again nor give me more, I took a first-class passage to Australia.

Since then my life had been one long peregrination—from the Orient to the Occident, from the Arctic to the Antarctic—to find myself at last, able seaman at thirty, in the full vigor of my manhood, drowning in San Francisco Bay because of a disastrously successful attempt to desert my ship.

My right leg was drawn up by the cramp, and I was suffering the keenest agony. A slight breeze stirred up a choppy sea, which washed into my mouth and down my throat, nor could I prevent it. Though I still contrived to keep afloat, it was merely mechanical, for I was rapidly becoming unconscious. I have a dim recollection of drifting past the seawall, and of catching a glimpse of an upriver steamer's starboard light; then everything became a blank.

I heard the low hum of insect life, and felt the balmy air of a spring morning fanning my cheek. Gradually it assumed a rhythmic flow, to whose soft pulsations my body seemed to respond. I floated on the gentle bosom of a summer's sea, rising and falling with dreamy pleasure on each crooning wave. But the pulsations grew stronger; the humming, louder; the waves, larger, fiercer—I was dashed about on a stormy sea. A great agony fastened upon me. Brilliant, intermittent sparks of light flashed athwart my inner consciousness; in my ears there was the sound of many waters; then a sudden snapping of an intangible something, and I awoke.

The scene, of which I was protagonist, was a curious one. A glance sufficed to inform me that I lay on the cabin floor of some gentleman's yacht, in a most uncomfortable posture. On either side, grasping my arms and working them up and down like pump handles, were two peculiarly clad, dark-skinned creatures. Though conversant with most aboriginal types, I could not conjecture their nationality. Some attachment had been fastened about my head, which connected my respiratory organs with the machine I shall next describe. My nostrils, however, had been closed, forcing me to breathe through the mouth. Foreshortened by the obliquity of my line of vision, I beheld two tubes, similar to small hosing but of different composition, which emerged from my mouth and went off at an acute angle from each other. The first came to an abrupt termination and lay on the floor beside me; the second traversed the floor in numerous coils, connecting with the apparatus I have promised to describe.

In the days before my life became tangential, I had dabbled not a little in science, and conversant with the appurtenances and general paraphernalia of the laboratory, I appreciated the machine I now beheld. It was composed chiefly of glass, the construction being of that crude sort which is employed for experimentative purposes. A vessel of water was surrounded by an air chamber, to which was fixed a vertical tube, surmounted by a globe. In the center of this was a vacuum gauge. The water of the tube moved upwards and downwards, creating alternate inhalations and exhalations, which were in turn communicated to me through the hose. With this, and the aid of the men who pumped my arms so vigorously, had the process of breathing been artificially carried on, my chest rising and falling and my lungs expanding and contracting, till nature could be persuaded to again take up her wonted labor.

As I opened my eyes the appliance about my head, nostrils and mouth was removed. Draining a stiff three fingers of brandy, I staggered to my feet to thank my preserver, and confronted—my father. But long years of fellowship with danger had taught me self-control, and I waited to see if he would recognize me. Not so; he saw in me no more than a runaway sailor and treated me accordingly.

Leaving me to the care of the blackies, he fell to revising the notes he had made on my resuscitation. As I ate of the handsome fare served up to me, confusion began on deck, and from the chanteys of the sailors and the

rattling of blocks and tackles I surmised that we were
getting under way. What a lark! Off on a cruise with my
recluse father into the wide Pacific! Little did I realize,
as I laughed to myself, which side the joke was to be on.
Aye, had I known, I would have plunged overboard and
welcomed the dirty fo'c'sle from which I had just
escaped.

I was not allowed on deck till we had sunk the Faral-
lones and the last pilot boat. I appreciated this fore-
thought on the part of my father and made it a point to
thank him heartily, in my bluff seaman's manner. I could
not suspect that he had his own ends in view, in thus
keeping my presence secret to all save the crew. He told
me briefly of my rescue by his sailors, assuring me that
the obligation was on his side, as my appearance had
been most opportune. He had constructed the appartus
for the vindication of a theory concerning certain biologi-
cal phenomena, and had been waiting for an opportunity
to use it.

"You have proved it beyond all doubt," he said; then
added with a sigh, "But only in the small matter of
drowning."

But, to take a reef in my yarn—he offered me an
advance of two pounds on my previous wages to sail with
him, and this I considered handsome, for he really did
not need me. Contrary to my expectations, I did not join
the sailor' mess, for'ard, being assigned to a comfortable
stateroom and eating at the captain's table. He had perceived that I was no common sailor, and I resolved to
take this chance for reinstating myself in his good graces.
I wove a fictitious past to account for my education and
present position, and did my best to come in touch with
him. I was not long in disclosing a predilection for scientific pursuits, nor he in appreciating my aptitude. I
became his assistant, with a corresponding increase in
wages, and before long, as he grew confidential and
expounded his theories, I was as enthusiastic as himself.

The days flew quickly by, for I was deeply interested
in my new studies, passing my waking hours in his well-
stocked library, or listening to his plans and aiding him

in his laboratory work. But we were forced to forgo many enticing experiments, a rolling ship not being exactly the proper place for delicate or intricate work. He promised me, however, many delightful hours in the magnificent laboratory for which we were bound. He had taken possession of an uncharted South Sea island, as he said, and turned it into a scientific paradise.

We had not been on the island long, before I discovered the horrible mare's nest I had fallen into. But before I describe the strange things which came to pass, I must briefly outline the causes which culminated in as startling an experience as ever fell to the lot of man.

Late in life, my father had abandoned the musty charms of antiquity and succumbed to the more fascinating ones embraced under the general head of biology. Having been thoroughly grounded during his youth in the fundamentals, he rapidly explored all the higher branches as far as the scientific world had gone, and found himself on the no-man's land of the unknowable. It was his intention to preempt some of this unclaimed territory, and it was at this stage of his investigations that we had been thrown together. Having a good brain, though I say it myself, I had mastered his speculations and methods of reasoning, becoming almost as mad as himself. But I should not say this. The marvelous results we afterwards obtained can only go to prove this sanity. I can but say that he was the most abnormal specimen of cold-blooded cruelty I have ever seen.

After having penetrated the dual mysteries of pathology and psychology, his thought had led him to the verge of a great field, for which, the better to explore, he began studies in higher organic chemistry, pathology, toxicology and other sciences and subsciences rendered kindred as accessories to his speculative hypotheses. Starting from the proposition that the direct cause of the temporary and permanent array of vitality was due to the coagulation of certain elements and compounds in the protoplasm, he had isolated and subjected these various substances to innumerable experiments. Since the temporary arrest of vitality in an organism brought coma, and a permanent arrest death, he held that by artificial means this coagulation of the protoplasm could be retarded, prevented, and even overcome in the extreme states of solidification. Or, to do away with the technical nomenclature, he argued that death, when not violent and in which none of the organs had suffered injury, was merely suspended vitality; and that, in such instances, life could be induced to resume its functions by the use of proper methods. This, then, was his idea: To discover the method—and by practical experimentation prove the possibility—of renewing vitality in a structure from which life had seemingly fled. Of course, he recognized the futility of such endeavor after decomposition had set in; he must have organisms which but the moment, the hour, or the day before, had been quick with life. With me, in a crude way, he had proved this theory. I was really drowned, really dead, when picked from the water of San Francisco Bay—but the vital spark had been renewed by means of his aerotherapeutical apparatus, as he called it.

Now to his dark purpose concerning me. He first showed me how completely I was in his power. He had sent the yacht away for a year, retaining only his two blackies, who were utterly devoted to him. He then made an exhaustive review of his theory and outlined the method of proof he had adopted, concluding with the startling announcement that I was to be his subject.

I had faced death and weighed my chances in many a desperate venture, but never in one of this nature. I can swear I am no coward, yet this proposition of journeying back and forth across the borderland of death put the yellow fear in me. I asked for time, which he granted at the same time assuring me that but the one course was open—I must submit. Escape from the island was out of the question; escape by suicide was not to be entertained, though really preferable to what it seemed I must undergo; my only hope was to destroy my captors. But this latter was frustrated through the precautions taken by my father. I was subjected to a constant surveillance, even in my sleep being guarded by one or the other of the blacks.

Having pleaded in vain, I announced and proved that I was his son. It was my last card, and I had placed all my hopes upon it. But he was inexorable; he was not a father but a scientific machine. I wonder yet how it ever came to pass that he married my mother or begat me, for there was not the slightest grain of emotion in his makeup. Reason was all in all to him, nor could he understand such things as love or sympathy in others, except as petty weaknesses which should be overcome. So he informed me that in the beginning he had given me life, and who had better right to take it away than he? Such, he said, was not his desire, however; he merely wished to borrow it occasionally, promising to return it punctually at that appointed time. Of course, there was a liability of mishaps, but I could do no more than take the chances, since the affairs of men were full of such.

The better to insure success, he wished me to be in the best possible condition, so I was dieted and trained like a great athlete before a decisive contest. What could I do? If I had to undergo the peril, it were best to be in good shape. In my intervals of relaxation he allowed me to assist in the arranging of the apparatus and in the various subsidary experiments. The interest I took in all such operations can be imagined. I mastered the work as thoroughly as he, and often had the pleasure of seeing some of my suggestions of alterations put into effect. After such events I would smile grimly, conscious of officiating at my own funeral.

He began by inaugurating a series of experiments in toxicology. When all was ready, I was killed by a stiff dose of strychnine and allowed to lie dead for some twenty hours. During that period my body was dead, absolutely dead. All respiration and circulation ceased; but the frightful part of it was, that while the protoplasmic coagulation proceeded, I retained consciousness and was enabled to study it in all its ghastly details.

The apparatus to bring me back to life was an airtight chamber, fitted to receive my body. The mechanism was simple—a few valves, a rotary shaft and crank, and an electric motor. When in operation, the interior atmosphere was alternately condensed and rarified, thus communicating to my lungs an artificial respiration without the agency of the hosing previously used. Though my body was inert, and, for all I knew, in the first stages of decomposition, I was cognisant of everything that transpired. I knew when they placed me in the chamber, and though all my senses were quiescent. I was aware of hypodermic injections of a compound to react upon the coagulatory process. Then the chamber was closed and the machinery started. My anxiety was terrible; but the circulation became gradually restored, the different organs began to carry on their respective functions, and in an hour's time I was eating a hearty dinner.

It cannot be said that I participated in this series, nor in the subsequent ones, with much verve; but after two ineffectual attempts at escape, I began to take quite an interest. Besides, I was becoming accustomed. My father was beside himself in success, and as the months rolled by his speculations took wilder and yet wilder flights. We ranged through the three great classes of poisons, the neurotics, the gaseous and the irritants, but carefully avoided some of the mineral irritants and passed up the whole group of corrosives. During the poison regime I became quite accustomed to dying, and had but one mishap to shake my growing confidence. Scarifying a number of lesser blood vessels in my arm, he introduced a minute quantity of that most frightful of poisons, the arrow poison, or curare. I lost consciousness at the start, quickly followed by the cessation of respiration and circulation, and so far had the solidification of the protoplasm advanced, that he gave up all hope. But at the last moment he applied a discovery he had been working upon, receiving such encouragement as to redouble his efforts.

In a glass vacuum, similar but not exactly like a

Crookes' tube was placed a magnetic field. When penetrated by polarized light, it gave no phenomena of phosphorescence nor of rectilinear projection of atoms, but emitted nonluminous rays, similar to the X ray. While the X ray could reveal opaque objects hidden in dense mediums, this was possessed of far subtler penetration. By this he photographed my body, and found on the negative an infinite number of blurred shadows, due to the chemical and electric motions still going on. This was infallible proof that the rigor mortis in which I lay was not genuine; that is, those mysterious forces, those delicate bonds which held my soul to my body, were still in action. The resultants of all other poisons were unapparent, save those of mercurial compounds, which usually left me languid for several days.

Another series of delightful experiments was with electricity. We verified Tesla's assertion that high currents were utterly harmless by passing 100,000 volts through my body. As this did not affect me, the current was reduced to 2,500, and I was quickly electrocuted. This time he ventured so far as to allow me to remain dead, or in a state of suspended vitality, for three days. It took four hours to bring me back.

Once, he superinduced lockjaw; but the agony of dying was so great that I positively refused to undergo similar experiments. The easiest deaths were by asphyxiation, such as drowning, strangling, and suffocation by gas; while those by morphine, opium, cocaine and chloroform, were not at all hard.

Another time, after being suffocated, he kept me in cold storage for three months, not permitting me to freeze or decay. This was without my knowledge, and I was in a great fright on discovering the lapse of time. I became afraid of what he might do with me when I lay dead, my alarm being increased by the predilection he was beginning to betray towards vivisection. The last time I was resurrected, I discovered that he had been tampering with my breast. Though he had carefully dressed and sewed the incisions up, they were so severe that I had to take to my bed for some time. It was during my convalescence that I evolved the plan by which I ultimately escaped.

While feigning unbounded enthusiasm in the work, I asked and received a vacation from my moribund occupation. During this period I devoted myself to laboratory work, while he was too deep in the vivisection of the many animals captured by the blacks to take notice of my work.

It was on these two propositions that I constructed my theory: First, electrolysis, or the decomposition of water into its constituent gases by means of electricity; and, second, by the hypothetical existence of a force, the converse of gravitation, which Astor has named "apergy." Terrestrial attention, for instance, merely draws objects together but does not combine them; hence apergy is merely repulsion. Now, atomic or molecular attraction not only draws objects together but intergrates them; and it was the converse of this, or a disintegrative force, which I wished to not only discover and produce, but to direct at will. Thus, the molecules of hydrogen and oxygen reacting on each other, separate and create new molecules, containing both elements and forming water. Electrolysis causes these molecules to split up and resume their original condition, producing the two gases separately. The force I wished to find must not only do this with two, but with all elements, no matter in what compounds they exist. If I could then entice my father within its radius, he would be instantly disintegrated and sent flying to the four quarters, a mass of isolated elements.

It must not be understood that this force, which I finally came to control, annihilated matter; it merely annihilated form. Nor, as I soon discovered, had it any effect on inorganic structure; but to all organic form it was absolutely fatal. This partiality puzzled me at first, though had I stopped to think deeper I would have seen through it. Since the number of atoms in organic molecules is far greater than in the most complex mineral molecules, organic compounds are characterized by their instability and the ease with which they are split up by physical forces and chemical reagents.

By two powerful batteries, connected with magnets constructed specially for this purpose, two tremendous forces were projected. Considered apart from each other, they were perfectly harmless; but they accomplished their purpose by focusing at an invisible point in midair. After practically demonstrating its success, besides narrowly escaping being blown into nothingness, I laid my trap. Concealing the magnets, so that their force made the whole space of my chamber doorway a field of death, and placing by my couch a button by which I could throw on the current from the storage batteries, I climbed into bed.

The blackies still guarded my sleeping quarters, one relieving the other at midnight. I turned on the current as soon as the first man arrived. Hardly had I begun to doze, when I was aroused by a sharp, metallic tinkle. There, on the mid-threshold, lay the collar of Dan, my father's St. Bernard. My keeper ran to pick it up. He disappeared like a gust of wind, his clothes falling to the floor in a heap. There was a slight whiff of ozone in the air, but since the principal gaseous components of his body were hydrogen, oxygen and nitrogen, which are equally colorless and odorless, there was no other manifestation of his departure. Yet when I shut off the current and removed the garments, I found a deposit of carbon in the form of animal charcoal; also other powders, the isolated, solid elements of his organism, such as sulphur, potassium and iron. Resetting the trap, I crawled back to bed. At midnight I got up and removed the remains of the second black, and then slept peacefully till morning.

I was awakened by the strident voice of my father, who was calling to me from across the laboratory. I laughed to myself. There had been no one to call him and he had overslept. I could hear him as he approached my room with the intention of rousing me, and so I sat up in bed, the better to observe his translation—perhaps apotheosis were a better term. He paused a moment at the threshold, then took the fatal step. Puff! It was like the wind

sighing among the pines. He was gone. His clothes fell
in a fantastic heap on the floor. Besides ozone, I noticed
the faint, garlic-like odor of phosphorous. A little pile of
elementary solids lay among his garments. That was all.
The wide world lay before me. My captors were no more.

THE OUTSIDER

by H. P. Lovecraft

Unhappy is he to whom the memories of childhood bring only fear and sadness. Wretched is he who looks back upon lone hours in vast and dismal chambers with brown hangings and maddening rows of antique books or upon awed watches in twilight groves of grotesque, gigantic, and vine-encumbered trees that silently wave twisted branches far aloft. Such a lot the gods gave to me—to me, the dazed, the disappointed; the barren, the broken. And yet I am strangely content and cling desperately to those sere memories, when my mind momentarily threatens to reach beyond to *the other*.

I know not where I was born, save that the castle was infinitely old and infinitely horrible, full of dark passages and having high ceilings where the eye could find only cobwebs and shadows. The stones in the crumbling corridors seemed always hideously damp, and there was an accursed smell everywhere, as of the piled-up corpses of dead generations. It was never light, so that I used sometimes to light candles and gaze steadily at them for relief, nor was there any sun outdoors, since the terrible trees grew high above the topmost accessible tower. There was one black tower which reached above the trees into the unknown outer sky, but that was partly ruined and could not be ascended save by a well-nigh impossible climb up the sheer wall, stone by stone.

I must have lived years in this place, but I can not measure the time. Beings must have cared for my needs, yet I can not recall any person except myself, or anything alive but the noiseless rats and bats and spiders. I think that whoever nursed me must have been shockingly aged, since my first conception of a living person was that of something mockingly like myself, yet distorted, shriveled and decaying like the castle. To me there was nothing grotesque in the bones and skeletons that strewed some of the stone crypts deep down among the foundations. I fantastically associated these things with everyday events, and thought them more natural than the colored pictures of living beings which I found in many of the moldy books. From such books I learned all that I know. No teacher urged or guided me, and I do not recall hearing any human voice in all those years—not even my own; for although I had read of speech, I had never thought to try to speak aloud. My aspect was a matter equally unthought of, for there were no mirrors in the castle, and I merely regarded myself by instinct as akin to the youthful figures I saw drawn and painted in the books. I felt conscious of youth because I remembered so little.

Outside, across the putrid moat and under the dark mute trees, I would often lie and dream for hours about what I read in the books; and would longingly picture myself amidst gay crowds in the sunny world beyond the endless forest. Once I tried to escape from the forest, but as I went farther from the castle the shade grew denser and the air more filled with brooding fear; so that I ran frantically back lest I lose my way in a labyrinth of nighted silence.

So through endless twilights I dreamed and waited, though I knew not what I waited for. Then in the shadowy solitude my longing for light grew so frantic that I could rest no more, and I lifted entreating hands to the single black ruined tower that reached above the forest into the unknown outer sky. And at last I resolved to scale the tower, fall though I might; since it were better to glimpse the sky and perish, than to live without ever beholding day.

In the dank twilight I climbed the worn and aged stone stairs till I reached the level where they ceased, and thereafter clung perilously to small footholds leading upward. Ghastly and terrible was that dead, stairless cylinder of rock; black, ruined, and deserted, and sinister with startled bats whose wings made no noise. But more ghastly and terrible still was the slowness of my progress; for climb as I might, the darkness overhead grew no thinner, and a new chill as of haunted and venerable mold assailed me. I shivered as I wondered why I did not reach the light, and would have looked down had I dared. I fancied that night had come suddenly upon me, and vainly groped with one free hand for a window embrasure, that I might peer out and above, and try to judge the height I had attained.

All at once, after an infinity of awesome, sightless crawling up that concave and desperate precipice, I felt my head touch a solid thing, and knew I must have gained the roof, or at least some kind of floor. In the darkness I raised my free hand and tested the barrier, finding it stone and immovable. Then came a deadly circuit of the tower, clinging to whatever holds the slimy wall could give; till finally my testing hand found the barrier yielding, and I turned upward again, pushing the slab or door with my head as I used both hands in my fearful ascent. There was no light revealed above, and as my hands went higher I knew that my climb was for the nonce ended; since the slab was the trap-door of an aperture leading to a level stone surface of greater circumference than the lower tower, no doubt the floor of some lofty and capacious observation chamber. I crawled through carefully, and tried to prevent the heavy slab from falling back into place, but failed in the latter attempt. As I lay exhausted on the stone floor I heard the eery echoes of its fall, but hoped when necessary to pry it up again.

Believing I was now at a prodigious height, far above the accursed branches of the wood, I dragged myself up from the floor and fumbled about for windows, that I might look for the first time upon the sky, and the moon and stars of which I had read. But on every hand I was disappointed; since all that I found were vast shelves of marble, bearing odious oblong boxes of disturbing size. More and more I reflected, and wondered what hoary secrets might abide in this high apartment so many eons cut off from the castle below. Then unexpectedly my hands came upon a doorway, where hung a portal of stone, rough with strange chiseling. Trying it, I found it locked; but with a supreme burst of strength I overcame all obstacles and dragged it open inward. As I did so there came to me the purest ecstasy I have ever known; for shining tranquilly through an ornate grating of iron, and down a short stone passageway of steps that ascended from the newly found doorway, was the radiant full moon, which I had never before seen save in dreams and in vague visions I dared not call memories.

Fancying now that I had attained the very pinnacle of the castle, I commenced to rush up the few steps beyond the door; but the sudden veiling of the moon by a cloud caused me to stumble, and I felt my way more slowly in the dark. It was still very dark when I reached the grating—which I tried carefully and found unlocked, but which I did not open for fear of falling from the amazing height to which I had climbed. Then the moon came out.

Most demoniacal of all shocks is that of the abysmally unexpected and grotesquely unbelievable. Nothing I had before undergone could compare in terror with what I now saw; with the bizarre marvels that sight implied. The sight itself was as simple as it was stupefying, for it was merely this: instead of a dizzying prospect of treetops seen from a lofty eminence, there stretched around me on the level through the grating nothing less than *the solid ground*, decked and diversified by marble slabs and columns, and overshadowed by an ancient stone church, whose ruined spire gleamed spectrally in the moonlight.

Half unconscious, I opened the grating and staggered out upon the white gravel path that stretched away in two directions. My mind, stunned and chaotic as it was, still held the frantic craving for light; and not even the fantastic wonder which had happened could stay my course. I neither knew nor cared whether my experience was insanity, dreaming, or magic; but was determined to gaze on brilliance and gayety at any cost. I knew not who I was or what I was, or what my surroundings might be; though as I continued to stumble along I became conscious of a kind of fearsome latent memory that made my progress not wholly fortuitous. I passed under an arch out of that region of slabs and columns, and wandered through the open country; sometimes following the visible road, but sometimes leaving it curiously to tread across meadows where only occasional ruins bespoke the ancient presence of a forgotten road. Once I swam across a swift river where crumbling, mossy masonry told of a bridge long vanished.

Over two hours must have passed before I reached what seemed to be my goal, a venerable ivied castle in a thickly wooded park, maddeningly familiar, yet full of perplexing strangeness to me. I saw that the moat was filled in, and that some of the well-known towers were demolished; whilst new wings existed to confuse the beholder. But what I observed with chief interest and delight were the open windows—gorgeously ablaze with light and sending forth sound of the gayest revelry. Advancing to one of these I looked in and saw an oddly dressed company, indeed; making merry, and speaking brightly to one another. I had never, seemingly, heard human speech before and could guess only vaguely what was said. Some of the faces seemed to hold expressions that brought up incredibly remote recollections, others were utterly alien.

I now stepped through the low window into the brilliantly lighted room, stepping as I did so from my single bright moment of hope to my blackest convulsion of despair and realization. The nightmare was quick to come, for as I entered, there occurred immediately one of the most terrifying demonstrations I had ever conceived. Scarcely had I crossed the sill when there descended upon the whole company a sudden and unheralded fear of hideous intensity, distorting every face and evoking the most horrible screams from nearly every throat. Flight was universal, and in the clamor and panic several fell in a swoon and were dragged away by their

madly fleeing companions. Many covered their eyes with
their hands, and plunged blindly and awkwardly in their
race to escape, overturning furniture and stumbling
against the walls before they managed to reach one of
the many doors.

The cries were shocking; and as I stood in the brilliant
apartment alone and dazed, listening to their vanishing
echoes, I trembled at the thought of what might be lurking near me unseen. At a casual inspection the room
seemed deserted, but when I moved toward one of the
alcoves I thought I detected a presence there—a hint
of motion beyond the golden-arched doorway leading to
another and somewhat similar room. As I approached
the arch I began to perceive the presence more clearly;
and then, with the first and last sound I ever uttered—a
ghastly ululation that revolted me almost as poignantly
as its noxious cause—I beheld in full, frightful vividness
the inconceivable, indescribable, and unmentionable
monstrosity which had by its simple appearance changed
a merry company to a herd of delirious fugitives.

I can not even hint what it was like, for it was a compound of all that is unclean, uncanny, unwelcome, abnormal, and detestable. It was the ghoulish shade of decay,
antiquity, and desolation; the putrid, dripping eidolon of
unwholesome revelation, the awful baring of that which
the merciful earth should always hide. God knows it was
not of this world—or no longer of this world—yet to my
horror I saw in its eaten-away and bone-revealing outlines a leering, abhorrent travesty on the human shape;
and in its moldy, disintegrating apparel an unspeakable
quality that chilled me even more.

I was almost paralyzed, but not too much so to make
a feeble effort toward flight; a backward stumble which
failed to break the spell in which the nameless, voiceless
monster held me. My eyes, bewitched by the glassy orbs
which stared loathsomely into them, refused to close,
though they were mercifully blurred, and showed the terrible object but indistinctly after the first shock. I tried
to raise my hand to shut out the sight, yet so stunned

were my nerves that my arm could not fully obey my
will. The attempt, however, was enough to disturb my
balance; so that I had to stagger forward several steps to
avoid falling. As I did so I became suddenly and agoniz-
ingly aware of the *nearness* of the carrion thing, whose
hideous hollow breathing I half fancied I could hear.
Nearly mad, I found myself yet able to throw out a hand
to ward off the fetid apparition which pressed so close;
when in one cataclysmic second of cosmic nightmarish-
ness and hellish accident *my fingers touched the rotting
outstretched paw of the monster beneath the golden arch.*

I did not shriek, but all the fiendish ghouls that ride
the night-wind shrieked for me as in that same second
they crashed down upon my mind a single and fleeting
avalanche of soul-annihilating memory. I knew in that
second all that had been; I remembered beyond the
frightful castle and the trees; and recognized the altered
edifice in which I now stood; I recognized, most terrible
of all, the unholy abomination that stood leering before
me as I withdrew my sullied fingers from its own.

But in the cosmos there is balm as well as bitterness,
and that balm is nepenthe. In the supreme horror of that
second I forgot what had horrified me, and the burst of
black memory vanished in a chaos of echoing images. In
a dream I fled from that haunted and accursed pile, and
ran swiftly and silently in the moonlight. When I returned
to the churchyard place of marble and went down the
steps I found the stone trap-door immovable; but I was
not sorry, for I had hated the antique castle and the
trees. Now I ride with the mocking and friendly ghouls
on the night wind, and play by day amongst the catacombs of Nephren-Ka in the sealed and unknown valley
of Hadoth by the Nile. I know that light is not for me,
save that of the moon over the rock tombs of Neb, nor
any gayety save the unnamed feasts of Nitokris beneath
the Great Pyramid; yet in my new wildness and freedom
I almost welcome the bitterness of alienage.

For although nepenthe has calmed me, I know always
that I am an outsider; stranger in this century and among

those who are still men. This I have known ever since I stretched out my fingers to the abomination within that great gilded frame; stretched out my fingers and touched *a cold and unyielding surface of polished glass.*

LIGEIA

by Edgar Allan Poe

And the will therein lieth, which dieth not. Who kno-weth the mysteries of the will, with its vigor? For God is but a great will pervading all things by nature of its intentness. Man doth not yield himself to the angels, nor unto death utterly, save only through the weakness of his feeble will.

—Joseph Glanvill.

I cannot, for my soul, remember how, when or even precisely where, I first became acquainted with the lady Ligeia. Long years have since elapsed, and my memory is feeble through much suffering. Or, perhaps, I cannot *now* bring these points to mind, because, in truth, the character of my beloved, her rare learning, her singular yet placid cast of beauty, and the thrilling and enthralling eloquence of her low musical language, made their way into my heart by paces so steadily and stealthily progres-sive that they have been unnoticed and unknown. Yet I believe that I met her first and most frequently in some large, old, decaying city near the Rhine. Of her family— I have surely heard her speak. That it is of a remotely ancient date cannot be doubted. Ligeia! Ligeia! Buried in studies of a nature more than all else adapted to deaden impressions of the outward world, it is by that sweet word alone—by Ligeia—that I bring before mine eyes in fancy the image of her who is no more. And now, while I write, a recollection flashes upon me that I have *never known* the paternal name of her who was my friend and my betrothed, and who became the partner of my studies, and finally the wife of my bosom. Was it a playful charge on the part of my Ligeia? or was it a test of my strength of affection, that I should institute no inquiries upon this point? or was it rather a caprice of my own— a wildly romantic offering on the shrine of the most passionate devotion? I but indistinctly recall the fact itself— what wonder that I have utterly forgotten the circumstances which originated or attended it? And, indeed, if ever that spirit which is entitled *Romance*—if ever she, the wan and the misty-winged *Ashtophet* of idolatrous Egypt, presided, as they tell, over marriages ill-omened, then most surely she presided over mine.

There is one dear topic, however, on which my memory fails me not. It is the *person* of Ligeia. In stature she was tall, somewhat slender, and, in her latter days, even emaciated. I would in vain attempt to portray the majesty, the quiet ease, of her demeanor, or the incomprehensible lightness and elasticity of her footfall. She came and departed as a shadow. I was never made aware of her entrance into my closed study save by the dear music of her low sweet voice, as she placed her marble hand upon my shoulder. In beauty of face no maiden ever equalled her. It was the radiance of an opium-dream— an airy and spirit-lifting vision more wildly divine than the phantasies which hovered about the slumbering souls of the daughters of Delos. Yet her features were not of that regular mould which we have been falsely taught to worship in the classical labors of the heathen. "There is no exquisite beauty," says Bacon, Lord Verulam, speaking truly of all the forms and *genera* of beauty, "without some *strangeness* in the proportion." Yet, although I saw that the features of Ligeia were not of a classic regularity—although I perceived that her loveliness was indeed "exquisite," and felt that there was much of "strangeness" pervading it, yet I have tried in vain to detect the irregularity and to trace home my own perception of "the strange." I examined the contour of the lofty and pale forehead—it was faultless—how cold indeed that word when applied to a majesty so divine!—the skin rivalling the purest ivory, the commanding extent and repose, the gentle prominence of the regions above the temples; and then the raven-black, the glossy, the luxuriant and naturally-curling tresses, setting forth the full force of the Homeric epithet, "hyacinthine!" I looked at the delicate outlines of the nose—and nowhere but in the graceful medallions of the Hebrews had I beheld a similar perfection. There were the same luxurious smoothness of surface, the same scarcely perceptible tendency to the aquiline, the same harmoniously curved nostrils speaking the free spirit. I regarded the sweet mouth. Here was indeed the triumph of all things heavenly—the magnificent turn of the short upper lip—the soft, voluptuous slumber of the under—the dimples which sported, and the color which spoke—the teeth glancing back, with a brilliancy almost startling, every ray of the holy light which fell upon them in her serene and placid, yet most exultingly radiant of all smiles. I scrutinized the formation of the chin—and here, too, I found the gentleness of breadth, the softness and the majesty, the fullness and the spirituality, of the Greek—the contour which the god Apollo revealed but in a dream, to Cleomenes, the son of the Athenian. And then I peered into the large eyes of Ligeia.

For eyes we have no models in the remotely antique. It might have been, too, that in these eyes of my beloved lay the secret to which Lord Verulam alludes. They were, I must believe, far larger than the ordinary eyes of our own race. They were even fuller than the fullest of the gazelle eyes of the tribe of the valley of Nourjahad. Yet it was only at intervals—in moments of intense excitement—that this peculiarity became more than slightly noticeable in Ligeia. And at such moments was her beauty—in my heated fancy thus it appeared perhaps—the beauty of beings either above or apart from the earth—the beauty of the fabulous Houri of the Turk. The hue of the orbs was the most brilliant of black, and, far over them, hung jetty lashes of great length. The brows, slightly irregular in outline, had the same tint. The "strangeness," however, which I found in the eyes, was of a nature distinct from the formation, or the color, or

the brilliancy of the features, and must, after all, be
referred to the *expression*. Ah, word of no meaning!
behind whose vast latitude of mere sound we intrench
our ignorance of so much of the spiritual. The expression
of the eyes of Ligeia! How for long hours have I pondered upon it! How have I, through the whole of a mid-
summer night, struggled to fathom it! What was it—that
something more profound than the well of Democritus—
which lay far within the pupils of my beloved? What *was*
it? I was possessed with a passion to discover. Those
eyes! those large, those shining, those divine orbs! they
became to me twin stars of Leda, and I to them devoutest
of astrologers.

There is no point, among the many incomprehensible
anomalies of the science of mind, more thrillingly exciting
than the fact—never, I believe, noticed in the schools—
that, in our endeavors to recall to memory something
long forgotten, we often find ourselves *upon the very
verge* of remembrance, without being able, in the end,
to remember. And thus how frequently, in my intense
scrutiny of Ligeia's eyes, have I felt approaching the full
knowledge of their expression—felt it approaching—yet
not quite be mine—and so at length entirely depart! And
(strange, oh strangest mystery of all!) I found, in the
commonest objects of the universe, a circle of analogies
to that expression. I mean to say that, subsequently to
the period when Ligeia's beauty passed into my spirit,
there dwelling as in a shrine, I derived, from many exis-
tences in the material world, a sentiment such as I felt
always aroused within me by her large and luminous
orbs. Yet not the more could I define that sentiment, or
analyze, or even steadily view it. I recognized it, let me
repeat, sometimes in the survey of a rapidly-growing
vine—in the contemplation of a moth, a butterfly, a
chrysalis, a stream of running water. I have felt it in the
ocean; in the falling of a meteor. I have felt it in the
glances of unusually aged people. And there are one or
two stars in heaven—(one especially, a star of the sixth
magnitude, double and changeable, to be found near the
large star in Lyra) in a telescopic scrutiny of which I have

been made aware of the feeling. I have been filled with
it by certain sounds from stringed instruments, and not
unfrequently by passages from books. Among innumerable other instances, I well remember something in a volume of Joseph Glanvill, which (perhaps merely from its
quaintness—who shall say?) never failed to inspire me
with the sentiment;—"And the will therein lieth, which
dieth not. Who knoweth the mysteries of the will, with
its vigor? For God is but a great will pervading all things
by nature of its intentness. Man doth not yield him to
the angels, nor unto death utterly, save only through the
weakness of his feeble will."

Length of years, and subsequent reflection, have
enabled me to trace, indeed, some remote connection
between this passage in the English moralist and a portion of the character of Ligeia. An *intensity* in thought,
action, or speech, was possibly, in her, a result, or at
least an index, of that gigantic volition which, during our
long intercourse, failed to give other and more immediate evidence of its existence. Of all the women whom I
have ever known, she, the outwardly calm, the ever-
placid Ligeia, was the most violently a prey to the tumul-
tuous vultures of stern passion. And of such passion I
could form no estimate, save by the miraculous expan-
sion of those eyes which at once so delighted and
appalled me—by the almost magical melody, modula-
tion, distinctness and placidity of her very low voice—
and by the fierce energy (rendered doubly effective by
contrast with her manner of utterance) of the wild words
which she habitually uttered.

I have spoken of the learning of Ligeia; it was
immense—such as I have never known in woman. In the
classical tongues was she deeply proficient, and as far as
my own acquaintance extended in regard to the modern
dialects of Europe, I have never known her at fault.
Indeed upon any theme of the most admired, because
simply the most abstruse of the boasted erudition of the
academy, have I *ever* found Ligeia at fault? How singu-
larly—how thrillingly, this one point in the nature of my
wife has forced itself, at this late period only, upon my

attention! I said her knowledge was such as I have never known in woman—but where breathes the man who has traversed, and successfully, *all* the wide areas of moral, physical, and mathematical science? I saw not then what I now clearly perceive, that the acquisitions of Ligeia were gigantic, were astounding; yet I was sufficiently aware of her infinite supremacy to resign myself, with a child-like confidence, to her guidance through the chaotic world of metaphysical investigation at which I was most busily occupied during the earlier years of our marriage. With how vast a triumph—with how vivid a delight— with how much of all that is ethereal in hope—did I *feel*, as she bent over me in studies but little sought—but less known—that delicious vista by slow degrees expanding before me, down whose long, gorgeous, and all untrodden path, I might at length pass onward to the goal of a wisdom too divinely precious not to be forbidden!

How poignant, then, must have been the grief with which, after some years, I beheld my well-grounded expectations take wings to themselves and fly away! Without Ligeia I was but as a child groping benighted. Her presence, her readings alone, rendered vividly luminous the many mysteries of the transcendentalism in which we were immersed. Wanting the radiant lustre of her eyes, letters, lambent and golden, grew duller than Saturnian lead. And now those eyes shone less and less frequently upon the pages over which I pored. Ligeia grew ill. The wild eyes blazed with a too-too glorious effulgence; the pale fingers became of the transparent waxen hue of the grave, and the blue veins upon the lofty forehead swelled and sank impetuously with the tides of the most gentle emotion. I saw that she must die—and I struggled desperately in spirit with the grim Azrael. And the struggles of the passionate wife were, to my astonishment, even more energetic than my own. There had been much in her stern nature to impress me with the belief that, to her, death would have come without its terrors;—but not so. Words are impotent to convey any just idea of the fierceness of resistance with which she wrestled with the Shadow. I groaned in anguish at the pitiable spectacle. I would have soothed—I would have reasoned; but, in the intensity of her wild desire for life—for life— *but* for life—solace and reason were alike the uttermost of folly. Yet not until the last instance, amid the most convulsive writhings of her fierce spirit, was shaken the external placidity of her demeanor. Her voice grew more gentle—grew more low—yet I would not wish to dwell upon the wild meaning of the quietly uttered words. My brain reeled as I hearkened entranced, to a melody more than mortal—to assumptions and aspirations which mortality had never before known.

That she loved me I should not have doubted; and I might have been easily aware that, in a bosom such as hers, love would have reigned no ordinary passion. But in death only, was I fully impressed with the strength of her affection. For long hours, detaining my hand, would she pour out before me the overflowing of a heart whose more than passionate devotion amounted to idolatry. How had I deserved to be so blessed by such confessions?—how had I deserved to be so cursed with the removal of my beloved in the hour of her making them? But upon this subject I cannot bear to dilate. Let me say only, that in Ligeia's more than womanly abandonment to a love, alas! all unmerited, all unworthily bestowed, I at length recognized the principle of her longing with so wildly earnest a desire for the life which was now fleeing so rapidly away. It is this wild longing—it is this eager vehemence of desire for life—*but* for life—that I have no power to portray—no utterance capable of expressing.

At high noon of the night in which she departed, beckoning me, peremptorily, to her side, she bade me repeat certain verses composed by herself not many days before. I obeyed her.—They were these:

> Lo! 't is a gala night
>   Within the lonesome latter years!
> An angel throng, bewinged, bedight
>   In veils, and drowned in tears,
> Sit in a theatre, to see
>   A play of hopes and fears,

While the orchestra breathes fitfully
   The music of the spheres.

Mimes, in the form of God on high,
   Mutter and mumble low,
And hither and thither fly—
   Mere puppets they, who come and go
At bidding of vast formless things
   That shift the scenery to and fro,
Flapping from out their Condor wings
   Invisible Wo!

That motley drama!—oh, be sure
   It shall not be forgot!
With its Phantom chased forever more,
   By a crowd that seize it not,
Through a circle that ever returneth in
   To the self-same spot,
And much of Madness and more of Sin
   And Horror the soul of the plot.

But see, amid the mimic rout,
   A crawling shape intrude!
A blood-red thing that writhes from out
   The scenic solitude!
It writhes!—it writhes!—with mortal pangs
   The mimes become its food,
And the seraphs sob at vermin fangs
   In human gore imbued.

Out—out are the lights—out all!
   And over each quivering form,
The curtain, a funeral pall,
   Comes down with the rush of a storm,
And the angels, all pallid and wan,
   Uprising, unveiling, affirm
That the play is the tragedy, "Man,"
   And its hero the Conqueror Worm.

"O God!" half shrieked Ligeia, leaping to her feet and

extending her arms aloft with a spasmodic movement, as I made an end of these lines—"O God! O Divine Father!—shall these things be undeviatingly so?—shall this Conqueror be not once conquered? Are we not part and parcel in Thee? Who—who knoweth the mysteries of the will with its vigor? Man doth not yield him to the angels, *nor unto death utterly*, save only through the weakness of his feeble will."

And now, as if exhausted with emotion, she suffered her white arms to fall, and returned solemnly to her bed of death. And as she breathed her last sighs, there came mingled with them a low murmur from her lips. I bent to them my ear and distinguished, again, the concluding words of the passage in Glanvill—*"Man doth not yield him to the angels, nor unto death utterly, save only through the weakness of his feeble will."*

She died;—and I, crushed into the very dust with sorrow, could no longer endure the lonely desolation of my dwelling in the dim and decaying city by the Rhine. I had no lack of what the world calls wealth. Ligeia had brought me far more, very far more than ordinarily falls to the lot of mortals. After a few months, therefore, of weary and aimless wandering, I purchased, and put in some repair, an abbey, which I shall not name, in one of the wildest and least frequented portions of fair England. The gloomy and dreary grandeur of the building, the almost savage aspect of the domain, the many melancholy and time-honored memories connected with both, had much in unison with the feelings of utter abandonment which had driven me into that remote and unsocial region of the country. Yet although the external abbey, with its verdant decay hanging about it, suffered but little alteration, I gave way, with a child-like perversity, and perchance with a faint hope of alleviating my sorrows, to a display of more than regal magnificence within.—For such follies, even in childhood, I had imbibed a taste and now they came back to me as if in the dotage of grief. Alas, I feel how much even of incipient madness might have been discovered in the gorgeous and fantastic draperies, in the solemn carvings of Egypt,

in the wild cornices and furniture, in the Bedlam patterns
of the carpets of tufted gold! I had become a bounden
slave in the trammels of opium, and my labors and my
orders had taken a coloring from my dreams. But these
absurdities I must not pause to detail. Let me speak only
of that one chamber, ever accursed, whither in a moment
of mental alienation, I led from the altar as my bride—as
the successor of the unforgotten Ligeia—the fair-haired and
blue-eyed Lady Rowena Trevanion, of Tremaine.

There is no individual portion of the architecture and
decoration of that bridal chamber which is not now visi-
bly before me. Where were the souls of the haughty family of the bride, when, through thirst of gold, they
permitted to pass the threshold of an apartment *so*
bedecked, a maiden and a daughter so beloved? I have
said that I minutely remember the details of the chamber—yet I am sadly forgetful on topics of deep moment—
and here there was no system, no keeping, in the fantastic display, to take hold upon the memory. The room lay
in a high turret of the castellated abbey, was pentagonal
in shape, and of capacious size. Occupying the whole
southern face of the pentagon was the sole window—an
immense sheet of unbroken glass from Venice—a single
pane, and tinted of a leaden hue, so that the rays of
either the sun or moon, passing through it, fell with a
ghastly lustre on the objects within. Over the upper portion of this huge window, extended the trellice-work of
an aged vine, which clambered up the massy walls of the
turret. The ceiling, of gloomy-looking oak, was exces-
sively lofty, vaulted, and elaborately fretted with the
wildest and most grotesque specimens of a semi-Gothic,
semi-Druidical device. From out the most central recess
of this melancholy vaulting, depended, by a single chain
of gold with long links, a huge censer of the same metal,
Saracenic in pattern, and with many perforations so contrived that there writhed in and out in them, as if endued
with a serpent vitality, a continual succession of parti-
colored fires.

Some few ottomans and golden candelabra, of Eastern
figure, were in various stations about—and there was the

couch, too—the bridal couch—of an Indian model, and low, and sculptured of solid ebony, with a pall-like canopy above. In each of the angles of the chamber stood on end a gigantic sarcophagus of black granite, from the tombs of the kings over against Luxor, with their aged lids full of immemorial sculpture. But in the draping of the apartment lay, alas! the chief phantasy of all. The lofty walls, gigantic in height—even unproportionably so—were hung from summit to foot, in vast folds, with a heavy and massive-looking tapestry—tapestry of a material which was found alike as a carpet on the floor, as a covering for the ottomans and the ebony bed, as a canopy for the bed, and as the gorgeous volutes of the curtains which partially shaded the window. The material was the richest cloth of gold. It was spotted all over, at irregular intervals, with arabesque figures, about a foot in diameter, and wrought upon the cloth in patterns of the most jetty black. But these figures partook of the true character of the arabesque only when regarded from a single point of view. By a contrivance now common, and indeed traceable to a very remote period of antiquity, they were made changeable in aspect. To one entering the room, they bore the appearance of simple monstrosities; but upon a farther advance, this appearance gradually departed; and step by step, as the visiter moved his station in the chamber, he saw himself surrounded by an endless succession of the ghastly forms which belong to the superstition of the Norman, or arise in the guilty slumbers of the monk. The phantasmagoric effect was vastly heightened by the artificial introduction of a strong continual current of wind behind the draperies—giving a hideous and uneasy animation to the whole.

In halls such as these—in a bridal chamber such as this—I passed, with the Lady of Tremaine, the unhallowed hours of the first month of our marriage—passed them with but little disquietude. That my wife dreaded the fierce moodiness of my temper—that she shunned me and loved me but little—I could not help perceiving; but it gave me rather pleasure than otherwise. I loathed her with a hatred belonging more to demon than to man.

My memory flew back, (oh, with what intensity of regret!) to Ligeia, the beloved, the august, the beautiful, the entombed. I revelled in recollections of her purity, of her wisdom, of her lofty, her ethereal nature, of her passionate, her idolatrous love. Now, then, did my spirit fully and freely burn with more than all the fires of her own. In the excitement of my opium dreams (for I was habitually fettered in the shackles of the drug) I would call aloud upon her name, during the silence of the night, or among the sheltered recesses of the glens by day, as if, through the wild eagerness, the solemn passion, the consuming ardor of my longing for the departed, I could restore her to the pathway she had abandoned—ah, *could* it be forever?—upon the earth.

About the commencement of the second month of the marriage, the Lady Rowena was attacked with sudden illness, from which her recovery was slow. The fever which consumed her rendered her nights uneasy; and in her perturbed state of half-slumber, she spoke of sounds, and of motions, in and about the chamber of the turret, which I concluded had no origin save in the distemper of her fancy, or perhaps in the phantasmagoric influences of the chamber itself. She became at length convalescent—finally well. Yet but a brief period elapsed, ere a second more violent disorder again threw her upon a bed of suffering; and from this attack her frame, at all times feeble, never altogether recovered. Her illnesses were, after this epoch, of alarming character, and of more alarming recurrence, defying alike the knowledge and the great exertions of her physicians. With the increase of the chronic disease which had thus, apparently, taken too sure hold upon her constitution to be eradicated by human means, I could not fail to observe a similar increase in the nervous irritation of her temperament, and in her excitability by trivial causes of fear. She spoke again, and now more frequently and pertinaciously of the sounds—of the slight sounds—and of the unusual motions among the tapestries, to which she had formerly alluded.

One night, near the closing in of September, she pressed this distressing subject with more than usual

emphasis upon my attention. She had just awakened
from an unquiet slumber and I had been watching, with
feelings half of anxiety, half of vague terror, the workings
of her emaciated countenance. I sat by the side of her
ebony bed, upon one of the ottomans of India. She partly
arose, and spoke, in an earnest low whisper, of sounds
which she *then* heard, but which I could not hear—of
motions which she *then* saw, but which I could not perceive. The wind was rushing hurriedly behind the tapestries, and I wished to show her (what, let me confess
it, I could not *all* believe) that those almost inarticulate
breathings, and those very gentle variations of the figures
upon the wall, were but the natural effects of that customary rushing of the wind. But a deadly pallor, over-
spreading her face, had proved to me that my exertion
to reassure her would be fruitless. She appeared to be
fainting, and no attendants were within call. I remembered where was deposited a decanter of light wine which
had been ordered by her physicians, and hastened across
the chamber to procure it. But, as I stepped beneath the
light of the censer, two circumstances of a startling nature
attracted my attention. I had felt that some palpable
although invisible object had passed lightly by my person;
and I saw that there lay upon the golden carpet, in the
very middle of the rich lustre thrown from the censer, a
shadow—a faint, indefinite shadow of angelic aspect—
such as might be fancied for the shadow of a shade. But
I was wild with the excitement of an immoderate dose
of opium, and heeded these things but little, nor spoke
to them to Rowena. Having found the wine, I recrossed
the chamber, and poured out a goblet-ful, which I held
to the lips of the fainting lady. She had now partially
recovered, however, and took the vessel herself, while I
sank upon an ottoman near me, with my eyes fastened
upon her person. It was then that I became distinctly
aware of a gentle foot-fall upon the carpet, and near the
couch; and in a second thereafter, as Rowena was in the
act of raising the wine to her lips, I saw, or may have
dreamed that I saw, fall within the goblet, as if from
some invisible spring in the atmosphere of the room,

three or four large drops of a brilliant and ruby colored fluid. If this I saw—not so Rowena. She swallowed the wine unhesitatingly, and I forbore to speak to her of a circumstance which must, after all, I considered, have been but the suggestion of a vivid imagination, rendered morbidly active by the terror of the lady, by the opium, and by the hour.

Yet I cannot conceal it from my own perception that, immediately subsequent to the fall of the ruby-drops, a rapid change for the worse took place in the disorder of my wife; so that, on the third subsequent night, the hands of her menials prepared her for the tomb, and on the fourth, I sat alone, with her shrouded body, in that fantastic chamber which had received her as my bride.— Wild visions, opium-engendered, flitted, shadow-like, before me. I gazed with unquiet eye upon the sarcophagi in the angles of the room, upon the varying figures of the drapery, and upon the writhing of the parti-colored fires in the censer overhead. My eyes then fell, as I called to mind the circumstances of a former night, to the spot beneath the glare of the censer where I had seen the faint traces of the shadow. It was there, however, no longer; and breathing with greater freedom, I turned my glances to the pallid and rigid figure upon the bed. Then rushed upon me a thousand memories of Ligeia—and then came back upon my heart, with the turbulent violence of a flood, the whole of that unutterable woe with which I had regarded *her* thus enshrouded. The night waned; and still, with a bosom full of bitter thoughts of the one only and supremely beloved, I remained gazing upon the body of Rowena.

It might have been midnight, or perhaps earlier, or later, for I had taken no note of time, when a sob, low, gentle, but very distinct, startled me from my revery.— I *felt* that it came from the bed of ebony—the bed of death. I listened in an agony of superstitious terror—but there was no repetition of the sound. I strained my vision to detect any motion in the corpse—but there was not the slightest perceptible. Yet I could not have been deceived. I *had* heard the noise, however faint, and my

soul was awakened within me. I resolutely and persever-
ingly kept my attention riveted upon the body. Many
minutes elapsed before any circumstance occurred tend-
ing to throw light upon the mystery. At length it became
evident that a slight, a very feeble, and barely noticeable
tinge of color had flushed up within the cheeks, and
along the sunken small veins of the eyelids. Through a
species of unutterable horror and awe, for which the language of mortality has no sufficiently energetic expression. I felt my heart cease to beat, my limbs grow rigid
where I sat. Yet a sense of duty finally operated to
restore my self-possession. I could no longer doubt that
we had been precipitate in our preparations—that Rowena
still lived. It was necessary that some immediate exertion
be made; yet the turret was altogether apart from the
portion of the abbey tenanted by the servants—there
were none within call—I had no means of summoning
them to my aid without leaving the room for many
minutes—and this I could not venture to do. I therefore
struggled alone in my endeavors to call back the spirit
still hovering. In a short period it was certain, however,
that a relapse had taken place; the color disappeared
from both eyelid and cheek, leaving a wanness even more
than that of marble; the lips became doubly shrivelled
and pinched up in the ghastly expression of death; a
repulsive clamminess and coldness overspread rapidly the
surface of the body; and all the usual rigorous stiffness
immediately supervened. I fell back with a shudder upon
the couch from which I had been so startlingly aroused,
and again gave myself up to passionate waking visions of
Ligeia.

An hour thus elapsed when (could it be possible?) I
was a second time aware of some vague sound issuing
from the region of the bed. I listened—in extremity of
horror. The sound came again—it was a sigh. Rushing
to the corpse, I saw—distinctly saw—a tremor upon the
lips. In a minute afterward they relaxed, disclosing a
bright line of the pearly teeth. Amazement now struggled
in my bosom with the profound awe which had hitherto
reigned there alone. I felt that my vision grew dim, that

my reason wandered; and it was only by a violent effort that I at length succeeded in nerving myself to the task which duty thus once more had pointed out. There was now a partial glow upon the forehead and upon the cheek and throat; a perceptible warmth pervaded the whole frame; there was even a slight pulsation at the heart. The lady *lived*; and with redoubled ardor I betook myself to the task of restoration. I chafed and bathed the temples and the hands, and used every exertion which experience, and no little medical reading, could suggest. But in vain. Suddenly, the color fled, the pulsation ceased, the lips resumed the expression of the dead, and, in an instant afterward, the whole body took upon itself the icy chilliness, the livid hue, the intense rigidity, the sunken outline, and all the loathsome peculiarities of that which has been, for many days, a tenant of the tomb.

And again I sunk into visions of Ligeia—and again, (what marvel that I shudder while I write?) *again* there reached my ears a low sob from the region of the ebony bed. But why shall I minutely detail the unspeakable horrors of that night? Why shall I pause to relate how, time after time, until near the period of the gray dawn, this hideous drama of revivification was repeated; how each terrific relapse was only into a sterner and apparently more irredeemable death; how each agony wore the aspect of a struggle with some invisible foe; and how each struggle was succeeded by I know not what of wild change in the personal appearance of the corpse? Let me hurry to a conclusion.

The greater part of the fearful night had worn away, and she who had been dead, once again stirred—and now more vigorously than hitherto, although arousing from a dissolution more appalling in its utter hopelessness than any. I had long ceased to struggle or to move, and remained sitting rigidly upon the ottoman, a helpless prey to a whirl of violent emotions, of which extreme awe was perhaps the least terrible, the least consuming. The corpse, I repeat, stirred, and now more vigorously than before. The hues of life flushed up with unwonted energy into the countenance—the limbs relaxed—and,

save that the eyelids were yet pressed heavily together,
and that the bandages and draperies of the grave still
imparted their charnel character to the figure, I might
have dreamed that Rowena had indeed shaken off,
utterly, the fetters of Death. But if this idea was not,
even then, altogether adopted, I could at least doubt no
longer, when, arising from the bed, tottering, with feeble
steps, with closed eyes, and with the manner of one
bewildered in a dream, the thing that was enshrouded
advanced boldly and palpably into the middle of the
apartment.

I trembled not—I stirred not—for a crowd of unutterable fancies connected with the air, the stature, the
demeanor of the figure, rushing hurriedly through my
brain, had paralyzed—had chilled me into stone. I stirred
not—but gazed upon the apparition. There was a mad
disorder in my thoughts—a tumult unappeasable. Could
it, indeed, be the *living* Rowena who confronted me?
Could it indeed be Rowena *at all*—the fair-haired, the
blue-eyed Lady Rowena Trevanion of Tremaine? Why,
why should I doubt it? The bandage lay heavily about
the mouth—but then might it not be the mouth of the
breathing Lady of Tremaine? And the cheeks—there
were the roses as in her noon of life—yes, these might
indeed be the fair cheeks of the living Lady of Tremaine.
And the chin, with its dimples, as in health, might it not
be hers?—but *had she then grown taller since her malady*?
What inexpressible madness seized me with that thought?
One bound, and I had reached her feet! Shrinking from
my touch, she let fall from her head, unloosened, the
ghastly cerements which had confined it, and there
streamed forth, into the rushing atmosphere of the chamber, huge masses of long and disheveled hair; *it was
blacker than the raven wings of midnight*! And now slowly
opened *the eyes* of the figure which stood before me.
"Here then, at least," I shrieked aloud, "can I never—
can I never be mistaken—these are the full, and the
black, and the wild eyes—of my lost love—of the lady—
of the LADY LIGEIA."

MOP-UP

by Arthur Porges

When he had quartered the stricken land in vain for almost two years without finding another living person, the man came upon a witch, a vampire, and a ghoul holding solemn parley by a gutted church.

As he broke through the tangled, untrimmed hedges into the weed-grown garden, the witch laughed shrilly; and as if mocking her own white hairs, danced widder-shins, cackling in delight, "There's one left, just as I thought, and a very pretty fellow, too!" She was a revolting old beldame, and he stared at her aghast.

The vampire, lean and elegant in a rusty black cloak, arose with his ruby eyes kindling. He crouched a little, and a pointed tongue flickered between full, soft lips. Catlike, he glided forward.

"Stop!" the witch cried. "He's the last, fool! Would you drink him dry? You must learn to use the blood of beasts. Remember, Baron—there's probably not another human in the whole world."

The vampire showed his enormous canines in a sly smile.

"You underestimate me, Mother. All I had in mind was a mere sip. It's been two years, and there's nothing quite like the fresh stuff, so strong and warm."

"No!" she protested. "He's mine. Not a drop. The poor darling's worn enough. There are plenty of animals left to suck on."

"Not for me—yet," was the lofty retort. "I prefer the blood banks. They'll keep me supplied for many years. People collected millions of pints, all nicely preserved,

232

carefully stored, rich and tasty—then never got to use them. What a pity! Still," he added, his voice wistful, "cold blood is hardly the drink for a nobleman of my lineage."

"Blood banks!" she chortled, displaying strong, discolored teeth. "So that's where you've been getting it all this time. I wondered." She nodded cynical approval. "Then there's no problem, because *his* kind"—with a contemptuous gesture towards the ghoul, huddled beast-like behind them—"are set for ages, too. Nothing to do but pick and choose." Her stringy jaw muscles knotted. "So the man is mine!"

The ghoul gave him a single wicked glance, and continued digging at his clogged incisors with fingernails like splinters of glass. The man's stomach heaved; he gulped down a sour taste.

"Don't be afraid, darling boy," the hag crooned. "You're safe with us. And it's worth a deal to be snug these days, I can tell you."

He stood there, haggard and feverish, thinking himself mad. Among the survivors, if any, he had expected the usual proportion of carrion crows, but nothing like this fantastic trio. Still, perhaps, even their company was better than the wrenching ache of complete isolation in a ravaged world. Two of them, at least, were outwardly human.

"You're not crazy," the witch reassured him, pinching his stubbled cheek. "You'll live long and well to serve me." She eyed him with a kind of leering coyness, utterly grotesque in an ugly old woman. "A fine, strong fellow. What a sweet lover he'll be for poor Mother Digby. I'll teach you the 435 ways—"

"Am I the last?" he muttered. "Really the last? I've searched. I—"

"Yes," the vampire said, with a melancholy smile. "Unfortunately, I fear you are." The ghoul tittered, and his eyes filmed over like oily, stagnant pools.

"Don't frighten him," she flared. "Sit down, my honey. Here, by me." She pulled him to her side, and dazed, he submitted.

"Tell me the truth," he begged again. "Am I actually the only one left?"

"Yes. First came the hydrogen bombs. It was something to see. I've been around a long time, my lad: the big Mississippi Quakes of 1815, Krakatoa, Hiroshima—they were nothing by comparison. The Baron knew it was coming—how did you know, hey? He won't tell." She snapped her fingers and laughed jeeringly; her bony elbow prodded the man. "Ah, it was the blood banks! I might have guessed—right?"

The Baron nodded coolly. "Yes. When they began to pyramid the stock piles, I suspected what would happen soon. That's when I told you to look out for fire. One atomic blast would have burnt your juiceless carcass to cinders." His lips twitched at her outraged expression. "As a nobleman, I was almost tempted to warn the more ancient monarchies of Europe. For the upstart Americans, with their absurd 'democracy' I care nothing. Rule by comic book! But in the Balkans—" He broke off with a sigh.

"Germs, Mother," the ghoul croaked suddenly, giving her a doglike glance of worship.

"Right, my pet. The germs came next. Every country had secret cultures, deadly soups of plagues old and new. How the people died! All but my lovely man here." She patted his thigh. "Why are you still alive, hey?"

He shook his head. "There was a new, untested serum in our lab—a last attempt. Just a tiny drop. I had nothing to lose." He brooded a moment in silence, then asked, "How about Europe—Asia?"

"Wiped out. Nobody left. Not one saucy little Mamselle, or golden Eurasian, or cool English girl for you. Take old Mother Digby, and be satisfied. Don't let my wrinkled face fool you! Wine long in the cask is best!"

He shuddered away from her. "How can you be sure? About Europe?"

"There are ways. Before we lost contact with our fellows, I received regular reports; and since then I've made many flights of my own. Paris, London, Belgrade,

Copenhagen—it's all the same. Some by bombs; more by disease."

"Where are Ours—the Others?" the ghoul demanded in a thick voice.

"Who knows?" she snapped, her lips tightening. "At the last Sabbath, few came. Maybe the old customs are dying as the silly humans died. Anyway, I've seen none for weeks now. Neither has the Baron." She turned back to the pale, bemused man. "Did you find any of your kind?"

"No," he admitted dully. "Only animals, and always huddled in groups. As if *they* were appalled, too. But—you're certain about the other countries?"

She flourished a veiny hand. "Clean sweep. From Tibet to Los Angeles. We cover oceans in hours, the Baron and I. *He*," sneering at the ghoul, "can only snuff about the ground." The ghoul winced. "You're the last human, all right. I knew one was about somewhere. I can tell. But no more rosy throats for the Baron, even if"—with a malicious smile—"he didn't prefer the easier method with blood banks!"

"Not much choice," was the unashamed reply. "And besides, people were getting harder to manage in these days of—ah—enlightenment. Even *he* was faced with a new problem: cremation."

A bubbling snarl came from the crouched ghoul.

"Never mind," the witch soothed him. "Your troubles have been over, these two years. No more cremation again, ever."

"We've just had cremation wholesale," the vampire pointed out. "And speaking of troubles," he jibed, "yours are not over, dear Mother. No orgies, no backsliding church folk to torment, and who's to care now if you dry up a cow?"

She ignored him, snuggling closer to the man. "Adam and Eve," she simpered, resting her white head on his shoulder.

"Don't!" He shrank away.

She glared at him. "Will you, will you," she hissed. "Don't cross me, my puling innocent, or—!"

"He's good for only a short time at best," the vampire reminded her, pleasantly solicitous. "After that—"

"You lie!" she screeched. "By my arts he'll live a thousand—ten thousand—years. He'll learn to love me. And if you dare to touch him—!"

The Baron shrugged. He winked at the man. "Ignore her threats to you. You're so valuable to the lecherous old hag that she wouldn't harm—what's that?" He rose to his full height, pointing.

Far out in the brush, a faint, bobbing light twinkled, then another.

"Fireflies," the witch said, indifferently. She stroked the man's hand, and tried to press her leathery cheek to his.

"No," said the ghoul. Doglike, he sniffed the air, his damp snout quivering.

A moment later, two rabbits hopped into the garden. One of them cautiously drew nearer. It stopped about ten feet away, and rose up on its hind paws, with ears up. Its button of a nose twitched. They watched the animal in amazement.

"They're certainly tame around here," the man muttered. He sensed a possible diversion, and alerted himself for escape. But he felt little hope. How could a lone mortal elude this dreadful trio?

The rabbit squeaked loudly, peremptorily, and a larger animal came up behind it, laboriously hauling in its jaws something that trailed on the ground.

"That's a beaver," said the man, unobtrusively edging away.

As the animal approached, they recognized its burden: a freshly felled sapling, one end gnawed to a rough point.

Suddenly the rabbit uttered a series of high, chirping sounds, strangely modulated. It waved one snowy paw in a gesture of command. The beaver responded with an irritable grunt, wrestling its clumsy stick forward. The dancing lights reappeared, very close now: tiny, flaming torches, gripped in the handlike paws of two raccoons, each running jerkily on three legs.

The rabbit made a new, imperious motion; it pointed directly at the squat, silent ghoul.

The witch broke into a laugh, and startled, the rabbit crouched, poised for flight. "Animals!" She jeered. "Attacking *us*!" She turned to the grave Baron. "You heard that rabbit—it's actually giving some sort of orders." She pointed a derisive finger at the rodent, small and wary, studying her with soft, luminous eyes. "Hey, there—do you think we're afraid of beavers and such vermin?"

"Wait." The vampire clutched her arm. "I doubt if they understand English. It's some simple language of their own. They've learned a lot in two years—if the whole thing didn't really begin much earlier. Mother, this is a serious matter. Don't you see? The stake's for me; the fire's for you; and for *him*, I imagine—"

The ghoul gave a hollow, moaning cry, and dived crashing into the nearest bushes. A moment after, there was a thin, bestial howl of pain. Then the underbrush crackled, and the ghoul stumbled back into the garden. He lurched blindly towards the witch, and they saw that his face was gone, leaving something like a wet sponge, soft and amorphous. The man stared in frozen horror, oblivious of his opportunity. There was a deep-chested growl from the weeds, and a great, shaggy form shambled out. It was a grizzly bear, grim and implacable, with bloody foam on its champing jaws.

Gasping, the witch leaped aside. The mangled ghoul groped for her, whimpering in fear. Silently the bear padded forward, its heavy coat rippling. But before it could close in, there was a quavering shriek like a woman in torment, a tawny blur, and a mountain lion, sickle claws wide spread, landed squarely upon the ghoul's back, smashing him to the ground.

Screaming hoarsely, the blinded monster writhed, clutching with thick, earth-stained fingers for his assailant. But the lion's hind legs were already gathered for the disembowelling stroke, and the ghoul had no chance. It was soon over; the quasi-human body lay still. The panther sat back, licking its great paws like any kitchen tabby. It paused once to give the man a sidelong, inscrutable glance. His pulse leaped to a new realization. Was the lion promising deliverance?

"Mother," the vampire said composedly, "this is the finish. Now we know where the Others went." There was a tinge of weariness in his accented voice. "Well, a nobleman does not fear—death." He pronounced the last word almost wonderingly.

"Idiot!" snarled the witch. "We're not earthbound like that," thrusting a finger at the torn ghoul.

The Baron gave a fatalistic shrug, met her challenging gaze, and smiled. He pulled his cloak tight, dislimned, and began to shrink. When he seemed about to vanish completely, there was a smoky flash, and a huge bat winged up from the garden, a spectral silhouette against the sunset sky. The black cloak lay empty on the grass.

A sonorous belling rang in the distance, harsh, yet mournfully musical, the call of a moose. Even in the circumstances, the man thrilled to the heady sound, recalling past hunts. The rabbit squealed in excitement, pointing upward. And they came, almost in military formation: a vast flight of birds, all predators of the air. Eagles, falcons, and hundreds of small piratical hawks, swift and rakish. They swooped with raucous cries; the sky throbbed to their wingbeats. A mighty golden eagle led the attack, hurtling 2,000 feet straight down, to strike with open talons. They heard the wind whistling through its stiff feathers and the crisp impact as the half-mile swoop reached a climax in that shattering blow.

The bat crumpled, disrupted in mid-air. It spun downward, erratic as a falling leaf, and there, in the weedy garden, the vampire reappeared, broken-backed.

As he squirmed, trying desperately to arise, the beaver drew near with its crudely-pointed sapling. Just out of reach, it paused, earnest and phlegmatic, its whiskered face indicating a solemn concern with the task ahead. The vampire glowered with concentrated malignance as a host of smaller animals pattered up. Sharp teeth and tenacious claws pinned the writhing thing, while four chipmunks held the stick upright in their facile paws, the point upon the heaving breast.

Then, from the darkening thicket, a bull moose emerged. He moved with stately tread, his split hooves clacking. On reaching the thrashing vampire, he snorted once, as if in profound distaste, and stood there waiting. The rabbit snapped its paw down in a vertical arc, and with a single blow of his massive forefoot, the moose drove the stake home.

Squawking imprecations, the witch abandoned her vain aerial search for an opening in the umbrella of birds, dropped heavily a dozen feet to the earth, and with ragged white locks streaming, crashed through the ranks of lesser animals. One of them grated in agony. But the witch halted abruptly, cowering. She looked about with darting, baleful eyes, a hunched figure of evil. They poured into the garden from all sides: bears, panthers, badgers, and two purebred bulls, wickedly horned and bellicose. Overhead, the hawks circled, watching with fierce yellow eyes. The man saw the beasts converge, backing her steadily toward the church wall, a fire-scarred, crazily tilted brick barrier. There were muffled sounds, and he heard clearly a wheezy sobbing. He smiled briefly, and some of the tension left him. The raccoons, like conspirators in their dark masks, raced in with torches, followed by dozens of beasts dragging twigs and bark. An old, gaunt cow ambled by with a fence rail in her worn jaws. She peeped at the man with liquidly compassionate eyes. Before long, the pyre flamed high against the blackened wall. There was a final wailing cry as the witch died.

He dropped to his knees emotionally exhausted. They had freed him. The beasts of the forest and farm: the burly, comical black bears, the sullen, feral grizzlies, the pretty rabbits and squirrels, even an old cow, doubtless filled with affection for some mouldering barnyard where children had laughed and people had once been kind. All these had joined to deliver the last man.

Touched, he peered through growing dusk at the rabbit, trying to convey his gratitude and delight. There would be a new Golden Age, wherein man and beast might live in loving harmony. He forced back guilty visions of timid deer horribly wounded, of dying birds cheerfully ravaged by his dog. But that was past. No more hunting for him. Instead, he would teach them man's wonders. He would—

The rabbit hopped aside, and four lean wolves pressed forward, licking black lips. A bull pawed the earth, bellowing. High above, an early owl hooted.

The rabbit faced the wolves, pointing to the man with one paw, the other poised in a familiar manner.

The man understood that pregnant signal, and the soft, purring sounds he had begun to make died in his throat. It was thumbs down.

CHARLIE

by Talmage Powell

Charlie came up out of the depths of her sleep, a gray mist taking small human form in the langorous Guatemalan night. She herself was in the dream, sitting cross-legged in her tent, face uplifted, watching the shifting change in the heavy blackness and wondering at first what it was all about.

And there was Charlie, struggling up from the pit to stand before her. In her dream state, she felt not the slightest twinge of alarm. In dreams, little boy mummies who go bump in the night are perfectly acceptable. Mummification had accented all his features, bringing out an ebonized aspect even if originally there had been none. He was ugly . . . ugly . . . and yet she felt the strongest compulsion to stretch out the maternal warmth of her fingertips and touch him. She sensed that he'd had a devilish time getting through to her. He was, after all, only about four years old—three thousand years old—and rather forlorn in his clinging tatters of long-decayed mummy wrappings.

"We found you, Charlie. Dr. Pangborn and I."

"Be grateful for the privilege."

"We searched long and hard for you. Not really you. Actually we didn't expect to find a little boy and girl in the old mini-pyramid tomb."

"I know."

"The exquisite little carving of time-blackened limestone . . . the ancient amulet the Quinch woman was wearing about her neck . . . it was our first tangible clue after weeks of searching the mountains and valleys, the forgotten glens and forests of Guatemala, Charlie. We were about to give up and return to civilization when we came to the village. It was beside the muddy little river Patchutx. There we saw the woman wearing the amulet, the artifact from a civilization that flourished when my race were savages in Europe."

"Your race continues in the original state."

"Now is that nice, Charlie?"

"I don't have to be nice to anyone," Charlie said. "I am a prince."

"My! Aren't we the snotty little brat!"

"Would you like to lose your head with that kind of talk? But I choose to care not for your opinion. Only that you came. It was written, of course."

"The amulet? The woman? She said her man had found the trinket in the Valley of Chauxtl. He refused to speak to us, that man of hers, and drew her away. Never mind. Our blood sang. We came to the valley, certain in our sense of discovery. As if an unseen finger pointed the way, we found the mini-pyramid . . . all this was written?"

"On the scrolls of Cacacluthcin," Charlie said as if he were about to pat back a yawn.

"I have never heard of the scrolls, Charlie."

"Your ignorance is deplorable."

"The scrolls . . . you must tell me . . ."

"I am beginning to feel bored," Charlie said.

And with that, there was a confused blurring in the dream. Where was Dr. Pangborn? The tough old archeologist should be here. No . . . he was on his way to Guatemala City and medical attention. He'd tripped on rubble and fractured his right arm badly at the dig site yesterday. Bitterly disappointed, he would have to leave the site almost at the moment of discovery. He'd picked two of the Indian laborers to accompany him in one of the Land Rovers. He'd argued against Marla staying at the site in his absence. She had accepted none of that nonsense. She'd explored digs from Angkor Wat to the Indus. She was armed and could shoot as well as any professional guide. She had four of the labor crew remaining with her, recruits from the hardy Qhotan tribe. She had the second Land Rover and plenty of supplies. Abandon the site for even a precious hour? Never on your life! She would have the mini-pyramid half cleared and catalogued when Dr. Pangborn returned with his arm in a cast a few days from now.

She stirred. She would explain the situation. "Charlie . . ."

But he was gone.

A light slashed her eyes, a silence crashed against her ears, and Marla Stone reared up on her canvas cot fighting for a breath. She clutched the cot railing during the moment her mind was sorting dream from reality. . . .

For eleven days they had worked their way along a dim Indian trail that wound through the valley, at one point fording the shallow stream called Chauxtl.

"The fellow who found the amulet had to come down this trail," Dr. Pangborn had reasoned. "At some point he turned aside to forage for food—and found the artifact." He'd scanned the primeval terrain, stretches of lowland jungle broken here and there by volcanic outcroppings. "Thank heaven for the Land Rovers!"

The twelfth day, ranging south of the trail, Marla's experienced gaze had noted the unnatural contours of a viny tangle. She'd slammed the Land Rover to a halt, jumped from the seat, and, assisted by two of the Indian crew, parted the morass of dead and green vines. Then she was whipping out the walkie-talkie antenna and gasping into the mike, "Dr. Pangborn . . . quickly! I've found rubble, ruins . . ."

By nightfall, they'd dropped exhausted at the campsite cleared and readied by a pair of the Qhotans. "Hardly anything left," Dr. Pangborn had said. "The jungle has reclaimed the farmlands, the streets, but it must have been a bustling little community, about three thousand years ago."

Hardly anything left . . . little had he known, that first night. The next day, today . . . no, now it was yesterday, Marla had discovered the small pyramid, a weedy crown on a low promontory east of the ruins. In an unreal haze of excitement, their machetes had hacked, their shovels and pickaxes had clanged, their levers had pried. "Carefully now . . ." And when the weathered limestone slab slid away, opening the cramped smallness of the entrance, their electric torches had probed into a three-thousand-year-old darkness . . . fingering the rearing statue of a feathered snake, limestone jars of food, delicately wrought pottery—and a low stone bier, sheeted with beaten gold, where a small boy and girl had lain side by side for three millenia.

It had been a moment beyond words, of simply staring and savoring a delicious giddiness. The immediate aftermath had been far less pleasant, Dr. Pangborn tripping, falling in the outside rubble as he'd rushed off for tools and camera. Sitting up with his creased, tough old face white from shock, cradling the broken arm with his left hand.

After his departure, Marla had worked inside the tomb, setting ranging poles, taking detailed pictures, calipering measurements, choosing samplings for carbon-14 dating. At day's end, she'd given the order for the removal of the little boy mummy. An obsessive desire to have him near had built within her. She ordered him placed on a low folding table in her tent.

Now, staring at the brightness of a new day that showed silver bands about the tent flap, her body steadied as the residue of the dream about Charlie faded.

She snapped her face about. Charlie of course was still there, right where they'd placed him. A tingling sensation began to crawl through her, unpleasantly. His sharp-visaged, blackened and saturnine little face was turned toward her, as if she was being studied by the black nothingness of the eyes. Charlie had moved during the night . . .

She sat stupefied, swallowing a dust-dryness. Am I losing my mind? She jerked her gaze away. In a froth, she thought: My imagination . . . whipped up to too fine an edge by the discovery of the tomb, Dr. Pangborn's accident, the sense of isolation after he was gone, the bone-rattling tiredness from too long a day, the dream. Cool it, Marla.

She swung her feet from the cot and reached for her hiking boots. They were atop the footlocker at the head of the cot. She upended the chukkas and shook, making sure a scorpion hadn't taken up squatter's rights. She had slept in poplin walking shorts and shirt after a tired sponging in the eddies of a nearby pool, where a rock formation partially dammed the stream.

Bending to fasten her shoe straps, she began to feel the quietness of the day. Too quiet. No sounds of movement. No back-and-forth banter in the Qhotan dialect.

She flung back the tent flap. The clearing lay before her. Empty. The small, two-man sleeping tents crouched limply. The portable table and folding canvas chairs, the Coleman stove, the pair of lanterns, the tins of food and water canteens were all arranged neatly in the center of the clearing, like a parting message from the departed Qhotans. They had abandoned her, but stolen nothing.

She clung to the tent post. Why? What had caused the secretive slipping away of nonthieves in the night?

She took comfort from the sight of the remaining Land Rover and the gasoline cans lashed to its rear. She didn't relish the thought of the trip out alone, but she could manage. Rejoin Dr. Pangborn in Guatemala City. Recruit a fresh crew. Be back here in a matter of a few days.

And leave Charlie? Charlie and the little girl mummy who continued her eternal sleep in the small pyramid?

No way. The first passing native would help himself to everything at the deserted campsite. Including Charlie. Charlie would be passed from hand to hand, trader to trader, until he finally arrived at . . . where? Some tourist-trap curio shop?

Charlie and the little girl . . . archeological discovery of the century. Their pyramid, their embalming and wrapping reflected Egyptian influence. Here were first proofs at last of the theory Marla had long held, that Mayan civilization did not magically appear on the Yucatán peninsula a thousand years before Christ. Civilization was an inheritable, loanable, borrowable product of the

human family. As in the case of Sumerian to Greek to
Roman to northern European civilization of another cut
had spread from Egypt to the western edges of Africa
and across the Atlantic on the wings of the westerlies.
Modern adventurers had reproduced the ancient boats of
reed and wood and retraced long-forgotten routes across
both major oceans. Perhaps the tales of Egyptian forebears had been told in Mayan writings. Who could say?
The Spanish conquistadores had destroyed Mayan libraries as works of the devil, and the surviving remnants of
Mayan literature had not yet been deciphered.

Marla turned, her mind zeroing on plans for loading
the Land Rover. She wouldn't need much food. Little
water. In the valleys between the towering volcanic
peaks, Guatemala was verdant and well-watered. Lakes
glittered in extinct volcanic craters. Streams spilled for
miles down through thick green bowers to feed the lower-
level jungles of hardwood, sapodilla, cacao, wild orchids,
morasses of vines, wild bananas, underbrush, mangrove.

"Well, Charlie, I propose we take a ride, you and I
and the little princess."

Standing over the gargoylean little mummy, she once
more experienced the senseless sensation that he'd moved,
was about to move.

Vagrant thoughts flicked, like impossible, out-of-sea-
son fireflies. Modern man . . . devotion to a materialism
he called science. Ancient Egypt . . . far longer, through
nearly forty dynasties, more than three thousand years
devoted to the study of death, afterdeath, a nonmaterial-
ism called science. . . . A person . . . lump of chemicals?
. . . or the weightless force called Life?

Charlie, so small, so incredibly long in the tomb. Was
he the repository of a power as unknown to Dr. Pangborn as electricity had been to Charlie's parents?

There were wheat kernels . . . yes, taken from an
Egyptian tomb . . . that began to grow when exposed to
fresh air and sunlight.

He's not a wheat kernel. He's a mummy.

And what is a mummy? We're making mummies right
now in the good old U.S. of A. Not many. One now and

then. Someone who believes and can afford the expenses of believing. Sufferers from incurable diseases frozen solid in tanks of liquid nitrogen to await the day of revival when the cures have been achieved. Mummies all, whether swathed in linen strips or nitrous ice. So what are the chances of it working? Maybe the secret doubters had asked the same question the day Charlie was sealed in total darkness to await his day.

" 'Allo!"

Marla gasped and slammed upright against the canvas slope of the tent.

Nothing. Silence.

"My God, have I started hearing voices?"

" 'Allo in there. Don't let me frighten you. It is I, a friend."

She let out a breath, lifted the heavy thirty-ought-six repeating rifle from its tent-pole sling, and stepped outside. Framed against the tent, she was an attractive image, lithe, leggy, tanned. Nicely put together face. Tousled, short black hair. And capable looking. Even dangerous, with the rifle cradled in the crook of her elbow.

The man in the center of the clearing looked at the gun and stood cautiously, making no move. He was an Indian of about thirty-five, lean, fit, light-toned mahagony. He looked rather ordinary in rough white-gray blouse and pantaloon, huaraches, and straw hat with a wide, floppy brim. Rather commonplace—except for the black reflections in the large, almond-shaped eyes.

"I am Somato," he said. He moved his right hand in a small gesture. "Please . . . the gun . . ."

"The gun is no threat," Marla said, "to my friends."

"I am that. Verdad! Your friend." He peeled the hat off the thick, coarse Indian hair and bent his body in a bow.

His movement dangled a fine golden neck chain. Marla's hands tightened on the gun. Sunlight caught in the swing of his neck chain amulet, the crest of the god Kukulcan. Older than three thousand years, Kukulcan was today's god in the hidden corners of Guatemala.

"I chanced upon one of your people," Somato said.

Liar, Marla thought; I'll bet you have watched us for days, priest of Kukulcan. And you came out of the night and spoke a word, and the Qhotans all ran away.

"The man I met," Somato ventured a step closer, "told me of your discoveries—and the accident. It is an evil place. Was his arm badly broken?"

"Yes."

"Too bad. All my wishes for his good health."

"Thank you. Now, I have a great deal to do."

"Is is not always so? I will be of help."

She shifted the gun an inch. "I can manage."

His intense gaze lifted from the gun barrel. "But I insist! You are the stranger, in my land. How can I be other than . . . how you say . . . hospitable?"

"You speak English quite well."

"I am in and out of Mazatenango where there are English speakers. I learn everything I can. I am interested in all things. Can I help being interested in your safety?" His face hovered, innocuous, foolish, except for the eyes.

His veiled threat brought a silence. Studying him, Marla knew he was here for a purpose and was not going to be easily discouraged. He appeared to be unarmed, even though men did not travel these remote pathways defenseless. He'd stashed machete or gun close by, wanting to allay quick fears or suspicions by making an unarmed appearance.

She felt the weight of the rifle for reassurance. Once the Land Rover was loaded, she would drive off and leave him, at gunpoint. No matter how tireless his legs, he could never overtake a motor vehicle.

Meanwhile, was he alone?

Somato had drawn several steps closer under her sharp, cold-eyed gaze. His perfect teeth flashed as he smiled.

"Please," he spread his hands, "you must accept my friendship. This is no place for a lone woman. You are surely self-reliant. But you are also—if I may say—very attractive. There are men without principles who would

. . . well, you know what I mean. It would be my pleasure to help you secure the camp and drive you out in the Land Rover."

He flung up a palm as she started to speak. "Not so," he said amiably, "I will not hear any ladylike protests. Later, you and Dr. Pangborn can return with a fresh crew of diggers. Perhaps, then, you will have friendly thoughts of Somato."

Don't force the issue prematurely, she cautioned herself. Don't paint either yourself or him into a corner. You must have time to prepare for departure.

She seemed to relax. Her lips hinted a smile. "Have you had breakfast, Señor Somato? I haven't."

His friendly laugh rang out. He rushed to the camp table in the center of the clearing. "It is my pleasure!" His hands darted about the tinned goods. "Would you have some sausage? Flapjacks with honey?"

"I said I hadn't had breakfast. I didn't say I was very hungry."

"Ah, but coffee! By all means. I see you have Guatemalan coffee, the rich dark beans grown high on the mountain slopes." He began pumping up pressure in the small fuel tank of the Coleman stove.

She kept him in the periphery of her vision as she washed up from a tin basin outside her tent and brushed the night-tousle from the dark thickness of her hair.

The clearing filled with the pleasant aroma of coffee, and a tin cup was before her, steaming, as she sat down across the table from him.

"Must you keep the gun on your knees, señorita?"

"Yes," she said, "I must."

He rocked back, relaxed, good-natured, seemingly indolent. "So be it. I have no fears, although I am a gentle man and the sight of firearms I find unpleasant. You would use the gun only in—how you say—extreme circumstances. Against an enemy. And I am your friend."

He was, at least, another human presence, and the coffee warmed a chill that was in her despite the growing heat of the humid day.

He looked at her over the rim of his coffee cup. "You found the pyramid."

A quick alarm flicked through her. The artifacts still in the pyramid . . . the little girl mummy . . . had Somato already . . .

He read her thought in her eyes, and broke in: "I have touched nothing, señorita. I have not entered the tomb. You should not have done so. The tomb never should have been opened."

"Why not?"

He shrugged. "There are words best never spoken, deeds best left undone, dark places best without light."

"Perhaps, in some cases. But this time, Señor Somato, I'm sure you are wrong."

He studied her, a flicker of regret in his deep, glistening eyes. "How was it you came to this place, señorita?"

"In the course of my work."

"But the world is wide. There are so many places you could explore. Why the lowlands of Guatemala?"

"I've been interested in Mayan culture, at long range, for a long time," she said. "Dr. Pangborn of course is the authority on Mayan antiquities. I met him several years ago when he was in the United States on a lecture tour and I was doing postgrad work. We corresponded, reams of it, while I did a lot of work in various places. Finally, the opportunity . . . and I came to Guatemala. It's a lovely country, Señor Somato—the ancient volcanic cones that tower thirteen thousand feet, the lushness of the lowlands. Beauty and mystery everywhere, in the jungle wilderness, in the tucked-away tribes untouched by time. Much beauty—except for the poverty."

"The poor continue," he said. "The rich, the kings, the powerful, they come, they enjoy, they go. The poor are forever. You must be very rich, renting expensive Land Rovers, equipping an expedition."

"I wish I were. Truth is, I joined Dr. Pangborn through a complicated morass of red tape. There was some grant money available at the National Endowment. There was a board of trustees who might have access to some of the money. There was a blooming army of

bureaucrats in Washington who had to be convinced that
a dig in Guatemala would be worth the price tag. You
have to hang in there, cut the tapes one at a time."

Somato lifted the pot from the Coleman burner and
topped off their cups. "Now you will be famous—if you
succeed in making your revelation to the world."

He was begging her, and he was warning her. She must
not take Charlie away. But, she thought, there will be a
revelation only if I get Charlie out. Without hard evidence, Dr. Pangborn and I will have told only a wives'
tale. And if I mess up this chance, there will never be
another. Before another expedition can return there'll be
no pyramid, no Charlie, no little girl mummy. Somato
can bring in a crew and wipe away the evidence, the
really important evidence, almost overnight.

"How do you call the little mummy?" he asked. "The
Qhotan I met and talked with said you have named him
Charlie."

"Why do you ask?"

"Curious. Is there a symbolism?"

He is attuned to symbolism, she thought, this priest of
an ageless religion. His omens and portents are everywhere, in the brassiness of a sky before a storm, in the
image of a feathered serpent, in the steaming entrails of
a sacrificial animal.

She shifted uncomfortably, feeling the total, uncross-
able gulf between herself and Somato. Aliens. Products
of diametric culture patterns. They might have been
beings from diverse planets meeting in this jungle clearing. Each thought of the other as a child of superstition.
And what was superstition? Space and time were absolute—until Einstein dismissed the absurd superstition.
Would the science of Einstein endure through a period
of nearly forty dynasties? Where did one superstition end
and another begin? Space was space, until a black hole
was discovered in it.

"No symbolism," she answered his question at last. "I
really don't know why I called the little fellow Charlie.
There was a ventriloquist's dummy in the United States,
very famous, named Charlie McCarthy. About the same

size as the mummy. There, the resemblance stops. In the hands of his creator, Mr. Bergen, Charlie McCarty was a happy, very nice little fellow . . ."

"I would like to see the mummy," Somato said, already on his feet. He started across the clearing toward Marla's tent.

She pushed up. "Señor Somato . . ."

Ignoring her, he stepped inside the tent. She ran across the short distance, hands firm on the rifle, and drew up in the inverted V of the tent opening. He had not touched Charlie. He was crouched over the mummy, fingering the amulet on his neck chain and murmuring soft and strange sounds under his breath. As their eyes locked and held, the eyes of Somato and the mummy, Marla caught her breath. It had to be a trick of the lighting, of her imagination. . . . The change in Charlie's eyes was not a glint of Life, not as she knew it. The expanding pupils were a blackness without bottom, a nothingness expression of anti-Life, anti-Light, anti-Spirit.

She backed off, holding the gun in desperately tight fingers, watching Somato. He haunched away from the mummy's side, tore his gaze away, and pushed to his feet. He slipped out into the sunlight and stood on spread, unsteady legs, wiping a hot, oily sheen from his brown face with a bandanna.

"He is Queaxtouxtl," he whispered.

"What?" she asked, keeping a safe distance between Somato and the rifle. "He is who?"

"The little prince from the seed of darkness. The Others . . . they fashioned him and the sister who would be his wife. The children grew like any children—until one day they drank of some water and sickened and died."

"Who were The Others?"

Somato pressed his wadded bandanna against his mouth for a moment. He lowered it slowly. "No one knows. It is said they came from beyond the stars. They came in a black bubble that ate the light. They had no shape or form. They made the two children in the image of our ancestors and went away in their black bubble. . . .

It is our legend, handed down through a thousand generations of Kukulcanites."

So was Troy a legend, Marla thought, until somebody thought of digging at the site.

Easing back, she glanced at shafted sunlight in the green of the surrounding jungle. She heard the rustling of a soft breeze. Reassuring realities.

She let herself slip close to the tent flap on a strange compulsion to put herself between Somato and Charlie. "Sometime I'd like to hear the rest of the legend, the details. But right now I must get started."

Somato nodded. "I will start striking the tents."

She started to speak, but he was rushing across the clearing. She watched as he went to one knee and detached the rope anchor from a tent peg.

She had a sense of moving. She saw the loss of sunlight as the shadows within her tent flowed over her. She turned and looked at Charlie. Ugly . . . ugly . . . so ugly he was cute . . . strangely winsome . . . such a defenseless little fellow . . .

She was on her knees beside him. "Charlie . . ."

She imagined a faint stirring of a tattered end among the dessicated wrappings across his chest. She groped a hand backward without taking her eyes from Charlie, feeling through the clutter of a tool chest. She lifted out a calipers. Bit by bit she measured Charlie, repeating the procedure she'd effected yesterday when Charlie had been in his tomb. Fingers, toes, sole to ankle, ankle to knee, knee to hip, fibulal, tibial, femural, ulnal, humerusal.

The rifle lay forgotten. Her mind computerized figures, comparisons of minute variations of measurements. She crouched back on her haunches, hands worrying the calipers while she stared at Charlie.

Growing . . . was he actually beginning to *grow?*

A slight sound caught through her. Marla whirled her face about. Somato's shadow filled the tent opening.

"So you are beginning to understand?" he said in a tight voice. "You must give me the little fellow."

"Charlie? Let you destroy Charlie? You idiot! You don't realize the importance—"

As she snarled out the words, she was grasping for the gun, clutching it, rearing up to her feet. But the Indian was very fast. His shadow enveloped her. His fist caught her on the jaw. Her senses spun. Somato's sweating, set face went out of focus. He had caught hold of the gun. She clung to the weapon, wrestling backward.

Somato's fist crashed hard against her chin. And his face disappeared altogether.

The darkness held; then shards of pain knifed through, a throbbing in her jaw, a pounding in her head. A soft cry parted her lips. Gritty light pushed the darkness away. She pushed up, and a wave of nausea washed through her. She hung on, half risen, propped by stiffened, extended arms. She pulled her face about and looked at the emptiness where Charlie had lain. A wild urgency swept her mind to clarity. Adrenalin poured forth.

Where had Somato taken Charlie? Insane priest of an ancient heathen religion . . . superstition-ridden anachronism who hadn't the slightest idea of what he was doing . . .

She looked quickly about for the gun, and saw it. It was lying on the ground in the back part of the tent. She made a quick movement, then stopped. The gun was twisted, bent. Somato had smashed it across the edge of the foot locker.

Her lips thinned. Okay, pally. She ran outside to the Land Rover, flipped open the narrow metal carrier bolted to its side, and lifted out the one remaining gun. It, too, was a thirty-ought-six. She checked the load and stood scanning the empty campsite. The lowlands jungle about her was suddenly very vast. Colors sprang at her, splotches of yellows, reds, purples strewn through the density of green and brown vines, trellises, thickets and trees. Somato's territory. How could she ever find him?

She worked her way along the perimeter of the clearing, straining for the sight of any hint, a broken twig, a crushed wildflower.

Even in her sharp-eyed state, she almost missed it, almost passed it up. She backed a step, looked a second time, and her hand shot out. Her fingers touched the tiny fragment of decayed mummy-wrapping that clung to a thorn.

As her fingers lifted and ground the bit of decayed cloth to dust, her eyes studied the narrowness where the undergrowth seemed less dense. She shifted the rifle from shoulder strap to two-handed grip and plunged into the pathway.

The dim trail led north, away from the lazy little river, toward higher ground. At times there seemed to be no trail at all, only a burrow through slashing briars and trailing vines. Her breath began to cut into her lungs; she felt the weight of her sweat-blackened shirt with its smothering stickiness. Salty droplets stung the corners of her eyes.

Her vision began to fuzz. She stumbled now and then as she pushed her way through wall after wall of yielding greenery. A great mass of bright plumage on a tree limb far ahead screamed out her foolishness at her.

She half tripped and stayed on her knees, using the rifle as a prop, butt on the ground, her exhausted fingers grasping the end of the barrel near the front sight. Perhaps the screeching macaw was right. She was beaten. She would never see Charlie again. And before Somato let her leave the jungle the little girl mummy would have vanished also.

Ease down . . . just for a moment . . . close your eyes . . . let the touch of a green fern cool your cheek . . .

The macaw was suddenly silent.

Marla lifted her head. What was different? What had changed? She drew a shallow breath, then a deeper one. The air . . . the faintest taint of smoke-smell was in the air.

She pushed downward on the rifle, climbing to her feet. The cessation of the giant parrot's outcries had left an unreal silence, a stillness, a hush.

A twig snapped with a sharp, clear sound as Marla pressed forward. A hundred yards up a steepening slope, and the smoke-smell was stronger. She picked her way, stepping over vines and gnarled upcroppings of giant roots, ducking and brushing her way through twilight patches where the sunlight was shut out.

She saw the first red wink of flame through heavy foliage ahead, and dropped into a crouch, moving on carefully.

She parted a green and pink thicket that smelled of honeysuckle. The cautious movement revealed to her a rocky and volcanic-ash clearing where strata had buckled and thrust when the earth was young. Somato was there, facing away from Marla, backing away a few steps from the heat of his fire. Its first crackling had become a continuous roar. The flames were spewing up to a height equaling Somato's own.

He nodded, as if in satisfaction. He turned, and for a fractured moment it seemed that he looked directly at Marla's face as it hovered in the thicket.

But he was focusing elsewhere. And straining up and forward, Marla saw Charlie. She saw Somato close the distance in half a dozen strides. She saw Somato pick up Charlie. Somato turned once more toward the voracious fire, his face white beneath its brown, his lips moving in frantic supplication.

Legs spread, back arched, Somato slowly lifted Charlie overhead, higher, yet higher, to the full extension of his arms.

And through the roar of the flames Marla listened, as if to a whisper. She heard it, but did not hear it. She felt it, and it was not less real. Charlie was mewling a cry for help, a piteous plea for mercy, a broken note of terror of the flames.

"Somato!"

Somato spun about, holding Charlie high, seeing her tear her way through the brush at the edge of the clearing.

"You were about to throw Charlie into the fire! You heathen . . . you superstitious fool!"

Slightly crouched, she padded toward him. He stared at the gun in her hands, his tongue rimming his dry lips.

"I? I the fool? You know nothing, señorita, only what your microscopes tell you . . . but when you look at brain tissue do you see a thought?"

"Put him down, Somato."

"I will die first. We both may die anyway. He is of the black seed. That part of the legend you heard. The rest you did not. The blackness in him . . ."

"No more, Somato! I will not listen to any more of this nonsense!"

"Then watch as I do what must be done." He turned, for a moment a regal figure in his peon's rough, ill-fitting cotton clothing.

His arms tensed for the casting, the hurling of Charlie into the inferno.

The gun crashed.

Marla felt the sound split through her head. She felt the pressure of her finger on the trigger. She sensed the beating of wings and scurryings and slitherings that swept through the forest in the vane of the alien echoes.

She saw the puff of dust, almost between the shoulder blades, where the high velocity bullet entered Somato and ripped and shattered its way through.

He stumbled, twisting sideways under the impact. His arms broke under Charlie's slight weight. His knees folded. His mouth opened on an unspoken word. He broke at the middle, rolled forward and lay still.

Marla groped her way across the short, stony waste. "Charlie . . ."

She wouldn't look at Somato. She kneeled beside Charlie, turned him onto his back, brushed the smear of dust from his sunken little cheek.

"I'm here, Charlie. Right beside you."

She picked him up gently.

"It's okay, Charlie. Everything is fine now. We'll go back to camp, and no one will disturb us. It's obvious that Somato came alone."

She arose, holding him.

"We'll pretend that Somato never happened. And I'll bring her to you, out of the pyramid, the little girl who belongs at your side."

She turned in the direction of her campsite and walked across the clearing. As Charlie's black-hole eyes passed, the light dimmed faintly. So faintly that Marla's eyes didn't see. The shift in the spectrum was too slight for any human eyes to note.

She carried Charlie away in the maternal cradle of her arms, pressing him tightly to her breast. And his little black-claw hand was curled slightly, childishly, as if to grip her shoulder. But perhaps it was only her own walking motion that caused his hand to do that.

IF THE RED SLAYER

by *Robert Sheckley*

I won't even try to describe the pain. I'll just say that it was unbearable even with anesthetics, and that I bore it because I didn't have any choice. Then it faded away and I opened my eyes and looked into the faces of the brahmins standing over me. There were three of them, dressed in the usual white operating gowns and white gauze masks. They say they wear those masks to keep germs out of us. But every soldier knows they wear them so we can't recognize them.

I was still doped up to the ears on anesthetics, and only chunks and bits of my memory were functioning. I asked, "How long was I dead?"

"About ten hours," one of the brahmins told me.

"How did I die?"

"Don't you remember?" the tallest brahmin asked.

"Not yet."

"Well," the tallest brahmin said, "you were with your platoon in Trench 2645B-4. At dawn your entire company made a frontal attack, trying to capture the next trench. Number 2645B-5."

"And what happened?" I asked.

"You stopped a couple of machine gun bullets. The new kind with the shock heads. Remember now? You took one in the chest and three more in the legs. When the medics found you, you were dead."

"Did we capture the trench?" I asked.

"No. Not this time."

"I see." My memory was returning rapidly as the anesthetic wore off. I remembered the boys in my platoon. I remembered our trench. Old 2645B-4 had been my home for over a year, and it was pretty nice as trenches go. The enemy had been trying to capture it, and our dawn assault had been a counter-attack, really. I remembered the machine gun bullets tearing me into shreds, and the wonderful relief I had felt when they did. And I remembered something else too . . .

I sat upright. "Hey, just a minute!" I said.

"What's the matter?"

"I thought eight hours was the upper limit for bringing a man back to life."

"We've improved our techniques since then," one of the brahmins told me. "We're improving them all the time. Twelve hours is the upper limit now, just as long as there isn't serious brain damage."

"Good for you," I said. Now my memory had returned completely, and I realized what had happened. "However, you made a serious mistake in bringing *me* back."

"What's the beef, soldier?" one of them asked in that voice only officers get.

"Read my dogtags," I said.

He read them. His forehead, which was all I could see of his face, became wrinkled. He said, "This *is* unusual!"

"Unusual!" I said.

"You see," he told me, "you were in a whole trench full of dead men. We were told they were all first-timers. Our orders were to bring the whole batch back to life."

"And you didn't read any dogtags first?"

"We were overworked. There wasn't time. I really am sorry, Private. If I'd known—"

"To hell with that," I said. "I want to see the Inspector General."

"Do you really think—"

"Yes I do," I said. "I'm no trench lawyer, but I've got a real beef. It's my right to see the I.G."

They went into a whispered conference, and I looked myself over. The brahmins had done a pretty good job on me. Not as good as they did in the first years of the war, of course. The skin grafts were sloppier now, and I felt a little scrambled inside. Also my right arm was about two inches longer than the left; bad joiner-work. Still, it was a pretty good job.

The brahmins came out of their conference and gave me my clothes. I dressed. "Now, about the Inspector General," one of them said. "That's a little difficult right now. You see—"

Needless to say, I didn't see the I.G. They took me to see a big, beefy, kindly old Master Sergeant. One of those understanding types who talks to you and makes everything all right. Except that I wasn't having any.

"Now, now, Private," the kindly old sarge said. "What's this I hear about you kicking up a fuss about being brought back to life?"

"You heard correct," I said. "Even a private soldier has his rights under the Articles of War. Or so I've been told."

"He certainly does," said the kindly old sarge.

"I've done my duty," I said. "Seventeen years in the army, eight years in combat. Three times killed, three times brought back. The orders read that you can requisition death after the third time. That's what I did, and it's stamped on my dogtags. But I wasn't *left* dead. Those damned medics brought me back to life again, and it isn't fair. I want to stay dead."

"It's much better staying alive," the sarge said. "Alive, you always have a chance of being rotated back to non-combat duties. Rotation isn't working very fast on account of the man-power shortage. But there's still a chance."

"I know," I said. "But I think I'd just as soon stay dead."

"I think I could promise you that in six months or so—"

"I want to stay dead," I said firmly. "After the third time, it's my privilege under the Articles of War."

"Of course it is," the kindly old sarge said, smiling at me, one soldier to another. "But mistakes happen in wartime. Especially in a war like this." He leaned back and clasped his hands behind his head. "I remember when the thing started. It sure looked like a pushbutton affair when it started. But both us and the Reds had a full arsenal of anti-missile-missiles, and that pretty well deadlocked the atomic stuff. The invention of the atomic damper clinched it. That made it a real infantry affair."

"I know, I know."

"But our enemies outnumbered us," the kindly old sarge said.

"They still do. All those millions and millions of Russians and Chinese! We had to have more fighting men. We had to at least hold our own. That's why the medics started reviving the dead."

"I know all this. Look, Sarge, I want us to win. I want it bad. I've been a good soldier. But I've been killed three times, and—"

"The trouble is," the sarge said, "the Reds are reviving their dead, too. The struggle for manpower in the front lines is crucial *right now*. The next few months will tell the tale, one way or the other. So why not forget about all this? The next time you're killed, I can promise you'll be left alone. So let's overlook it this time."

"I want to see the Inspector General," I said.

"All right, Private," the kindly old sarge said, in a not very friendly tone. "Go to Room 303."

I went to 303, which was an outer office, and I waited. I was feeling sort of guilty about all the fuss I was kicking up. After all, there was a war on. But I was angry, too. A soldier has his rights, even in a war. Those damned brahmins . . .

It's funny how they got that name. They're just medics, not Hindus or Brahmins or anything like that. They got the name because of a newspaper article a couple years ago, when all this was new. The guy who wrote the article told about how the medics could revive dead men now, and make them combat-worthy. It was pretty hot stuff then. The writer quoted a poem by Emerson. The poem starts out—

If the red slayer thinks he slays,
  Or if the slain thinks he is
  slain,
They know not well the subtle
  always.
I keep, and pass, and turn
  again.

That's how things were. You could never know, when you killed a man, whether he'd stay dead, or be back in the trenches shooting at you the next day. And you didn't know whether you'd stay dead or not if you got killed. Emerson's poem was called "Brahma," so our medics got to be called brahmins.

Being brought back to life wasn't bad at first. Even with the pain, it was good to be alive. But you finally reach a time when you get tired of being killed and brought back and killed and brought back. You start wondering how many deaths you owe your country, and if it might not be nice and restful staying dead a while. You look forward to the long sleep.

The authorities understood this. Being brought back too often was bad for morale. So they set three revivals as the limit. After the third time you could choose rotation or permanent death. The authorities preferred you to choose death; a man who's been dead three times has a very bad effect on the morale of civilians. And most combat soldiers preferred to stay dead after the third time.

But I'd been cheated. I had been brought back to life for the fourth time. I'm as patriotic as the next man, but this I wasn't going to stand for.

At last I was allowed to see the Inspector-General's adjutant. He was a colonel, a thin, gray, no-nonsense type. He'd already been briefed on my case, and he wasted no time on me. It was a short interview.

"Private," he said, "I'm sorry about this, but new orders have been issued. The Reds have increased their rebirth rate, and we have to match them. The standing order now is six revivals before retirement.

"But that order hadn't been issued at the time I was killed."

"It's retroactive," he said. "You have two deaths to go. Good-bye and good luck, Private."

And that was it. I should have known you can't get anywhere with top brass. They don't know how things are. They rarely get killed more than once, and they just don't understand how a man feels after four times. So I went back to my trench.

I walked back slowly, past the poisoned barbed wire, thinking hard. I walked past something covered with a khaki tarpaulin stenciled *Secret Weapon*. Our sector is filled with secret weapons. They come out about once a week, and maybe one of them will win the war.

But right now I didn't care. I was thinking about the next stanza of that Emerson poem. It goes:

> Far or forgot to me is near;
>   Shadow and sunlight are the
>   same;
> The vanished gods to me appear;
>   And one to me are shame and
>   fame.

Old Emerson got it pretty right, because that's how it is after your fourth death. Nothing makes any difference, and everything seems pretty much the same. Don't get me wrong, I'm no cynic. I'm just saying that a man's viewpoint is bound to change after he's died four times.

At last I reached good old Trench 2645B-4, and greeted all the boys. I found out we were attacking again at dawn. I was still thinking.

I'm no quitter, but I figured four times dead was enough. In this attack, I decided I'd make sure I stayed dead. There would be no mistakes this time.

We moved out at first light, past the barbed wire and the rolling mines, into the no-man's-land between our trench and 2645B-5. This attack was being carried out in battalion strength, and we were all armed with the new homing bullets. We moved along pretty briskly for a while. Then the enemy really opened up.

We kept on gaining ground. Stuff was blowing up all around me, but I hadn't a scratch yet. I started to think we would make it this time. Maybe I wouldn't get killed.

Then I got it. An explosive bullet through the chest. Definitely a mortal wound. Usually after something like that hits you, you stay down. But not me. I wanted to make sure of staying dead this time. So I picked myself up and staggered forward, using my rifle as a crutch. I made another fifteen yards in the face of the damnedest cross-fire you've ever seen. Then I got it, and got it right. There was no mistaking it on this round.

I felt the explosive bullet slam into my forehead. There was the tiniest fraction of a second in which I could feel my brains boiling out, and I knew I was safe this time. The brahmins couldn't do anything about serious head injuries, and mine was really serious.

Then I died.

I recovered consciousness and looked up at the brahmins in their white gowns and gauze masks.

"How long was I dead?" I asked.

"Two hours."

Then I remembered. "But I got it in the head!"

The gauze masks wrinkled, and I knew they were grinning. "Secret weapon," one of them told me. "It's been in the works for close to three years. At last we and the engineers perfected a de-scrambler. Tremendous invention!"

"Yeah?" I said.

"At last medical science can treat serious head injuries," the brahmin told me. "Or any other kind of injury. We can bring any man back now, just as long as we can collect seventy percent of his pieces and feed them to the de-scrambler. This is really going to cut down our losses. It may turn the tide of the whole war!"

"That's fine," I said.

"By the way," the brahmin told me, "you've been awarded a medal for your heroic advance under fire after receiving a mortal wound."

"That's nice," I said. "Did we take 2645B-5?"

"We took it this time. We're massing for an assault against Trench 2645B-6."

I nodded, and in a little while I was given my clothes and sent back to the front. Things have quieted down now, and I must admit it's kind of a pleasant to be alive. Still, I think I've had all I want of it.

Now I've got just one more death to go before I'll have my six.

If they don't change the orders again.

THE CHARNEL GOD

by *Clark Ashton Smith*

"Mordiggian is the god of Zul-Bha-Sair," said the inn-keeper with unctuous solemnity. "He has been the god from years that are lost to man's memory in shadow deeper than the subterranes of his black temple. There is no other god in Zul-Bha-Sair. And all who die within the walls of the city are sacred to Mordiggian. Even the kings and the optimates, at death, are delivered into the hands of his muffled priests. It is the law and the custom. A little while, and the priests will come for your bride."

"But Elaith is not dead," protested the youth Phariom for the third or fourth time, in piteous desperation. "Her malady is one that assumes the lying likeness of death. Twice before has she lain insensible, with a pallor upon her cheeks, and a stillness in her very blood, that could hardly be distinguished from those of the tomb; and twice she has awakened after an interim of days."

The inn-keeper peered with an air of ponderous unbelief at the girl who lay white and motionless as a mown lily on the bed in the poorly furnished attic chamber.

"In that case you should not have brought her into Zul-Bha-Sair," he averred in a tone of owlish irony. "The physician has pronounced her dead; and her death has been reported to the priests. She must go to the temple of Mordiggian."

"But we are outlanders, guests of a night. We have come from the land of Xylac, far in the north; and this morning we should have gone on through Tasuun, toward Pharaad, the capital of Yoros, which lies near to the southern sea. Surely your god could have no claim upon Elaith, even if she were truly dead."

"All who die in Zul-Bha-Sair are the property of Mordiggian," insisted the taverner sententiously. "Outlanders are not exempt. The dark maw of his temple yawns eternally, and no man, no child, no woman, throughout the years, has evaded its yawning. All mortal flesh must become, in due time, the provender of the god."

Phariom shuddered at the oily and portentous declaration.

"Dimly have I heard of Mordiggian, as a legend that travellers tell in Xylac," he admitted. "But I had forgotten the name of his city; and Elaith and I came ignorantly into Zul-Bha-Sair . . . . Even had I known, I should have doubted the terrible custom of which you inform me . . . . What manner of deity is this, who imitates the hyena and the vulture? Surely he is no god, but a ghoul."

"Take heed, lest you utter blasphemy," admonished the inn-keeper. "Mordiggian is old and omnipotent as death. He was worshipped in former continents, before the lifting of Zothique from out the sea. Through him, we are saved from corruption and the worm. Even as the people of other places devote their dead to the consuming flame, so we of Zul-Bha-Sair deliver ours to the god. Awful is the fane, a place of terror and obscure shadow untrod by the sun, into which the dead are borne by his priests and are laid on a vast table of stone to await his coming from the nether vault in which he dwells. No living men, other than priests, have ever beheld him; and the faces of the priests are hidden behind masks of silver, and even their hands are shrouded, that men may not gaze on them that have seen Mordiggian."

"But there is a king in Zul-Bha-Sair, is there not? I shall appeal to him against this heinous and horrible injustice. Surely he will heed me."

"Phenquor is the king; but he could not help you even if he wished. Your appeal will not even be heard. Mordiggian is above all kings, and his law is sacred. Hark!— for already the priests come."

Phariom, sick at heart with the charnel terror and cruelty of the doom that impended for his girlish wife in this unknown city of nightmare, heard an evil, stealthy creaking on the stairs that led to the attic of the inn. The sound drew nearer with inhuman rapidity, and four strange figures came into the room, heavily garbed in funereal purple, and wearing huge masks of silver graven in the likeness of skulls. It was impossible to surmise their actual appearance, for, even as the taverner had hinted, their very hands were concealed by fingerless gloves; and the purple gowns came down in loose folds that trailed about their feet like unwinding cerecloths. There was a horror about them, of which the macabre masks were only a lesser element; a horror that lay partly in their unnatural, crouching attitudes, and the beast-like agility with which they moved, unhampered by their cumbrous habiliments.

Among them, they carried a curious bier, made from interwoven strips of leather, and with monstrous bones that served for frame and handles. The leather was greasy and blackened as if from long years of mortuary use. Without speaking to Phariom or the innkeeper, and with no delay or formality of any sort, they advanced toward the bed on which Elaith was lying.

Undeterred by their more than formidable aspect, and wholly distraught with grief and anger, Phariom drew from his girdle a short knife, the only weapon he possessed. Disregarding the minatory cry of the taverner, he rushed wildly upon the muffled figures. He was quick and muscular, and, moreover, was clad in light, close-fitting raiment, such as would seemingly have given him a brief advantage.

The priests had turned their backs on him; but, as if they had foreseen his every action, two of them wheeled about with the swiftness of tigers, dropping the handles of bone that they carried. One of them struck the knife from Phariom's hand with a movement that the eye could barely follow in its snaky darting. Then both assailed him, beating him back with terrible flailing blows of their shrouded arms, and hurling him half across the room into an empty corner. Stunned by his fall, he lay senseless for a term of minutes.

Recovering dazedly, with eyes that blurred as he opened them, he beheld the fact of the stout taverner stooping above him like a tallow-colored moon. The thought of Elaith, more sharp than the thrust of a dagger, brought him back to agonizing consciousness. Fearfully he scanned the shadowy room, and saw that the cere-mented priests were gone, that the bed was vacant. He heard the orotund and sepulchral croaking of the tav-erner.

"The priests of Mordiggian are merciful, they make allowance for the frenzy and distraction of the newly bereaved. It is well for you that they are compassionate, and considerate of mortal weakness."

Phariom sprang erect, as if his bruised and aching body were scorched by a sudden fire. Pausing only to retrieve his knife, which still lay in the middle of the room, he started toward the door. He was stopped by the hand of the hosteler, clutching greasily at his shoulder.

"Beware, lest you exceed the bounds of the mercy of Mordiggian. It is an ill thing to follow his priests—and a worse thing to intrude upon the deathly and sacred gloom of his temple."

Phariom scarcely heard the admonition. He wrenched himself hastily away from the odious fingers and turned to go; but again the hand clutched him.

"At least, pay me the money that you owe for food and lodging, ere you depart," demanded the innkeeper. "Also, there is the matter of the physician's fee, which I can settle for you, if you will entrust me with the proper sum. Pay now—for there is no surety that you will return."

Phariom drew out the purse that contained his entire worldly wealth, and filled the greedily cupped palm before him with coins that he did not pause to count. With no parting word or backward glance, he descended the moldy and musty stairs of the worm-eaten hostelry, as if spurred by an incubus, and went out into the gloomy, serpentine streets of Zul-Bha-Sair.

Perhaps the city differed little from others, except in being older and darker; but to Phariom, in his extremity of anguish, the ways that he followed were like subterrene corridors that led only to some profound and monstrous charnel. The sun had risen above the overjutting houses, but it seemed to him that there was no light, other than a lost and doleful glimmering such as might descend into mortuary depths. The people, it may have been, were much like other people, but he saw them under a malefic aspect, as if they were ghouls and demons that went to and fro on the ghastly errands of a necropolis.

Bitterly, in his distraction, he recalled the previous evening, when he had entered Zul-Bha-Sair at twilight with Elaith, the girl riding on the one dromedary that had survived their passage of the northern desert, and he walking beside her, weary but content. With the rosy purple of afterglow upon its walls and cupolas, with the deepening golden eyes of its lit windows, the place had seemed a fair and nameless city of dreams, and they had planned to rest there for a day or two before resuming the long, arduous journey to Pharaad, in Yoros.

This journey had been undertaken only through necessity. Phariom, an impoverished youth of noble blood, had been exiled because of the political and religious tenets of his family, which were not in accord with those of the reigning emperor, Caleppos. Taking his newly wedded wife, Phariom had set out for Yoros, where certain allied branches of the house to which he belonged had already established themselves, and would give him a fraternal welcome.

They had travelled with a large caravan of merchants, going directly southward to Tasuun. Beyond the borders of Xylac, amid the red sands of the Celotian waste, the caravan had been attacked by robbers, who had slain many of its members and dispersed the rest. Phairom and his bride, escaping with the dromedaries, had found themselves lost and alone in the desert, and, failing to regain the road toward Tasuun, had taken inadvertently another track, leading to Zul-Bha-Sair, a walled metropolis on the southwestern verge of the waste, which their itinerary had not included.

Entering Zul-Bha-Sair, the couple had repaired for reasons of economy to a tavern in the humbler quarter. There, during the night, Elaith had been overcome by the third seizure of the cataleptic malady to which she was liable. The earlier seizures, occurring before her marriage to Phariom, had been recognized in their true character by the physicians of Xylac, and had been palliated by skilful treatment. It was hoped that the malady would not recur. The third attack, no doubt, had been induced by the fatigues and hardships of the journey. Phariom had felt sure that Elaith would recover; but a doctor of Zul-Bha-Sair, hastily summoned by the innkeeper, had insisted that she was actually dead; and, in obedience to the strange law of the city, had reported her death without delay to the priests of Mordiggian. The frantic protests of the husband had been utterly ignored.

There was, it seemed, a diabolic fatality about the whole train of circumstances through which Elaith, still living, though with that outward aspect of the tomb which her illness involved, had fallen into the grasp of the devotees of the charnel god. Phariom pondered this fatality almost to madness, as he strode with furious, aimless haste along the eternally winding and crowded streets.

To the cheerless information received from the taverner, he added, as he went on, more and more of the tardily remembered legends which he had heard in Xylac. Ill and dubious indeed was the renown of Zul-Bha-Sair, and he marvelled that he should have forgotten it, and cursed himself with black curses for the temporary but fatal forgetfulness. Better would it have been if he and Elaith had perished in the desert, rather than enter the wide gates that stood always open, gaping for their prey, as was the custom of Zul-Bha-Sair.

The city was a mart of trade, where outland travellers came, but did not care to linger, because of the repulsive cult of Mordiggian, the invisible eater of the dead, who was believed to share his provender with the shrouded priests. It was said that the bodies lay for days in the dark temple and were not devoured till corruption had begun. And people whispered of fouler things than necrophagism, of blasphemous rites that were solemnized in the ghoul-ridden vaults, and nameless uses to which the dead were put before Mordiggian claimed them. In all outlying places, the fate of those who died in Zul-Bha-Sair was a dreadful byword and a malediction. But to the people of that city, reared in the faith of the ghoul-ish god, it was merely the usual and expected mode of mortuary disposal. Tombs, graves, catacombs, funeral pyres, and other such nuisances, were rendered needless by this highly utilitarian deity.

Phariom was surprised to see the people of the city going about the common businesses of life. Porters were passing with bales of household goods upon their shoulders. Merchants were squatting in their shops like other merchants. Buyers and sellers chaffered loudly in the public bazars. Women laughed and chattered in the doorways. Only by their voluminous robes of red, black and violet, and their strange, uncouth accents, was he able to distinguish the men of Zul-Bha-Sair from those who were outlanders like himself. The murk of nightmare began to lift from his impressions; and gradually, as he went on, the spectacle of everyday humanity all about him helped to calm a little his wild distraction and desperation. Nothing could dissipate the horror of his loss, and the abominable fate that threatened Elaith. But now, with a cool logic born of the cruel exigence, he began to consider the apparently hopeless problem of rescuing her from the ghoul-god's temple.

He composed his features, and constrained his febrile pacing to an idle saunter, so that none might guess the preoccupations that racked him inwardly. Pretending to be interested in the wares of a seller of men's apparel, he drew the dealer into converse regarding Zul-Bha-Sair and its customs, and made such inquiries as a traveller from far lands might make. The dealer was talkative, and Phariom soon learned from him the location of the temple of Mordiggian, which stood at the city's core. He also learned that the temple was open at all hours, and that people were free to come and go within its precincts. There were, however, no rituals of worship, other than certain private rites that were celebrated by the priesthood. Few cared to enter the fane, because of a superstition that any living person who intruded upon its gloom would return to it shortly as the provender of the god.

Mordiggian, it seemed, was a benign deity in the eyes of the inhabitants of Zul-Bha-Sair. Curiously enough, no definite personal attributes were ascribed to him. He was, so to speak, an impersonal force akin to the elements—a consuming and cleansing power, like fire. His hierophants were equally mysterious; they lived in the temple and emerged from it only in the execution of their funereal duties. No one knew the manner of their recruiting, but many believed that they were both male and female, thus renewing their numbers from generation to generation with no ulterior commerce. Others thought that they were not human beings at all, but an order of subterranean earth-entities, who lived for ever, and who fed upon corpses like the god himself. Through this latter belief, of late years, a minor heresy had risen, some holding that Mordiggian was a mere hieratic figment, and the priests were the sole devourers of the dead. The dealer, quoting this heresy, made haste to disavow it with pious reprobation.

Phariom chatted for awhile on other topics, and then continued his progress through the city, going as forthrightly toward the temple as the obliquely running thoroughfares would permit. He had formed no conscious plan, but desired to reconnoiter the vicinage. In that which the garment-dealer had told him, the one reassuring detail was the openness of the fane and its accessibility to all who dared enter. The rarity of visitors, however, would make Phariom conspicuous, and he wished above all to avoid attention. On the other hand, any effort to remove bodies from the temple was seemingly unheard of—a thing audacious beyond the dreams of the people of Zul-Bha-Sair. Through the very boldness of his design, he might avoid suspicion, and succeed in rescuing Elaith.

The streets that he followed began to tend downward, and were narrower, dimmer and more tortuous than any he had yet traversed. He thought for awhile that he had lost his way, and he was about to ask the passers to redirect him, when four of the priests of Mordiggian, bearing one of the curious litter-like biers of bone and leather, emerged from an ancient alley just before him.

The bier was occupied by the body of a girl, and for one moment of convulsive shock and agitation that left him trembling, Phariom thought that the girl was Elaith. Looking again, he saw his mistake. The gown that the girl wore, though simple, was made of some rare exotic stuff. Her features, though pale as those of Elaith, were crowned with curls like the petals of heavy black poppies. Her beauty, warm and voluptuous even in death, differed from the blond pureness of Elaith as tropic lilies differ from narcissi.

Quietly, and maintaining a discreet interval, Phariom followed the sullenly shrouded figures and their lovely burden. He saw that people made way for the passage of the bier with awed, unquestioning alacrity; and the loud voices of hucksters and chafferers were hushed as the priests went by. Overhearing a murmured conversation between two of the townsfolk, he learned that the dead girl was Arctela, daughter of Quaos, a high noble and magistrate of Zul-Bha-Sair. She had died very quickly and mysteriously, from a cause unknown to the physicians, which had not marred or wasted her beauty in the least. There were those who held that an indetectable poison, rather than disease, had been the agency of death; and others deemed her the victim of malefic sorcery.

The priests went on, and Phariom kept them in sight as well as he could in the blind tangle of streets. The way steepened, without affording any clear prospect of the levels below, and the houses seemed to crowd more closely, as if huddling back from a precipice. Finally the youth emerged behind his macabre guides in a sort of circular hollow at the city's heart, where the temple of Mordiggian loomed alone and separate amid pavements

of sad onyx, and funerary cedars whose green had blackened as if with the undeparting charnel shadows
bequeathed by dead ages.

The edifice was built of a strange stone, hued as with
the blackish purple of carnal decay: a stone that refused
the ardent luster of noon, and the prodigality of dawn
or sunset glory. It was low and windowless, having the
form of a monstrous mausoleum. Its portals yawned
sepulchrally in the gloom of the cedars.

Phariom watched the priests as they vanished within
the portals, carrying the girl Arctela like phantoms who
bear a phantom burden. The broad area of pavement
between the recoiling houses and the temple was now
deserted, but he did not venture to cross it in the blare
of betraying daylight. Circling the area, he saw that there
were several other entrances to the great fane, all open
and unguarded. There was no sign of activity about the
place; but he shuddered at the thought of that which was
hidden within its walls, even as the feasting of worms is
hidden in the marble tomb.

Like a vomiting of charnels, the abominations of which
he had heard rose up before him in the sunlight; and
again he drew close to madness, knowing that Elaith
must lie among the dead, in the temple, with the foul
umbrage of such things upon her; and that he, consumed
with unremitting frenzy, must wait for the favorable
shrouding of darkness before he could execute his nebu-
lous, doubtful plan of rescue. In the meanwhile, she
might awake, and perish from the mortal horror of her
surroundings . . . Or worse even than this might befall,
if the whispered tales were true. . . .

Abnon-Tha, sorcerer and necromancer, was felicitating
himself on the bargain he had made with the priests of
Mordiggian. He felt, perhaps justly, that no one less
clever than he could have conceived and executed the
various procedures that had made possible this bargain,
through which Arctela, daughter of the proud Quaos,
would become an unquestioning slave. No other lover,
he told himself, could have been resourceful enough to
obtain a desired woman in this fashion. Arctela, betrothed

to Alos, a young noble of the city, was seemingly beyond the aspiration of a sorcerer. Abnon-Tha, however, was no common hedge-wizard, but an adept of long standing in the most awful and profound arcana of the black arts. He knew the spells that kill more quickly and surely than knife or poison, at a distance; and he knew also the darker spells by which the dead can be reanimated, even after years or ages of decay. He had slain Arctela in a manner that none could detect, with a rare and subtle invultuation that had left no mark; and her body lay now among the dead, in Mordiggian's temple. Tonight, with the tacit connivance of the terrible, shrouded priests, he would bring her back to life.

Abnon-Tha was not native to Zul-Bha-Sair, but had come many years before from the infamous, half-mythic isle of Sotar, lying somewhere to the east of the huge continent of Zothique. Like a sleek young vulture, he had established himself in the very shadow of the charnel fane, and had prospered, taking to himself pupils and assistants.

His dealings with the priests were long and extensive, and the bargain he had just made was far from being the first of its kind. They had allowed him the temporary use of bodies claimed by Mordiggian, stipulating only that these bodies should not be removed from the temple during the course of any of his experiments in necromancy. Since the privilege was slightly irregular from their viewpoint, he had found it necessary to bribe them—not, however, with gold, but with the promise of a liberal purveyance of matters more sinister and corruptible than gold. The arrangement had been satisfactory enough to all concerned: cadavers had poured into the temple with more than their usual abundance ever since the coming of the sorcerer; the god had not lacked for provender; and Abnon-Tha had never lacked for subjects on which to employ his more baleful spells.

On the whole, Abnon-Tha was not ill-pleased with himself. He reflected, moreover, that, aside from his mastery of magic and his sleightful ingenuity, he was about to manifest a well-nigh unexampled courage. He

had planned a robbery that would amount to dire sacri-
lege: the removal of the reanimated body of Arctela from
the temple. Such robberies (either of animate or exani-
mate corpses) and the penalty attached to them, were a
matter of legend only; for none had occurred in recent
ages. Thrice terrible, according to common belief, was
the doom of those who had tried and failed. The necromancer was not blind to the risks of his enterprise; nor,
on the other hand, was he deterred or intimidated by
them.

His two assistants, Narghai and Vemba-Tsith, apprised
of his intention, had made with all due privity the necessary preparations for their flight from Zul-Bha-Sair. The
strong passion that the sorcerer had conceived for Arctela was not his only motive, perhaps, in removing from
that city. He was desirous of change, for he had grown
a little weary of the odd laws that really served to restrict
his necromantic practices, while facilitating them in a
sense. He planned to travel southward, and establish
himself in one of the cities of Tasuun, an empire famous
for the number and antiquity of its mummies.

It was now sunset-time. Five dromedaries, bred for
racing, waited in the inner courtyard of Abnon-Tha's
house, a high and moldering mansion that seemed to lean
forward upon the open, circular area belonging to the
temple. One of the dromedaries would carry a bale containing the sorcerer's most valuable books, manuscripts,
and other impedimenta of magic. Its fellows would bear
Abnon-Tha, the two assistants—and Arctela.

Narghai and Vemba-Tsith appeared before their master to tell him that all was made ready. Both were much
younger than Abnon-Tha; but, like himself, they were
outlanders in Zul-Bha-Sair. They came of the swart and
narrow-eyed people of Naat, an isle that was little less
infamous than Sotar.

"It is well," said the necromancer, as they stood before
him with lowered eyes, after making their announcement. "We have only to await the favorable hour. Mid-
way between sunset and moonrise, when the priests are
at their supper in the nether adytum, we will enter the

temple and perform that which must be done for the raising of Arctela. *They* feed well tonight, for I know that many of the dead grow ripe on the great table in the upper sanctuary; and it may be that Mordiggian feeds also. None will come to watch us at our doings."

"But, master," said Narghai, shivering a little beneath his robe of nacarat red, "is it wise, after all, to do this thing? Must you take the girl from the temple? Always, ere this, you have contented yourself with the brief loan that the priests allow, and have rendered back the dead in the required state of exanimation. Truly, is it well to violate the law of the god? Men say that the wrath of Mordiggian, though seldom loosed, is more dreadful than the wrath of all other deities. For this reason, none has dared to defraud him in latter years, or attempt the removal of any of the corpses from his fane. Long ago, it is told, a high noble of the city bore hence the cadaver of a woman he had loved, and fled with it to the desert; but the priests pursued him, running more swiftly than jackals . . . and the fate that overtook him is a thing whereof the legends whisper but dimly."

"I fear neither Mordiggian nor his creatures," said Abnon-Tha, with a solemn vainglory in his voice. "My dromedaries can outrun the priests—even granting that the priests are not men at all, but ghouls, as some say. And there is small likelihood that they will follow us: after their feasting tonight, they will sleep like gorged vultures. The morrow will find us far on the road to Tasuun, ere they awake."

"The master is right," interpolated Vemba-Tsith. "We have nothing to fear."

"But they say that Mordiggian does not sleep," insisted Narghai, "and that he watches all things eternally from his black vault beneath the temple."

"So I have heard," said Abnon-Tha, with a dry and learned air. "But I consider that such beliefs are mere superstition. There is nothing to confirm them in the real nature of corpse-eating entities. So far, I have never beheld Mordiggian, either sleeping or awake; but in all likelihood he is merely a common ghoul. I know these demons and their habits. They differ from hyenas only through their monstrous shape and size, and their immortality."

"Still, I must deem it an ill thing to cheat Mordiggian," muttered Narghai beneath his breath.

The words were caught by the quick ears of Abnon-Tha. "Nay, there is no question of cheating. Well have I served Mordiggian and his priesthood, and amply have I larded their black table. Also, I shall keep, in a sense, the bargain I have made concerning Arctela: the providing of a new cadaver in return for my necromantic privilege. Tomorrow, the youth Alos, the betrothed of Arctela, will lie in her place among the dead. Go now, and leave me, for I must devise the inward invultuation that will rot the heart of Alos, like a worm that awakens at the core of fruit."

To Pahriom, fevered and distraught, it seemed that the cloudless day went by with the sluggishness of a corpse-clogged river. Unable to calm his agitation, he wandered aimlessly through the thronged bazars, till the western towers grew dark on a heaven of saffron flame, and the twilight rose like a gray and curdling sea among the houses. Then he returned to the inn where Elaith had been stricken, and claimed the dromedary which he had left in the tavern stables. Riding the animal through dim thoroughfares, lit only by the covert gleam of lamps or tapers from half-closed windows, he found his way once more to the city's center.

The dusk had thickened into darkness when he came to the open area surrounding Mordiggian's temple. The windows of mansions fronting the area were shut and lightless as dead eyes, and the fane itself, a colossal bulk of gloom, was rayless as any mausoleum beneath the gathering stars. No one, it seemed, was abroad, and though the quietude was favorable to his project, Pahriom shivered with a chill of deathly menace and desolation. The hoofs of his camel rang on the pavement with a startling and preternatural clangor, and he thought that the ears of hidden ghouls, listening alertly behind the silence, must surely hear them.

However, there was no stirring of life in that sepulchral gloom. Reaching the shelter of one of the thick groups of ancient cedars, he dismounted and tied the dromedary to a low-growing branch. Keeping among the trees, like a shadow among shadows, he approached the temple with infinite wariness, and circled it slowly, finding that its four doorways, which corresponded to the four quarters of the Earth, were all wide open, deserted, and equally dark. Returning at length to the eastern side, on which he had tethered his camel, he emboldened himself to enter the blackly gaping portals.

Crossing the threshold, he was engulfed instantly by a dead and clammy darkness, touched with the faint fetor of corruption, and a smell as of charred bone and flesh. He thought that he was in a huge corridor, and feeling his way forward along the right-hand wall, he soon came to a sudden turn, and saw a bluish glimmering far ahead, as if in some central adytum where the hall ended. Massy columns were silhouetted against the glimmering; and across it, as he drew nearer, several dark and muffled figures passed, presenting the profiles of enormous skulls. Two of them were sharing the burden of a human body which they carried in their arms. To Phariom, pausing in the shadowy hall, it appeared that the vague taint of putrescence upon the air grew stronger for a few instants after the figures had come and gone.

They were not succeeded by any others, and the fane resumed its mausolean stillness. But the youth waited for many minutes, doubtful and trepidant, before venturing to go on. An oppression of mortuary mystery thickened the air, and stifled him like the noisome effluvia of catacombs. His ears became intolerably acute, and he heard a dim humming, a sound of deep and viscid voices indistinquishably blent, that appeared to issue from crypts beneath the temple.

Stealing at length to the hall's end, he peered beyond into what was obviously the main sanctuary: a low and many-pillared room, whose vastness was but half-revealed by the bluish fires that glowed and flickered in numerous urn-like vessels borne aloft on slender stelae.

Phariom hesitated upon that awful threshold, for the mingled odors of burnt and decaying flesh were heavier on the air, as if he had drawn nearer to their sources; and the thick humming seemed to ascend from a dark stairway in the floor, beside the left-hand wall. But the room, to all appearance, was empty of life, and nothing stirred except the wavering lights and shadows. The watcher discerned the outlines of a vast table in the center, carved from the same black stone as the building itself. Upon the table, half lit by the flaming urns, or shrouded by the umbrage of the heavy columns, a number of people lay side by side; and Phariom knew that he had found the black altar of Mordiggian, whereon were disposed the bodies claimed by the god.

A wild and stifling fear contended with a wilder hope in his bosom. Trembling, he went toward the table; and a cold clamminess, wrought by the presence of the dead, assailed him. The table was nearly thirty feet in length, and it rose waist-high on a dozen mighty legs. Beginning at the nearer end, he passed along the row of corpses, peering fearfully into each upturned face. Both sexes, and many ages and differing ranks were represented. Nobles and rich merchants were crowded by beggars in filthy rags. Some were newly dead, and others, it seemed, had lain there for days, and were beginning to show the marks of corruption. There were many gaps in the ordered row, suggesting that certain of the corpses had been removed. Phariom went on in the dim light, searching for the loved features of Elaith. At last, when he was nearing the further end, and had begun to fear that she was not among them, he found her.

With the cryptic pallor and stillness of her strange malady upon her, she lay unchanged on the chill stone. A great thankfulness was born in the heart of Phariom, for he felt sure that she was not dead—and that she had not awakened at any time to the horrors of the temple. If he could bear her away from the hateful purlieus of Zul-

Bha-Sair without detection, she would recover from her death-simulating sickness.

Cursorily, he noted that another woman was lying beside Elaith, and recognized her as the beautiful Arctela, whose bearers he had followed almost to the portals of the fane. He gave her no second glance, but stooped to lift Elaith in his arms.

At that moment, he heard a murmur of low voices in the direction of the door by which he had entered the sanctuary. Thinking that some of the priests had returned, he dropped swiftly on hands and knees and crawled beneath the ponderous table, which afforded the only accessible hiding-place. Retreating into shadow beyond the glimmering shed from the lofty urns, he waited and looked out between the pillar-thick legs.

The voices grew louder, and he saw the curiously sandalled feet and shortish robes of three persons who approached the table of the dead and paused in the very spot where he himself had stood a few instants before. Who they were, he could not surmise; but their garments of light and swarthy red were not the shroudings of Mordiggian's priests. He was uncertain whether or not they had seen him; and crouching in the low space beneath the table, he plucked his dagger from its sheath.

Now he was able to distinguish three voices, one solemn and unctuously imperative, one somewhat guttural and growling, and the other shrill and nasal. The accents were alien, differing from those of the men of Zul-Bha-Sair, and the words were often strange to Phariom. Also, much of the converse was inaudible.

". . . here . . . at the end," said the solemn voice. "Be swift. . . . We have no time to loiter."

"Yes, Master," came the growling voice. "But who is this other? . . . Truly, she is very fair."

A discussion seemed to take place, in discreetly lowered tones. Apparently the owner of the guttural voice was urging something that the other two opposed. The listener could distinguish only a word or two here and there; but he gathered that the name of the first person was Vemba-Tsith, and that the one who spoke in a nasal shrilling was called Narghai. At last, above the others, the grave accents of the man addressed only as the Master were clearly audible:

"I do not altogether approve. . . . It will delay our departure . . . and the two must ride on one dromedary. But take her, Vemba-Tsith, if you can perform the necessary spells unaided. I have no time for a double incantation. . . . It will be a good test of your proficiency."

There was a mumbling as of thanks or acknowledgement from Vemba-Tsith. Then the voice of the Master: "Be quiet now, and make haste." To Phariom, wondering vaguely and uneasily as to the import of this colloquy, it seemed that two of the three men pressed closer to the table, as if stooping above the dead. He heard a rustling of cloth upon stone, and an instant later, he saw that all three were departing among the columns and stelae, in a direction opposite to that from which they had entered the sanctuary. Two of them carried burdens that glimmered palely and indistinctly in the shadows.

A black horror clutched at the heart of Phariom, for all too clearly he surmised the nature of those burdens— and the possible identity of one of them. Quickly he crawled forth from his hiding-place and saw that Elaith was gone from the black table, together with the girl Arctela. He saw the vanishing of shadowy figures in the gloom that zoned the chamber's western wall. Whether the abductors were ghouls, or worse than ghouls, he could not know, but he followed swiftly, forgetful of all caution in his concern for Elaith.

Reaching the wall, he found the mouth of a corridor, and plunged into it headlong. Somewhere in the gloom ahead, he saw a ruddy glimmering of light. Then he heard a sullen, metallic grating; and the glimmer narrowed to a slit-like gleam, as if the door of the chamber from which it issued were being closed.

Following the blind wall, he came to that slit of crimson light. A door of darkly tarnished bronze had been left ajar, and Phariom peered in on a weird, unholy scene, illumined by the blood-like flames that flared and soared unsteadily from high urns upborne on sable pedestals.

The room was full of sensuous luxury that accorded strangely with the dull, funereal stone of that temple of death. There were couches and carpets of superbly figured stuffs, vermilion, gold, azure, silver; and jewelled censers of unknown metals stood in the corners. A low table at one side was littered with curious bottles, and occult appliances such as might be used in medicine or sorcery.

Elaith was lying on one of the couches, and near her, on a second couch, the body of the girl Arctela had been disposed. The abductors, whose faces Phariom now beheld for the first time, were busying themselves with singular preparations that mystified him prodigiously. His impulse to invade the room was repressed by a sort of wonder that held him enthralled and motionless.

One of the three, a tall, middle-aged man whom he identified as the Master, had assembled certain peculiar vessels, including a small brazier and a censer, and had set them on the floor beside Arctela. The second, a younger man with lecherously slitted eyes, had placed similar impedimenta before Elaith. The third, who was also young and evil of aspect, merely stood and looked on with an apprehensive, uneasy air.

Phariom divined that the men were sorcerers when, with a deftness born of long practice, they lit the censers and braziers, and began simultaneously the intonation of rhythmically measured words in a strange tongue, accompanied by the sprinkling, at regular intervals, of black oils that fell with a great hissing on the coals in the braziers and sent up enormous clouds of pearly smoke. Dark threads of vapor serpentined from the censers, interweaving themselves like veins through the dim, misshapen figures as of ghostly giants that were formed by the lighter fumes. A reek of intolerably acrid balsams filled the chamber, assailing and troubling the senses of Phariom, till the scene wavered before him and took on a dream-like vastness, a narcotic distortion.

The voices of the necromancers mounted and fell as if

in some unholy paean. Imperious, exigent, they seemed to implore the consummation of forbidden blasphemy Like thronging phantoms, writhing and swirling with malignant life, the vapors rose about the couches on which lay the dead girl and the girl who bore the outward likeness of death.

Then, as the fumes were riven apart in their baleful seething, Phariom saw that the pale figure of Elaith had stirred like a sleeper who awakens, that she had opened her eyes and was lifting a feeble hand from the gorgeous couch. The younger necromancer ceased his chanting on a sharply broken cadence; but the solemn tones of the other still went on, and still there was a spell on the limbs and senses of Phariom, making it impossible for him to stir.

Slowly the vapors thinned like a rout of dissolving phantoms. The watcher saw that the dead girl, Arctela, was rising to her feet like a somnambulist. The chanting of Abnon-Tha, standing before her, came sonorously to an end. In the awful silence that followed, Phariom heard a weak cry from Elaith, and then the jubilant, growling voice of Vemba-Tsith, who was stooping above her:

"Behold, O Abnon-Tha! My spells are swifter than yours, for she that I have chosen awakened before Arctela!"

Phariom was released from his thralldom, as if through the lifting of an evil enchantment. He flung back the ponderous door of darkened bronze, that ground with protesting clangors on its hinges. His dagger drawn, he rushed into the room.

Elaith, her eyes wide with piteous bewilderment, turned toward him and made an ineffectual effort to arise from the couch. Arctela, mute and submissive before Abnon-Tha, appeared to heed nothing but the will of the necromancer. She was alike a fair and soulless automaton. The sorcerers, turning as Phariom entered, sprang back with instant agility before his onset, and drew the short, cruelly crooked swords which they all carried. Narghai struck the knife from Phariom's fingers with a darting blow that shattered its thin blade at the hilt, and

Vemba-Tsith, his weapon swinging back in a vicious arc, would have killed the youth promptly if Abnon-Tha had not intervened and bade him stay.

Phariom, standing furious but irresolute before the lifted swords, was aware of the darkly searching eyes of Abnon-Tha, like those of some nyctalopic bird of prey.

"I would know the meaning of this intrusion," said the necromancer. "Truly, you are bold to enter the temple of Mordiggian."

"I came to find the girl who lies yonder," declared Phariom. "She is Elaith, my wife, who was claimed unjustly by the god. But tell me, why have you brought her to this room from the table of Mordiggian, and what manner of men are you, that raise up the dead as you have raised this other woman?"

"I am Abnon-Tha, the necromancer, and these others are my pupils, Narghai and Vemba-Tsith. Give thanks to Vemba-Tsith, for verily he has brought back your wife from the purlieus of the dead with a skill excelling that of his master. She awoke ere the incantation was finished!"

Phariom glared with implacable suspicion at Abnon-Tha. "Elaith was not dead, but only as one in trance," he averred. "It was not your pupil's sorcery that awakened her. And verily, whether Elaith be dead or living is not a matter that should concern any but myself. Permit us to depart, for I wish to remove with her from Zul-Bha-Sair, in which we are only passing travellers."

So speaking, he turned his back on the necromancers, and went over to Elaith, who regarded him with dazed eyes but uttered his name feebly as he clasped her in his arms.

"Now this is a remarkable coincidence," purred Abnon-Tha. "I and my pupils are also planning to depart from Zul-Bha-Sair, and we start this very night. Perhaps you will honor us with your company."

"I thank you," said Phariom, curtly. "But I am not sure that our roads lie together. Elaith and I would go toward Tasuun."

"Now, by the black altar of Mordiggian, that is a still

stranger coincidence, for Tasuun is also our destination. We take with us the resurrected girl Arctela, whom I have deemed too fair for the charnel god and his ghouls."

Phariom divined the dark evil that lay behind the oily, mocking speeches of the necromancer. Also, he saw the furtive and sinister sign that Abnon-Tha had made to his assistants. Weaponless, he could only give a formal assent to the sardonic proposal. He knew well that he would not be permitted to leave the temple alive, for the narrow eyes of Narghai and Vemba-Tsith, regarding him closely, were alight with the red lust of murder.

"Come," said Abnon-Tha, in a voice of imperious command, "It is time to go." He turned to the still figure of Arctela and spoke an unknown word. With vacant eyes and noctambulistic paces, she followed at his heels as he stepped toward the open door. Phariom had helped Elaith to her feet, and was whispering words of reassurance in an effort to lull the growing horror and confused alarm that he saw in her eyes. She was able to walk, albeit slowly and uncertainly. Vemba-Tsith and Narghai drew back, motioning that she and Phariom should precede them; but Phariom, sensing their intent to slay him as soon as his back was turned, obeyed unwillingly and looked desperately about for something that he could seize as a weapon.

One of the metal braziers, full of smoldering coals, was at his very feet. He stooped quickly, lifted it in his hands, and turned upon the necromancers. Vemba-Tsith, as he had suspected, was prowling toward him with upraised sword, and was making ready to strike. Phariom hurled the brazier and its glowing contents full in the necromancer's face, and Vemba-Tsith went down with a terrible, smothered cry. Narghai, snarling ferociously, leapt forward to assail the defenseless youth. His simitar gleamed with a wicked luster in the lurid glare of the urns as he swung it back for the blow. But the weapon did not fall; and Phariom, steeling himself against the impending death, became aware that Narghai was staring beyond him as if petrified by the vision of some Gorgonian specter.

As if compelled by another will than his own, the youth turned—and saw the thing that had arrested Narghai's blow. Arctela and Abnon-Tha, pausing before the open door, were outlined against a colossal shadow that was not wrought by anything in the room. It filled the portals from side to side, it towered above the lintel—and then, swiftly, it became more than a shadow: it was a bulk of darkness, black and opaque, that somehow blinded the eyes with a strange dazzlement. It seemed to suck the flame from the red urns and fill the chamber with a chill of utter death and voidness. Its form was that of a worm-shapen column, huge as a dragon, its further coils still issuing from the gloom of the corridor; but it changed from moment to moment, swirling and spinning as if alive with the vortical energies of dark eons. Briefly it took the semblance of some demoniac giant with eyeless head and limbless body; and then, leaping and spreading like smoky fire, it swept forward into the chamber.

Abnon-Tha fell back before it, with frantic mumblings of malediction or exorcism; but Arctela, pale and slight and motionless, remained full in its path, while the thing enfolded her and enveloped her with a hungry flaring until she was hidden wholly from view.

Phariom, supporting Elaith, who leaned weakly on his shoulder as if about to swoon, was powerless to move. He forgot the murderous Narghai, and it seemed that he and Elaith were but faint shadows in the presence of embodied death and dissolution. He saw the blackness grow and wax with the towering of fed flame as it closed about Arctela; and he saw it gleam with eddying hues of somber iris, like the spectrum of a sable sun. For an instant, he heard a soft and flame-like murmuring. Then, quickly and terribly, the thing ebbed from the room. Arctela was gone, as if she had dissolved like a phantom on the air. Borne on a sudden gust of strangely mingled heat and cold, there came an acrid odor, such as would rise from a burnt-out funeral pyre.

"Mordiggian!" shrilled Narghai, in hysteric terror. "It was the god Mordiggian! He has taken Arctela!"

It seemed that his cry was answered by a score of sardonic echoes, unhuman as the howling of hyenas, and yet articulate, that repeated the name Mordiggian. Into the room, from the dark hall, there poured a horde of creatures whose violet robes alone identified them in Phariom's eyes as the priests of the ghoul-god. They had removed the skull-like masks, revealing heads and faces that were half anthropomorphic, half canine, and wholly diabolic. Also, they had taken off the fingerless gloves . . . . There were at least a dozen of them. Their curving talons gleamed in the bloody light like the hooks of darkly tarnished metal; their spiky teeth, longer than coffin-nails, protruded from snarling lips. They closed like a ring of jackals on Abnon-Tha and Narghai, driving them back into the farthest corner. Several others, entering tardily, fell with a bestial ferocity on Vemba-Tsith, who had begun to revive, and was moaning and writhing on the floor amid the scattered coals of the brazier.

They seemed to ignore Phariom and Elaith, who stood looking on as if in some baleful trance. But the hindmost, ere he joined the assailants of Vemba-Tsith, turned to the youthful pair and addressed them in a hoarse, hollow voice, like a tomb-reverberate barking:

"Go, for Mordiggian is a just god, who claims only the dead, and has no concern with the living. And we, the priests of Mordiggian, deal in our own fashion with those who would violate his law by removing the dead from the temple."

Phariom, with Elaith still leaning on his shoulder, went out into the dark hall, hearing a hideous clamor in which the screams of men were mingled with a growling of jackals, a laughter as of hyenas. The clamor ceased as they entered the blue-lit sanctuary and passed toward the outer corridor; and the silence that filled Mordiggian's fane behind them was deep as the silence of the dead on the black altar-table.

IT

by Theodore Sturgeon

It walked in the woods.

It was never born. It existed. Under the pine needles the fires burn, deep and smokeless in the mold. In heat and in darkness and decay there is growth. There is life and there is growth. It grew, but it was not alive. It walked unbreathing through the woods, and thought and saw and was hideous and strong, and it was not born and it did not live. It grew and moved about without living.

It crawled out of the darkness and hot damp mold into the cool of a morning. It was huge. It was lumped and crusted with its own hateful substances, and pieces of it dropped off as it went its way, dropped off and lay writhing, and stilled, and sank putrescent into the forest loam.

It had no mercy, no laughter, no beauty. It had strength and great intelligence. And—perhaps it could not be destroyed. It crawled out of its mound in the wood and lay pulsing in the sunlight for a long moment. Patches of it shone wetly in the golden glow, parts of it were nubbled and flaked. And whose dead bones had given it the form of a man?

It scrabbled painfully with its half-formed hands, beating the ground and the bole of a tree. It rolled and lifted itself up on its crumbling elbows, and it tore up a great handful of herbs and shredded them against its chest, and it paused and gazed at the gray-green juices with intelligent calm. It wavered to its feet, and seized a young sapling and destroyed it, folding the slender trunk back on itself again and again, watching attentively the useless, fibered splinters. And it squealed, snatching up a fear-

291

frozen field-creature, crushing it slowly, letting blood and pulpy flesh and fur ooze from between its fingers, run down and rot on the forearms.

It began searching.

Kimbo drifted through the tall grasses like a puff of dust, his bushy tail curled tightly over his back and his long jaws agape. He ran with an easy lope, loving his freedom and the power of his flanks and furry shoulders. His tongue lolled listlessly over his lips. His lips were black and serrated, and each tiny pointed liplet swayed with his doggy gallop. Kimbo was all dog, all healthy animal.

He leaped high over a boulder and landed with a startled yelp as a long-eared cony shot from its hiding place under the rock. Kimbo hurtled after it, grunting with each great thrust of his legs. The rabbit bounced just ahead of him, keeping its distance, its ears flattened on its curving back and its little legs nibbling away at a distance hungrily. It stopped, and Kimbo pounced, and the rabbit shot away at a tangent and popped into a hollow log. Kimbo yelped again and rushed snuffling at the log, and knowing his failure, curvetted but once around the stump and ran on into the forest. The thing that watched from the wood raised its crusted arms and waited for Kimbo.

Kimbo sensed it there, standing dead-still by the path. To him it was a bulk which smelled of carrion not fit to roll in, and he snuffled distastefully and ran to pass it.

The thing let him come abreast and dropped a heavy twisted fist on him. Kimbo saw it coming and curled up tight as he ran, and the hand clipped stunningly on his rump, sending him rolling and yipping down the slope. Kimbo straddled to his feet, shook his head, shook his body with a deep growl, came back to the silent thing with green murder in his eyes. He walked stiffly, straight-legged, his tail as low as his lowered head and a ruff of fury round his neck. The thing raised its arms again, waited.

Kimbo slowed, then flipped himself through the air at

the monster's throat. His jaws closed on it; his teeth clicked together through a mass of filth, and he fell choking and snarling at its feet. The thing leaned down and struck twice, and after the dog's back was broken, it sat beside him and began to tear him apart.

"Be back in an hour or so," said Alton Drew, picking up his rifle from the corner behind the wood box. His brother laughed.

"Old Kimbo 'bout runs your life, Alton," he said.

"Ah, I know the ol' devil," said Alton. "When I whistle for him for half an hour and he don't show up, he's in a jam or he's treed something wuth shootin' at. The ol' son of a gun calls me by not answerin'."

Cory Drew shoved a full glass of milk over to his nine-year-old daughter and smiled. "You think as much o' that houn'-dog o' yours as I do of Babe here."

Babe slid off her chair and ran to her uncle. "Gonna catch me the bad fella, Uncle Alton?" she shrilled. The "bad fella" was Cory's invention—the one who lurked in corners ready to pounce on little girls who chased the chickens and played around mowing machines and hurled green apples with a powerful young arm at the sides of the hogs, to hear the synchronized thud and grunt; little girls who swore with an Austrian accent like an ex-hired man they had had; who dug caves in haystacks till they tipped over, and kept pet crawfish in tomorrow's milk cans, and rode work horses to a lather in the night pasture.

"Get back here and keep away from Uncle Alton's gun!" said Cory. "If you see the bad fella, Alton, chase him back here. He has a date with Babe here for that stunt of hers last night." The preceding evening, Babe had kind-heartedly poured pepper on the cows' salt block.

"Don't worry, kiddo," grinned her uncle, "I'll bring you the bad fella's hide if he don't get me first."

Alton Drew walked up the path toward the wood, thinking about Babe. She was a phenomenon—a pampered farm child. Ah well—she had to be. They'd both

loved Clissa Drew, and she'd married Cory, and they
had to love Clissa's child. Funny thing, love. Alton was
a man's man, and thought things out that way; and his
reaction to love was a strong and frightened one. He
knew what love was because he felt it still for his brother's wife and would feel it as long as he lived for Babe.
It led him through his life, and yet he embarrassed himself by thinking of it. Loving a dog was an easy thing,
because you and the old devil could love one another
completely without talking about it. The smell of gun
smoke and the smell of wet fur in the rain were perfume
enough for Alton Drew, a grunt of satisfaction and the
scream of something hunted and hit were poetry enough.
They weren't like love for a human, that choked his
throat so he could not say words he could not have
thought of anyway. So Alton loved his dog Kimbo and
his Winchester for all to see, and let his love for his
brother's women, Clissa and Babe, eat at him quietly
and unmentioned.

His quick eyes saw the fresh indentations in the soft
earth behind the boulder, which showed where Kimbo
had turned and leaped with a single surge, chasing the
rabbit. Ignoring the tracks, he looked for the nearest
place where a rabbit might hide, and strolled over to the
stump. Kimbo had been there, he saw, and had been
there too late. "You're an ol' fool," muttered Alton. "Y'
can't catch a cony by chasin' it. You want to cross him
up some way." He gave a peculiar trilling whistle, sure
that Kimbo was digging frantically under some nearby
stump for a rabbit that was three counties away by now.
No answer. A little puzzled, Alton went back to the path.
"He never done this before," he said softly. There was
something about this he didn't like.

He cocked his .32-40 and cradled it. At the county fair
someone had once said of Alton Drew that he could
shoot at a handful of salt and pepper thrown in the air
and hit only the pepper. Once he split a bullet on the
blade of a knife and put two candles out. He had no
need to fear anything that could be shot at. That's what
he believed.

*   *   *

The thing in the woods looked curiously down at what it had done to Kimbo, and moaned the way Kimbo had before he died. It stood a minute storing away facts in its foul, unemotional mind. Blood was warm. The sunlight was warm. Things that moved and bore fur had a muscle to force the thick liquid through tiny tubes in their bodies. The liquid coagulated after a time. The liquid on rooted green things was thinner and the loss of a limb did not mean loss of life. It was very interesting, but the thing, the mold with a mind, was not pleased. Neither was it displeased. Its accidental urge was a thirst for knowledge, and it was only—interested.

It was growing late, and the sun reddened and rested awhile on the hilly horizon, teaching the clouds to be inverted flames. The thing threw up its head suddenly, noticing the dusk. Night was ever a strange thing, even for those of us who have known it in life. It would have been frightening for the monster had it been capable of fright, but it could only be curious; it could only reason from what it had observed.

What was happening? It was getting harder to see. Why? It threw its shapeless head from side to side. It was true—things were dim, and growing dimmer. Things were changing shape, taking on a new and darker color. What did the creatures it had crushed and torn apart see? How did they see? The larger one, the one that had attacked, had used two organs in its head. That must have been it, because after the thing had torn off two of the dog's legs it had struck at the hairy muzzle; and the dog, seeing the blow coming, had dropped folds of skin over the organs—closed its eyes. Ergo, the dog saw with its eyes. But then after the dog was dead, and its body still, repeated blows had had no effect on the eyes. They remained open and staring. The logical conclusion was, then, that a being that had ceased to live and breathe and move about lost the use of its eyes. It must be that to lose sight was, conversely, to die. Dead things did not walk about. They lay down and did not move. Therefore the thing in the wood concluded that it must be dead, and so it lay down by the path, not far away from Kimbo's scattered body, lay down and believed itself dead.

Alton Drew came up through the dusk to the wood. He was frankly worried. He whistled again, and then called, and there was still no response, and he said again, "The ol' flea-bus never done this before," and shook his heavy head. It was past milking time, and Cory would need him. "Kimbo!" he roared. The cry echoed through the shadows, and Alton flipped on the safety catch of his rifle and put the butt on the ground beside the path. Leaning on it, he took off his cap and scratched the back of his head, wondering. The rifle butt sank into what he thought was soft earth; he staggered and stepped into the chest of the thing that lay beside the path. His foot went up to the ankle in its yielding rottenness, and he swore and jumped back.

"*Whew!* Sompn sure dead as hell there! Ugh!" He swabbed at his boot with a handful of leaves while the monster lay in the growing blackness with the edges of the deep footprint in its chest sliding into it, filling it up. It lay there regarding him dimly out of its muddy eyes, thinking it was dead because of the darkness, watching the articulation of Alton Drew's joints, wondering at this new uncautious creature.

Alton cleaned the butt of his gun with more leaves and went on up the path, whistling anxiously for Kimbo.

Clissa Drew stood in the door of the milk shed, very lovely in red-checked gingham and a blue apron. Her hair was clean yellow, parted in the middle and stretched tautly back to a heavy braided knot. "Cory! Alton!" she called a little sharply.

"Well?" Cory responded gruffly from the barn, where he was stripping off the Ayrshire. The dwindling streams of milk plopped pleasantly into the froth of a full pail.

"I've called and called," said Clissa. "Supper's cold, and Babe won't eat until you come. Why—where's Alton?"

Cory grunted, heaved the stool out of the way, threw over the stanchion lock and slapped the Ayrshire on the rump. The cow backed and filled like a towboat, clattered down the line and out into the barnyard. "Ain't back yet."

"Not back?" Clissa came in and stood beside him as he sat by the next cow, put his forehead against the warm flank. "But, Cory, he said he'd—"

"Yeh, yeh, I know. He said he'd be back fer the milkin'. I heard him. Well, he ain't."

"And you have to— Oh, Cory, I'll help you finish up. Alton would be back if he could. Maybe he's—"

"Maybe he's treed a blue jay," snapped her husband. "Him an' that damn dog." He gestured hugely with one hand while the other went on milking. "I got twenty-six head o' cows to milk. I got pigs to feed an' chickens to put to bed. I got to toss hay for the mare and turn the team out. I got harness to mend and a wire down in the night pasture. I got wood to split an' carry." He milked for a moment in silence, chewing on his lip. Clissa stood twisting her hands together, trying to think of something to stem the tide. It wasn't the first time Alton's hunting had interfered with the chores. "So I got to go ahead with it. I can't interfere with Alton's spoorin'. Every damn time that hound o' his smells out a squirrel I go without my supper. I'm gettin' sick an'—"

"Oh, I'll help you!" said Clissa. She was thinking of the spring, when Kimbo had held four hundred pounds of raging black bear at bay until Alton could put a bullet in its brain, the time Babe had found a bearcub and started to carry it home, and had fallen into a freshet, cutting her head. You can't hate a dog that has saved your child for you, she thought.

"You'll do nothin' of the kind!" Cory growled. "Get back to the house. You'll find work enough there. I'll be along when I can. Dammit, Clissa, don't cry! I didn't mean to— Oh, shucks!" He got up and put his arms around her. "I'm wrought up," he said. "Go on now. I'd no call to speak that way to you. I'm sorry. Go back to Babe. I'll put a stop to this for good tonight. I've had enough. There's work here for four farmers an' all we've got is me an' that . . . that huntsman. Go on now, Clissa."

"All right," she said into his shoulder. "But, Cory, hear him out first when he comes back. He might be unable to come back this time. Maybe he . . . he—"

"Ain't nothin' kin hurt my brother that a bullet will hit. He can take care of himself. He's got no excuse good enough this time. Go on, now. Make the kid eat."

Clissa went back to the house, her young face furrowed. If Cory quarreled with Alton now and drove him away, what with the drought and the creamery about to close and all, they just couldn't manage. Hiring a man was out of the question. Cory'd have to work himself to death, and he just wouldn't be able to make it. No one man could. She sighed and went into the house. It was seven o'clock, and the milking not done yet. Oh, why did Alton have to—

Babe was in bed at nine when Clissa heard Cory in the shed, slinging the wire cutters into a corner. "Alton back yet?" they both said at once as Cory stepped into the kitchen; and as she shook her head he clumped over to the stove, and lifting a lid, spat into the coals. "Come to bed," he said.

She lay down her stitching and looked at his broad back. He was twenty-eight, and he walked and acted like a man ten years older, and looked like a man five years younger. "I'll be up in a while," Clissa said.

Cory glanced at the corner behind the wood box where Alton's rifle usually stood, then made an unspellable, disgusted sound and sat down to take off his heavy muddy shoes.

"It's after nine," Clissa volunteered timidly. Cory said nothing, reaching for house slippers.

"Cory, you're not going to—"

"Not going to what?"

"Oh, nothing. I just thought that maybe Alton—"

"Alton!" Cory flared. "The dog goes hunting field mice. Alton goes hunting the dog. Now you want me to go hunting Alton. That's what you want?"

"I just— He was never this late before."

"I won't do it! Go out lookin' for him at nine o'clock in the night? I'll be damned! He has no call to use us so, Clissa."

Clissa said nothing. She went to the stove, peered into the wash boiler, set it aside at the back of the range. When she turned around, Cory had his shoes and coat on again.

"I knew you'd go," she said. Her voice smiled though she did not.

"I'll be back durned soon," said Cory. "I don't reckon he's strayed far. It is late. I ain't feared for him, but—" He broke his 12-gauge shotgun, looked through the barrels, slipped two shells in the breech and a box of them into his pocket. "Don't wait up," he said over his shoulder as he went out.

"I won't," Clissa replied to the closed door, and went back to her stitching by the lamp.

The path up the slope to the wood was very dark when Cory went up to it, peering and calling. The air was chill and quiet, and a fetid odor of mold hung in it. Cory blew the taste of it out through impatient nostrils, drew it in again with the next breath, and swore. "Nonsense," he muttered. "Houn'-dog. Huntin', at ten in th' night, too. Alton!" he bellowed. "Alton Drew!" Echoes answered him, and he entered the wood. The huddled thing he passed in the dark heard him and felt the vibrations of his footsteps and did not move because it thought it was dead.

Cory strode on, looking around and ahead and not down since his feet knew the path.

"Alton!"

"That you, Cory?"

Cory Drew froze. That corner of the wood was thickly set and as dark as a burial vault. The voice he heard was choked, quiet, penetrating.

"Alton?"

"I found Kimbo, Cory."

"Where the hell have you been?" shouted Cory furiously. He disliked this pitch-blackness; he was afraid at the tense hopelessness of Alton's voice, and he mistrusted his ability to stay angry at his brother.

"I called him, Cory. I whistled at him, an' the ol' devil didn't answer."

"I can say the same for you, you . . . you louse. Why weren't you to milkin'? Where are you? You caught in a trap?"

"The houn' never missed answerin' me before, you know," said the tight, monotonous voice from the darkness.

"Alton! What the devil's the matter with you? What do I care if your mutt didn't answer? Where—"

"I guess because he ain't never died before," said Alton, refusing to be interrupted.

"You *what?*" Cory clicked his lips together twice and then said. "Alton, you turned crazy? What's that you say?"

"Kimbo's dead!"

"Kim . . . oh! Oh!" Cory was seeing that picture again in his mind—Baby sprawled unconscious in the freshet, and Kimbo raging and snapping against a monster bear, holding her back until Alton could get there. "What happened, Alton?" he asked more quietly.

"I aim to find out. Someone tore him up."

"*Tore him up?*"

"There ain't a bit of him left tacked together, Cory. Every damn joint in his body tore apart. Guts out of him."

"Good God! Bear, you reckon?"

"No bear, nor nothin' on four legs. He's all here. None of him's been et. Whoever done it just killed him an'— tore him up."

"Good God!" Cory said again. "Who could've—" There was a long silence, then. "Come 'long home," he said almost gently. "There's no call for you to set up by him all night."

"I'll set. I aim to be here at sunup, an' I'm goin' to start trackin', an' I'm goin' to keep trackin' till I find the one done this job on Kimbo."

"You're drunk or crazy, Alton."

"I ain't drunk. You can think what you like about the rest of it. I'm stickin' here."

"We got a farm back yonder. Remember? I ain't going to milk twenty-six head o' cows again in the mornin' like I did jest now, Alton."

"Somebody's got to. I can't be there. I guess you'll just have to, Cory."

"You dirty scum!" Cory screamed. "You'll come back with me now or I'll know why!"

Alton's voice was still tight, half-sleepy. "Don't you come no nearer, Bud."

Cory kept moving toward Alton's voice.

"I said"—the voice was very quiet now—"*stop where you are.*" Cory kept coming. A sharp click told of the release of the .32-40's safety. Cory stopped.

"You got your gun on me, Alton?" Cory whispered.

"That's right, Bud. You ain't a-trompin' up these tracks for me. I need 'em at sun-up."

A full minute passed, and the only sound in the blackness was that of Cory's pained breathing. Finally:

"I got my gun, too, Alton. Come home."

"You can't see to shoot me."

"We're even on that."

"We ain't. I know just where you stand, Cory. I been here four hours."

"My gun scatters."

"My gun kills."

Without another word Cory Drew turned on his heel and stamped back to the farm.

Black and liquescent it lay in the blackness, not alive, not understanding death, believing itself dead. Things that were alive saw and moved about. Things that were not alive could do neither. It rested its muddy gaze on the line of trees at the crest of the rise, and deep within its thoughts trickled wetly. It lay huddled, dividing its new-found facts, dissecting them as it had dissected live things when there was light, comparing, concluding, pigeon-holing.

The trees at the top of the slope could just be seen,

as their trunks were a fraction of a shade lighter than the
dark sky behind them. At length they, too, disappeared,
and for a moment sky and trees were a monotone. The
thing knew it was dead now, and like many a being
before it, it wondered how long it must stay like this.
And then the sky beyond the trees grew a little lighter.
That was a manifestly impossible occurrence, thought the
thing, but it could see it and it must be so. Did dead
things live again? That was curious. What about dismem-
bered dead things? It would wait and see.

The sun came hand over hand up a beam of light. A
bird somewhere made a high yawning peep, and as an
owl killed a shrew, a skunk pounced on another, so that
the night-shift deaths and those of day could go on without cessation. Two flowers nodded archly to each other,
comparing their pretty clothes. A dragonfly nymph
decided it was tired of looking serious and cracked its
back open, to crawl out and dry gauzily. The first golden
ray sheared down between the trees, through the grasses,
passed over the mass in the shadowed bushes. "I am
alive again," thought the thing that could not possibly
live. "I am alive, for I see clearly," It stood up on its
thick legs, up into the golden glow. In a little while the
wet flakes that had grown during the night dried in the
sun, and when it took its first steps, they cracked off and
a little shower of them fell away. It walked up the slope
to find Kimbo, to see if he, too, were alive again.

Babe let the sun come into her room by opening her
eyes. Uncle Alton was gone—that was the first thing that
ran through her head. Dad had come home last night
and had shouted at mother for an hour. Alton was plumb
crazy. He'd turned a gun on his own brother. If Alton
ever came ten feet into Cory's land, Cory would fill him
so full of holes he'd look like a tumbleweed. Alton was
lazy, shiftless, selfish, and one or two other things of
questionable taste but undoubted vividness. Babe knew
her father. Uncle Alton would never be safe in this
county.

She bounced out of bed in the enviable way of the

very young, and ran to the window. Cory was trudging
down to the night pasture with two bridles over his arm,
to get the team. There were kitchen noises from downstairs.

Babe ducked her head in the washbowl and shook off
the water like a terrier before she toweled. Trailing clean
shirt and dungarees, she went to the head of the stairs,
slid into the shirt, and began her morning ritual with the
trousers. One step down was a step through the right
leg. One more, and she was into the left. Then, bouncing
step by step on both feet, buttoning one button per step,
she reached the bottom fully dressed and ran into the
kitchen.

"Didn't Uncle Alton come back a-tall, Mum?"

"Morning, Babe. No, dear." Clissa was too quiet,
smiling too much, Babe thought shrewdly. Wasn't happy.

"Where'd he go, Mum?"

"We don't know, Babe. Sit down and eat your
breakfast."

"What's a misbegotten, Mum?" the Babe asked suddenly. Her mother nearly dropped the dish she was drying. "Babe! You must never say that again!"

"Oh. Well, why is Uncle Alton, then?"

"Why is he what?"

Babe's mouth muscled around an outsize spoonful of
oatmeal. "A misbe—"

"Babe!"

"All right, Mum," said Babe with her mouth full.
"Well, why?"

"I told Cory not to shout last night," Clissa said half
to herself.

"Well, whatever it means, he isn't," said Babe with
finality. "Did he go hunting again?"

"He went to look for Kimbo, darling."

"Kimbo? Oh Mummy, is Kimbo gone, too? Didn't he
come back either?"

"No, dear. Oh, please, Babe, stop asking questions!"

"All right. Where do you think they went?"

"Into the north woods. Be quiet."

Babe gulped away at her breakfast. An idea struck

her; and as she thought of it she ate slower and slower, and cast more and more glances at her mother from under the lashes of her tilted eyes. It would be awful if daddy did anything to Uncle Alton. Someone ought to warn him.

Babe was halfway to the woods when Alton's .32-40 sent echoes giggling up and down the valley.

Cory was in the south thirty, riding a cultivator and cussing at the team of grays when he heard the gun. "Hoa," he called to the horses, and sat a moment to listen to the sound. "One-two-three. Four," he counted. "Saw someone, blasted away at him. Had a chance to take aim and give him another, careful. My God!" He threw up the cultivator points and steered the team into the shade of three oaks. He hobbled the gelding with swift tosses of a spare strap, and headed for the woods. "Alton a killer," he murmured, and doubled back to the house for his gun. Clissa was standing just outside the door.

"Get shells!" he snapped and flung into the house. Clissa followed him. He was strapping his hunting knife on before she could get a box off the shelf. "Cory—"

"Hear that gun, did you? Alton's off his nut. He don't waste lead. He shot at someone just then, and he wasn't fixin' to shoot pa'tridges when I saw him last. He was out to get a man. Gimme my gun."

"Cory, Babe—"

"You keep her here. Oh, God, this is a helluva mess! I can't stand much more." Cory ran out the door.

Clissa caught his arm. "Cory, I'm trying to tell you. Babe isn't here. I've called, and she isn't here."

Cory's heavy, young-old face tautened. "Babe— Where did you last see her?"

"Breakfast." Clissa was crying now.

"She say where she was going?"

"No. She asked a lot of questions about Alton and where he'd gone."

"Did you say?"

Clissa's eyes widened, and she nodded, biting the back of her hand.

"You shouldn't ha' done that, Clissa," he gritted, and ran toward the woods. Clissa looked after him, and in that moment she could have killed herself.

Cory ran with his head up, straining with his legs and lungs and eyes at the long path. He puffed up the slope to the woods, agonized for breath after the forty-five minutes' heavy going. He couldn't even notice the damp smell of mold in the air.

He caught a movement in a thicket to his right, and dropped. Struggling to keep his breath, he crept forward until he could see clearly. There was something in there, all right. Something black, keeping still. Cory relaxed his legs and torso completely to make it easier for his heart to pump some strength back into them, and slowly raised the 12-gauge until it bore on the thing hidden in the thicket.

"Come out!" Cory said when he could speak.

Nothing happened.

"Come out or by God I'll shoot!" rasped Cory.

There was a long moment of silence, and his finger tightened on the trigger.

"You asked for it," he said, and as he fired the thing leaped sideways into the open, screaming.

It was a thin little man dressed in sepulchral black, and bearing the rosiest little baby-face Cory had ever seen. The face was twisted with fright and pain. The little man scrambled to his feet and hopped up and down saying over and over, "Oh, my hand! don't shoot again! Oh, my hand! Don't shoot again!" He stopped after a bit, when Cory had climbed to his feet, and he regarded the farmer out of sad china-blue eyes. "You shot me," he said reproachfully, holding up a little bloody hand. "Oh, my goodness!"

Cory said, "Now, who the hell are you?"

The man immediately became hysterical, mouthing such a flood of broken sentences that Cory stepped back a pace and half-raised his gun in self-defense. It seemed to consist mostly of "I lost my papers," and "I didn't do it," and "It was horrible. Horrible. Horrible," and "The dead man," and "Oh, don't shoot again!"

Cory tried twice to ask him a question, and then he stepped over and knocked the man down. He lay on the ground writhing and moaning and blubbering and putting his bloody hand to his mouth where Cory had hit him.

The man rolled over and sat up. "I didn't do it!" he sobbed. "I didn't! I was walking along and I heard the gun and I heard some swearing and an awful scream and I went over there and peeped and I saw the dead man and I ran away and you came and I hid and you shot me and—"

"*Shut up!*" The man did, as if a switch had been thrown. "Now," said Cory, pointing along the path, "you say there's a dead man up there?"

The man nodded and began crying in earnest. Cory helped him up. "Follow this path back to my farmhouse," he said. "Tell my wife to fix up your hand. *Don't* tell her anything else. And wait there until I come. Hear?"

"Yes. Thank you. Oh, thank you. *Snff.*"

"Go on now." Cory gave him a gentle shove in the right direction and went alone, in cold fear, up the path to the spot where he had found Alton the night before.

He found him here now, too, and Kimbo. Kimbo and Alton had spent several years together in the deepest friendship; they had hunted and fought and slept together, and the lives they owed each other were finished now. They were dead together.

It was terrible that they died the same way. Cory Drew was a strong man, but he gasped and fainted dead away when he saw what the thing of the mold had done to his brother and his brother's dog.

The little man in black hurried down the path, whimpering and holding his injured hand as if he rather wished he could limp with it. After a while the whimper faded away, and the hurried stride changed to a walk as the gibbering terror of the last hour receded. He drew two deep breaths, said: "My goodness!" and felt almost normal. He bound a linen handkerchief around his wrist, but the hand kept bleeding. He tried the elbow, and that made it hurt. So he stuffed the handkerchief back in his pocket and simply waved the hand stupidly in the air until the blood clotted.

It wasn't much of a wound. Two of the balls of shot had struck him, one passing through the fleshy part of his thumb and the other scoring the side. As he thought of it, he became a little proud that he had borne a gunshot wound. He strolled along in the midmorning sunlight, feeling a dreamy communion with the boys at the front. "The whine of shot and shell—" Where had he read that? Ah, what a story this would make! "And there beside the"—what was the line? —"the embattled farmer stood." Didn't the awfulest things happen in the nicest places? This was a nice forest. No screeches and snakes and deep dark menaces. Not a story-book wood at all. Shot by a gun. How exciting! He was now—he strutted— a gentleman adventurer. He did not see the great moist horror that clumped along behind him, though his nostrils crinkled a little with its foulness.

The monster had three little holes close together on its chest, and one little hole in the middle of its slimy forehead. It had three close-set pits in its back and one on the back of its head. These marks were where Alton Drew's bullets had struck and passed through. Half of the monster's shapeless face was sloughed away, and there was a deep indentation on its shoulder. This was what Alton Drew's gun butt had done after he clubbed it and struck at the thing that would not lie down after he put his four bullets through it. When these things happened the monster was not hurt or angry. It only wondered why Alton Drew acted that way. Now it followed the little man without hurrying at all, matching his stride step by step and dropping little particles of muck behind it.

The little man went on out of the wood and stood with his back against a big tree at the forest's edge, and he thought. Enough had happened to him here. What good would it do to stay and face a horrible murder inquest, just to continue this silly, vague quest? There was supposed to be the ruin of an old, old hunting lodge deep in this wood somewhere, and perhaps it would hold the evidence he wanted. But it was a vague report—vague enough to be forgotten without regret. It would be the height of foolishness to stay for all the hick-town red tape that would follow that ghastly affair back in the wood. Ergo, it would be ridiculous to follow that farmer's advice, to go to his house and wait for him. He would go back to town.

The monster was leaning against the other side of the big tree.

The little man snuffled disgustedly at a sudden overpowering odor of rot. He reached for his handkerchief, fumbled and dropped it. As he bent to pick it up, the monster's arm *whuffed* heavily in the air where his head had been—a blow that would certainly have removed that baby-faced protuberance. The man stood up and would have put the handkerchief to his nose had it not been so bloody. The creature behind the tree lifted its arms again just as the little man tossed the handkerchief away and stepped out into the field, heading across country to the distant highway that would take him back to town. The monster pounced on the handkerchief, picked it up, studied it, tore it across several times and inspected the tattered edges. Then it gazed vacantly at the disappearing figure of the little man, and finding him no longer interesting, turned back into the woods.

Babe broke into a trot at the sound of the shots. It was important to warn Uncle Alton about what her father had said, but it was more interesting to find out what he had bagged. Oh, he'd bagged it, all right. Uncle Alton never fired without killing. This was about the first time she had ever heard him blast away like that. Must be a bear, she thought excitedly, tripping over a root, sprawling, rolling to her feet again, without noticing the tumble. She'd love to have another bearskin in her room. Where would she put it? Maybe they could line it and she could have it for a blanket. Uncle Alton could sit on it and read to her in the evening— Oh, no. No. Not with this trouble between him and dad. Oh, if she could only do something! She tried to run faster, worried and anticipating, but she was out of breath and went more slowly instead.

At the top of the rise by the edge of the woods she stopped and looked back. Far down in the valley lay the south thirty. She scanned it carefully, looking for her father. The new furrows and the old were sharply defined, and her keen eyes saw immediately that Cory had left the line with the cultivator and had angled the team over to the shade trees without finishing his row. That wasn't like him. She could see the team now, and Cory's pale-blue denim was not in sight.

A little nearer was the house; and as her gaze fell on it she moved out of the cleared pathway. Her father was coming; she had seen his shotgun and he was running. He could really cover ground when he wanted to. He must be chasing her, she thought immediately. He'd guessed that she would run toward the sound of the shots, and he was going to follow her tracks to Uncle Alton and shoot him. She knew that he was as good a woodsman as Alton; he would most certainly see her tracks. Well, she'd fix him.

She ran along the edge of the wood, being careful to dig her heels deeply into the loam. A hundred yards of this, and she angled into the forest and ran until she reached a particularly thick grove of trees. Shinnying up like a squirrel, she squirmed from one close-set tree to another until she could go no farther back toward the path, then dropped lightly to the ground and crept on her way, now stepping very gently. It would take him an hour to beat around for her trail, she thought proudly, and by that time she could easily get to Uncle Alton. She giggled to herself as she thought of the way she had fooled her father. And the little sound of laughter drowned out, for her, the sound of Alton's hoarse dying scream.

She reached and crossed the path and slid through the brush beside it. The shots came from up around here somewhere. She stopped and listened several times, and then suddenly heard something coming toward her, fast. She ducked under cover, terrified, and a little babyfaced man in black, his blue eyes wide with horror, crashed blindly past her, the leather case he carried catching on the branches. It spun a moment and then fell right in front of her. The man never missed it.

Babe lay there for a long moment and then picked up the case and faded into the woods. Things were happening too fast for her. She wanted Uncle Alton, but she dared not call. She stopped again and strained her ears. Back toward the edge of the wood she heard her father's voice, and another's—probably the man who had dropped the brief case. She dared not go over there. Filled with enjoyable terror, she thought hard, then snapped her fingers in triumph. She and Alton had played Injun many times up here; they had a whole repertoire of secret signals. She had practiced birdcalls until she knew them better than the birds themselves. What would it be? Ah—blue jay. She threw back her head and by some youthful alchemy produced a nerve-shattering screech that would have done justice to any jay that ever flew. She repeated it, and then twice more.

The response was immediate—the call of a blue jay, four times, spaced two and two. Babe nodded to herself happily. That was the signal that they were to meet immediately at The Place. The Place was a hide-out that he had discovered and shared with her, and not another soul knew of it; an angle of rock beside a stream not far away. It wasn't exactly a cave, but almost. Enough so to be entrancing. Babe trotted happily toward the brook. She had just known that Uncle Alton would remember the call of the blue jay, and what it meant.

In the tree that arched over Alton's scattered body perched a large jay bird, preening itself and shining in the sun. Quite unconscious of the presence of death, hardly noticing the Babe's realistic cry, it screamed again four times, two and two.

*   *   *

It took Cory more than a moment to recover himself from what he had seen. He turned away from it and leaned weakly against a pine, panting. Alton. That was Alton lying there, in—parts.

"God! God, God, God—"

Gradually his strength returned, and he forced himself to turn again. Stepping carefully, he bent and picked up the .32-40. Its barrel was bright and clean, but the butt and stock were smeared with some kind of stinking rottenness. Where had he seen the stuff before? Somewhere—no matter. He cleaned it off absently, throwing the befouled bandanna away afterward. Through his mind ran Alton's words—was that only last night?—"*I'm goin' to start trackin. An' I'm goin' to keep trackin' till I find the one done this job on Kimbo.*"

Cory searched shrinkingly until he found Alton's box of shells. The box was wet and sticky. That made it—better, somehow. A bullet wet with Alton's blood was the right thing to use. He went away a short distance, circled around till he found heavy footprints, then came back.

"I'm a-trackin' for you, Bud," he whispered thickly, and began. Through the brush he followed its wavering spoor, amazed at the amount of filthy mold about, gradually associating it with the thing that had killed his brother. There was nothing in the world for him any more but hate and doggedness. Cursing himself for not getting Alton home last night, he followed the tracks to the edge of the woods. They led him to a big tree there, and there he saw something else—the footprints of the little city man. Nearby lay some tattered scraps of linen, and—what was that?

Another set of prints—small ones. Small, stub-toed ones. Babe's.

"Babe!" Cory screamed. "Babe!"

No answer. The wind sighed. Somewhere a blue jay called.

Babe stopped and turned when she heard her father's voice, faint with distance, piercing.

"Listen at him holler," she crooned delightedly. "Gee,

he sounds mad." She sent a jay bird's call disrespectfully back to him and hurried to The Place.

It consisted of a mammoth boulder beside the brook. Some upheaval in the glacial age had cleft it, cutting out a huge V-shaped chunk. The widest part of the cleft was at the water's edge, and the narrowest was hidden by bushes. It made a little ceilingless room, rough and uneven and full of pot-holes and cavelets inside, and yet with quite a level floor. The open end was at the water's edge.

Babe parted the bushes and peered down the cleft.

"Uncle Alton!" she called softly. There was no answer. Oh, well, he'd be along. She scrambled in and slid down to the floor.

She loved it here. It was shaded and cool, and the chattering little stream filled it with shifting golden lights and laughing gurgles. She called again, on principle, and then perched on an outcropping to wait. It was only then she realized that she still carried the little man's brief case.

She turned it over a couple of times and then opened it. It was divided in the middle by a leather wall. On one side were a few papers in a large yellow envelope, and on the other some sandwiches, a candy bar, and an apple. With a youngster's complacent acceptance of manna from heaven, Babe fell to. She saved one sandwich for Alton, mainly because she didn't like its highly spiced bologna. The rest made quite a feast.

She was a little worried when Alton hadn't arrived, even after she had consumed the apple core. She got up and tried to skim some flat pebbles across the roiling brook, and she stood on her hands, and she tried to think of a story to tell herself, and she tried just waiting. Finally, in desperation, she turned again to the brief case, took out the papers, curled up by the rocky wall and began to read them. It was something to do, anyway.

There was an old newspaper clipping that told about strange wills that people had left. An old lady had once left a lot of money to whoever would make the trip from the Earth to the Moon and back. Another had financed a home for cats whose masters and mistresses had died. A man left thousands of dollars to the first man who could solve a certain mathematical problem and prove his solution. But one item was blue-penciled. It was:

One of the strangest of wills still in force is that of Thaddeus M. Kirk, who died in 1920. It appears that he built an elaborate mausoleum with burial vaults for all the remains of his family. He collected and removed caskets from all over the country to fill the designated niches. Kirk was the last of his line; there were no relatives when he died. His will stated that the mausoleum was to be kept in repair permanently, and that a certain sum was to be set aside as a reward for whoever could produce the body of his grandfather, Roger Kirk, whose niche is still empty. Anyone finding this body is eligible to receive a substantial fortune.

Babe yawned vaguely over this, but kept on reading because there was nothing else to do. Next was a thick sheet of business correspondence, bearing the letterhead of a firm of lawyers. The body of it ran:

In regard to your query regarding the will of Thaddeus Kirk, we are authorized to state that his grandfather was a man about five feet, five inches, whose left arm had been broken and who had a triangular silver plate set into his skull. There is no information as to the whereabouts of his death. He disappeared and was declared legally dead after the lapse of fourteen years.

The amount of the reward as stated in the will, plus accrued interest, now amounts to a fraction over sixty-two thousand dollars. This will be paid to anyone who produces the remains, providing that said remains answer descriptions kept in our private files.

There was more, but Babe was bored. She went on to the little black notebook. There was nothing in it but penciled and highly abbreviated records of visits to libraries; quotations from books with titles like "History of

Angelina and Tyler Counties" and "Kirk Family History." Babe threw that aside, too. Where could Uncle Alton be?

She began to sing tunelessly, "Tumalumalum tum, ta ta ta," pretending to dance a minuet with flowing skirts like a girl she had seen in the movies. A rustle of the bushes at the entrance to The Place stopped her. She peeped upward, saw them being thrust aside. Quickly she ran to a tiny cul-de-sac in the rock wall, just big enough for her to hide in. She giggled at the thought of how surprised Uncle Alton would be when she jumped out at him.

She heard the newcomer come shuffling down the steep slope of the crevice and land heavily on the floor. There was something about the sound—what was it? It occurred to her that though it was a hard job for a big man like Uncle Alton to get through the little opening in the bushes, she could hear no heavy breathing. She heard no breathing at all!

Babe peeped out into the main cave and squealed in utmost horror. Standing there was, not Uncle Alton, but a massive caricature of a man: a huge thing like an irregular mud doll, clumsily made. It quivered and parts of it glistened and parts of it were dried and crumby. Half of the lower left part of its face was gone, giving it a lopsided look. It had no perceptible mouth or nose, and its eyes were crooked, one higher than the other, both a dingy brown with no whites at all. It stood quite still looking at her, its only movement a steady unalive quivering of its body.

It wondered about the queer little noise Babe had made.

Babe crept far back against a little pocket of stone, her brain running round and round in tiny circles of agony. She opened her mouth to cry out, and could not. Her eyes bulged and her face flamed with the strangling effort, and the two golden ropes of her braided hair twitched and twitched as she hunted hopelessly for a way out. If only she were out in the open—or in the wedge-shaped half-cave where the thing was—or home in bed!

The thing clumped toward her, expressionless, moving with a slow inevitability that was the sheer crux of horror. Babe lay wide-eyed and frozen, mounting pressure of terror stilling her lungs, making her heart shake the whole world. The monster came to the mouth of the little pocket, tried to walk to her and was stopped by the sides. It was such a narrow little fissure; and it was all Babe could do to get in. The thing from the wood stood straining against the rock at its shoulders, pressing harder and harder to get to Babe. She sat up slowly, so near to the thing that its odor was almost thick enough to see, and a wild hope burst through her voiceless fear. It couldn't get in! It couldn't get in because it was too big!

The substance of its feet spread slowly under the tremendous strain, and at its shoulder appeared a slight crack. It widened as the monster unfeelingly crushed itself against the rock, and suddenly a large piece of the shoulder came away and the being twisted slushily three feet farther in. It lay quietly with its muddy eyes fixed on her, and then brought one thick arm up over its head and reached.

Babe scrambled in the inch farther she had believed impossible, and the filthy clubbed hand stroked down her back, leaving a trail of muck on the blue denim of the shirt she wore. The monster surged suddenly and, lying full length now, gained the last precious inch. A black hand seized one of her braids, and for Babe the lights went out.

When she came to, she was dangling by her hair from that same crusted paw. The thing held her high, so that her face and its featureless head were not more than a foot apart. It gazed at her with a mild curiosity in its eyes, and it swung her slowly back and forth. The agony of her pulled hair did what fear could not do—gave her a voice. She screamed. She opened her mouth and puffed up her powerful young lungs, and she sounded off. She held her throat in the position of the first scream, and her chest labored and pumped more air through the frozen throat. Shrill and monotonous and infinitely piercing, her screams.

The thing did not mind. It held her as she was, and watched. When it had learned all it could from this phenomenon, it dropped her jarringly, and looked around the half-cave, ignoring the stunned and huddled Babe. It reached over and picked up the leather brief case and tore it twice across as if it were tissue. It saw the sandwich Babe had left, picked it up, crushed it, dropped it.

Babe opened her eyes, saw that she was free, and just as the thing turned back to her she dove between its legs and out into the shallow pool in front of the rock, paddled across and hit the other bank screaming. A vicious little light of fury burned in her; she picked up a grapefruit-sized stone and hurled it with all her frenzied might. It flew low and fast, and struck squashily on the monster's ankle. The thing was just taking a step toward the water; the stone caught it off balance, and its unpracticed equilibrium could not save it. It tottered for a long, silent moment at the edge and then splashed into the stream. Without a second look Babe ran shrieking away.

Cory Drew was following the little gobs of mold that somehow indicated the path of the murderer, and he was nearby when he first heard her scream. He broke into a run, dropping his shotgun and holding the .32-40 ready to fire. He ran with such deadly panic in his heart that he ran right past the huge cleft rock and was a hundred yards past it before she burst out through the pool and ran up the bank. He had to run hard and fast to catch her, because anything behind her was that faceless horror in the cave, and she was living for the one idea of getting away from there. He caught her in his arms and swung her to him, and she screamed on and on and on.

Babe didn't see Cory at all, even when he held her and quieted her.

The monster lay in the water. It neither liked nor disliked the new element. It rested on the bottom, its massive head a foot beneath the surface, and it curiously considered the facts that it had garnered. There was the little humming noise of Babe's voice that sent the monster questing into the cave. There was the black material of the brief case that resisted so much more than green things when he tore it. There was the little two-legged one who sang and brought him near, and who screamed when he came. There was this new cold moving thing he had fallen into. It was washing his body away. That had never happened before. That was interesting. The monster decided to stay and observe this new thing. It felt no urge to save itself; it could only be curious.

The brook came laughing down out of its spring, ran down from its source beckoning to the sunbeams and embracing freshets and helpful brooklets. It shouted and played with streaming little roots, and nudged the minnows and pollywogs about in its tiny backwaters. It was a happy brook. When it came to the pool by the cloven rock it found the monster there, and plucked at it. It soaked the foul substances and smoothed and melted the molds, and the waters below the thing eddied darkly with its diluted matter. It was a thorough brook. It washed all it touched, persistently. Where it found filth, it removed filth; and if there were layer on layer of foulness, then layer by foul layer it was removed. It was a good brook. It did not mind the poison of the monster, but took it up and thinned it and spread it in little rings around rocks downstream, and let it drift to the rootlets of water plants, that they might grow greener and lovelier. And the monster melted.

"I am smaller," the thing thought. "That is interesting. I could not move now. And now this part of me which thinks is going, too. It will stop in just a moment, and drift away with the rest of the body. It will stop thinking and I will stop being, and that, too, is a very interesting thing."

So the monster melted and dirtied the water, and the water was clean again, washing and washing the skeleton that the monster had left. It was not very big, and there was a badly healed knot on the left arm. The sunlight flickered on the triangular silver plate set into the pale skull, and the skeleton was very clean now. The brook laughed about it for an age.

*   *   *

They found the skeleton, six grim-lipped men who came to find a killer. No one had believed Babe, when she told her story days later. It had to be days later because Babe had screamed for seven hours without stopping, and had lain like a dead child for a day. No one believed her at all, because her story was all about the bad fella, and they knew that the bad fella was simply a thing that her father had made up to frighten her with. But it was through her that the skeleton was found, and so the men at the bank sent a check to the Drews for more money than they had ever dreamed about. It was old Roger Kirk, sure enough, that skeleton, though it was found five miles from where he had died and sank into the forest floor where the hot molds builded around his skeleton and emerged—a monster.

So the Drews had a new barn and fine new livestock and they hired four men. But they didn't have Alton. And they didn't have Kimbo. And Babe screams at night and has grown very thin.

WHERE THE
WOODBINE TWINETH

by Manly Wade Wellman

After he'd helped wash and wipe the supper dishes, young Jess Warrick climbed the ladder to his loft over the cabin; and when he swung down again, his mother asked, "How come you're all dressed up, boy?"

He'd put on his new jeans and a clean hickory shirt, with the sleeves rolled up his strong brown arms. "I felt sticky in the clothes I chopped weeds in today," he said.

"Thought you swum in the fish pond before supper," spoke up his father from where by the table lamp he read Virgil's *Aeneid* in Latin. No saying how many times Clay Warrick had been through that and all the other twenty books shelved on the fireboard. Clay Warrick was schooled, though he didn't let it hurt him.

"I still feel sticky," said Jess. "Reckon I'll go in again. It's a good moon up over Dogged Mountain."

He stood taller than his father, taller than his married brother George living four miles off in Sky Notch, taller than would have been air Warrick man if more had lived through the last fight with the Mair family fifty years back; taller than his grandsire Big Tobe, head of the Warrick clan, who'd died knifing it out with Burt Mair; taller than Big Tobe's two brothers and his son Bob; all of them tall but none as tall as Jess had got to be. His hair was Indian-black; he had dark eyes and scooped-out tan cheeks and a straight nose. Girls through those parts of the mountains called him good-looking.

"I'd not love to swim by strong moonlight," said Clay Warrick, but Jess made out like as if he didn't hear.

"The spring high's flowed off Walnut Creek," he said. "Water's clear enough there to show you a fish ten foot down."

"You be careful," warned his mother, like as if Jess was only six instead of twenty.

"And don't stay out late, hear?" said Clay Warrick. "We got to work high on the hill field tomorrow."

Jess raised the wooden latch and stepped out into the shiny night. A bat grabbed a bug in front of him. Another flopped higher. Jess had heard his father tell that Lord Byron thought bats were bad luck. He strode past the mail box and along the dirt road. When he got to where his mother couldn't watch and see, he cut left up Dogged Mountain's slope, toward where the Warricks and the Mairs had butchered one another that long-ago night.

Maybe he'd nair know the whole truth of that battle, for none who'd fought it lived to tell of it. His grandmother used to moan out her sad notion, before she died when Jess was ten. His father hadn't been but seven at the time. Nor could air soul guess just why the two clans had fought to the last man. Their bad feelings had gone back to the start of things among these mountains.

So they'd got to shooting from behind trees and rail fences, nibbling off enemies here and there. Till the night Big Tobe Warrick pulled together his brothers and nephews and his oldest boy Bob and went with loaded guns toward where the Mairs lived. But the Mairs had got out that night too, and in a brushy hollow on Dogged Mountain they'd wiped one another out. Big Tobe got his hands on Burt Mair and they'd each chopped the other to death with hunting knives. Dead, they'd clung to such a grapple the neighbor folks who'd found them couldn't drag them apart. So while the ten others who'd been killed were carried off to family burying grounds, the two chiefs were buried right where they'd died, with no prayer for them. Old Mr. Sam Upchurch, the store-keeper and township trustee, had said drive a locust-tree stake through both of them, to keep them from ever walking out and making fresh trouble. Dirt and rocks were heaped on them, and next week two preachers and the sheriff and the superior court judge had come around to beg the lady folks left alive in both families to swear peace and no more killing forever.

Peace was there, only once in a while at night there'd be a knock at a cabin door, and when you opened it, nobody came in. The hollow was named Lost Soul, and it grew up in the years with brush and with Virginia creeper and honeysuckle, two sorts of vines different folks call woodbine. No Mair and no Warrick air went near the place, except for Jess Warrick and, from the Mairs, a slim, tawny-haired girl named Midge. Because there, they figured, neither bunch of their hating folks would pester them from loving one another.

In the bright moonlight Jess trotted along a path where cows grazed by day. His long legs ate up a mile of ground his feet knew. In his mind, all unasked, ran a song he'd used to hear his grandmother hum:

> . . . Gone where the woodbine twineth,
> With the vine on the broken wall,
> 'Neath the shade of the weeping willow
> Where its drooping branches fall . . .

Round the jaw of the slope, now, would be Lost Soul Hollow.

Somebody moved in front of him, somebody in a long, shiny-gray gown. His heart jumped. Midge must be coming to meet him.

But, "Jess?" half-sang a low voice not Midge's. "Jess Warrick? Why are you out tonight, as if I didn't already know."

Air soul in those mountains knew Haidee Bettisthorne's voice. Jess stopped and she winnowed toward him, Haidee Bettisthorne folks called the witch-woman, moon-bright and bright as the moon. She was as tall as Jess

himself, and her fine proud shape showed through the
gray dress. Her hair made a black shadow around her
shoulders, her full dark mouth smiled, her eyes shone
green like an animal's.

"So," she half-sang at him, "you break your family's
rule and come to your grandsire's grave."

Witchcraft had told her he'd be out, the way it told
her how to whisper corn dead in the field, hogs dead in
the pen, or lame or blind you if you made her mad. "I
didn't make that rule, Miss Haidee," he said.

Laughing, she stood before him, her green eyes digging into his dark ones. She was beautiful but, gentlemen, she was creepy. Jess wondered how old or how
young she was.

"You know what they say walks here," she said.
"Tracks have been seen. Sometimes the two hind feet,
big and flat with claws. Sometimes the front feet too,
marking the earth like hands. Ever wonder what makes
them kind of tracks, Jess?"

He'd wondered. He'd seen the tracks, by light of day,
more or less near woodbiney Lost Hollow. But he had
made himself come there by night anyway.

"Some allow it's your dog," he said, and she laughed.
"It's mine, but it's not a dog." Her eyes glowed. "It
does me errands, it fetches me news."

He wondered if she was funning him. But for once she
sounded like the truth.

"Is Midge Mair worth coming here for?" Haidee Bettisthorne inquired him. "That little pan-of-milk girl?"
Her green eyes ran up and down him like fingers. "I
reckon you could do better than that, Jess."

Right then she looked no older than Jess, only smarter
and another sight wickeder. "Good job I'm the only one
know you two meet," she said. "A Warrick and a Mair.
Else the two clans would fetch out to look at you with
something in their hand besides a field glass."

"We're up to no harm," said Jess. "Not to one another
nor yet to our folks either side."

An owl hallooed in a tree over them.

"You think you're in love," she said, like a charge in law court.

"Yessum. It's a natural thing, Miss Haidee."

"Don't call me Miss Haidee; you sound like a little boy with his school teacher." A lick of her lips. "Though I might could teach you a thing or two at that."

She stirred her rich body inside the gown. "Maybe you want to be coaxed."

"I just want to get along this here trail."

"Well," and the moonlight spilled over her like pale fire, "why coax you? I have choice friends other places."

"I hear tell your sort goes in bands," said Jess, recollecting talk about witch covens.

"You sound scornful." She stood so close she almost touched against him. "Is that wise, Jess?"

"I don't claim much wisdom. I don't mean to say bad against you, just what I've heard tell for a fact."

"You're a fool," she smiled.

"We won't quarrel about that," said Jess. "Every day I try to be less of one, find out something new."

"Shall I teach you?" She was close. He smelled perfume of night flowers.

"No, ma'am, thank you anyway."

"You're not only a fool, Jess. You're afraid of me."

"I reckon I'd be twice foolish not to be kindly afraid of you," he agreed with her.

"You don't have the sense to know what I could give you, or the nerve to take it," said Haidee Bettisthorne. "Good night."

She slid out of his way and he passed her, quick as he could set foot. She laughed behind him. The owl hallooed again, and off yonder, some direction, a slap-slap-slap like the echo of guns going off in the dark. On the high ground to his left, a sense of things watching, figuring on him.

But he made the turn in the trail, and he saw Midge at the mouth of the dip of Lost Soul Hollow, saw her fair as an angel with her tawny hair bright in the moon and her two hands lifting to him. They came together and their arms flew round one another.

She was small and slim against him like that. He thought, how real Midge is, how flesh and blood and how good. Her mouth lived against his, eager but not greedy, a love kiss. She drew back and looked at him.

"You're pale," she whispered.

"That's moonwash on my face. Hark at me, Midge, I just saw Haidee Bettisthorne. She knows about us meeting."

"That old witch." Wide eyes in Midge's round face. "What'll she do?"

Jess felt they were being watched and harked at. "She allowed that our folks on both sides might fight again if they found us."

"That's no new thought to me. Why is she meddling, Jess?"

"Witch nature," he said. "Wanting to fetch on trouble. A witch is sworn to evil. I've heard tell of goings-on up in Avery County, down at the sea towns. Haidee Bettisthorne's made a many folks miserable. Now she wants to start in on us."

"She can't, Jess. Witches don't prevail against a clean heart, and we both got that."

A tree, a weeping willow like in his grandmother's song, hung low to where they held each other at the hollow's edge, with down in the dark the place where their dead grandfathers lay buried and staked down. Not a comfortable tree, nor yet the bushes clumped in the moonlight, like things with heads betwixt hunched shoulders. Flecks of light made eyes in them. They looked to have snouts. The willow reached down branches, like arms with long twig fingers. It was embarrassing to be watched like that when you were with your true love.

"That's right, Midge," Jess said. "If there's evil on this earth, there must be good. We couldn't last a minute else."

"I wouldn't come here but to meet you," she said back. "Good and strong as you are. How long can we go on, Jess?"

He took hold of her smooth, round arms. "Let's not

go on like this at all," he said all of a sudden. "Let's run off together."

"Off where?" she asked him, ready to go.

"Anywhere. I've got some money saved up. We'll take a bus, find a town where I can work. Hark, Midge, what if this is what our folks need? Us two loving one another, maybe softening up this old hate and madness, one family against the other?"

"When shall we go?" she asked him, ready.

"Right now." He made up his mind as he said it. "Tonight. Soon as your folks are asleep, put on your best dress and shoes and take what you can bring that you'll need. Come back here and so will I. We'll head for the highway, to where we can flag that early-morning bus. Buy tickets to some big town where they can't seek us out."

Her kiss was strong and glad. "I'll be here," she said.

They left, two ways. It seemed the willow reached for them to hold them there, but that might have been moon shadows. And whatever watched them from around Lost Soul Hollow, it watched Jess as he went.

On the way home he thought something moved ahead of him, but couldn't be sure. In the cabin again, he made a big yawn and allowed he'd go up to bed. He got a few things together in the loft, a shirt and socks and some underwear to put in a croker sack, and he tied on a black tie and got a jacket and his Stetson hat. From behind a rafter he scooped the little purse that held maybe eighty dollars and some change. He wrote a note on a paper bag and left it on the pillow. Then he blew out the light and sat on the cot and waited and waited.

He heard his parents go to their room and saw the light die out from below. He kept waiting. They must be asleep now. He hiked up the loft window, slow and quiet, swung out of it into the tree behind, the way he used to when playing as a boy.

Down he climbed. Pod, the old mule, stamped in the shed, but the cows made nair sound. Jess moved quietly around the cabin and to the trail, taking the way he'd taken once tonight to meet Midge Mair.

Only now there'd come a fog of cloud in the sky, making the moon look like a dab of butter, and away off there he heard a noise, half like a laugh, half like a strangle. Following the trail, he looked up slope. He saw Haidee Bettisthorne, no missing the glow of her gray dress, and something with her. It was a dark shape, stood up before her with humped shoulders, its face close to hers, whatever face it had. Then it dropped down and moved beyond her on all fours. She said something to it as it went.

Jess felt glad he was going to leave that place, to some part of the world where he'd see no more of that witch-woman or that thing she said wasn't a dog.

On he went in the muggy night that had lost half its shine, his feet finding the way along for him. Around the turn upslope, and there ahead was Lost Soul Hollow, all black in the gray ground, all full of woodbine and brush, and there was Midge.

"Jess!" she breathed hard at him. "Somebody's coming!"

"There sure enough is," he said, for up-slope behind her moved black shapes, moved a string of black shapes, three or four. "Duck down in the hollow, quick."

"They're coming from below after you, Jess."

Then he looked round, and there were more black things, strung out and closing in from the other direction. For God's sake, what were they?

Whatever they were, both bunches hemmed him and Midge in there by Lost Soul Hollow. He pulled her down among the mess of brush and woodbine.

"You Warricks think you'll hide out on us?" bawled a voice from up the mountain. "Come out and fight like a man!"

"Ain't hiding no such thing!" came back another loud voice from down the slope, and Jess knew it. "No Warrick air yet hid out from all the Mairs in the world!"

Now he knew. It wasn't witch stuff, it was real and it was mean. Midge's folks and his folks had come together there and meant to fight it out, though they'd sworn never to fight again. And Jess and Midge were at the hollow, betwixt the two clans.

"Wish I could get me a hold of a gun," he said, out loud to himself.

"No guns," Midge wailed. "What did guns ever get for our folks but grief? If somebody's got to be shot, they can shoot me."

He grabbed her back from climbing out of the tangle of vines. "You stay down," he ordered, like as if he owned her. "I'll go up, I'll talk to them—"

If he could just have a club. He rummaged both hands amongst the vines and grabbed onto a stob there. It felt like a pick handle. He gave a twist and a yank, he rocked it to and fro. It came clear, like pulling up a big carrot. It was big enough to bat sense into a head with. "Stay here," he told Midge again and scrambled out of there, on his knees and one hand, the other holding that chunk of wood. On the ground above he stood up.

"Which Mair's that, daring me?" howled the voice he knew.

"It's me, P'," he called back.

"I hear a Warrick," came a yell from the up side. "Stand off, youins, I'm a-going to shoot."

Jess was glad for the foggy night. Maybe it wouldn't be good aim against him. He hunched down a bit and heard scrambling below.

"I said stay down, Midge," he said, but it wasn't Midge coming up.

Two shapes climbed to the top beside him. Big men, flapping rags of clothes, making deep-breath noises. They held one another by the hand; they were both broad and near as tall as Jess, and he could see them.

Could see them in the dark cloudiness, because there was some sort of fox-fire light on them, enough to see their faces. Their dark, crinkled faces, like tree bark, with teeth.

"Don't shoot," wailed one of them, in a woolly kind of voice, like as if his insides was full of the fog.

"Who's that talking?" snarled somebody from up there, and that must be Midge's father, a black shadow off there with the black shadow of a rifle slanting across in its hands.

"You know me, Lee," said the woolly voice. "You know me, Lee Mair, my son."

"Pa!" That was a wail. The Mairs had come close, but they'd stopped. The shape that had spoken moved out of the bushes toward them. It must have let go the other one's hand. The other one paced down-slope towards the Warrick bunch, pacing slowly, as if its knees and feet were sore. The soft light of it flickered.

Jess heard both sets of folks jabbering out things, but he couldn't make out what. The two things out of the hollow kept on the move, slow but steady, each headed for one of the clans. Looking this way and that, Jess saw them lift their arms up wide and high. Those arms were gaunt as bones, with old dark rags of sleeves falling away from them.

He made out that the two bunches who'd come after him and Midge, the Mairs and the Warricks, might could want to run, but neither was running. The two things came at the two families, and Jess heard the voices, moany sighs of voices. Somebody or other answered in a living voice, purely scared but talking. Then, and it was like long hours later, though it couldn't be that long, the two fox-fiery shapes turned and came back toward Lost Soul Hollow, each from its errand. All Jess could do was stand and wait for them to come in from the up side and the down side. He'd not done aught but stand and wait the whole while, with that stick in his hand.

Closer they came. Closer. He looked back and forth at them. They were dark in the crinkly faces, but their heads looked ashy white on top, with streaky strands of hair. Through their rags he thought he saw bones moving. They were close enough for him to hit them now, but he didn't hit. Back down in the hollow they went, each from his side, and amongst the brush and vines. Midge gave a whimper, as if she couldn't raise the breath to scream, and she came climbing up beside Jess.

"What were they?" she made out to say. "Oh, what—"

"Can't rightly say, Midge," he replied her, though he was beginning to guess.

Now those two bunches of folks came toward them. Jess and Midge stood and waited, and at last Jess hefted the club in his hand.

"Boy," he heard his father saying, "what you up to out here?"

"Come home, Midgie," said somebody from the other side. It had to be Lee Mair.

Both bunches came and stood at the sides of the hollow, looking across at one another and at Midge and Jess.

"If youins got to shoot, start shooting," said Clay Warrick. "I can't, not after what I was told just now."

"Nor me," said Lee Mair back. "The shooting's over and past."

Both of them started talking and others chimed in. Both crowds, the Mairs and the Warricks, had been told not to shoot. It was Tobe Warrick had told his family, and Burt Mair had told his.

"My pa said, him and Tobe Warrick had laid side by side, spiked together, for what felt like a million years," Midge's father said. "Told me, they'd learned to know one another, be friends. Said it was for us, the living ones, to be friends, too, start looking one another in the face."

"My pa told me the same," owned up Clay Warrick. "Said if we didn't, him and your pa would come back and see why not. And I don't want them to come back, never no more."

"Never no more," Lee Mair repeated him. The two fathers looked just then how Tobe Warrick and Burt Mair might could have looked, long ago, if somebody had made them listen to sense and reason.

"Hark at me one time," spoke up Jess. Tired-feeling, he leaned on his club. "How come youins both to be out here?"

"It was Haidee Bettisthorne," his father replied him. "Come and said Midge Mair was a-going to tole you off to where her folks could kill you."

"That's what she told us!" came out Lee Mair. "She swore up and down Jess was out to kill Midge, we'd better come and save her."

"She lied to both of us," said Clay Warrick. "Lee Mair, she wanted to get the shooting started all over. That's a witch way, making trouble and grief. Just for the making."

"We should ought to make Haidee Bettisthorne scarce and hard to find," said Jess's brother George, the first he'd said yet.

All of them started talking. How sorry they were they'd been mad with each other, how glad they were it hadn't come to bloodshed, how it was Haidee Bettisthorne's doing. Finally Jess drew a big breath of air into him and flung the club down on the ground.

"What's that, son?" his father inquired him, stooping for it. "I swanny, it's a piece of old locust tree, big as a fence post."

"I got it down there amongst the vines," said Jess.

"A stake driven there," said Midge softly. "That's what it was."

And that's what it had been. The locust stake, driven fifty years ago through Tobe Warrick and Burt Mair, where they'd died grappling one another, to keep them in their grave. The stake Jess had yanked out, to fight what fight he didn't rightly know. And it had turned them loose to come out and speak to their kinfolks, and now they'd gone back, and now maybe they were at rest.

Things turned out pretty much to the good. When Jess and Midge got married, Burt Mair gave the bride away and Clay Warrick stood up with his son. But nobody did aught about Haidee Bettisthorne. Because when folks went looking for her, she couldn't be found, ever again in those parts of the mountains. As to whatever helped her that wasn't her dog, it seems to be gone too, though once in a while somebody sees funny tracks. Funny, but not laughing-at funny.

AFTERWARD

by Edith Wharton

"Oh, there *is* one, of course, but you'll never know it."

The assertion, laughingly flung out six months earlier in a bright June garden, came back to Mary Boyne with a new perception of its significance as she stood, in the December dusk, waiting for the lamps to be brought into the library.

The words had been spoken by their friend Alida Stair, as they sat at tea on her lawn at Pangbourne, in reference to the very house of which the library in question was the central, the pivotal "feature." Mary Boyne and her husband, in quest of a country place in one of the southern or southwestern counties, had, on their arrival in England, carried their problem straight to Alida Stair, who had successfully solved it in her own case; but it was not until they had rejected, almost capriciously, several practical and judicious suggestions that she threw out: "Well, there's Lyng, in Dorsetshire. It belongs to Hugo's cousins, and you can get it for a song."

The reason she gave for its being obtainable on these terms—its remoteness from a station, its lack of electric light, hot water pipes, and other vulgar necessities—were exactly those pleading in its favor with two romantic Americans perversely in search of the economic drawbacks which were associated, in their tradition, with unusual architectural felicities.

"I should never believe I was living in an old house unless I was thoroughly uncomfortable," Ned Boyne, the more extravagant of the two, had jocosely insisted; "the least hint of convenience would make me think it had been bought out of an exhibition, with the pieces numbered, and set up again." And they had proceeded to enumerate, with humorous precision, their various doubts and demands, refusing to believe that the house their cousin recommended was *really* Tudor till they learned it had no heating system, or that the village church was literally in the grounds till she assured them of the deplorable uncertainty of the water supply.

"It's too uncomfortable to be true!" Edward Boyne had continued to exult as the avowal of each disadvantage was successively wrung from her; but he had cut short his rhapsody to ask, with a relapse to distrust: "And the ghost? You've been concealing from us the fact that there is no ghost!"

Mary, at the moment, had laughed with him, yet almost with her laugh, being possessed of several sets of independent perceptions, had been struck by a note of flatness in Alida's answering hilarity.

"Oh, Dorsetshire's full of ghosts, you know."

"Yes, yes; but that won't do. I don't want to have to drive ten miles to see somebody else's ghost. I want one of my own on the premises. *Is* there a ghost at Lyng?"

His rejoinder had made Alida laugh again, and it was then that she had flung back tantalizing: "Oh, there *is* one, of course, but you'll never know it."

"Never know it?" Boyne pulled her up. "But what in the world constitutes a ghost except the fact of its being known for one?"

"I can't say. But that's the story."

"That there's a ghost, that nobody knows it's a ghost?"

"Well—not till afterward, at any rate."

"Till afterward?"

"Not till long long afterward."

"But if it's once been identified as an unearthly visitant, why hasn't it *signalement* been handed down in the family? How has it managed to preserve its incognito?"

Alida could only shake her head. "Don't ask me. But it has."

"And then suddenly"—Mary spoke up as if from cavernous depths of divination—"suddenly, long afterward, one says to one's self *That was it?*'"

She was startled at the sepulchral sound with which her question fell on the banter of the other two, and she saw the shadow of the same surprise flit across Alida's pupils. "I suppose so. One just has to wait."

"Oh, hang waiting!" Ned broke in. "Life's too short for a ghost who can only be enjoyed in retrospect. Can't we do better than that, Mary?"

But it turned out that in the event they were not destined to, for within three months of their conversation with Mrs. Stair they were settled at Lyng, and the life they had yearned for, to the point of planning it in advance in all its daily details, had actually begun for them.

It was to sit, in the thick December dusk, by just such a wide-hooded fireplace, under just such black oak rafters, with the sense that beyond the mullioned panes the downs were darkened to a deeper solitude: it was for the ultimate indulgence of such sensations that Mary Boyne, abruptly exiled from New York by her husband's business, had endured for nearly fourteen years the soul-deadening ugliness of a Middle Western town, and that Boyne had ground on doggedly at his engineering till, with a suddenness that still made her blink, the prodigious windfall of the Blue Star mine had put them at a stroke in possession of life and the leisure to taste it. They had never for a moment meant their new state to be one of idleness; but they meant to give themselves only to harmonious activities. She had her vision of painting and gardening (against a background of grey walls), he dreamed of the production of his long-planned book on the "Economic Basis of Culture"; and with such absorbing work ahead no existence could be too sequestered: they could not get far enough from the world, or plunge deep enough into the past.

Dorsetshire had attracted them from the first by an air of remoteness out of all proportion to its geographical position. But to the Boynes it was one of the ever-recurring wonders of the whole incredibly compressed island—

a nest of counties, as they put it—that for the production
of its effects so little of a given quality went so far: that
so few miles made a distance, and so short a distance a
difference.

"It's that," Ned had once enthusiastically explained,
"that gives such depth to their effects, such relief to their
contrasts. They've been able to lay the butter so thick
on every delicious mouthful."

The butter had certainly been laid on thick at Lyng:
the old house hidden under a shoulder of the downs had
almost all the finer marks of commerce with a protracted
past. The mere fact that it was neither large nor exceptional made it, to the Boynes, abound the more completely in its special charm—the charm of having been
for centuries a deep dim reservoir of life. The life had
probably not been of the most vivid order: for long peri-
ods, no doubt, it had fallen as noiselessly into the past
as the quiet drizzle of autumn fell, hour after hour, into
the fish pond between the yews; but these backwaters of
existence sometimes breed, in their sluggish depths,
strange acuities of emotion, and Mary Boyne· had felt
from the first the mysterious stir of intenser memories.

The feeling had never been stronger than on this particular afternoon when, waiting in the library for the
lamps to come, she rose from her seat and stood among
the shadows of the hearth. Her husband had gone off,
after luncheon, for one of his long tramps on the downs.
She had noticed of late that he preferred to go alone;
and, in the tried security of their personal relations, had
been driven to conclude that his book was bothering him,
and that he needed the afternoons to turn over in solitude the problems left from the morning's work. Certainly the book was not going as smoothly as she had
thought it would, and there were lines of perplexity
between his eyes such as had never been there in his
engineering days. He had often, then, looked fagged to
the verge of illness, but the native demon of worry had
never branded his brow. Yet the few pages he had so
far read to her—the introduction, and a summary of the

opening chapter—showed a firm hold on his subject, and an increasing confidence in his powers.

The fact threw her into deeper perplexity, since, now that he had done with business and its disturbing contingencies, the one other possible source of anxiety was eliminated. Unless it were his health, then? But physically he had gained since they had come to Dorsetshire, grown robuster, ruddier and fresher eyed. It was only within the last week that she had felt in him the undefinable change which made her restless in his absence, and as tongue-tied in his presence as though it were *she* who had a secret to keep from him!

The thought that there *was* a secret somewhere between them struck her with a sudden rap of wonder, and she looked about her down the long room.

"Can it be the house?" she mused.

The room itself might have been full of secrets. They seemed to be piling themselves up, as evening fell, like the layers and layers of velvet shadow dropping from the low ceiling, the rows of books, the smoke-blurred sculpture of the hearth.

"Why, of course—the house is haunted!" she reflected.

The ghost—Alida's imperceptible ghost—after figuring largely in the banter of their first month or two at Lyng, had been gradually left aside as too ineffectual for imaginative use. Mary had, indeed, as became the tenant of a haunted house, made the customary inquiries among her rural neighbors, but beyond, a vague "They do say so, Ma'am," the villagers had nothing to impart. The elusive specter had apparently never had sufficient identity for a legend to crystallize about it, and after a time the Boynes had set the matter down to their profit-and-loss account, agreeing that Lyng was one of the few houses good enough in itself to dispense with supernatural enhancements.

"And I suppose, poor ineffectual demon, that's why it beats its beautiful wings in vain in the void," Mary had laughingly concluded.

"Or rather," Ned answered in the same strain, "why

amid so much that's ghostly, it can never affirm its separate existence as *the* ghost." And thereupon their invisible housemate had finally dropped out of their references, which were numerous enough to make them soon unaware of the loss.

Now, as she stood on the hearth, the subject of their earlier curiosity revived in her with a new sense of its meaning—a sense gradually acquired through daily contact with the scene of the lurking mystery. It was the house itself, of course, that possessed the ghost-seeing faculty, that communed visually but secretly with its own past; if one could only get into close enough communion with the house, one might surprise its secret, and acquire the ghost sight on one's own account. Perhaps, in his long hours in this very room, where she never trespassed till the afternoon, her husband *had* acquired it already, and was silently carrying about the weight of whatever it had revealed to him. Mary was too well versed in the code of the spectral world not to know that one could not talk about the ghosts one saw: to do so was almost as great a breach of taste as to name a lady in a club. But this explanation did not really satisfy her. "What, after all, except for the fun of the shudder," she reflected, "would he really care for any of their old ghosts?" And thence she was thrown back once more on the fundamental dilemma: the fact that one's greater or less susceptibility to spectral influences had no particular bearing on the case, since, when one *did* see a ghost at Lyng, one did not know it.

"Not till long afterward," Alida Stair had said. Well, supposing Ned *had* seen one when they first came, and had known only within the last week what had happened to him? More and more under the spell of the hour, she threw back her thoughts to the early days of their tenancy, but at first only to recall a lively confusion of unpacking, settling, arranging of books, and calling to each other from remote corners of the house as, treasure after treasure, it revealed itself to them. It was in this particular connection that she presently recalled a certain soft afternoon of the previous October, when, passing from the first rapturous flurry of exploration to a detailed inspection of the old house, she had pressed (like a novel heroine) a panel that opened on a flight of corkscrew stairs leading to a flat ledge of the roof—the roof which, from below, seemed to slope away on all sides too abruptly for any but practiced feet to scale.

The view from this hidden coign was enchanting, and she had flown down to snatch Ned from his papers and give him the freedom of her discovery. She remembered still how, standing at her side, he had passed his arm about her while their gaze flew to the long tossed horizon line of the downs, and then dropped contentedly back to trace the arabesque of yew hedges about the fish pond, and the shadow of the cedar on the lawn.

"And now the other way," he had said, turning her about within his arm; and closely pressed to him, she had absorbed, like some long satisfying draught, the picture of the grey-walled court, the squat lions on the gates, and the lime avenue reaching up to the highroad under the downs.

It was just then, while they gazed and held each other, that she had felt his arm relax, and heard a sharp "Hullo!" that made her turn to glance at him.

Distinctly, yes, she now recalled that she had seen, as she glanced, a shadow of anxiety, of perplexity, rather, fall across his face; and, following his eyes, had beheld the figure of a man—a man in loose greyish clothes, as it appeared to her—who was sauntering down the lime avenue to the court with the doubtful gait of a stranger who seeks his way. Her shortsighted eyes hàd given her but a blurred impression of slightness and greyishness, with something foreign, or at least unlocal, in the cut of the figure or its dress; but her husband had apparently seen more—seen enough to make him push past her with a hasty "Wait!" and dash down the stairs without pausing to give her a hand.

A slight tendency to dizziness obliged her, after a provisional clutch at the chimney against which they had been leaning, to follow him first more cautiously; and when she had reached the landing she paused again, for a less definite reason, leaning over the banister to strain her eyes through the silence of the brown sun-flecked depths. She lingered there till, somewhere in those depths, she heard the closing of a door; then, mechanically impelled, she went down the shallow flights of steps till she reached the lower hall.

The front door stood open on the sunlight of the court, and hall and court were empty. The library door was open, too, and after listening in vain for any sound of voices within, she crossed the threshold, and found her husband alone, vaguely fingering the papers on his desk.

He looked up, as if surprised at her entrance, but the shadow of anxiety had passed from his face, leaving it even, as she fancied, a little brighter and clearer than usual.

"What was it? Who was it?" she asked.

"Who?" he repeated, with the surprise still all on his side.

"The man we saw coming toward the house."

He seemed to reflect. "The man? Why, I thought I saw Peters; I dashed after him to say a word about the stable drains, but he had disappeared before I could get down."

"Disappeared? But he seemed to be walking so slowly when we saw him."

Boyne shrugged his shoulders. "So I thought; but he must have got up steam in the interval. What do you say to our trying a scramble up Meldon Steep before sunset?"

That was all. At the time the occurrence had been less than nothing, had, indeed, been immediately obliterated by the magic of their first vision from Meldon Steep, a height which they had dreamed of climbing ever since they had first seen its bare spine rising above the roof of Lyng. Doubtless it was the mere fact of the other incident's having occurred on the very day of their ascent to Meldon that had kept it stored away in the fold of memory from which it now emerged; for in itself it had no mark of the portentous. At the moment there could have been nothing more natural than that Ned should dash

himself from the roof in the pursuit of dilatory tradesmen. It was the period when they were always on the
watch for one or the other of the specialists employed
about the place; always lying in wait for them, and rushing out at them with questions, reproaches or reminders.
And certainly in the distance the grey figure had looked
like Peters.

Yet now, as she reviewed the scene, she felt her husband's explanation of it to have been invalidated by the
look of anxiety on his face. Why had the familiar appearance of Peters made him anxious? Why, above all, if it
was such prime necessity to confer with him on the subject of the stable drains, had the failure to find him produced such a look of relief? Mary could not say that any
one of these questions had occurred to her at the time,
yet, from the promptness with which they now mar-
shalled themselves at her summons, she had a sense that
they must all along have been there, waiting their hour.

II

Weary with her thoughts, she moved to the window. The
library was now quite dark, and she was surprised to see
how much light the outer world still held.

As she peered out into it across the court, a figure
shaped itself far down the perspective of bare limes: it
looked a mere blot of deeper grey in the greyness, and
for an instant, as it moved toward her, her heart thumped
to the thought "It's the ghost!"

She had time, in that long instant, to feel suddenly
that the man of whom, two months earlier, she had had
a distant vision from the roof, was now, at his predes-
tined hour, about to reveal himself as *not* having been
Peters; and her spirit sank under the impending fear of
the disclosure. But almost with the next tick of the clock
the figure, gaining substance and character, showed itself
even to her weak sight as her husband's; and she turned
to meet him, as he entered, with the confession of her
folly.

"It's really too absurd," she laughed out, "but I never *can* remember!"

"Remember what?" Boyne questioned as they drew together.

"That when one sees the Lyng ghost one never knows it."

Her hand was on his sleeve, and he kept it there, but with no response in his gesture or in the lines of his preoccupied face.

"Did you think you'd seen it?" he asked, after an appreciable interval.

"Why, I actually took *you* for it, my dear, in my mad determination to spot it!"

"Me—just now?" His arm dropped away, and he turned from her with a faint echo of her laugh. "Really, dearest, you'd better give it up, if that's the best you can do."

"Oh, yes, I give it up. Have *you?*" she asked, turning round on him abruptly.

The parlormaid had entered with letters and a lamp, and the light struck up into Boyne's face as he bent above the tray she presented.

"Have *you!*" Mary perversely insisted, when the servant had disappeared on her errand of illumination.

"Have I what?" he rejoined absently, the light bringing out the sharp stamp of worry between his brows as he turned over the letters.

"Given up trying to see the ghost." Her heart beat a little at the experiment she was making.

Her husband, laying his letters aside, moved away into the shadow of the hearth.

"I never tried," he said, tearing open the wrapper of a newspaper.

"Well, of course," Mary persisted, "the exasperating thing is that there's no use trying, since one can't be sure till so long afterward."

He was unfolding the paper as if he had hardly heard her; but after a pause, during which the sheets rustled spasmodically between his hands, he looked up to ask, "Have you any idea *how long?*"

Mary had sunk into a low chair beside the fireplace. From her seat she glanced over, startled, at her husband's profile, which was projected against the circle of lamplight.

"No; none. Have *you?*" she retorted, repeating her former phrase with an added stress of intention.

Boyne crumpled the paper into a bunch, and then, inconsequently, turned back with it toward the lamp.

"Lord, no! I only meant," he exclaimed, with a faint tinge of impatience, "is there any legend, any tradition, as to that?"

"Not that I know of," she answered; but the impulse to add "What makes you ask?" was checked by the reappearance of the parlormaid, with tea and a second lamp.

With the dispersal of shadows, and the reception of the daily domestic office, Mary Boyne felt herself less oppressed by that sense of something mutely imminent which had darkened her afternoon. For a few moments she gave herself to the details of her task, and when she looked up from it she was struck to the point of bewilderment by the change in her husband's face. He had seated himself near the farther lamp, and was absorbed in the perusal of his letters; but was it something he had found in them, or merely the shifting of her own point of view, that had restored his features to their normal aspect? The longer she looked the more definitely the change affirmed itself. The lines of tension had vanished, and such traces of fatigue as lingered were of the kind easily attributable to steady mental effort. He glanced up, as if drawn by her gaze, and met her eyes with a smile.

"I'm dying for my tea, you know; and here's a letter for you," he said.

She took the letter he held out in exchange for the cup she proffered him, and, returning to her seat, broke the seal with the languid gesture of the reader whose interests are all enclosed in the circle of one cherished presence.

Her next conscious motion was that of starting to her

feet, the letter falling to them as she rose, while she held out to her husband a newspaper clipping.

"Ned! What's this? What does it mean?"

He had risen at the same instant, almost as if hearing her cry before she uttered it; and for a perceptible space of time he and she studied each other, like adversaries watching for an advantage, across the space between her chair and his desk.

"What's what? You fairly made me jump!" Boyne said at length, moving toward her with a sudden half-exasperated laugh. The shadow of apprehension was on his face again, not now a look of fixed foreboding, but a shifting vigilance of lips and eyes that gave her the sense of his feeling himself invisibly surrounded.

Her hand shook so that she could hardly give him the clipping. "This article—from the *Waukesha Sentinel*— that a man named Elwell has brought suit against you— that there was something wrong about the Blue Star Mine. I can't understand more than half."

They continued to face each other as she spoke, and to her astonishment she saw that her words had the almost immediate effect of dissipating the strained watchfulness of his look.

"Oh, *that*!" He glanced down the printed slip, and then folded it with the gesture of one who handles something harmless and familiar. "What's the matter with you this afternoon, Mary? I thought you'd got bad news."

She stood before him with her undefinable terror subsiding slowly under the reassurance of his tone.

"You knew about this, then—it's all right?"

"Certainly I knew about it; and it's all right."

"But what *is* it? I don't understand. What does this man accuse you of?"

"Pretty nearly every crime in the calendar." Boyne had tossed the clipping down, and thrown himself into an armchair near the fire. "Do you want to hear the story? It's not particularly interesting—just a squabble over interests in the Blue Star."

"But who is this Elwell? I don't know the name."

"Oh, he's a fellow I put into it—gave him a hand up. I told you all about him at the time."

"I dare say. I must have forgotten." Vainly she strained back among her memories. "But if you helped him, why does he make this return?"

"Probably some shyster lawyer got hold of him and talked him over. It's all rather technical and complicated. I thought that kind of thing bored you."

His wife felt a sting of compunction. Theoretically, she deprecated the American wife's detachment from her husband's professional interests, but in practice she had always found it difficult to fix her attention on Boyne's report of the transactions in which his varied interests involved him. Besides, she had felt during their years of exile, that, in a community where the amenities of living could be obtained only at the cost of efforts as arduous as her husband's professional labors, such brief leisure as he and she could command should be used as an escape from immediate preoccupations, a flight to the life they always dreamed of living. Once or twice, now that this new life had actually drawn its magic circle about them, she had asked herself if she had done right; but hitherto such conjectures had been no more than the retrospective excursions of an active fancy. Now, for the first time, it startled her a little to find how little she knew of the material foundation on which her happiness was built.

She glanced at her husband, and was again reassured by the composure of his face; yet she felt the need of more definite grounds for her assurance.

"But doesn't this suit worry you? Why have you never spoken to me about it?"

He answered both questions at once. "I didn't speak of it at first because it *did* worry me—annoyed me, rather. But it's all ancient history now. Your correspondent must have got hold of a back number of the *Sentinel*."

She felt a quick thrill of relief. "You mean it's over? He's lost his case?"

There was a just perceptible delay in Boyne's reply. "The suit's been withdrawn—that's all."

But she persisted, as if to exonerate herself from the inward charge of being too easily put off. "Withdrawn it because he saw he had no chance?"

"Oh, he had no chance," Boyne answered.

She was still struggling with a dimly felt perplexity at the back of her thoughts.

"How long ago was it withdrawn?"

He paused, as if with a slight return to his former uncertainty. "I've just had the news now; but I've been expecting it."

"Just now—in one of your letters?"

"Yes; in one of my letters."

She made no answer, and was aware only, after a short interval of waiting, that he had risen, and, strolling across the room, had placed himself on the sofa at her side. She felt him, as he did so, pass an arm about her, she felt his hand seek hers and clasp it, and turning slowly, drawn by the warmth of his cheek, she met his smiling eyes.

"It's all right—it's all right?" she questioned, through the flood of her dissolving doubts; and "I give you my word it was never righter!" he laughed back at her, holding her close.

III

One of the strangest things she was afterward to recall out of all the next day's strangeness was the sudden and complete recovery of her sense of security.

It was in the air when she woke in her low-ceiled, dusky room; it went with her downstairs to the breakfast table, flashed out at her from the fire, and reduplicated itself from the flanks of the urn and the sturdy flutings of the Georgian teapot. It was as if in some roundabout way, all her diffused fears of the previous day, with their moment of sharp concentration about the newspaper article—as if this dim questioning of the future, and startled return upon the past, had between them liquidated the arrears of some haunting moral obligation. If she had indeed been careless of her husband's affairs, it was, her new state seemed to prove, because her faith in him instinctively justified such carelessness; and his right to her faith had now affirmed itself in the very face of menace and suspicion. She had never seen him more untroubled, more naturally and unconsciously himself, than after the cross-examination to which she had subjected him: it was almost as if he had been aware of her doubts, and had wanted the air cleared as much as she did.

It was as clear, thank heaven, as the bright outer light that surprised her almost with a touch of summer when she issued from the house for her daily round of the gardens. She had left Boyne at his desk, indulging herself, as she passed the library door, by a last peep at his quiet face, where he bent, pipe in mouth, above his papers; and now she had her own morning's task to perform. The task involved, on such charmed winter days, almost as much happy loitering about the different quarters of her domain as if spring were already at work there. There were such endless possibilities still before her, such opportunities to bring out the latent graces of the old place, without a single irreverent touch of alteration, that the winter was all too short to plan what spring and autumn executed. And her recovered sense of safety gave, on this particular morning, a peculiar zest to her progress through the sweet still place. She went first to the kitchen garden, where the espaliered pear trees drew complicated patterns on the walls, and pigeons were fluttering and preening about the silvery-slated roof of their cot. There was something wrong about the piping of the hothouse, and she was expecting an authority from Dorchester, who was to drive out between trains and make a diagnosis of the boiler. But when she dipped into the damp heat of the greenhouses, among the spiced scents and waxy pinks and reds of old-fashioned exotics—even the flora of Lyng was in the note!—she learned that the great man had not arrived, and, the day being too rare to waste in an artificial atmosphere, she came out again and paced along the springy turf of the bowling green to the gardens behind the house. At their farther end rose a grass terrace, looking across the fish pond and yew hedges to the long house front with its twisted chimney stacks and blue roof angles all drenched in the pale gold moisture of the air.

Seen thus, across the level tracery of the gardens, it sent her, from open windows and hospitably smoking chimneys, the look of some warm human presence, of a mind slowly ripened on a sunny wall of experience. She had never before had such a sense of her intimacy with it, such a conviction that its secrets were all beneficent, kept, as they said to children, "for one's good," such a trust in its power to gather up her life and Ned's into the harmonious pattern of the long long story it sat there weaving in the sun.

She heard steps behind her, and turned, expecting to see the gardener accompanied by the engineer from Dorchester. But only one figure was in sight, that of a youngish slightly built man, who, for reasons she could not on the spot have given, did not remotely resemble her notion of an authority on hothouse boilers. The newcomer, on seeing her, lifted his hat, and paused with the air of a gentleman—perhaps a traveler—who wishes to make it known that his intrusion is involuntary. Lyng occasionally attracted the more cultivated traveler, and Mary half expected to see the stranger dissemble a camera, or justify his presence by producing it. But he made no gesture of any sort, and after a moment she asked, in a tone responding to the courteous hesitation of his attitude: "Is there anyone you wish to see?"

"I came to see Mr. Boyne," he answered. His intonation, rather than his accent, was faintly American, and Mary, at the note, looked at him more closely. The brim of his soft felt hat cast a shade on his face, which, thus obscured, wore to her shortsighted gaze a look of seriousness, as of a person arriving on business, and civilly but firmly aware of his rights.

Past experience had made her equally sensible to such claims; but she was jealous of her husband's morning hours, and doubtful of his having given anyone the right to intrude on them.

"Have you an appointment with my husband?" she asked.

The visitor hesitated, as if unprepared for the question. "I think he expects me," he replied.

It was Mary's turn to hesitate. "You see this is his time for work: he never sees anyone in the morning."

He looked at her a moment without answering; then, as if accepting her decision, he began to move away. As he turned, Mary saw him pause and glance up at the peaceful house front. Something in his air suggested weariness and disappointment, the dejection of the traveler who has come from far off and whose hours are limited by the timetable. It occurred to her that if this were the case her refusal might have made his errand vain, and a sense of compunction caused her to hasten after him.

"May I ask if you have come a long way?"

He gave her the same grave look. "Yes—I have come a long way."

"Then, if you'll go to the house, no doubt my husband will see you now. You'll find him in the library."

She did not know why she had added the last phrase, except from a vague impulse to atone for her previous inhospitality. The visitor seemed about to express his thanks, but her attention was distracted by the approach of the gardener with a companion who bore all the marks of being the expert from Dorchester.

"This way," she said, waving the stranger to the house; and an instant later she had forgotten him in the absorption of her meeting with the boiler maker.

The encounter led to such far-reaching results that the engineer ended by finding it expedient to ignore his train, and Mary was beguiled into spending the remainder of the morning in absorbed confabulation among the flower pots. When the colloquy ended, she was surprised to find that it was nearly luncheon time, and she half expected, as she hurried back to the house, to see her husband coming out to meet her. But she found no one in the court but an undergardener raking the gravel, and the hall, when she entered it, was so silent that she guessed Boyne to be still at work.

Not wishing to disturb him, she turned into the drawing room, and there, at her writing table, lost herself in renewed calculations of the outlay to which the morning's conference had pledged her. The fact that she could permit herself such follies had not yet lost its novelty; and somehow, in contrast to the vague fears of the previous days, it now seemed an element of her recovered security, of the sense that, as Ned had said, things in general had never been "righter."

She was still luxuriating in a lavish play of figures when the parlormaid, from the threshold, roused her with an inquiry as to the expediency of serving luncheon. It was one of their jokes that Trimmle announced luncheon as if she were divulging a state secret, and Mary, intent upon her papers, merely murmured an absent-minded assent.

She felt Trimmle wavering doubtfully on the threshold, as if in rebuke of such unconsidered assent; then her retreating steps sounded down the passage, and Mary, pushing away her papers, crossed the hall and went to the library door. It was still closed, and she wavered in her turn, disliking to disturb her husband, yet anxious that he should not exceed his usual measure of work. As she stood there, balancing her impulses, Trimmle returned with the announcement of luncheon, and Mary, thus impelled, opened the library door.

Boyne was not at his desk, and she peered about her, expecting to discover him before the bookshelves, somewhere down the length of the room; but her call brought no response, and gradually it became clear to her that he was not there.

She turned back to the parlormaid.

"Mr. Boyne must be upstairs. Please tell him that luncheon is ready."

Trimmle appeared to hesitate between the obvious duty of obedience and an equally obvious conviction of the foolishness of the injunction laid on her. The struggle resulted in her saying: "If you please, Madam, Mr. Boyne's not upstairs."

"Not in his room? Are you sure?"

"I'm sure, Madam."

Mary consulted the clock. "Where is he, then?"

"He's gone out," Trimmle announced, with the superior air of one who has respectfully waited for the question that a well-ordered mind would have put first.

Mary's conjecture had been right, then. Boyne must have gone to the gardens to meet her, and since she had missed him, it was clear that he had taken the shorter way by the south door, instead of going round to the court. She crossed the hall to the French window opening directly on the yew garden, but the parlormaid, after another moment of inner conflict, decided to bring out: "Please, Madam, Mr. Boyne didn't go that way."

Mary turned back. "Where *did* he go? And when?"

"He went out the front door, up the drive, Madam." It was a matter of principle with Trimmle never to answer more than one question at a time.

"Up the drive? At this hour?" Mary went to the door herself, and glanced across the court through the tunnel of bare limes. But its perspective was as empty as when she had scanned it on entering.

"Did Mr. Boyne leave no messages?"

Trimmle seemed to surrender herself to a last struggle with the forces of chaos.

"No, Madam. He just went out with the gentleman."

"The gentleman? What gentleman?" Mary wheeled about, as if to front this new factor.

"The gentleman who called, Madam," said Trimmle resignedly.

"When did a gentleman call? Do explain yourself, Trimmle!"

Only the fact that Mary was very hungry, and that she wanted to consult her husband about the greenhouses, would have caused her to lay so unusual an injunction on her attendant; and even now she was detached enough to note in Trimmle's eye the dawning defiance of the respectful subordinate who has been pressed too hard.

"I couldn't exactly say the hour, Madam, because I didn't let the gentleman in," she replied, with an air of discreetly ignoring the irregularity of her mistress's course.

"You didn't let him in?"

"No, Madam. When the bell rang I was dressing, and Agnes—"

"Go and ask Agnes, then," said Mary.

Trimmle still wore her look of patient magnanimity. "Agnes would not know, Madam, for she had unfortunately burnt her hand in trimming the wick of the new lamp from town"—Trimmle, as Mary was aware, had always been opposed to the new lamp—"and so Mrs. Dockett sent the kitchenmaid instead."

Mary looked again at the clock. "It's after two! Go and ask the kitchenmaid if Mr. Boyne left any word."

She went into luncheon without waiting, and Trimmle presently brought her there the kitchenmaid's statement that the gentleman had called about eleven o'clock, and that Mr. Boyne had gone out with him without leaving any message. The kitchenmaid did not even know the caller's name, for he had written it on a slip of paper, which he had folded and handed to her, with the injunction to deliver it at once to Mr. Boyne.

Mary finished her luncheon, still wondering, and when it was over, and Trimmle had brought the coffee to the drawing room, her wonder had deepened to a first faint tinge of disquietude. It was unlike Boyne to absent himself without explanation at so unwonted an hour, and the difficulty of identifying the visitor whose summons he had apparently obeyed made his disappearance the more unaccountable. Mary Boyne's experience as the wife of a busy engineer, subject to sudden calls and compelled to keep irregular hours, had trained her to the philosophic acceptance of surprises; but since Boyne's withdrawal from business he had adopted a Benedictine regularity of life. As if to make up for the dispersed and agitated years, with their "stand-up" lunches, and dinners rattled down to the joltings of the dining cars, he cultivated the last refinements of punctuality and monotony, discouraging his wife's fancy for the unexpected, and declaring that to a delicate taste there were infinite gradations of pleasure in the recurrences of habit.

Still, since no life can completely defend itself from the unforeseen, it was evident that all Boyne's precautions would sooner or later prove unavailable, and Mary concluded that he had cut short a tiresome visit by walking with his caller to the station, or at least accompanying him for part of the way.

This conclusion relieved her from further preoccupation, and she went out herself to take up her conference with the gardener. Thence she walked to the village post office, a mile or so away; and when she returned toward home the early twilight was setting in.

She had taken a footpath across the downs, and as Boyne, meanwhile, had probably returned from the station by the highroad, there was little likelihood of their meeting. She felt sure, however, of his having reached the house before her; so sure that, when she entered it herself, without even pausing to inquire of Trimmle, she made directly for the library. But the library was still empty, and with an unwonted exactness of visual memory she observed that the papers on her husband's desk lay precisely as they had lain when she had gone in to call him to luncheon.

Then of a sudden she was seized by a vague dread of the unknown. She had closed the door behind her on entering, and as she stood alone in the long silent room, her dread seemed to take shape and sound, to be there breathing and lurking among the shadows. Her short-sighted eyes strained through them, half-discerning an actual presence, something aloof, that watched and knew; and in the recoil from the intangible presence she threw herself on the bell rope and gave it a sharp pull.

The sharp summons brought Trimmle in precipitately with a lamp, and Mary breathed again at this sobering reappearance of the usual.

"You may bring tea if Mr. Boyne is in," she said, to justify her ring.

"Very well, Madam. But Mr. Boyne is not in," said Trimmle, putting down the lamp.

"Not in? You mean he's come back and gone out again?"

"No, Madam. He's never been back."

The dread stirred again, and Mary knew that now it had her fast.

"Not since he went out with—the gentleman?"

"Not since he went out with the gentleman."

"But who *was* the gentleman?" Mary insisted, with the shrill note of someone trying to be heard through a confusion of noises.

"That I couldn't say, Madam." Trimmle, standing there by the lamp, seemed suddenly to grow less round and rosy, as though eclipsed by the same creeping shade of apprehension.

"But the kitchenmaid knows—wasn't it the kitchenmaid who let him in?"

"She doesn't know either, Madam, for he wrote his name on a folded paper."

Mary, through her agitation, was aware that they were both designating the unknown visitor by a vague pronoun, instead of the conventional formula which, till then, had kept their allusions within the bounds of conformity. And at the same moment her mind caught at the suggestion of the folded paper.

"But he must have a name! Where's the paper?"

She moved to the desk, and began to turn over the documents that littered it. The first that caught her eye was an unfinished letter in her husband's hand, with his pen lying across it, as though dropped there at a sudden summons.

"My dear Parvis"—who was Parvis?—"I have just received your letter announcing Elwell's death, and while I suppose there is now no further risk of trouble, it might be safer—"

She tossed the sheet aside, and continued her search; but no folded paper was discoverable among the letters and pages of manuscript which had been swept together in a heap, as if by a hurried or a startled gesture.

"But the kitchenmaid *saw* him. Send her here," she commanded, wondering at her dullness in not thinking sooner of so simple a solution.

Trimmle vanished in a flash, as if thankful to be out of the room, and when she reappeared, conducting the

agitated underling, Mary had regained her self-possession, and had her questions ready.

The gentleman was a stranger, yes—that she understood. But what had he said? And, above all, what had
he looked like? The first question was easily enough
answered, for the disconcerting reason that he had said
so little—had merely asked for Mr. Boyne, and, scrib-
bling something on a bit of paper, had requested that it
should at once be carried in to him.

"Then you don't know what he wrote? You're not sure
it *was* his name?"

The kitchenmaid was not sure, but supposed it was,
since he had written it in answer to her inquiry as to
whom she should announce.

"And when you carried the paper in to Mr. Boyne,
what did he say?"

The kitchenmaid did not think that Mr. Boyne had
said anything, but she could not be sure, for just as she
had handed him the paper and he was opening it, she
had become aware that the visitor had followed her into
the library, and she had slipped out, leaving the two gentlemen together.

"But then, if you left them in the library, how do you
know that they went out of the house?"

This question plunged the witness into a momentary
inarticulateness, from which she was rescued by Trimmle, who, by means of ingenious circumlocutions, elicited the statement that before she could cross the hall to
the back passage she had heard the two gentlemen
behind her, and had seen them go out of the front door
together.

"Then, if you saw the strange gentleman twice, you
must be able to tell me what he looked like."

But with this final challenge to her powers of expression it became clear that the limit of the kitchenmaid's
endurance had been reached. The obligation of going to
the front door to "show in" a visitor was in itself so
subversive of the fundamental order of things that it had
thrown her faculties into hopeless disarray, and she could

only stammer out, after various panting efforts: "His hat, mum, was different-like as you might say—"

"Different? How different?" Mary flashed out, her own mind, in the same instant, leaping back to an image left on it that morning, and then lost under layers of subsequent impressions.

"His hat had a wide brim, you mean, and his face was pale—a youngish face?" Mary pressed her, with a white-lipped intensity of interrogation. But if the kitchenmaid found any adequate answer to this challenge, it was swept away for her listener down the rushing current of her own convictions. The stranger—the stranger in the garden! Why had Mary not thought of him before? She needed no one now to tell her that it was he who had called for her husband and gone away with him. But who was he, and why had Boyne obeyed him?

IV

It leaped out at her suddenly, like a grin out of the dark, that they had often called England so little—"such a confoundedly hard place to get lost in."

A confoundedly hard place to get lost in! That had been her husband's phrase. And now, with the whole machinery of official investigation sweeping its flashlights from shore to shore, and across the dividing straits; now, with Boyne's name blazing from the walls of every town and village, his portrait (how that wrung her!) hawked up and down the country like the image of a hunted criminal; now the little compact populous island, so policed, surveyed and administered, revealed itself as a Sphinxlike guardian of abysmal mysteries, staring back into his wife's anguished eyes as if with the wicked joy of knowing something they would never know!

In the fortnight since Boyne's disappearance there had been no word of him, no trace of his movements. Even the usual misleading reports that raise expectancy in tortured bosoms had been few and fleeting. No one but the kitchenmaid had seen Boyne leave the house, and no one else had seen "the gentleman" who accompanied him. All inquiries in the neighborhood failed to elicit the memory of a stranger's presence that day in the neighborhood of Lyng. And no one had met Edward Boyne, either alone or in company, in any of the neighboring villages, or on the road across the downs, or at either of the local railway stations. The sunny English noon had swallowed him as completely as if he had gone out into Cimmerian night.

Mary, while every official means of investigation was working at its highest pressure, had ransacked her husband's papers for any trace of antecedent complications, of entanglements or obligations unknown to her, that might throw a ray into the darkness. But if any such had existed in the background of Boyne's life, they had vanished like the slip of paper on which the visitor had written his name. There remained no possible thread of guidance except—if it were indeed an exception—the letter which Boyne had apparently been in the act of writing when he received his mysterious summons. That letter, read and reread by his wife, and submitted by her to the police, yielded little enough to feed conjecture.

"I have just heard of Elwell's death, and while I suppose there is now no further risk of trouble, it might be safer—" That was all. The "risk of trouble" was easily explained by the newspaper clipping which had apprised Mary of the suit brought against her husband by one of his associates in the Blue Star enterprise. The only new information conveyed by the letter was the fact of its showing Boyne, when he wrote it, to be still apprehensive of the results of the suit, though he had told his wife that it had been withdrawn, and though the letter itself proved that the plaintiff was dead. It took several days of cabling to fix the identity of the "Parvis" to whom the fragment was addressed, but even after these inquiries had shown him to be a Waukesha lawyer, no new facts concerning the Elwell suit were elicited. He appeared to have had no direct concern in it, but to have been conversant with the facts merely as an acquaintance, and possible intermediary; and he declared himself unable to guess with what object Boyne intended to seek his assistance.

This negative information, sole fruit of the first fortnight's search, was not increased by a jot during the slow weeks that followed. Mary knew that the investigations were still being carried on, but she had a vague sense of their gradually slackening, as the actual march of time seemed to slacken. It was as though the days, flying horror-struck from the shrouded image of the one inscrutable day, gained assurance as the distance lengthened, till at last they fell back into their normal gait. And so with the human imaginations at work on the dark event. No doubt it occupied them still, but week by week and hour by hour it grew less absorbing, took up less space, was slowly but inevitably crowded out of the foreground of consciousness by the new problems perpetually bubbling up from the cloudy caldron of human experience.

Even Mary Boyne's consciousness gradually felt the same lowering of velocity. It still swayed with the incessant oscillations of conjecture; but they were slower, more rhythmical in their beat. There were even moments of weariness when, like the victim of some poison which leaves the brain clear, but holds the body motionless, she saw herself domesticated with the Horror, accepting its perpetual presence as one of the fixed conditions of life.

These moments lengthened into hours and days, till she passed into a phase of stolid acquiescence. She watched the routine of daily life with the incurious eye of a savage on whom the meaningless processes of civilization make but the faintest impression. She had come to regard herself as part of the routine, a spoke of the wheel, revolving with its motion; she felt almost like the furniture of the room in which she sat, an insensate object to be dusted and pushed about with the chairs and tables. And this deepening apathy held her fast at Lyng, in spite of the entreaties of friends and the usual medical recommendation of "change." Her friends supposed that her refusal to move was inspired by the belief that her husband would one day return to the spot from which he had vanished, and a beautiful legend grew up about this imaginary state of waiting. But in reality she had no such belief: the depths of anguish enclosing her were no longer lighted by flashes of hope. She was sure that Boyne would never come back, that he had gone out of her sight as completely as if Death itself had waited that day on the threshold. She had even renounced, one by one, the various theories as to his disappearance which had been advanced by the press, the police, and her own agonized imagination. In sheer lassitude her mind turned from these alternatives of horror, and sank back into the blank fact that he was gone.

No, she would never know what had become of him—no one would ever know. But the house *knew*; the library in which she spent her long lonely evenings knew. For it was here that the last scene had been enacted, here that the stranger had come, and spoken the word which had caused Boyne to rise and follow him. The floor she trod had felt his tread; the books on the shelves had seen his face; and there were moments when the intense consciousness of the old dusky walls seemed about to break out into some audible revelation of their secret. But the revelation never came, and she knew it would never come. Lyng was not one of the garrulous old houses that betray the secrets entrusted to them. Its very legend proved that it had always been the mute accomplice, the incorruptible custodian, of the mysteries it had surprised. And Mary Boyne, sitting face to face with its silence, felt the futility of seeking to break it by any human means.

V

"I don't say it *wasn't* straight, and yet I don't say it *was* straight. It was business."

Mary, at the words, lifted her head with a start, and looked intently at the speaker.

When, half an hour before, a card with "Mr. Parvis" on it had been brought up to her, she had been immediately aware that the name had been a part of her consciousness ever since she had read it at the head of Boyne's unfinished letter. In the library she had found awaiting her a small sallow man with a bald head and gold eyeglasses, and it sent a tremor through her to know that this was the person to whom her husband's last known thought had been directed.

Parvis, civilly, but without vain preamble—in the manner of a man who has his watch in his hand—had set forth the object of his visit. He had "run over" to England on business, and finding himself in the neighborhood of Dorchester, had not wished to leave it without paying his respects to Mrs. Boyne; and without asking her, if the occasion offered, what she meant to do about Bob Elwell's family.

The words touched the spring of some obscure dread in Mary's bosom. Did her visitor, after all, know what Boyne had meant by his unfinished phrase? She asked for an elucidation of his question, and noticed at once that he seemed surprised at her continued ignorance of the subject. Was it possible that she really knew as little as she said?

"I know nothing—you must tell me," she faltered out; and her visitor thereupon proceeded to unfold his story. It threw, even to her confused perceptions, an imperfectly initiated vision, a lurid glare on the whole hazy episode of the Blue Star Mine. Her husband had made his money in that brilliant speculation at the cost of "getting ahead" of someone less alert to seize the chance; and the victim of his ingenuity was young Robert Elwell, who had "put him on" to the Blue Star scheme.

Parvis, at Mary's first cry, had thrown her a sobering glance through his impartial glasses.

"Bob Elwell wasn't smart enough, that's all; if he had been, he might have turned round and served Boyne the same way. It's the kind of thing that happens every day in business. I guess it's what the scientists call the survival of the fittest—see?" said Mr. Parvis, evidently pleased with the aptness of his analogy.

Mary felt a physical shrinking from the next question she tried to frame: it was as though the words on her lips had a taste that nauseated her.

"But then—you accused my husband of doing something dishonorable?"

Mr. Parvis surveyed the question dispassionately. "Oh, no, I don't. I don't even say it wasn't straight." He glanced up and down the long lines of books, as if one of them might have supplied him with the definition he sought. "I don't say it *wasn't* straight, and yet I don't say it *was* straight. It was business." After all, no definition in his category could be more comprehensive than that.

Mary sat staring at him with a look of terror. He seemed to her like the indifferent emissary of some evil power.

"But Mr. Elwell's lawyers apparently did not take your view, since I suppose the suit was withdrawn by their advice."

"Oh, yes; they knew he hadn't a leg to stand on, technically. It was when they advised him to withdraw the suit that he got desperate. You see, he'd borrowed most of the money he lost in the Blue Star, and he was up a tree. That's why he shot himself when they told him he had no show."

The horror was sweeping over Mary in great deafening waves.

"He shot himself? He killed himself because of *that*?"

"Well, he didn't kill himself, exactly. He dragged on two months before he died." Parvis emitted the statement as unemotionally as a gramophone grinding out its record.

"You mean that he tried to kill himself, and failed? And tried again?"

"Oh, he didn't have to *try* again," said Parvis grimly.

They sat opposite each other in silence, he swinging his eyeglasses thoughtfully about his finger, she, motionless, her arms stretched along her knees in an attitude of rigid tension.

"But if you knew all this," she began at length, hardly able to force her voice above a whisper, "how is it that when I wrote you at the time of my husband's disappearance you said you didn't understand his letter?"

Parvis received this without perceptible embarrassment: "Why, I didn't understand it—strictly speaking. And it wasn't the time to talk about it, if I had. The Elwell business was settled when the suit was withdrawn. Nothing I could have told you would have helped you to find your husband."

Mary continued to scrutinize him. "Then why are you telling me now?"

Still Parvis did not hesitate. "Well, to begin with, I supposed you knew more than you appear to—I mean about the circumstances of Elwell's death. And then people are talking of it now; the whole matter's been raked up again. And I thought if you didn't know you ought to."

She remained silent, and he continued: "You see, it's only come out lately what a bad state Elwell's affairs were in. His wife's a proud woman, and she fought on as long as she could, going out to work, and taking sewing at home when she got too sick—something with the heart, I believe. But she had his mother to look after, and the children, and she broke down under it, and finally had to ask for help. That called attention to the case, and the papers took it up, and a subscription was started. Everybody out there liked Bob Elwell, and most of the prominent names in the place are down on the list, and people began to wonder why—"

Parvis broke off to fumble in an inner pocket. "Here," he continued, "here's an account of the whole thing from the *Sentinel*—a little sensational, of course. But I guess you'd better look it over."

He held out a newspaper to Mary, who unfolded it slowly, remembering, as she did so, the evening when, in the same room, the perusal of a clipping from the *Sentinel* had first shaken the depths of her security.

As she opened the paper, her eyes, shrinking from the glaring headlines, "Widow of Boyne's Victim Forced to Appeal for Aid," ran down the column of text to two portraits inserted in it. The first was her husband's, taken from a photograph made the year they had come to England. It was the picture of him that she liked best, the one that stood on the writing table upstairs in her bedroom. As the eyes in the photograph met hers, she felt it would be impossible to read what was said of him, and closed her lids with the sharpness of the pain.

"I thought if you felt disposed to put your name down—" she heard Parvis continue.

She opened her eyes with an effort, and they fell on the other portrait. It was that of a youngish man, slightly built, with features somewhat blurred by the shadow of a projecting hat brim. Where had she seen that outline before? She stared at it confusedly, her heart hammering in her ears. Then she gave a cry.

"This is the man—the man who came for my husband!"

She heard Parvis start to his feet, and was dimly aware that she had slipped backward into the corner of the sofa, and that he was bending above her in alarm. She straightened herself and reached out for the paper, which she had dropped.

"It's the man! I should know him anywhere!" she persisted in a voice that sounded to her own ears like a scream.

Parvis's answer seemed to come to her from far off, down endless fog-muffled windings.

"Mrs. Boyne, you're not very well. Shall I call somebody? Shall I get a glass of water?"

"No, no, no!" She threw herself toward him, her hand frantically clutching the newspaper. "I tell you, it's the man! I *know* him! He spoke to me in the garden!"

Parvis took the journal from her, directing his glasses to the portrait. "It can't be, Mrs. Boyne. It's Robert Elwell."

"Robert Elwell?" Her white stare seemed to travel into space. "Then it was Robert Elwell who came for him."

"Came for Boyne? The day he went away from here?" Parvis's voice dropped as hers rose. He bent over, laying a fraternal hand on her, as if to coax her gently back into her seat. "Why, Elwell was dead! Don't you remember?"

Mary sat with her eyes fixed on the picture, unconscious of what he was saying.

"Don't you remember Boyne's unfinished letter to me—the one you found on his desk that day? It was written just after he'd heard of Elwell's death." She noticed an odd shake in Parvis's unemotional voice. "Surely you remember!" he urged her.

Yes, she remembered: that was the profoundest horror of it. Elwell had died the day before her husband's disappearance; and this was Elwell's portrait; and it was the portrait of the man who had spoken to her in the garden. She lifted her head and looked slowly about the library. The library could have borne witness that it was also the portrait of the man who had come in that day to call Boyne from his unfinished letter. Through the misty surgings of her brain she heard the faint boom of half-forgotten words—words spoken by Alida Stair on the lawn at Pangbourne before Boyne and his wife had ever seen the house at Lyng, or had imagined that they might one day live there.

"This was the man who spoke to me," she repeated.

She looked again at Parvis. He was trying to conceal his disturbance under what he probably imagined to be an expression of indulgent commiseration; but the edges of his lips were blue. "He thinks me mad; but I'm not mad," she reflected; and suddenly there flashed upon her a way of justifying her strange affirmation.

She sat quiet, controlling the quiver of her lips, and waiting till she could trust her voice; then she said, looking straight at Parvis: "Will you answer me one question, please? When was it that Robert Elwell tried to kill himself?"

"When—when?" Parvis stammered.

"Yes; the date. Please try to remember."

She saw that he was growing still more afraid of her. "I have a reason," she insisted.

"Yes, yes. Only I can't remember. About two months before I should say."

"I want the date," she repeated.

Parvis picked up the newspaper. "We might see here," he said, still humoring her. He ran his eyes down the page. "Here it is. Last October—the—"

She caught the words from him. "The 20th, wasn't it?" With a sharp look at her, he verified. "Yes, the 20th. Then you *did* know?"

"I know now." Her gaze continued to travel past him. "Sunday, the 20th—that was the day he came first."

Parvis's voice was almost inaudible. "Came *here* first?"

"Yes."

"You saw him twice, then?"

"Yes, twice." She just breathed it at him. "He came first on the 20th of October. I remember the date because it was the day we went up to Meldon Steep for the first time." She felt a faint gasp of inward laughter at the thought that but for that she might have forgotten.

Parvis continued to scrutinize her, as if trying to intercept her gaze.

"We saw him from the roof," she went on. "He came down the lime avenue toward the house. He was dressed just as he is in that picture. My husband saw him first. He was frightened, and ran down ahead of me; but there was no one there. He had vanished.

"Elwell had vanished?" Parvis faltered.

"Yes." Their two whispers seemed to grope for each other. "I couldn't think what had happened. I see now. He *tried* to come then; but he wasn't dead enough—he couldn't reach us. He had to wait for two months to die; then he came back again—and Ned went with him."

She nodded at Parvis with the look of triumph of a child who has worked out a difficult puzzle. But suddenly she lifted her hands with a desperate gesture, pressing them to her temples.

"Oh, my God! I sent him to Ned—I told him where to go! I sent him to this room!" she screamed.

She felt the walls of books rush toward her, like inward falling ruins; and she heard Parvis, a long way off, through the ruins, crying to her, and struggling to get at her. But she was numb to his touch, she did not know what he was saying. Through the tumult she heard but one clear note, the voice of Alida Stair, speaking on the lawn at Pangbourne.

"You won't know till afterward," it said. "You won't know till long, long afterward."

DAW

Welcome to DAW's Gallery of Ghoulish Delights!

BACK FROM THE DEAD
Martin H. Greenberg and Charles G. Waugh, editors
  Let the living beware when what has gone beyond returns!
☐ UE2472 $4.99

CULTS OF HORROR
Martin H. Greenberg and Charles G. Waugh, editors
  Tales of Terror as frightening as today's news stories.
☐ UE2437 $4.50

DEVIL WORSHIPERS
Martin H. Greenberg and Charles G. Waugh, editors
  On unhallowed ground they gather to rouse the powers of
  night, the forces of fear. . . .
☐ UE2420 $4.50

INTENSIVE SCARE
Karl Edward Wagner, editor
  Scalpel-edged tales from terror's operating room!
☐ UE2402 $3.95

PHANTOMS
Martin H. Greenberg and Rosalind M. Greenberg, editors
  Original tales of terror—from the Phantom of the Paris Opera
  to a soap opera cursed by a ghostly doom. . . .
☐ UE2348 $3.95

THE YEAR'S BEST HORROR STORIES
Karl Edward Wagner, editor
  ☐ Series XVII   UE2381—$3.95
  ☐ Series XVIII   UE2446—$4.95

PENGUIN USA

P.O. Box 999, Bergenfield, New Jersey 07621

Please send me the DAW BOOKS I have checked above. I am enclosing $_____
(check or money order—no currency or C.O.D.'s). Please include the list price plus
$1.00 per order to cover handling costs. Prices and numbers are subject to change
without notice. (Prices slightly higher in Canada.)

Name _____

Address _____

City _____ State _____ Zip _____
Please allow 4-6 weeks for delivery.

DAW

Don't Miss These Exciting DAW Anthologies

DAW

Enter the Magical Worlds of

Tanya Huff

☐ **GATE OF DARKNESS, CIRCLE OF LIGHT** (UE2386—$3.95)

The Wild Magic was loose in Toronto, for an Adept of Darkness had broken through the barrier into the everyday mortal world. And in this age when only fools and innocents still believed in magic, who was there to fight against this invasion by evil? But Toronto did have its unexpected champions of the Light: a street musician, a "simple" young girl, a bag lady, an over-worked social worker, a streetwise cat, and Evan, Adept of Light, summoned to stand with these mortals in the ultimate war!

THE NOVELS OF CRYSTAL

☐ **CHILD OF THE GROVE: Book 1** (UE2432—$3.95)

Ardhan is a world slowly losing its magic. But one wizard still survives, a master of evil bent on world domination. No mere mortal can withstand him—and so the Elder Races must inter-vene. Their gift of hope to Ardhan is Crystal, the Child of the Grove, daughter of Power and the last-born wizard who will ever walk this world!

☐ **THE LAST WIZARD: Book 2** (UE2331—$3.95)

Kraydak, the evil sorcerer was dead, and Crystal's purpose for existing was gone. For in a world terrified of wizards, a land where only Lord Death was her friend, what future was there for Crystal, the last wizard ever to walk the world? Then she used her power to save a mortal's life and forged one final bond to humanity—a bond that would take her on a quest to destroy a long-dead wizard's stronghold of magic, a place which had lured many to their doom.

DAW

Great Masterpieces of Fantasy!

Tad Williams

☐ **TAILCHASER'S SONG** (UE2374—$4.95)

Meet Fritti Tailchaser, a ginger tomcat of rare courage and curiosity, a born survivor in a world of heroes and villains, of powerful gods and whiskery legends about those strange, furless, erect creatures called M'an. Join Tailchaser on his magical quest to rescue his catfriend Hushpad—a quest that takes him all the way to cat hell and beyond.

Memory, Sorrow and Thorn

THE DRAGONBONE CHAIR: Book 1
☐ **Hardcover Edition** (0-8099-003-3—$19.50)
☐ **Paperback Edition** (UE2384—$5.95)

A war fueled by the dark powers of sorcery is about to engulf the long-peaceful land of Osten Ard—as the Storm King, undead ruler of the elvishlike Sithi, seeks to regain his lost realm through a pact with one of human royal blood. And to Simon, a former castle scullion, will go the task of spearheading the quest that offers the only hope of salvation . . . a quest that will see him fleeing and facing enemies straight out of a legendmaker's worst nightmares!

STONE OF FAREWELL: Book 2
☐ **Hardcover Edition** (UE2435—$21.95)

As the dark magic and dread minions of the undead Sithi ruler spread their seemingly undefeatable evil across the land, the tattered remnants of a once-proud human army flee in search of a last sanctuary and rallying point, and the last survivors of the League of the Scroll seek to fulfill missions which will take them from the fallen citadels of humans to the secret heartland of the Sithi.
